CURTIS HAD THE FEELING HE AND LOUCH HAD DIED AND WERE MAKING THEIR WAY IN UTTER DARKNESS FROM ONE RING OF HELL TO ANOTHER. . . .

They crept, step by step, up the triangular iron rungs of the spiral stairway, placing each foot with the kind of terrifying care a surgeon must use for every scalpel stroke. At each floor, Curtis made a slow sweep of the blackness with the Noctron sensor. Then Louch moved the lens from side to side with slow precision, racking in and out of focus on things near and far.

Perhaps it was the silence, or the total blackness, or the total lack of communication. Curtis had the desolate feeling of isolation that drowning men feel in midocean, that the climber feels trapped on a glacier face.

They were looking for K-7, the lethal, supersensitive explosive that would blow the Trocadéro to smithereens. They had found nothing. Time was running out . . .

"Another blockbuster."—*Library Journal*

TROCADERO

LESLIE WALLER

A DELL BOOK

Published by
DELL PUBLISHING CO., INC.
1 Dag Hammarskjold Plaza
New York, N.Y. 10017

Dell ® TM 681510, Dell Publishing Co., Inc.

ISBN: 0–440–18613–7

Reprinted by arrangement with Delacorte Press
Printed in the United States of America
First Dell printing—November 1979

FOREWORD

What really happened? No, it's not in newspapers or history books. They arrange pieces of the truth. What *really* happened? Unknowable.

So we readers of newspapers and histories settle for someone's arrangement. Or keep looking for a version that better matches our bias.

But facts don't exist until someone sees and arranges them. So yet another bias is applied, like a flawed lens whose projected image is not—quite—factual. Durrell calls it "selected" fiction. You can call it rigorously selected by experts, if you wish. Still, it's not quite what really happened.

But work that bears the unmistakable fiction label? Fiction enjoys the awesome power of paradox. Being candidly fictitious, it tells no lies. Can we approach the unknowable heart of what really happened through fiction? Through the licensed distortion of a storyteller's (sometimes cracked) lens? You bet we can.

Even so, fiction has factual debts to acknowledge. My thanks go to Horace Marston, Norma and Joseph Walsh and Ruth Taffy Holland, for help with that Martian outpost called France. Also to a few honest *flics;* to Namet, Dieter and the original Principessa herself, and her files.

Lastly, closer to home: to Jeanne Bernkopf, with appreciation; to *The New York Times*, with fascination; to Pat, with love.

LESLIE WALLER

PART ONE

APRIL IN PARIS

1

Curtis got out of bed before eight in the morning and padded on bare feet to the window. He drew back one of the lace curtains and stared out at the rain. His landlady's idea, the curtains. He realized now, as he let the curtain fall and hide the dull, leaden sky, that curtains had their uses.

There is a certain morning sky in Paris, he thought as he showered and shaved, that is a view into a remote corner of Hell.

Something about the air and oppressive darkness, something about the streaming rain and the limitless expanse of lowering gunmetal sky, made him resent even more the errand he had to run this morning.

Curtis made himself a mug of American-style coffee and sipped it black. He penciled notes for the day on a small file card. He was being summoned to the presence of a customer as if he were an errand boy.

It grated on Curtis. He hated to be reminded that he was not acting alone, that he inhabited a niche in an organization. It disturbed his sense of who he was.

He finished his coffee and his file card at about the same time, dressed in a red-and-white tattersall-checked shirt, dark brown trousers and a light brown sports jacket. Tie or no tie?

Mrs. Irish would expect an UBCO errand boy to wear a tie. In New York United Bank and Trust Company errands were run by assistant vice-presidents, occasionally even a full VP. Curtis grinned lopsided as he pictured how carefully, with what exquisite attention to each fold and dimple, these men would tie their ties.

Carelessly, he knotted a khaki-colored tie around his neck, failing to fasten the top button of his shirt or to pull the tie tight. He was not one of UBCO's white-faced bankers.

Curtis's job had no name. The post was labeled "Internal Security (Eur.)," a deliberately nondescript phrase. Using as his base this small Paris apartment on Rue Washington off the Champs-Elysées, Curtis roamed Western Europe, rounding up UBCO officers in their middle years who had suddenly absconded with what they hoped were enough funds to buy them the youth they already knew was lost. Occasionally a debtor on the run excited Curtis's interest.

And very occasionally, as this morning, an errand.

Netta Irish would be arriving at Charles de Gaulle Airport at 7:55 A.M. on Air France 070 from New York. She would have almost an hour to transfer to a smaller plane for 070's concluding leg down to Nice. She intended to use that time to convey something of importance to Curtis.

He tucked the scribbled file card in his breast pocket and switched on his security systems as he left. A perimeter-sensitive alarm stood watch over the apartment's windows and doors. An internal proximity-alarm system guarded Curtis's files.

The airport at Roissy is a great circular core surrounded by satellites that shoot out at several levels, like the random arms of some gigantic barrel cactus. Each satellite is linked to the center by slanting runways traversed by long moving sidewalks of rubber into which one steps deeply, as into the mossy floor of a forest.

Curtis made his way up one of these slanted tubes, glancing out through the transparent covering at nearby tubes running in other directions. He felt like a particle in the bloodstream of a giant and found himself wondering if he were something benign, like a white corpuscle, or a loose cancer cell looking for a likely host.

Netta Irish deplaned in a puff of orchestrated confusion. As the 747's first-class compartment door opened, the first to emerge was a steward, cheeks red with effort, lugging two heavy, pale blue alligator vanity cases and two pale blue garment carriers.

The owner of this surely over-legal-weight array of carry-on luggage emerged next, a woman Curtis knew to be about forty, with the quick, confident strut of a Las Vegas showgirl who had rehearsed each move, chalk marks and all, for hours. Her pale blue suede jeans and short jacket emphasized her long-legged, high-waisted look.

A showgirl, Curtis told himself, who still seemed less than thirty.

There was a long pause after she left the plane and then a second passenger emerged. Because he had made it his business to dig up a photograph of Oscar Ferguson, Curtis was able to recognize the man. He looked slightly older than Netta Irish but was, if Curtis remembered accurately—and he always remembered accurately—in his midthirties, like Curtis himself.

Ferguson was Netta's height—in heels she was well over six feet tall—but where she was dark-haired and ivory-skinned, Ferguson was reddish-blond and sandy, as if he'd originally been meant as a Scots dialect comedian but thought better of it.

Netta Irish paused just inside the arrival gate and stared about her with a certain hauteur. Curtis, who knew something of Mrs. Irish's background, was aware that the attitude was not a contrived one.

When Mignon Antoinette Darcy married Minton Irish some years before, she effectively welded the ailing and backruptcy-headed Darcy Industries to IBI, the multinational conglomerate Minton Irish had put together since World War II. She also wiped out the

array of debts she'd inherited on the death of Jim
Darcy, her first husband. And, finally, she provided
the proper provenance and background for Leila
Darcy, her daughter.

Curtis took a step forward as the rest of the 747's
passengers began to move out behind Ferguson and
Mrs. Irish.

Curtis lifted his hand and caught the woman's attention. He indicated a long, low line of leather-
bound couches to one side of the arrival area.

"Mr. Curtis?"

He nodded. "Mrs. Irish?"

Ferguson came between them, exuding a double
aroma of intimidating richness: Curtis could detect
an expensive cologne and the dying shards of an even
more expensive cognac. "Isn't there some more private place?" Ferguson asked in an abrupt way, as if
Curtis had designed the airport.

"We're private here," Curtis said, indicating the
space between them and the rest of the deplaning
passengers. "You had something for me?" he asked,
turning back to Mrs. Irish.

Up close, her dark brown eyes looked enormous.
Curtis felt as if he were being screened by powerful
television lenses. Her oval face was framed by touseled
hair of a black so deep it held glints of blue in it, the
lights deep in a bottle of ink.

Marriage to an adventurous and often bankrupt
Jim Darcy had left no lines in the woman's face. Nor
had Jim's death in an auto crash. Nor had marriage
to Minton Irish, who had already tormented and discarded two previous wives, one to suicide, another to
a sanitarium. Nor had Minton's death by cerebral
stroke less than six months ago.

Nothing showed. Curtis saw neither lines nor shadows. The face was a map of rather chilly beauty,
almost formal in its design, like one of those topiary
gardens that surround an extensive château, each ele-

ment balanced in an orderly arrangement with nothing . . . absolutely nothing left to chance.

"Let's have some kind of identification," Ferguson
was saying in his husky voice.

Curtis realized suddenly that he had been staring
at Mrs. Irish. He turned to the other man. "Mr.
Ferguson," he began in a flat, unaccented tone, "I am
not some kind of cop."

"It's all right, Oscar." Her voice was low but with
a harsh note to it, as if she had spent much of her life
communicating across great distances over high winds.

She smiled at Curtis. "Oscar has been overly pro-
tective of me since Minton's death." Smile off. "It's
Leila."

Curtis waited a beat or two to indicate that he was
busy remembering who Leila was. "Your daughter?"

"She's been in Paris most of this year," Netta Irish
went on, her eyes moving past Curtis's face to watch
the disembarking passengers. "She's penniless by now,
of course."

"By now?"

"She had a small bequest from her grandmother,
twenty thousand or so. I'm sure it's all spent." Her
glance kept darting to other parts of the airport.
Curtis wondered whether she was afraid of missing
something or simply wasn't terribly interested in what
she was telling him.

"Mrs. Irish," he said, trying to rivet her attention.
"Do you have Leila's address?"

The big dark eyes flicked back to regard Curtis.
"Care of American Express," she said with a wry
smile.

"Just like that?"

The dark-haired woman's face went dead again. "I
want her to have two thousand a month. You'll see
to it, won't you?"

"Dollars?"

"Dollars." The woman's dark-rouged mouth was
full to the point of generosity. Her lower lip

thinned. "I think that ought to be more than enough to keep the little idiot out of trouble."

"On the contrary," Oscar Ferguson said in a brash voice. He seemed used to contradicting her. "You give the girl that much and she'll be a target for every thief and fortune hunter in Paris."

Curtis eyed the man coolly. Ferguson stood taller than Curtis by almost a head, and bigger by—at a glance—fifty pounds. There was no sense, Curtis told himself with utter calm, in pointing out that when it came to fortune hunters, Ferguson himself gave off signs of being an expert.

"A thousand a month," the sandy man told Curtis.

Curtis glanced at Mrs. Irish questioningly. "Very well," she said in her faintly cracked voice. "But promptly on the first of every month."

"I'll make sure someone does that," Curtis assured her.

"No. You, yourself. Personally."

"I'm not always in Paris. I travel a lot."

"Then as close to the first of the month as you can make it. But I want you to take personal responsibility. The girl's a fool, alone, rebellious, but she is my daughter. I have to know you'll take this on yourself."

Curtis suppressed a sharp sigh of anger. "I'll do my best. Another person may have to substitute for me on occasion."

"No good," Ferguson butted in.

Netta Irish had been about to agree with Curtis. Now she seemed to reconsider it. "But, Oscar, if he travels . . . ?"

"Your husband's companies, his art collections and his estate," Ferguson reeled off, "are damned good customers of UBCO. Billion-dollar customers, Netta." His pale tan eyes regarded Curtis. "Do I make myself clear?"

Curtis nodded. "You do. What about you, Mrs. Irish?"

"I . . ."

"She agrees," Ferguson said impatiently.

Curtis grinned at him. "Thank you, Mrs. Irish."

The sandy man had the good grace to blush. "Sorry. Netta?"

"I will take Mr. Curtis's word that he'll try to handle it himself as often as possible."

The hoarse, chilly tone in which this was said was directed, Curtis hoped, at Ferguson, not at him. The man was some sort of authority on art, Curtis recalled, a boy wonder who had shot to easy prominence in the museum world and been hired by Minton Irish a few years ago to oversee the growing collection of paintings and sculpture into which the head of IBI was plowing tax-sheltered income.

"Naturally," Ferguson added then, "you'll make sure Leila picks it up each month."

Curtis started to launch what he hoped would come out as a prudently worded attack on the idea that he spend days, perhaps weeks, lurking around the American Express office waiting for someone to ask for Leila's check.

But before he could begin, Ferguson glanced at his watch and twitched. "The connecting plane." He took Mrs. Irish's hand. "Come on, Netta." His aroma of cologne grew suddenly stronger. The smell of old cognac had gone stale. Curtis was happy to see him go.

"I don't suppose—" Mrs. Irish stopped in the middle of asking Curtis something, then picked up again, ". . . I mean, a mother wants to know with whom her daughter is associating . . ." Her big eyes measured Curtis's reaction. "There's a terribly unsuitable boy she was seeing in New York. He may have gotten himself to Paris by now . . ." Again her faintly hoarse voice died out. "Dominic Brown he calls himself. A totally unsuitable person who—"

"Netta, you're babbling." Ferguson was pulling her along. "We'll miss the flight."

"Mr. Curtis, can't you—?"

"Netta!"

They made a picture of even more carelessly orchestrated confusion as they ran off toward one of the glassed-in tubes that would convey them to another part of the terminal.

Suddenly, Mrs. Irish stopped and turned back to Curtis. "You're a love, Mr. Curtis," she called. "Be sure it's paid in cash!"

She blew him a kiss and disappeared into the arterial innards of Charles de Gaulle Airport.

2

Not many people knew Louch. That is to say, in his own arrondissement, the Sixth on the Left Bank, Louch was known to the tobacconist who sold him two packs of Gitanes every morning. The concierge of the apartment house where Louch lived knew him. The gendarme on the beat and the paper seller did, too. The woman who ran the neighborhood *épicerie* sold Louch a tenth of a kilo of country pâté most nights or perhaps two *œufs en gelée*.

For a man the size of Louch, the woman in the *épicerie* would often think, he didn't eat enough to keep alive even a small street sparrow. Of course, she realized that a bachelor like Louch ate out a great deal.

As a matter of fact, Louch was now, and always had been, on a diet. A real, weight-loss, no-nonsense diet. In his fifty-two years he had lost hundreds of kilos of flab from around his midriff. But there was always the bulge over his abdomen and now, in recent years, another bulge just above it, a kind of Buddha spare tire.

Louch was tall for a Frenchman, almost two meters, easily as tall as De Gaulle was. But Louch affected an air of plump jolliness unlike le Grand Charlie's distant gloom.

Louch believed his outwardly happy demeanor disarmed most people. He was right. Louch was usually right. In his business, he had to be.

He was also, surprisingly for his size, an inconspicuous man. He had, for example, sat down in the shade of an outdoor café across the street from the American Express office on Rue Scribe. It was August and hot. There were no Parisians in Paris, of course, and Louch should have stood out somewhat from the run of visiting Americans, Germans and Scandinavians.

But even the waiter had forgotten Louch was there. The coffee Louch had ordered at 9:00 A.M., when the American Express doors opened, had been consumed long ago, but the waiter had neglected to come back for another order.

Louch had the outward look of a man at peace. He usually did. It was part of the disarming character he presented to the world. A man neither impatient nor ill at ease. A man at peace with himself and everyone else, come what may. Not sitting there with a smirky smile, but simply sitting there. At rest.

At the same time, Louch missed very little. From time to time he shifted his big frame on the small, cane-bottomed chair. He recrossed his legs. He rubbed the bulbous tip of his longish, narrow nose. He occasionally pulled at one of his long ears. But the lids over his faintly bulging eyes never really closed for more than a blink. Louch was too much a professional to brag that he missed nothing. Conceivably, something might elude him at some time, but not very often.

And all this despite the fact that Louch's usual place was not at an outdoor café watching who came and went at the American Express office. Far from it. His normal posture was seated, yes, but behind the desk of a rather large, impressive office in a small, dingy building off the Quai des Orfèvres.

He came and went each day with studied irregularity, like a clock whose outside is trustworthy and plain, but whose works have been tampered with by a demon. Some mornings the two sergeants who manned his office would find him busy at his desk when they arrived for the day's work. Sometimes he didn't appear for days, but telephoned from unlikely places like Cannes or Le Havre or Marseilles.

This hot summer morning, for instance, he had gone directly to the outdoor café. As the sun moved higher, the temperature under the shade of the awning began to rise, too. By ten-fifteen Louch was perspiring. He signaled for the waiter and had some difficulty making the man see him.

"*Un Perrier avec des glaçons.*"

He sipped the chilled soda water slowly, with the eye of an engineer of hydraulics, making sure there was still a bit of ice left to cool the last sip as thoroughly as the first. At the same time, another part of Louch's mind registered the fact that his total caloric intake this morning, since he took his coffee unsweetened and black, was zero.

As a matter of fact, Louch had taken a science degree from the Sorbonne some years ago, after the Algerian troubles. The degree had very little to do with his job. It was just that Louch felt his mind needed the discipline of the scientific method.

His job . . .

Originally Louch had been placed in charge of narcotics: not the catching of street dealers, but the finding and extermination of supply routes. He had traveled a lot in those days, when he had been some kilos thinner. The less sedentary life had led him from Vietnam and the Golden Triangle to Turkey and Corsica and Marseilles, even to Montreal and New York.

Eventually, however, because he had been so good with the Lebanese and Turks and Moroccans who ran the routes, Louch had been moved into a new area of work, with a higher title and more pay. He had taught himself Arabic in those more active days, and now he was placed in charge of terrorism.

In a career of almost thirty years with his offshoot branch of the police, Louch had seen the drug problem in France grow from a small matter of opium and laudanum, or the odd hashish cigarette, to a raging fire that consumed thousands of young people each year and had raised the crime rate in France alone to at least double what it had been when he had started fighting the drug traffic.

Five or six years before, when he'd been placed in charge of terrorism, there had been one group of Provence-for-Provençals separatists operating in the Camargue, with ties to the Basque movement in Spain, one Algerian cell operating in Paris and a PLO fund-raising network eking out a chancy existence along the Riviera, near Monte Carlo.

Now France seemed honeycombed with terrorist groups. Louch's department had identified two dozen of them with Arab affiliations alone, without even attempting to categorize the splinter cells from the Baader-Meinhof Gruppe who had infiltrated Alsace, the Breton apparatus that had linked itself with the IRA and the various separatist groups as far away as Croatia and Slovakia who seemed to thrive in the freer air of France.

Louch, even in his most introspective moments, even during a night of insomnia and the corrosive thoughts of the small hours, never once blamed his own performance, or lack of it, for the burgeoning success of the drug trade and the plaguelike spread of terrorist groups.

Neither did his superiors. Nor would any other Frenchman. The drug trade, after all, was an American affair. The ultimate market was always the States. And as for terror, the Israelis seemed to go out of their way to attract it to themselves. Why blame a Frenchman for any of this?

As he finished the last of his Perrier, Louch saw the boy.

He seemed no more than twenty-five years of age, if that, but it wasn't always easy to know how old

Third World people were. In any event, people that age were still "boys" to Louch.

He was good-looking in a dark, Bedouin way, with an olive skin and black eyes, high cheekbones as sharp as knives that ran straight out from a beaky nose to the sides of his narrow face in perfectly horizontal slashes. He had a big chin and he smiled a lot because his teeth were perfect.

The perfection, Louch decided now, of a well-to-do childhood. Lots of milk and dental care. No starvation in this boy's family.

Louch had been keeping an eye on him ever since the evening, some six months before, when a certain Dr. Hakkad, a PLO strategist, had put aside time for the boy during a busy visit to Paris. If someone meant that much to Hakkad, Louch reasoned, he was a person of importance, against all outward evidence. Perhaps the boy was only being groomed for importance. Perhaps the Palestinians saw in him what Louch had also noted, a certain air, a charisma, signs of a personality from which people unquestioningly took leadership. Unfortunately.

He had come up the street from the Boulevard de la Madeleine and he was so green at his work—or was it only a hobby?—that by his glance and his manner, he telegraphed to Louch that he was here to meet someone. Louch checked his watch. Ten-thirty, the busiest time at American Express for youngsters looking for mail and money from home. The first post was sorted. If today were to bring a check, it would now be ready.

The boy sauntered past Louch twice without seeing him. Then his face went totally dead and he seemed to lose interest in whatever he was here for. That gave Louch his clue to look down the street in the opposite direction.

She was a small girl, not more than five feet tall, if that. But the boy was short, too, Louch noted. And both of them were fashionably thin in their tight, overwashed jeans, wide leather belts and skimpy, sleeveless shirts.

The girl was possibly a shade better at this than the boy, Louch noted. She moved past him without taking notice of his presence, crossed the street and disappeared inside the American Express office. Louch sat back and waited.

Then minutes later she was outside again in the hot sun, her eyes hidden behind immense dark glasses. Her thick blond hair had been frizzed into tight kinks that seemed to glitter in the sunlight.

Although it was hard to see her face—the fright-wig hair and the immense dark glasses covered much of it—Louch felt sure that he'd never seen the girl before. She was so petite in a world of big, lubberly young people, that Louch would have remembered her. Not that he knew every face in Paris. After all, who could? But for the younger faces, his memory was acute. It didn't include her.

Louch decided she was no better at this business than the boy because the grin on her tiny face was a radiogram to the world that her check had come in. Or was it something more? Louch saw that she had stuffed something bulky into the back pockets of her jeans. Not a check. Cash?

The packets looked like money, disturbing the smooth, swelling curve of her rear end as she wiggled off down the street. The boy followed at an ever-decreasing distance until, at the corner near the Opéra, they were walking together.

Louch glanced at his watch and grunted as he got to his feet. He made his way back to a telephone booth inside the restaurant, dialed a number and waited. The sergeants weren't answering.

"Louch," a voice at his elbow said in English, "you're turning into a dirty old man."

Louch revolved slowly. He always took care to do things in an easy, disarming way, but the tightness of his elbow, cocked to deliver a crippling sideways blow, was fairly obvious. He completed his turn and found himself looking at an American with thin pale hair combed straight across his head, and a mocking grin on his face.

"Hello, Curtis," Louch said in a grumpy tone. He hated to be caught out.

3

The Duomo is not the tallest building in Milan. Its lovely, lacy spires, a wild effusion of stone, are dwarfed now by a number of structures in and around Milan's lively stock exchange, the Borsa. Having rendered unto God the thing which is God's, Milan has busied itself rendering only unto Caesar.

The Gagnelli Building is not the tallest structure either, but its slim tower of green glass, rising forty stories into the air over Milan, gives one of the city's loftier views. A mixed breed of building, the Gagnelli. Financed by the powerful family whose name it bears, the structure is only partly devoted to offices. It also has a theater, television studios and, near the top, several floors of terribly expensive apartments with their own express elevator.

George Brown, seated in one of the low, puffy modern sofas, his fat knees almost touching his chin, stared out through the expanse of tinted plate glass. A December gloom had settled over the city, but Brown seemed impervious to it. *"Che bella vista,"* he murmured.

"Giorgio," the woman across from him said in excellent English, "please give up trying to speak Italian, like a good boy?"

"Thanks, Princess."

The woman smiled slightly. She had chosen a severe plastic and chrome chair to sit in for the very good reason that if she had settled into one of the cream-puff sofas, she would have disappeared from view.

La Principessa Claudia Carloni was under five feet in height, although no one knew it. Whatever the fashions, she had always worn five-inch heels. It was only one of her lovers who might have known, or perhaps her bodyguard, Nico, who had seen her in a bikini at her private pool in the far south.

The Principessa's business address was this lavishly ultramodern apartment forty floors above Milan. Her private life, what little she had, was spent in Calabria, the province in the toe of the boot that is Italy, where she had a villa in the hills overlooking the Ionic Sea.

George Brown interested her. Otherwise he would never have gained entrance merely by presenting his card, as he had today.

The Principessa Carloni had never laid eyes on Brown before but his reputation had preceded him. She had heard of him, with respect, for many years now, not just from other Americans like himself, but from some of her powerful friends in Europe as well.

She watched him through the huge, rimless sunglasses she always wore in this all-glass apartment. Even now in winter, the green-tinted windows didn't spare her.

The Principessa was afraid of squint lines at the outer corners of her small eyes. She spent a lot of time making them look bigger, adding outrageously false lashes, glitter and shadow, until they seemed of a size for a man to fall into. But the squint lines would undo all that. As he started to topple, a man would see the lines and wonder: how old is she?

The same problem attended the movements of her mouth. As most Italians, she spoke animatedly, with facial gestures. She lived in fear that these exertions, too—pursing her lips, grinning, God knew what else! —could produce those vertical creases of age that slashed through one's lips, as if they had been sewn together with coarse thread.

She was a wealthy woman, almost as rich as the man who sat across from her at this moment, and a handsome one. But the look she had created for herself over the years cost money, too. The Principessa often wondered if she would end her days paying out her vast hoard to plastic surgeons and cosmeticians. A silly business, vanity, she often told herself. Silly and inevitable.

"Giorgio, *caro*," she purred, "do you come as a buyer or a seller?"

Brown shrugged. "A buyer. But it's crossed my head, Princess, that maybe I have a swap."

She laughed softly so as not to disarrange her face. She had worn a pair of lounging pajamas, black velours, with a halter top made of two broad vertical straps that came up over her breasts and tied behind her neck. When she laughed her breasts jiggled visibly. She had turned her profile to her visitor in order to look over her bare shoulder at him.

"What do you seek?" she asked.

Brown hunched forward on the too-comfortable sofa. "Skeletons in the IBI closet," he said. "Minnie Irish cut a wide swath while he was alive. I need details."

"Not about the women," the Principessa said. "Nobody pays for that sort of scandal anymore."

"Business dirt. Back in the States there's a big market in business dirt."

"You don't have to tell me, *caro*. I created that market." She laughed again and watched his eyes drift down to the place where he could just begin to see one of her breasts, or live in hope thereof. "And what have you brought me?"

"Some more for the same file."

"I beg your pardon?"

"I have IBI stuff to trade for IBI stuff. Is that fair?"

"Not if my file is full."

She put a long cigarette into an even longer holder and placed the end in her mouth. The idea of lighting it for her struggled slowly to the surface of George Brown's brain, but not fast enough. Nico, who had represented Italy in light heavyweight boxing at the last Olympics, appeared out of nowhere with a lighter already bearing a flame. As always, his footwork was dazzling.

"You see," the Princess went on, blowing smoke at the departing Nico, "to be a true swap, I must name what I want. And it would not be anything about IBI. Business scandal bores me."

"And pays your rent."

She lowered her enormous eyelashes by way of acknowledgement. "George Brown," she said then, as if she'd only just heard the name. "Bruno Giordano, born in 1926 at Castellamare del Golfo, brought to the States as an infant. *Sotto-capo* to Stefano Magaddino of Buffalo. Business associate of Meyer Lansky, Sam Giancana, Moey Dalitz and Santo Trafficante in Cuba. Until—"

"Moey had almost no investments in Cuba," Brown corrected her.

"Si, ricordo." She blew another plume of cigarette smoke, this time in his direction. "You are a man of great respect," she mused. "Your sons, too. They do you honor. All but the youngest boy. The handsome, tall one who broke his leg at Klosters a year ago."

Her visitor grinned. "Princess, you're good. Real good."

She shrugged negligently. "I remember his photograph in one of the gossip magazines. There is nothing magic about the way I work."

"Not much."

"The youngest is a stone in your shoe," she mused, but it was obvious that she had started thinking of something else. "George Brown. Yes! You have been sent here by the gods! I know *exactly* what you can sell to me."

He blinked. "What?"

"I have heard it so often I cannot believe it is only a malicious rumor. I have heard about it from so many secondhand sources. But you are a firsthand source."

"For what?" The American sounded bewildered by her, but enjoyably so.

"The microcassette."

"Huh?"

"*Si, è vero*. It exists. The girl was wired."

"Princess . . ."

"Don't bother to deny it, *caro*. I don't know how one wires a girl naked in bed with the President of the United States, but you Americans are all technical geniuses anyway."

Brown's face went utterly blank for a long moment. He watched the tiny princess with something like new respect, a heightened wariness where there had only been sexual interest.

This was the moment the Principessa always worked for in dealing with men. They enjoyed what they saw, a pretty toy. It wasn't until later that she hit them an unsuspected blow to the ego. What? This little toy knows about the microcassette?

The heavyset American was on his feet. He walked over to the window and stared down forty floors at the commercial heart of a city where commerce had been king for a thousand years.

"There isn't enough stuff in your files," he said then, his voice a bit hoarse with emotion, "to trade for what you're talking about."

"Then it exists."

"If you had it, who in Christ's name would buy it from you?"

The smile that wreathed the Principessa's face was so broad, and created so many wrinkles, that she would have been dismayed to see herself in a mirror.

4

Netta Irish had finished five hard sets with Françoise, a woman she knew only by sight at the club, but who was a nationally ranked tennis player.

At New Year's the tennis club at Beaulieu-sur-Mer is a place for serious enthusiasts of the sport. Januaries on the Riviera are never warm enough for anyone to sit in a sunny corner and sip an aperitif. One has to be out on one of many red-clay courts, working hard, just to stay warm.

It was, in fact, perhaps the most unfashionable time of the year to be anywhere along this mist-shrouded coast. January was meant, Netta knew, for the other shore of the Mediterranean, for Morocco and Tunisia, or for the Caribbean.

But Oscar had business in Saint-Paul-de-Vence, something to do with Matisse cartoons that had just come to light. They seemed to be preliminary sketches for the immense work of decorating the chapel there. And, whatever the price, Oscar felt the Minton Irish Collection needed these stray scrawls and blots for its very own.

The Matisse Chapel in Vence left Netta cold. She found the work ungainly and ugly in a useless way, that is, ugliness that didn't even stir or bother her or violently wrench her way of seeing. Just ugly.

Of course, Netta was only a bystander along the high-speed raceway of modern art, and knew it. Oscar was the great authority. He had staked out his early, fast-blooming career on the chapel work of Matisse and Chagall. It had been Oscar's M.A. thesis on the Chagall windows in the Rockefeller Church at Pocantico, New York, that had elevated him to international prominence.

How Oscar had come to be chosen by Minton Irish was something Netta had never fully understood. The Irish Collection had been deadly overboard on Sure Things: Rembrandts, El Grecos, Titians and Rubens, with a spattering of Renoirs and Van Goghs. The older paintings had been bought in the late nineteenth century by Minton's father for what Minton had always referred to as "a song." The French Impressionists were Minton's own addition to the period between the two great wars, bought at even more musical prices.

It had been the disaster of Irish's life that none of his wives had presented him with a son, or any other offspring, for that matter. His fantasy was that his son would swoop down into the arena of modern art and accumulate for yet another song the flux of Motherwells, De Koonings, Tobeys and Pollocks then coming to market.

Netta finished showering and dried herself in the women's dressing room at the club. She eyed Françoise and was forcibly reminded of the difference in figures between a woman who plays serious tennis every day of the year, and someone like herself who does it in spasms, more to kill time than to keep in trim.

Netta had a lot of time to kill on this trip. Oscar was away every day, mousing about cellars in the hill towns around Vence or arguing learnedly with the curators at the Maeght Foundation nearby. From a young man who had made his name on church art, Oscar Ferguson had blossomed into a world figure, whose slightest pronouncement on any aspect of art, from Minoan tomb vases to the most recent rendering of Arabic numerals by Jasper Johns, was listened to with terrified respect. He was, after all, curator of the most valuable private art collection in the world.

This ambition and the aggressive drive had certainly impressed Minton Irish. In his last years, Netta's husband had become a caricature of all the unpleasant traits of his earlier life: caustic, brutal, vulgar and mean. Yet he had so much confidence in Oscar that in his will he had left the full right of decision in all matters relating to the Collection jointly to Oscar and his widow. Their signatures were all that was needed to buy, sell, shift or in any other way manipulate this immense hoard of art.

The Collection was the core of the estate left by her husband as the Minton Irish Foundation. And it was this tax-free entity which controlled a large chunk of IBI shares, something Netta tended to forget, but which IBI's executives tended to keep close track of.

Netta had no idea how much the Collection was worth. Oscar was no help in this respect. His words always grew vague and his arms would begin to churn as he rattled off a mélange of "no telling what the market price would be," accompanied by warnings that, like a government selling gold bullion, the Irish Collection had to be very careful what it offered for sale, for fear of depressing prices in the art world generally.

Netta watched as Françoise bundled up for the January chill outside, layering a wool sweater over a flannel shirt. The two women smiled at each other as Netta pulled on her own sweater.

Françoise asked: "Cacharel?"

Netta nodded.

"There's a shop in St. Jean," Françoise said with sudden animation, "where the Cacharels are on sale now. You know the place? Jujube, on the left as you drive out. Between the center of town and the post office?"

Netta's glance went blank. How French, she thought, to know where all the sales were. "This sweater is from New York," she said by way of answer.

Françoise's face relaxed into a look as blank as

Netta's. She finished dressing, bade her partner good-bye and left.

Netta collapsed on one of the slatted benches. After five ferocious sets, one had to sit down. She stared at the door through which the younger Frenchwoman had left.

Françoise is probably Oscar's age, Netta thought. And, as it had for some time now since Oscar had become her lover, Netta reminded herself that it was not always easy for a woman in her early forties to keep up with people as much as ten years her junior.

As always, when she thought of someone younger, she thought of Leila.

Leaning back against a row of shelves and letting her tired muscles regenerate themselves, Netta tried to picture what her daughter's life was these days. The man, Curtis, was maddeningly skimpy with news. Leila *was* collecting her money. She *looked* to be in good health. She obviously still was living in Paris and still consorting with strange, exotic people.

A telephone call Netta had placed to Curtis in December, she in Athens, he in London at that moment, had been less than satisfactory.

He had nothing to say about Leila's companions, not even the one she'd warned him about. "Dominic Brown?" he'd asked, as if hearing the name for the first time.

"Surely you remember my—"

"You know, Mrs. Irish, UBCO is your bank, not your private detective agency. If you need to know more than I'm telling you, I can suggest the names of several reputable Paris firms that—"

Netta sat up straight on the dressing room bench, then got to her feet. Leila was almost exactly the image of her father. Jim Darcy had that same opinionated streak of utter self-confidence that inevitably leads to disaster.

For Jim the world had never been a hostile place, even in the small things. Jim Darcy had never missed a bus on a rainy day with the next one not due for twenty minutes. When Jim Darcy passed another car on a narrow curve, he never found an auto in the other lane racing toward a head-on collision with him. It wasn't just that these ugly patches of life were in some magic way shielded from Jim. He never admitted their existence.

Until too late. Until all the credit had gone and all the extensions on loans had lapsed and all the luck on narrow, curving mountain roads had . . . run out. Pf. End of the magic.

Netta shrugged into a navy blue sailor's pea coat and buttoned it up to her throat. She drew on gloves and left the dressing room, moving quickly through the bar, past the deserted dining room to the outdoor area under now-leafless trees. In season small tables and chairs made it possible to while away a pleasant afternoon here.

She walked briskly out of the parklike setting into the curving road where in summer cars were parked bumper to bumper. Now only her little rented orange Renault 5 stood. She drove off toward Cap Ferrat, the peninsula of rocky land that reaches out into the Mediterranean from Beaulieu-sur-Mer.

Leila had been born Christmas Day. That was why Netta had called Curtis in December, to try to get a message through to her daughter. Undelivered, as always. Or not accepted.

Leila was twenty now. In another year she would inherit everything Netta's parents had left her. It had always seemed more than enough in Netta's world, until she entered the larger world of Minton Irish and IBI. His business holdings were so vast, and so layered with the impenetrable cloak of multinational bookkeeping, that Netta had no idea how much she would eventually leave to Leila.

At the Voile d'Or, as she turned over the R-5 to a bellman, Netta was met by Mr. Lorenzi, the manager, who seemed perturbed almost to the point of distress.

"I am terribly sorry, madame, but he insisted that you expected him."

"Him?"

They were moving through the lobby now, conferring in undertones. "But I know that the radiogram did not arrive until this morning, after you left for the club, madame. So I know you had no warning."

"Who is he?"

"A M'sieur . . ." He managed, in his south-of-France accent, with its Italian overtones, to pronounce the name as "Sandwich."

"I don't know any Mr. Sandwich, I assure you."

Mr. Lorenzi fussed in a vest pocket and produced a rectangle of parchment. "His card, madame."

"Netta!" a man called.

She glanced up to see him striding across the lobby floor toward her, looking tanned and fit as ever, his heels making sharp, decisive explosions like the bark of guns as he approached, arms spread to embrace her.

"Sandweg!" she shrieked, laughing. "I thought it was Sand—" She stopped, not wanting to offend Mr. Lorenzi. "Tom, what brings you at this ungodly season?"

He folded her in a strong hug and kissed her cheek just to one side of her mouth. "Mmm. Vivará."

"How did you know that?" she asked, stepping back. Tom Sandweg had a reputation for being bright, but there was no reason to imagine that he could identify a Pucci perfume.

She stared frankly at him. Tom had been her first husband's "best" friend, whatever that meant in the world of business. They'd both come up the same route, from the Wharton School of Business, Jim Darcy on family money he finally blew to the four winds, Tom on nothing but what he earned and invested.

Tom had been one of the directors of Darcy Industries who, after Jim's death, had worked to merge the near-bankrupt company into IBI, on whose board he also sat. In fact, Tom had been the one to introduce Netta, hardly used to her new role as widow, to Minton Irish.

Netta had always wondered about Tom's motives for making the introduction. But, like all victims of matchmaking, she seldom cared to examine the question too closely. With his consummate tact and his awfully real smile, Tom brought a new and higher level of corporate meaning to the term "pimp."

In any event, within a year she'd become Mrs. Irish and Darcy Industries, a subsidiary of IBI, whose executive vice-president, directly under Minton Irish, was, of course, Tom.

Since Minton's fatal stroke, the board had met several times to appoint a new chief executive officer and president. They had failed to agree. In the interim, Tom had run IBI and . . . hoped for the best.

"What could bring me to this desolate shore indeed," Sandweg was saying, "what else but the thought of seeing you?"

Netta took another step back out of the powerful ring of magnetic energy that seemed to surround Tom Sandweg like high-voltage plasma.

He had let his dark brown hair grow longer and grayer at the temples, in keeping with his new, hoped-for, titan-of-industry position. He had always been attractive to women. Netta calculated the grayer Tom would be even more attractive to them now.

She gave him a wry smile, a kind of let's-not-kid-an-old-friend look. "In other words," she said, "you need my signature on something."

Sandweg burst out laughing. He turned to Mr. Lorenzi. "This is the most formidable woman in the world. I warn you."

The manager nodded. At this season any guests were welcome, especially wealthy ones, but he felt uneasy at having them stage such public events as this reunion was becoming. Glancing at his watch, he said, "Will you be my guests for an aperitif?"

Having carefully led them to the comfortable bar that overlooked the tiny bay and yacht harbor, the manager sipped a Campari and then smoothly removed himself.

"Now, then, Netta."

"Now, then, Tom."

They stared at each other with a curiosity from which almost all sexual questions had been removed. Tom Sandweg had his women, Netta knew, probably dozens of them. The King of the One-Night Stand, Jim Darcy had once called him, as always to his face.

"How's Oscar coming along with his mission?"

Netta sipped an Italian bitters. "Poking around for lost, stolen and strayed scrawls by Matisse. As if the hill towns around Vence haven't been combed a hundred times before."

"But not by someone with Oscar's fine-toothed golden rake."

"Um."

A pause, while Tom fiddled with the ice in his drink. "You two getting along?"

Netta started to respond with an abrupt request that Tom keep out of her private life. Instead she hesitated. She supposed his question had been only the usual stage-setting social chitchat he'd use with anyone. It was the equivalent of what he'd ask a male friend: "Getting much?"

"You'd think it was a lot," Netta replied then in a husky voice.

He glanced up at her, caught off guard. Then, smoothly: "That's just fine. I have to talk to both of you and it's better if you're being friendly this week."

"Oscar and I have a remarkably level life together," Netta told him. "We rarely quarrel."

"No downs. Not many ups." He nodded. "Very wise."

She smiled at him. "My dear Tom. Advice about long-term relationships from you?"

He opened his mouth and, when he threw his head back to laugh at the joke on him, Netta was able to count perhaps more teeth—strong, white, shiny—than are normally allotted to human beings. "You drew blood that time, Netta."

His laughter bounded out of the bar and across the lobby, making one of the bellmen turn inquisitively toward them. Because she saw this, she also saw Oscar arrive at that moment, hear the laugh and turn in the same direction. He recognized Sandweg and came toward the bar in a stealthy, padding way, like a cat stalking. Tom's back was to him.

"We're in a thin patch at the moment, Netta," Sandweg was saying. "Nothing to worry about, long-term, but the immediate cash position of one big subsidiary is thin."

Netta made a brushing gesture before her long, perfectly motionless face. Her big eyes swung from Tom to Oscar, who had tiptoed up behind him. "You of all people," she said, "should know how little I understand of IBI affairs."

"It's the new contracts for Jet-Tech."

"Tom, please."

"Well, maybe I can get Oscar to listen."

"You have my undivided attention," Oscar boomed in his aggressive voice. Tom Sandweg blinked, but failed to flinch. He sat motionless for a long moment.

Then he turned slowly around on his high-back white wicker chair. "Oscar," he said in faintly taunting tone, "sit down."

"I'm fine here. What did you come for?"

Netta watched the sandy-haired man shift from foot to foot, as if testing his stance in case, without an eye blink of warning, he had to spring out of Tom Sandweg's grasp. The two men hated each other. No, Netta corrected herself, it wasn't as active an emotion as hate.

Had no use for each other. Oscar had not been part of Tom Sandweg's advance planning when Tom married Netta to the head of IBI. Tom hadn't counted on the young curator looming so powerfully in the arrangement, or taking such an overbearing part in Netta's life even before Minton Irish died.

"You'd better have a seat," Tom warned him.

"Say what you have to say."

Tom's voice still had a faint edge to it. "We have to sell some paintings, Oscar. We have to raise, say, twenty million."

Ferguson was silent for a long moment. Then he looked at Netta. He had light-irised eyes, the color of coffee with a lot of cream in it, approaching so close to yellow that they resembled the eyes of a tiger. Not always, Netta told herself. But they did now.

"Netta?" Oscar asked. "Are we together on this?"

"As always."

Oscar's smile was tight. "We have no intention of bailing you out, Tom. The Collection is an independent, tax-exempt foundation. It takes one hell of a lot of gall for a man to try short-circuiting that independence just to bail out some inept management error."

Tom's smile was relaxed. "A lot of gall," he echoed, "or else a compelling need."

"Forget it."

"A need," Tom went on, raising his voice slightly, "so compelling that it affects the future of the estate and, naturally," his glance swung back to Netta, "your own financial security."

"That's nonsense," Oscar countered.

He came around from behind Tom's chair and sat on the sofa next to Netta. "Netta's always able to live in her accustomed style with or without the estate. She can always sell a few sketches if she has to." His voice had grown less truculent, more reasonable. "If the need arises, she can even sell a painting now and then. But under no circumstances could we think of liquidating twenty million dollars' worth of paintings simultaneously. You just don't understand the art market, Sandweg."

"I understand that under Minton Irish's will, this independent foundation of yours is inextricably tied up with the same estate that owns a majority interest in IBI. I understand, Oscar, that if we don't make the connection I suggest and flog a few paintings, there may come a time when IBI's creditors will make the connection for us."

"What the hell is that meant to suggest?"

"They may force the foundation to sell paintings when it least wants to, in order to satisfy their demands."

Oscar sat there silently for a moment. Then he looked at Netta. She had seen him look many ways— passionate, depressed, joyous, scheming—but she had never before seen him looking as he did now.

Frightened.

5

In Turin, the Vicolo Dodici Apostoli, not far from the Piazza Castello, is too narrow for any automobile, even the tiny Fiat 500. Along this twisting passage three old houses, known as Number 20, have been gutted to make one of Turin's more popular shopping places.

One could pass Number 20 without knowing it was the retail outlet where the people of Turin buy many of their radios, refrigerators, television sets and other appliances. Everything is in its original carton. Only the prices give a clue that everything at Number 20 is stolen goods.

Marco, the young Sicilian who ran Number 20, had the face of an artist and premature gray in his glossy black hair. In this cold, bustling, money-oriented city, Marco rarely missed the sunny scenes in his native island.

His presence in Turin was a piece of history peculiarly Italian. In Mussolini's day, when the thugs of his secret Ovra had finished torturing information from a Communist or other radical, if nothing incriminating came forth, some punishment was still necessary. So, lacking a confession, the Fascists meted out a penalty that would seem devastating only to an Italian, perhaps: banishment from his hometown.

Political people, artists and writers who ran afoul of the Fascists would be shipped to some town at the opposite end of the peninsula from their beloved home. Many was the poem, the painting, the book of anguish and longing that resulted from such exile.

The punishment still sits on the books. Today it is meted out especially to those *mafiosi* clever enough to cover their tracks. Lacking evidence, the police still exile such men, usually from the south to a chill, unfriendly northern city. Around such banished criminals a subfamily instantly springs up, always with nationwide connections.

As a result, therefore, the Italian government has managed to distribute organized crime throughout every remote corner of the land, even in places where it never existed before. Marco, and the thriving business at Number 20, were direct results of the policy.

The man walking up the Vicolo Dodici Apostoli was expected. Marco stood in awe of him or, rather, of the man who had sent him. When the expected visitor arrived, in an American-style trench coat and pulled-down suede hat, his narrow face in shadow, Marco rushed forward, hand outstretched.

"Signore Groark," he enthused, "such a pleasure to meet you."

Whatever he made of the way Marco pronounced his name—"Grog" was as close as he came—the arrival nodded and allowed himself to be led into Marco's private office.

"I need sompin special," he said in an accent that had originated close to the Bronx. "Hasta be flat. You dig?"

"Flat? Like a pack of cigarettes?"

Groark shook his narrow head. "Flatter." He indicated between thumb and forefinger a distance of about a quarter of an inch.

Marco frowned importantly. *"Aspetta uno momento."* He disappeared long enough for Groark to smoke a cigarette, Then he returned with a brown plastic portfolio in imitation alligator, the kind elegant young executives might carry aboard a supersonic transport.

Groark opened the portfolio. There was room inside for perhaps a dozen sheets of paper. "What's the range?" he asked.

"Five hundred meters."

"Say, uh, five hundred yards, huh? How's it work?"

Marco warmed to his task. He liked to know about such things himself. An untrained immigrant took pleasure in learning, and in teaching another. "In here," he began, "is the, ah, *batteria*."

"It don't look thick enough," Groark objected.

"A new type. Flat strips of zinc." Marco turned over the portfolio. "Here, the device. All cheeps," he added proudly.

"Cheap?"

"Cheeps. Cheeps." Marco dug his fingernail into the wood of his desk and dislodged a flake of paint. "Cheeps like these."

"Chips!" Groark said. "Subminiaturized chips. I dig."

"And the *microfono* connects h—"

"No microphone," Groark stopped him. "Not necessary."

Marco looked crestfallen. "Truly no?"

Groark's dead, narrow-set eyes fixed him. "Truly no."

Questions boiled up in Marco. This was a very sophisticated device, the latest way of trapping unfaithful mates or dishonest business partners. But some things are more powerful than curiosity. Mafia discipline is one of them. Mario composed his face. "Certainly," he murmured, "*sensa microfono*."

"How much, goombar?"

Marco produced an elegant shrug. "I have sold this for as much as five million lire, Signore Groark."

"But to me?"

"Two million."

The American closed one small eye to help him figure the cost in dollars. "Say twenty-five hundred bucks? So, look, I pay in hundred-dollar bills. Make it an even two grand, okay?"

Marco's face went dead. It wasn't the price. Even at two thousand dollars he made a profit of a thousand. No, it was the bargaining. In circles of respect, once a special price was made, there was no bargaining. However, he had to remember that in dealing with Groark, he was actually selling to someone Groark represented, a figure of the highest respect.

"Two thousand," he agreed.

Later, as Marco stared after the departing Groark, he wondered how sane Americans could be. No microphone? If a man was curious, what a bizarre tale he might learn of the adventures that portfolio would have. If a man was curious, Marco added privately, or no longer valued his life.

6

The house is over two hundred years old. It was much smaller in the 1790s when Williamstown was just a tiny Massachusetts village and Williams College only recently established there. Since then the house has been enlarged several times until its two-story, white-clapboard shape budges at unlikely angles with ells and additions of whimsical size. The heating system has been engineered along the same let's-stick-on-a-new-piece-here system.

Nick Brown stared at the dirty white radiator in his room. The place was always too hot or too cold. If he had elected to live in one of the modern dorm buildings—which usually meant having a roommate—he could have been assured of regular temperatures. He might even have avoided the galelike blasts of February wind that lanced at him from cracks around the ancient window frame of his room.

But he'd wanted privacy. He'd chosen this ramshackle room in the rambling house and, except for being alternately roasted and frozen, he loved it.

The room represented the first time in his life he'd lived by himself. In looking back on his twenty-two years, Nick could never remember a time without people pressing in on him from every side, touching, talking, laughing, urging food on him, demanding answers . . . intruding.

He knew families were like that, especially big families . . . and especially Sicilian families. That much was taken for granted. But being an American of Sicilian origin didn't necessarily mean having no life alone, did it?

Even now, finishing his much-delayed senior year, he had to put up with constant telephone calls from his mother and weekend visits from one or another of his brothers and their families. "Let's not let Nickie alone for a goddamn second," seemed to be the family motto.

Nick had arranged his heavy desk at a window that looked out on the main street of Williamstown. Since the village itself was devoted mostly to the College and the Clark Art Museum, anything that passed by could be viewed from this vantage point.

He liked that. He liked being a spectator. All his life, it seemed to Nick, he was being urged to *take part*. The hell with it. The Browns were a great do-it family. But here was one Brown who liked to sit back and watch the passing parade.

The trouble was the endless numbers of siblings who served as examples, urgers-on, pep-talking coaches and guidance counselors. Mom and Pop didn't need to say a word. Being the baby of a family of eight boys and two girls meant that he had seven brothers, two brothers-in-law and two sisters to help him Shape Up.

He sat at the desk and watched three college girls in brightly colored crocheted caps struggle across the highway in a strong wind. They bent into it, eyes tearing, books clutched for protection from the blast.

Nick picked up his pen and started the letter for the fourth time. "Dear Leila."

He stared at the two words. His handwriting looked like a kindergarten scrawl. She hadn't answered his last letter. Was there any reason to think she'd answer this one? That she even got his letters?

He knew all about getting mail at American Express offices in Europe, and the fact that letters lingered there without being picked up or returned to the sender for long periods of time. He sighed unhappily and continued writing.

"Sorry to keep doing this number on your head, but who else can I unload on? It's a year since I saw you. I think a lot about getting my act together and splitting for Paris. Don't think I don't think of doing that."

He paused and stared out the window again. A young man he knew was flipping a Day-Glo orange Frisbee to a young woman. The wind caught it and sent the disc whirling skyward like a chip of fire.

"But I am not going to split this scene," he went on writing, "till they goddamn well hand me the B.A. I know it's a lot of crap. But I have to have the piece of paper if I want to live my own life."

Of course, he noted to himself, to get the B.A. he still had to complete his thesis. It was a term paper, actually, but a most important one, since the grade he earned on it was the grade he got in his major, political science. Something about the awesome finality of it had prevented him from doing the thesis. It was still blocking him. And for this delay he could only blame himself, not his family.

It wasn't, Nick reminded himself, that his family downgraded a college diploma. Far from it. Brother Vinnie was a lawyer. Brother-in-law Sal was an accountant. Two of the other boys had B.A.'s. So did both girls. Good schools, too.

The problem was him. There was no one in his superclose family who didn't know Nick's problem and lay it out for him in endless detail.

"You got no goal, Nickie."

"You got no specialty, kid, and in this world you need a specialty."

"You just gotta take aim at something and zoom in on it. Whatever."

"Man, pick your thing and . . . do it!"

It didn't help, either, that in a family of short, wide people, Nick was nearly six feet tall and thin. Nor was it any comfort to him that even his eyes—that intensely pale blue that mysteriously crops up in

Sicilians now and then—set him apart from his family.

Staring out the window at the highway, Nick's gaze unfocused till everything blurred. Why did he have to come from such a highly motivated bunch? Every goddamn one of them was an over-achiever. It was no wonder the George Brown family's holdings were the biggest of any of the families.

All the holdings, the legit ones that were run legitimately and even paid taxes, as well as the ones that nobody talked about in front of the kids at Sunday dinner, the businesses that were strictly the province of the men of the family and provided the cash flow for the rest of the empire . . . all these affairs were flourishing. If he were to draw them as an organizational chart, he'd need a piece of paper the size of a beach towel. And every enterprise doing well. Or floundering badly and producing the tax losses, if that was what it had been designed to do.

Nick made his eyes focus on the letter that lay before him. "Once I get the diploma," he wrote, frowning with the effort of putting his thoughts into words, "I am my own man. Nobody else's."

He sat back and felt a wave of depression wash over him. Leila wouldn't understand what he was talking about. She might not even be *there*, for Christ's sake. It was just an act of dumb faith to assume she was still in Paris and still collecting mail.

He wished he had the guts to fly to Paris during intersession vacation, and find her. It wasn't as if she was his girl anymore. She had been once, but . . . but she was still the only one he could talk to. He was still crazy about her, even though she'd dropped him. Maybe she wouldn't want to see him, once he got over there. Maybe she was tearing up his letters without even reading them.

Even if she were reading his words, how would she understand what the hell he was getting at? She was an only child. She hadn't even lived with her family in years. There was no family, just her mother. The distance between the WASP life of the Darcys and Irishes and the Sicilian smother of his own family was light years.

And if that were not enough, there was another difference, one so immense that it blotted out everything else.

It was well and good to say that people like Leila's stepfather, with their hotshot lawyers and lobbyists, were committing crimes all over the globe, exploiting, upheaving governments that got in their way, corrupting those amenable to it. That was, after all, only business.

His mouth twisted sideways in a bitter grin. Only business. And what was his father but a businessman? What were the Brown brothers and brothers-in-law and cousins and uncles? The whole thing was business.

The humiliating part was that he'd never been able to earn enough to free himself from them. They were right. Nick Brown had no specialty.

Even after he finally finished his thesis—assuming it was approved—and they handed him his B.A., what was it but a piece of paper that said he'd majored in political science? And what was that?

Anybody who'd grown up in the bosom of the Brown family knew that the politics taught in school was a lot of nonsense. Maybe that was why he'd stalled around so long picking a subject for his thesis. Maybe he didn't believe in any of it enough to do the work.

The real political experts weren't the poli sci professors but men like his own father. The real textbook on politics was carried in his father's head, never to be written . . . on pain of death.

7

For an hour the thin-faced man with the narrow-set eyes had been parked in front of the George V Hotel. As he sat behind the wheel of his little Fiat 128, anonymous in its mouse-colored paint job, he tried to keep an eye on the hotel entrance while at the same time watch for the arrival of one of the Parisian meter maids who patrolled this area, writing traffic tickets on cars parked for even a moment in the no-parking zones. They had the reputation of being devoted, sharp-eyed, incorruptible sadists.

On the seat beside him, hidden under a map of Paris, Groark had set up a small, battery-operated FM radio. The thin whine coming from its speaker was unvarying and—to Groark, who had been listening to it for several days now—unnerving.

At the far end of the block, a young woman with a grave face, dark blue jacket and skirt, black mesh stockings and patent leather pumps with high heels began writing traffic tickets. Groark sighed unhappily.

Then his ear registered something different—at last —about the whine coming from the FM receiver. It was getting louder. Groark produced one of his pinched-lip smiles.

A long, dark brown Mercedes 600 limousine appeared at the head of the street and purred softly to a halt in front of the hotel. An immense sable coat with a small woman inside it emerged from the George V and was ushered into the limousine by a chauffeur in a chocolate brown uniform and cap.

Groark followed the big car as it left the neighborhood. He had been following the lady in the car—la Principessa Carloni—since their meeting three days ago in Milan, when Groark had sold her some papers, neatly packaged in an imitation alligator leather portfolio.

The miserly smile on his lips grew microscopically wider. When one's lips were as frugal as his, no smile ever got generous.

The brown limousine stopped in front of the Avenue Kléber entrance of the triangular Sogegarde Building. The Princess went inside. The Mercedes drove off and Groark paused to consider his alternatives.

The whine from the radio transmitter in the leatherette portfolio had grown slightly fainter, but not by much. Obviously it had gone inside this building with the Princess. He had no idea what the building was, nor did its exterior give him many clues, but it wouldn't hurt, he reasoned, to circle the place a few times.

The first time around, Groark noticed a young man with dull blond hair in the doorway of the Hôtel Residence Trocadéro on Avenue Poincaré. He paid little attention.

On his second circuit, Groark saw the young man standing in front of a post office that occupied one storefront's space on the Rue de Longchamp side of the triangular building. He was medium in height, with a long torso encased in blue jeans, white T-shirt and a short denim jacket with metal buttons.

The third time Groark circled the Sogegarde Building, the boy was staring into the windows of a paperback store on Kléber. An old hand at such matters, Groark surmised that the boy was using the store's window as a mirror to continue his surveillance.

The Mercedes 600 turned into the block and parked in front of the entrance to the triangular building. Groark double-parked his Fiat for a moment. In a minute or two, the Princess got in the limousine and it drove away.

Groark frowned, listening to the FM radio on the seat beside him. As the limousine disappeared from view, the whining sound remained constant. Groark nodded his squeezed-in head. The Princess had deposited the fake leather folder inside this building. It was inside this place where she kept her famous hoard of blackmail goodies. He would have to report this to his boss immediately.

Just then the boy examining the paperback bookstore strolled to the corner of Longchamp and stood for a moment in front of Le Carrefour Buffet. Groark couldn't be sure the young man had seen him, not that it made much difference.

Almost at once, the young man walked down Longchamp to an open alleyway at about Number 46. Groark watched him disappear through the opening.

Once more he drove the Fiat on a circuit of the triangular building and this time he caught a glimpse of the boy—who obviously thought he was hidden from casual view—busily writing something in a spiral-bound notebook.

To a man like Groark, it was obvious that the boy was casing the triangular building, noting who came and went, and when, not only via the Kléber entrance, but the ones on Poincaré and Longchamp.

Groark checked his watch. It was a bit later than noon. He headed for his apartment, calculating that a call to Miami Beach now would surely waken his boss. But the news warranted it.

"Wha'?" a sleepy voice said.

"It's Neil, boss."

"G'head."

Groark placed his telephone in a scrambler device. "That little lady," he said into the scrambler phone, "took me to Paris."

"She stash it?"

Groark described the triangular building and its

location. "She has her whole act squirreled away in there," he concluded.

The silence on the line lasted a long time.

"Hello?" Groark asked.

"I'm here," George Brown grunted unhappily. "You know what that place is?"

"Some kinda bank?"

"Ha." Another long pause. "That half-pint guinea broad has foxed us."

"How d'y'figure?"

"It's the one joint we can't bust. Son of a bitch."

"Somebody else has eyes for this crib. I spotted a kid casing it. No pro, but no schnook, neither."

"Good luck to him."

"Any harm in me bracing him?" Groark asked.

"Go ahead. Maybe he's some kinda Houdini. What can we lose?"

"That's what I say, boss." Groark's stingy mouth flattened in what was, for him, a self-congratulatory grin. "What can we lose?"

PART TWO

THE FOLLOWING MARCH

8

Curtis supposed he had a sort of thing for Netta Irish. There was something about her racehorse good looks that rang a bell deep in Curtis's sexual soul. Otherwise he wouldn't have let her get away with the things she did.

Paris had been unusually cold and, apparently, so had the Riviera. At any rate, that was what Netta— Mrs. Irish, Curtis corrected himself—had been complaining of in her phone calls. In March she was coming to Paris with Oscar Ferguson.

Would Curtis alert Sogegarde and arrange for a private viewing room?

He really had no time to run errands of such a clerklike nature. At the moment he was gathering evidence that one of UBCO's assistant managers in Paris was diverting funds to a private currency-speculation scheme of his own—which was doing badly. But Curtis had to be in the Trocadéro neighborhood anyway and it gave him a chance to brush up his acquaintance with M. Hardy, the *chef de la sécurité* at Sogegarde, a most useful contact for anyone in Curtis's business.

And besides, anything for Netta.

Accordingly, after making the necessary telephone call, Curtis set out on foot. It would be a brisk twenty-minute walk from his flat in the Rue Washington, part of it along the Avenue George V, toward the river. He reached the Seine at the Place de l'Alma where the *bateaux mouches* tie up during the day.

Their many-faceted glass roofs twinkled in the pale morning sunlight.

At Avenue du Président Wilson, at about 10:00 A.M., Curtis swung off the river route before it reached the d'Iena bridge to the Eiffel Tower across the Seine. On this cold, breezy morning, the tower stood against a background of fast-moving clouds that gave Curtis the illusion the tower, not the clouds, was drifting past.

Curtis was hiking along Avenue Wilson now, past the Musée d'Arts Modernes. In a moment, the half-circle of grass called the Place du Trocadéro was visible, old, brown-green, spotty and chartreuse yellow in places. Marshal Foch astride his bronze-thewed horse stared due south along the *allée* between the two main buildings of the Palais de Chaillot toward the Eiffel Tower itself. There was a look on Foch's face as if to say: "A bit more to the left, men. That's it."

Curtis turned right at the corner where the Avenue Kléber ran into the Place du Trocadéro. He looked up at the eight-story building which housed Sogegarde, a vast, safe-deposit complex run by one of France's largest banks. Like so many other places in Paris, this area was a focus of major avenues converging like spokes of a wheel whose hub, in this case, was the Place du Trocadéro. The Sogegarde building was triangular, since it stood between the converging Kléber and the Avenue Raymond Poincaré.

Triangular was perhaps not the proper word, Curtis corrected himself. The apex of the triangle had been truncated where the two avenues ran into the Trocadéro, so that, instead of coming to a point, the apex had been flattened to accommodate two cafés, a Métro station entrance and a pastry shop.

From this blunted apex the elderly building ran a full block back to the baseline of its triangle, Rue de Longchamp. About halfway along this block of Kléber, across the street from Number 14 where a paperbook bookstore stood, was the entrance to Sogegarde. It was just an entrance, nothing prepossessing. In fact the entire building, except for its immense bulk and lack of identification, was in no way conspicuous in the Trocadéro neighborhood.

It was hard to believe what lay inside this anonymous structure. Two years ago when he had first heard what Sogegarde actually was—from Louch in one of their drunken evenings on the town—Curtis had not believed the story at all. The next day, once he'd sobered up, Curtis had made a pilgrimage to the Eiffel Tower to stand in one of the long, patient lines of tourists waiting for the elevator ride skyward.

Curtis had never been up in the tower before. Like any other tourist, he boarded the elevator to the second-stage lifts and emerged finally into the perpetual wind that blows at the Troisiéme Etage of the tower, the peak of the thing itself, beyond which only technicians working on the overhead television mast can go.

He had faced toward the Palais de Chaillot and its magnificent double spread of fountains. Following along a line beyond the palais to the Place du Trocadéro, he had spotted the triangular Sogegarde building at once.

Sure enough, it was hollow. Not solid at all but, as Louch had promised him, with a great, hollow, inner courtyard in which sat an enormous . . . what?

Curtis had fished in his pocket and found two one-franc pieces which he'd fed into the coin-operated telescope. After some fiddling around, he was staring intently at the thing in the inner courtyard of the Sogegarde Building. It was a . . . well . . . it was as high as the building itself, eight stories at least. It was round, a cylinder in a triangular space. It looked like a reinforced concrete grain elevator. Or perhaps, Curtis had decided, a giant oil tank, with a shallow conical top, braced by wires and catwalks crisscrossing it.

A network of wire fencing—some of it probably

charged with electricity—barred anyone from jumping across from any part of the main building to the
top of the round inner structure. This—silo?—seemed
isolated by both design and space from contact with
the main Sogegarde structure. And, if Louch had been
telling him the complete truth, this inner, silolike
thing was approachable by only one route.

Apparently its base inside the courtyard was a moat
filled with tens of thousands of gallons of water.
Under the moat, lined in concrete, a single tunnel
ran from the outside world into the center of the
mysterious cylinder. At night, so Louch swore, some
of the moat water was drained into this tunnel, flooding it to the ceiling.

This rather medieval security system was nothing,
Louch had said, compared to the sophisticated sensors
and alarms with which the rest of the interior was
fitted out.

"You see, the moat and the tunnel are relics of the
nineteenth-century mind," he had explained to Curtis. "The thing was finished during the first great war,
you know, and the military mind was still living back
in the Franco-Prussian era. So, in the years since, the
place has been gone over by security experts and
wired to within an inch of its life against burglary."

The Société Générale, one of France's three na-
tionalized banks, operated Sogegarde. As such it maintained regular, and presumably friendly, relations
with most international banks of any size. Since
UBCO was the largest American commercial bank,
and serviced many clients in France, it was natural
that Curtis would have made himself known to his
opposite number in security at the Société.

This brisk March morning, with its pale sun, Curtis
entered the Kléber side of Sogegarde, aware that as
he approached the outer doors he was already being
picked up on closed-circuit television. He walked inside a smallish area and saw a second camera pick

him up as he approached a microphone set into the wall.

"*M. Curtis pour M. Hardy, s'il vous plaît.*"

Somewhere inside, the guard who kept a vigil before the television screens would already have buzzed Hardy. This was not Curtis's first visit to the Trocadéro, but only Hardy, the *chef de la sécurité*, knew him on sight.

Waiting impatiently, Curtis supposed this super-French organization was necessary, but there was something silly about it, nevertheless, and also something very offputtingly French, as if the arrangements had been devised not only to identify visitors, but to give them as well a strong feeling of inferiority. Specimens under observation.

A door clicked open and Curtis advanced into yet another detention-pen area where yet another camera picked him up. He repeated his request into a second microphone, resisting the inner urge to make a face at the camera lens.

The door now buzzed open and Curtis stepped inside a third area.

Hardy stood there, peering at him through bullet-proof plate glass. Behind him, two burly guards with drawn guns waited attentively.

Hardy was a small man, shorter than Curtis and older, with a neatly trimmed gray mustache and a tonsure of bald scalp surrounded by dark hair with no trace of gray. He wore pince-nez glasses, did M. Hardy (Ahr-dee, Curtis repeated to himself silently), but perhaps out of a concession to modernity, they were attached to his lapel not by a grosgrain ribbon but by a thin cord.

He removed them to stare at Curtis through the bulletproof glass that separated visitors from insiders. Curtis could see the cruel little bites in the bridge of M. Hardy's nose where the pince-nez had clung.

The bald head bobbed up and down and the look of inquiry, faintly tinged with disdain, was replaced

on M. Hardy's small face by a slight smile tinged
with suspicion. He made a mixing motion with his
hands as if chastising the entrance guard for keeping
Curtis waiting.

Hardy's hand was small, thin and papery dry as
he shook Curtis's hand. "We seldom get to see you
here," he said, leading the newcomer along a corridor to his office.

"One of our clients will be visiting here," Curtis
said as he sat down in the chair Hardy indicated. "A
rather large private room is needed and the services
of two or three men to bring objects and remove
them."

Hardy sat down behind his large desk and almost
disappeared from view. Small as he was, Hardy was
mostly legs. His trunk was no taller than a child's
and he had difficulty looking over the top of the pen
set to Curtis's face.

There was a longish pause. Curtis knew from past
experience at Trocadéro Tower that Hardy would
never dream of asking a client's name, although he
knew most of them by sight. Deposits here were by
numbered account anyway, quite like the celebrated
anonymous Swiss accounts, and it would have been as
much a breach of protocol for Hardy to ask a name
as for Curtis to volunteer one.

Nevertheless, Hardy had to have some indication
of the scope of the request. "A morning visit, then?"
he managed to ask.

Curtis nodded. "I think this will be an all-day
review. Some rather large pieces." He paused. Then:
"Two people, I think."

"Among them you?"

Curtis shook his head from side to side. "I'll be in
Basel."

"Basel." Hardy's narrow face grew cunning. He sat
forward so that his chin almost touched the top of
his desk. "M'sieur Curtis, a favor. Just between us."

"Certainly."

"You know those Alsan capsules, the Gerovital 12, I think they're called?"

Curtis nodded again. These eternal-youth pills were sold all over Switzerland, the product of an amazing Rumanian woman scientist. Next to tourist trips to Dracula's castle, her rejuvenating medicines were probably her nation's most profitable source of income.

"They're damned expensive," Hardy was saying, tilting sideways to pull out his wallet. He flipped through to some five-hundred-franc notes, removed one and pushed it across the desk. "A bottle of one hundred?"

"Consider it done."

"It's not for me," Hardy said then.

Curtis had been expecting this. The pills were never for the person buying them. If he were any judge of character, he'd say that Hardy would mention an ancient aunt, or perhaps his wife, as the ultimate consumer of the capsules.

But Hardy surprised Curtis. "A certain lady friend," he said then, producing a frosty smile that engaged only one side of his mouth. "It's a delicate matter. You do me a tremendous favor."

"Not at all," Curtis said, pocketing the bill. "I'll return from Basel Sunday. So, the next day, I'll drop off the bottle here."

"Er, suitably wrapped."

Curtis held his hands palms out. "In a safe-deposit box, if you wish."

Hardy produced a tiny chirrup of a laugh. "Be sure to ask for me and hand the package over in person, like a good fellow."

"Of course."

This out of the way, the two men tried to find a way of bringing the interview to a quick close. They had no further business with each other, nor were they, in any manner of speaking, friends. Business was full of such moments, Curtis thought, in which there is simply no reason to prolong the matter, but manners required some sort of social maneuver. He had never learned the right one.

He got to his feet. "Always good to see you, M. Hardy."

The little man stood up and came around his desk to lead the way to the Avenue Kléber entrance. In the distance, along a corridor that must have run the full length of the building, Curtis could see a parade of workmen in overalls, each pushing a small, four-wheeled cart.

There were a dozen men with carts, perhaps more, and they moved slowly, as though this were a solemn occasion of state. About to usher Curtis out, Hardy paused and watched the parade for a moment as it drew closer. *"Merveilleux,"* he murmured.

"I beg your pardon?"

"It's the Cellini saltcellars," Hardy said. "I am supposed to let no one see this—" He stopped himself and stood aside to give Curtis a better view.

The parade was on top of them now, moving into another corridor that branched out at right angles from the long one. Each cart bore only one object, an epergne, a saltcellar or some other form of table decoration. They seemed to be solid gold, by the tight-faced concern with which each workman pushed his cart. The gold was inlaid with surprisingly large rubies, topaz and stones Curtis took to be emeralds.

"Lovely workmanship," he murmured.

"Worth billions."

"Of francs?"

"Naturellement." Hardy watched the last workman disappear into the distance. The moment was past. But the air seemed to vibrate with the sound and the—electric aura, was it?—of great riches.

"They're Hapsburg, originally," he volunteered, "part of the collection that's normally kept near the Hofburg in Vienna, in the art history museum."

His voice had a hushed quality to it, as though he

were not used to the proximity of such great wealth. It had been so unusual for him to let Curtis catch even this tiny glimpse that the moment had become a special one.

"Billions," Hardy said then. "And yet they fit into only one little corner of Trocadéro Tower." The small man seemed lost in thought. "How much is the rest of our inventory worth?" he asked then. "No way of knowing," Hardy went on in a helpless voice, as if the idea were too big for him. "Astronomical. When you think of what's stored here." He had popped on his nasty little spectacles, which clung to his nose like a bird with sharp claws. The pale sunlight on the street reflected for a moment in the lenses, giving Hardy a blank, blind look.

"When you think of the museums who use our resources even temporarily, as in the case of the Kunsthistorisches Museum, or the private dealers, the galleries, who store everything with us during their off-seasons. Or the hundreds of families, like your client, who keep their paintings and sculpture here. Or the business concerns who store documents with us. Yes, and the governments, too. It's amazing what governments bring to us. Not just works of art, but documents of great value, as if their own facilities were not secure enough."

The two men stood silently for a moment, thinking of this. "Governments come and go," Curtis said then. "The Trocadéro Tower remains."

Hardy nodded. "Even I have little idea what is hidden here," he said in a small, awed voice. "When the Louvre or the Jeu de Paume closes a wing for renovation, everything is stored here. Out of season, all the galleries—here in Paris, in the south, in Milan and Frankfurt and London and Madrid—all use our facilities.

"The families, Curtis. Everyone, Pahlavi, Niarchos, Rockefeller, your own Irish collection, Getty, Agnelli, Krupp, even the Windsors, they all come here, if only for a time. There is never a moment when we don't have things from the Tate, the Metropolitan, the Prado, the British Museum." His voice dropped. "The Hermitage in Leningrad. Yes!"

Curtis could see that the little man rarely found anyone trustworthy enough to tell these things to, or rarely experienced such a moment of ecstasy in which such confidences tumbled forth.

"But the money value is only extrinsic, Curtis. It is nothing, compared to the intrinsic value, the political significance, the value to world civilization, to the humanities, to scholarship, history, to . . ." His voice died away.

"Quite a responsibility," Curtis said then.

Hardy's spectacles were two moons of reflected light from the street behind Curtis. "I think often of the riches here," the little man went on in his amazed murmur. "I dream of it often."

"The stuff of dreams."

"Yes," Hardy agreed solemnly. "The cultural heritage of the West."

Curtis had never seen the little gray-mustached man in such an emotional state. With his blank Orphan Annie eyes and his bald monk's pate, his girlfriend in need of youth and his librarian's pince-nez, M. Hardy was a classic figure of fun. But Curtis found it impossible to smile.

The two men shook hands. Curtis left. Outside the March wind had lessened. The day was warmer. It always gave Curtis the creeps inside any place as impervious and tomblike as the Trocadéro Tower. It was a tomb. The cultural heritage of the West. But hidden from the eye of man.

Despite the sudden warmth of the sunshine, Curtis shivered.

9

In any big city there are permanent and temporary neighborhoods. Some sections of Paris, for example, have remained more or less as they were in the time of Napoleon. There are dark corners of the city where even François Villon might still know his way.

But new, temporary quarters of town also spring up, often in the wake of some disaster, and seem to materialize overnight, full-blown. Such a neighborhood surrounds that part of the old Marais quarter where the great glass-and-steel roofs of Les Halles once spread their wings over one of the largest markets in the world.

Where the stalls of flower sellers, grocers and butchers once stood, teeming with noise in the dark hours before dawn, there now exists a solemn wilderness of excavation, dust and mud. The politest name the Parisians have for this empty area—where some mysterious municipal construction has been under way for years—is "The Hole."

Around it a Little America has sprung up, a shops-and-cafés area catering to the pressing need of Parisian young people for cheeseburgers and chili con carne, for Levi's and Frye boots and for sweat shirts on which are stenciled legends relating to marijuana smoking or intellectual bons mots of the nature of "Fuck You."

One of the narrow streets leading away from The Hole is the Rue de la Grande Truanderie which ends three blocks west at the Boulevard de Sebastopol. The street has a few sex shops and small bars, a boutique for kinky clothes called The Great Mischief, in a rough translation of the street's name, and a restaurant-bar of some charm known as Mother's.

Mother's repeats in painstaking detail the brick-walled look of an East Side Manhattan pub like P.J. Clarke's with a long, ancient mahogany bar and several dining rooms, menus chalked on blackboards, many varieties of beer on tap.

Mother's is not cheap, although its mainstay dishes are hamburgers and fried potatoes. Nor is it easy to find a table. The usual lines of expectant diners wait with apparent good nature, often for an hour. Part of the business of eating at places like Mother's is being seen there. Standing in line for a table is an even more conspicuous way of achieving that result, and without paying for the food.

It was one of Louch's favorite places.

Not to be seen. But to see. Louch's favorite vantage point for seeing was not actually in Mother's. He had an arrangement with the madame of a *hôtel d'accommodation* across the street. Louch got Room 7 whenever he required it. Sometimes this meant ousting a couple who had just checked in for an hour of joy. Louch was always truly apologetic when this happened. He insisted on paying the female of the couple what she would have earned if he hadn't interrupted her working schedule.

Although he had his Sorbonne science degree, and the budget to buy the most sophisticated apparatus designed to eavesdrop, record and photograph, Louch believed in simple, direct measures. He carried around in a pocket of his much-worn jacket a small pair of folding binoculars of the type used by serious opera buffs. These glasses, and the encyclopedia of faces Louch kept in his head, were enough. Well, almost enough.

When Mother's had opened for business some years before, Louch had also implanted listening devices. He saw no reason for Mother's to be the only

place in the lively new area without them. His spo-
radic use of the bugs indicated that the investment
was sound. As the new neighborhood stopped mush-
rooming and settled into a semblance of stability,
Mother's became Louch's most useful listening post,
so much so that he came to an agreement with one
of the captains. For a monthly stipend and Louch's
assurance that the man's previous record of drug con-
victions would be overlooked, the captain served as
Louch's eyes on those occasions—tonight was one—
when Louch needed to know who was sitting where.

He had followed the boy from the Chatelet station
of the Métro, trailing him by several blocks. The boy
had been with two friends, one also Arabic looking,
all in their early twenties. It was a warm evening in
March. They had strolled. None of them had noticed
Louch, even in the subway car. He had followed them
to Mother's and indicated them to the captain. With
a nod of his head, Louch signaled that he would be in
his usual post across the street.

It was a busy night in Mother's, hardly ten o'clock,
but already quite full. As Louch sat in the window of
Room 7, binoculars still in his pocket, he knew that
it would be some time before the captain was able to
tell him which table the three boys had finally gotten.

Louch followed no set routine in keeping an eye
on them. He had been interested in the handsome
one for some time now, the one who in Louch's files
bore the code name Aziz.

The dossier on Aziz was filling up. Since last summer, when Louch had spotted him at the American
Express office and been caught at it by Curtis, he had
assembled a lot of new material on Aziz.

He was twenty-three, with a French last name that
belonged to his father, a reputable hotelier in the
Baie des Singes area of Tunis. His good looks came
from his mother, who had been a Schiaparelli model
in the 1950s. Aziz retained the lean desert aspect of
her Touareg family. He'd gone to schools both in

Tunisia and France and had taken special courses in Libya as well. He traveled a lot, occasionally out of France, and always alone.

Louch also knew something of the second young man with Aziz tonight, a German. The third, who looked Arabic, was new to him. Louch's system, or lack of it, depended on his own memory for faces. Eventually his files contained photographs, but none of them were as sharp or as memorable as those he carried in his head.

He lighted one of his Gitanes and filled the air of Room 7 with the fat, acid smell of Turkish tobacco. Time passed. On such nights, it passed more slowly, Louch knew, because the life of this quarter was an active one on pleasant nights like this. Prostitutes and drug dealers moved in and out among the strolling couples. He noted several plainclothesmen of his acquaintance among the passing parade.

A large party of well-to-do Germans and their ladies of the evening arrived in three cabs. From his vantage point one story up and across the street, Louch watched the captain regretfully inform the Germans —with that experienced blend of outward civility and not-so-hidden malice—that he couldn't possibly promise a table for twelve people in under ninety minutes. Would M'sieur like to come back at . . . oh, say, eleven-thirty?

Louch's grin matched the captain's as the German party huffily stalked off to find another eating place. There would be several with room for a large party, but without the cachet of Mother's.

Instead of returning inside, the captain stood for a moment, arms folded. He let his glance flick upward. It almost met Louch's glance, but didn't. Then his right hand, visible against his left forearm, arranged itself so that three fingers were showing. The captain held the position for a moment, then showed two fingers silhouetted against his dark denim jacket.

Three-two. Louch got to his feet and lumbered over

to the small medicine cabinet that stood above the tiny porcelain sink in the corner of Room 7, a one-tap sink where the women who used this room made quick dabs at cleanliness before returning to the street.

Louch opened the door of the cabinet and then reached in and pulled out the rear wall. A baked-metal panel displayed several dozen tiny toggle switches. Louch counted them row by row, then flicked one. He picked up a roll of insulated wire hanging from the switchboard, plugged in one end and unrolled the wire as he moved backward across the room to his seat at the window. The wire ended in a small earphone of the hearing-aid kind. Louch tucked it into one of his big ears with their queerly dangling lobes.

He sat down and listened. The microphone at the table was one of the contact variety. Some acoustical genius had convinced Louch that by adhering the thing to the underside of a table, the entire surface acted as a collector of sound, moreover of just the immediate sounds of those talking around this particular table.

In this the genius had been correct. But neither he nor Louch had foreseen that this method also picked up giant rumbles, explosions, thuds and crashes that were the commonplace traffic of plates, glasses and silverware being moved about on the table's surface.

Louch winced as one of the three boys emphasized something he was saying—in Arabic—by rapping the table, probably with the handle of a spoon. Louch gritted his teeth and listened . . . listened.

He noted almost absentmindedly that the boy he believed to be German spoke almost as fluent Arabic as the other two. Germans were good at languages, Louch decided. And even better at terror.

Good God but humans were boring. He found himself wondering if the small talk of his drinking companions was quite as dull as these three young men, endlessly arguing politics and money and tactics.

So repetitive were most people, and so fuzzy in expressing themselves, that only a tenth of what they finally did say meant much. If given to him as court-reporter transcript, Louch could reduce each page of conversation to a sentence and miss nothing of importance.

". . . says she will do it."

"First she promises. Then she reneges."

". . . ways of making sure she keeps her word."

"But she assures me that she . . ."

"You haven't started believing everything she . . ."

". . . exact a solemn promise, under oath."

"She has already given me her word."

"Please don't insult our intelligence."

". . . have to treat her as a person of honor."

"And for this reason, she will . . ."

Louch closed his eyes. Sleepytime talk. Endless, repetitive, like Arabic music with its little finger thuds, again, again, and the skirling quarter tones twisting in and out again, again.

Over and over again. Louch spit out the end of his cigarette and lighted a second. If it weren't for his knowledge that Aziz bore watching, he could be doing something more useful tonight. Even going to bed early was preferable to this self-imposed boredom.

Most people in the terrorist cells and movements were young, many as young as Aziz. Only the Germans tended to be older. And most of the young people, like youths everywhere, were quite naive, in Louch's view. One could call them idealists. Louch called them dumbbells.

Unlike most of the government people assigned to antiterrorist work, Louch felt no hatred or fear of the people he was trying to outwit. To him they seemed . . . brain-damaged. Louch felt that some very important genes had been left out of these young people, so that, as they grew up, they had somehow lost the most important link in human endeavor, the one between public and private good.

No Frenchman needed to be reminded of self-interest. A law in his own interest, the Frenchman obeyed. Any other law—those about taxes, for example—he spent time and ingenuity outwitting. Louch was enough of a man of the world to know that the French were by no means unique in this respect.

But there were times when even a Frenchman understood that his own interest ran head-on into the public interest and it was there, Louch reasoned, that heroes were born.

He had seen it happen in the Underground during the war. A man or woman, one of the Maquis, would embark on something so devoid of self-interest that death awaited the outcome. It didn't matter, Louch knew, whether this hero-in-the-making had reached such a pass deliberately, or was trapped into it by mistakes or blind bad luck.

No, what mattered was whether the person accepted danger or backed away from it. Defended the public interest, or held tightly to his own. Was, in short, a dead hero or a live coward.

Thinking these things as he half-listened to the table chatter of the three young men, Louch smiled slightly. By no stretch of the imagination did today's young people qualify as heroes. Not for him.

He sat forward suddenly. The girl was coming down the street, the tiny one with the frizzy hair. The one Louch privately referred to as Curtis's girl.

Maddening. Curtis was his friend—well, perhaps not a friend as one counted the true friends of childhood—but Curtis steadfastly refused to identify the girl for Louch. She was American, like Curtis, and obviously of a well-to-do family, customers of UBCO, or Curtis would not be taking an interest in her affairs.

Louch knew only that Curtis deposited cash for her

once a month. He had had the girl followed by his men and she had lost them, not once, but several times. She was very good (or his men were worse than Louch had suspected), and her connection with all of this remained tantalizingly hazy.

Louch had asked Curtis to let him mark some of the bills, or register their serial numbers, so that they could be traced later. In this way Louch could determine if the money found its way into the terror underground. Curtis had refused. It had put a serious strain on their friendship.

"What you're asking is out of the question," Curtis had insisted.

"When lives are at stake, nothing is out of the question."

"What lives?"

"These are dangerous children," Louch had explained. "They are idealists. They struggle for the betterment of man. So, naturally, a human life means nothing to them."

"Oh, Christ, Louch. Stop exaggerating."

"Assassination? Hijacking? *These* are the exaggerations. I only witness these things, these monstrous exaggerations of human violence."

"Lighten up, Louch. Are you saying this girl and her Bedouin buddies have been—?"

"No. No violence. Yet."

"Then back off."

"Until people die, is that it? Wait until then?"

But he'd made no further headway with Curtis. It wasn't that the man was amoral or stupid, Louch knew. It was that he had a keen sense of the perimeters of his job, his mandate from UBCO and from the bank's customer. And it obviously didn't extend to cooperation with an obscure branch of an obscure bureau whose activities might put the tiny girl behind bars.

Oh, Louch knew these efficient American agent

types. He'd dealt with them in Vietnam and along the heroin routes. They never stepped beyond the boundaries of their job. This was the secret of their efficiency: do no more than you're asked. It was also the secret of their failures, since life never unreels in neat, individual bobbins of thread. Everything is tied to everything else.

And when the roles reversed, Louch told himself now, Curtis would expect cooperation. When this darling little wool-topped daughter of the idle rich stopped playing her games because they'd brought her too close to the edge of chaos—when she wanted out, wanted a reprieve, an exoneration—then Curtis would beg for cooperation.

Were all streets in America one-way? Louch wondered.

He watched the girl enter Mother's. He sat back and a long moment later had the dismal satisfaction of hearing her voice at Table 32. Out of deference to the fact that she seemed to speak very little Arabic, the boys switched to French.

Almost at once, too, the talk came into a sharper focus. Maybe it was the shift in language. Arabic is after all the language of delay, of indolence. French is the language of science, emotion, achievement, Louch told himself.

Or perhaps it was just that the three young men wanted to seem more efficient in the eyes of this American efficiency expert. She was pretty and perhaps her cash was keeping all these boys in shoe leather. In any event, from endless ruminations, the talk now shifted almost at once to precise descriptions.

"He's dead. An eye disease. The infection spread."

"But the infirmary . . ."

"There is no infirmary. Our village is in the hills."

"In the city there are hospitals."

"For those with money."

"The clinic at Al Akhmein is free."

"But only to the American families from the missile base."

"Then we can't count on him?"

"Nor his proximity fuses."

"Tais-toi, imbecile!"

It was Aziz's whisper cutting through like a hot branding iron. Mother's may have been a fashionable place to spend the American girl's money, Louch decided, but it was no place for idle chatter about— what had he mentioned?—proximity fuses. Sweet Christ, a bombing?

As if they had been a quartet of actors handed a new script, the four young people began talking about something else entirely.

". . . needs an abortion," the girl was saying. "Do we know a doctor for her?"

"There's a very good man in the Eleventh Arrondissement."

"I have one of ours for her. Habib knows him."

"Where did he train, Beirut?"

"Paris. And Basel."

"Isn't there a woman doctor who . . ."

"Mm. Maybe."

"It's bad news about Karim dying."

"Death is never good news."

"But especially now."

"Why now?"

"My information about the shipment. After expecting it for so long, too. And now that the time's come . . . no Karim."

Louch sat forward. The word "shipment" had been concrete enough, in this maze of mists, to jostle his attention.

"The pickup is scheduled no later than Good Friday."

"That means . . . ?"

"The Christian Easter."

"Ah."

They were silent for a long moment. Louch's mind tangled with the odd words. "Scheduled" and "pick-up" were nice, concrete words. How did they fit in with proximity fuses?

". . . no longer living with Mamoud."

"That sort of thing never lasts."

"Don't be a fool."

"She was far too intelligent for Mamoud."

". . . petit bourgeois pimp."

"Mm. Maybe."

Louch's attention flagged again. Whatever else they were, the children were disciplined. Not entirely, of course, or they would not have surfaced at Mother's. This was no place for dedicated fighters for the freedom of the Third World, this decadent watering hole for gilded wastrels of the petite bourgeoisie. Hard-core activists ate gruel in unheated garrets.

As a matter of fact, following them from the Métro, Louch had been surprised to see them turn in at Mother's, but the arrival of their American benefactor solved that problem. She would be the one to want it both ways: political idealism and radical chic.

It was nearly eleven o'clock now and none of them had ordered anything but beer. Louch yawned and smoked another Gitane. He suspected there wouldn't be much more to listen to. They had enough sense not to talk about anything very interesting in such a place. Then why go there?

Louch straightened up. A car had turned into the Rue de la Grande Truanderie. There were fewer people on the sidewalks now. The neighborhood had settled down to indoor pleasures. The car was moving slowly as if the chauffeur had never been on this street before.

Some modification had been made to the normal chassis of a long, black, seven-passenger Fleetwood. The big Cadillac's doors had been extended a few inches up into the roof so that people could get in and out of the car without stooping.

Louch drew back from the window and pulled binoculars from the pocket of his wrinkled jacket. He focused through one of the Fleetwood's large windows. Two men sat there for a moment. The one nearest Louch seemed older, heavier. He hadn't stirred from his seat, but was gesticulating. The other man was preparing to leave the car.

It had stopped directly in front of Mother's. Louch could only see the chauffeur and the older man in back. The captain of the restaurant had come to the door. He watched for a moment, then swung the door open.

The man who was leaving got out of the black car and closed the door behind him. He was thin, with a very narrow face, as if his head had been squeezed together. He wore an American raincoat and a suede hat. Without looking back, he headed into Mother's.

The heavyset man in the rear set gestured. The car moved forward, turned the corner and was gone. Louch put away the binoculars. As he did, through the tiny earphone he was surprised to hear the newcomer being seated at Table 32.

"We are waiting for an hour," Aziz said in a cold voice. He had switched to English and his command of the language was imperfect.

"Let me handle him," the girl said. "Look—"

"Shut up." The man's voice was high and scratchy. Louch could hear scraping sounds. "Here it is," the man grunted.

The earphone went dead.

Louch got up and checked the connection behind the medicine cabinet. It seemed all right. So the man had found the contact microphone and removed it. Louch's face went blank for a moment, then his mouth twisted in an unhappy grin. A professional's touch at last, he thought.

But all was not lost. He could no longer listen to the conversation, but he had recognized the heavyset man in the back of the Fleetwood sedan. One didn't need Louch's almost photographic memory for faces the recognize an international figure like George Brown.

10

La Principessa Claudia Carloni, bundled up in an immense sable greatcoat and cossack hat that hid everything except her eyes, with their extra-long lashes and hint of added glitter, perched in the back of the Mercedes 600, a car in which ten people her size could fit.

The rented Mercedes was the same dark brown as her furs. For Nico, who served as chauffeur, she had rented a dark brown uniform. It was true that the Principessa's business visits to Paris were usually of a confidential nature, but did that mean that *le tout Paris* couldn't know she was, indeed, cutting her usual swath through the City of Light? Even in the Principessa's delicate business, publicity never hurt.

Her first appointment at Sogegarde's Trocadéro Tower was for three in the afternoon. The sable brown Mercedes moved with sumptuous languor along the Avenue Raymond Poincaré toward the Place du Trocadéro. At the corner of Rue de Longchamp, the Principessa glanced left at the beginning of the Sogegarde building in which the tower was hidden. On the opposite corner stood a small office of the Paribas Bank, the beginning of a long block of mostly residential buildings that led eventually to the Place itself.

Nico maneuvered the heavy car slowly. The Principessa, glancing idly to her right, saw the entrance to the embassy of Bahrain. Several doors farther along was the Ugandan embassy. Incongruously, a big

Kawasaki motorcycle was chained to the fence at its entrance. The Principessa frowned. No class, these emerging nations.

"Nico, più veloce, caro. Siamo in retardo."

He guided the Mercedes around the semicircular Place, where the statue of Marshal Foch sat eternally on his gigantic bronze war horse, past the Passy Cemetery where the Principessa would be transacting some business later in the afternoon and then, taking a sharp left, past the facade of the Palais de Chaillot and left again to the corner of the Avenue Kléber.

It was a ceremonial procession of one. The big auto moved at a parade pace in a circle around the monument until it turned into Kléber and approached the entrance to Sogegarde. Nico was braking smoothly to a stop in front when the Principessa's sharp eyes spotted three people emerging from the building.

She sank lower in the back seat until nothing at all was visible except her eyes. Not that any of the three people knew her. The woman was the Widow Irish and the man holding her arm was the art-expert lover with some sort of Scottish name. The other man was Tom Sandweg. It was he who led the other two back down Kléber toward the Place du Trocadéro.

"Presto, Nico!"

She ordered the car forward again and left at Rue Didier, then left again on Poincaré. Once more the dark brown Mercedes passed the two embassies. The Kawasaki was gone, the Principessa noted. At the corner of the Place, she had Nico pull to the curb in the space between the Hotel Residence Trocadéro, a pleasant small hotel, and at the corner, the triangular Café du Trocadéro.

As they waited, the three Americans came around the Kléber corner and headed into the Café Malakoff. The Principessa glanced at her watch. Exactly three o'clock. She made a face, then tried to smooth away the muscular furrows she had produced.

"*Aspetta, caro*," she called, letting herself out of the car and dashing wildly across Poincaré to the far corner. She gave the appearance of a small puffball of dark brown fluff, borne on a wind of near hurricane speed. She slipped into the Café Malakoff by a side entrance and, without the waiter seeing her, materialized at a table behind the American trio with her back to them.

The widow and her lover had ordered coffee, Sandweg a whisky and soda with ice. Now he was saying something in an undertone that the Principessa strained to her. Her English was quite good, but her hearing left a bit to be desired.

The burly art expert the Principessa dismissed as impossible, the type of bully who was too easy to handle to be very interesting. The woman she despised for her tall good looks and infinite supply of money, none of which she had earned. The other man, Sandweg, with his graying hair and animal health, intrigued the Principessa. He was upwardly mobile. Such men took chances. And where the high risk went, there went la Principessa Claudia Carloni.

". . . goddamned dog-in-the-manger attitude, Oscar," Sandweg complained.

"Bullshit." The burly man was silent for a long moment. Then: "The sight of you pleading poverty is about as impressive as when Netta complains she hasn't a thing to wear." He produced a mirthless laugh in which no one joined. "Is that why you tagged along to Paris, just to stick out your hand and beg? I resent you even being here, Sandweg. And you sure as hell had no business horning in on us at the Trocadéro."

"Nevertheless," the woman said, and stopped.

The waiter put down various drinks and left. "Nevertheless," Sandweg picked up, "if you people don't liquidate something substantial, there could be an ugly bankruptcy and all sorts of creditors searching for assets."

"Will you cut that?" the art expert demanded. "You've been crying wolf ever since Cap Ferrat."

"You don't give me an alternative," Sandweg said with barely controlled anger. "I have yet to hear you say, 'Okay, Tom, we're all in the same boat. If I can't do this, maybe I can do something else.' All I get from you is a flat no."

"Something else?" the sandy-haired man asked. "Like what? A few spare Picassos or the odd Rembrandt sketch? What the hell are you nattering about?"

"I've been checking other assets," Sandweg persisted. "What about the château at Senlis?"

"What about it?" the woman wanted to know.

"Is it worth anything?"

"It's as full of crap as a Christmas turkey," the art expert said. "The artwork is second-rate, but the sculpture and the books and the . . ." His voice died away. "Hm."

"Hm," Sandweg repeated.

"You're really that desperate?" the other man asked.

"Do you want me to get down on my knees?"

None of them spoke for a while. The waiter came over to the Principessa's table. "Madame?"

She shook her finger at him and demanded a menu. He disappeared. The Principessa got up and moved as inconspicuously as possible out the side entrance of the Café Malakoff.

She got back in the brown Mercedes and proceeded to the Kléber entrance of Trocadéro Tower by the same circular route. It was three-fifteen. She still had plenty of time to get to her vaults, remove the documents for which she'd come and make her four o'clock appointment at Passy Cemetery, near the grave of Debussy, where someone would hand over many thousand-franc Swiss notes in return for those documents.

As she went about the business of signing in at Trocadéro Tower, the Principessa ran over in her mind the conversation she had made it her business to listen to. Some of it made sense, but none of it seemed very promising. Creditors. Bankruptcy. Still, with a little discreet detective work, it could be developed into something more.

At two minutes to four, as the brown Mercedes swept up to the Avenue Georges Mandel entrance to Passy Cemetery, the three Americans left the Café Malakoff. The Principessa's sharp, glittering eyes spotted them at once, but she didn't ask Nico to slow the car.

It was because she had been thus distracted for an instant that she failed to spot the Kawasaki motorcycle slightly down the street from the corner of the Place du Trocadéro, where the Rue Greuze curves into Mandel.

She was sharp, the Principessa, but no one could hope to see everything in such a busy town as Paris.

11

The telephone call had not been a complete surprise to Curtis. When Netta Irish had arrived in Paris, he had first had a call from Oscar Ferguson demanding to know, in his usual officious manner, if everything had been arranged at Sogegarde for their one day of reviewing paintings and sculpture in the guarded fastness of its keep. Curtis had barely been able to get out a "yes" when Ferguson had, without saying good-bye, hung up.

A day later, however, after the visit, the call was from Mrs. Irish.

The late March weather had turned rainy. Curtis had come home to his apartment from a wet day of minor frustrations. He had successfully traced the funds being diverted from Paris by the UBCO assistant manager. They had turned up, as he had suspected, in Basel. The man had been confronted with his crime, a restitution plan had been agreed to, and he had been allowed to resign. Now Curtis had a new problem. Bill Elston in the New York office had asked him to check the whereabouts of the Czech minister for trade who was two days overdue for an off-the-record chat with a consortium of banks whose only American member was UBCO. The prospective loan was large and lucrative, the minister powerful enough to authorize it on his signature alone.

It had taken Curtis most of the day to locate the rest of the trade mission, housed in various modestly priced Paris hotels. Of the minister himself, there was no trace. Perhaps tomorrow?

On his return to the apartment in the Rue Washington, Curtis checked his answering-service tape recorder and found that Netta Irish had called at four and again at five. It was now six, totally dark outside the windows, a nasty March wind prying at the glass, rattling, searching for entry. Curtis made himself a tall Scotch and soda and waited for the telephone to ring. It did so at one minute after six.

"You're in," Netta Irish began. "What luck. I thought you'd left Paris."

"I thought you had."

"Only Oscar. He's up in Senlis at the château."

Curtis sat back and put his feet up on an ottoman. He sipped his drink. "What château?"

"Something my late husband owned, an estate, a château, a topiary garden, a small *hameau* and dozens of dreary Greuzes and Watteaus and Delacroix and immense bronze caryatids by Vaincre."

Curtis frowned at his drink. "What's a Vaincre?"

"Late eighteenth-century sculptor of dryads, maenads, seraphim, nymphs, fountain statuary . . ." Her voice died away. Then: "Are you free for dinner tonight?"

Over the rim of his glass, Curtis could see his kitchen, where in the refrigerator sat his usual dinner, cold sausage and cheese, enlivened, if he felt ambitious, by a cup of soup from a can. "I'm afraid not," he said then. "I'm due now for dinner with someone."

"Oh." Downturn in the usually confident voice. "And after?"

"After dinner?" Curtis sat up straight in the easy chair and let his legs drop to the floor. She meant business, did she? "A drink or something?"

"Or something."

He arrived at her suite in the Ritz about ten. He'd

seen the inside of this particular kind of suite often enough. It was the one his own visiting UBCO brass usually rented, two bedrooms, a service kitchen and a huge living room with a dozen windows overlooking the Place Vendôme.

She had used some restraint, Curtis saw, in that she was still dressed more or less as she might have been for dinner at a restaurant, in a black knit dress that clung to her long body. The V neck plunged deeply enough to show cleavage in most women, but not her. The skirt was the new, slightly shorter length, Curtis noted, which crossed her long, lean legs just above the knee. She made them drinks and indicated a sofa facing the array of windows overlooking the city below.

"It's stopped raining," Curtis said. Good-looking, dark-haired women didn't necessarily tongue-tie him, even when they invited him to their hotel suite after hours. But UBCO clients were another matter. Tightrope act.

"Let's just relax," she said, extending her legs to the dark walnut coffee table and letting her heels click down on the thick, plate-glass top.

Curtis admired her legs for a while. Then: "Why is Mr. Ferguson at the château? Selling it?"

"Possibly." She touched the bottom of his glass and moved it gently upward in a please-drink gesture. "He hates everything in it, but he's canny enough to know it's worth a lot. He's down there with a perfectly sweet little man who knows antiques the way Oscar knows art."

"The Duc de Clary?"

"That's the one."

Curtis tried to look impressed. "Then the château is worth quite a bit. The duke doesn't play with trifles."

"He'd like to play with Oscar, I think."

Both of them sipped their drinks and sat silently for a while. "He'll be several days," Mrs. Irish said, more to herself than to Curtis, but it did conjure up a long, Oscarless period of time.

"And you?"

"I'm supposed to go up there tomorrow."

"But—?"

She shrugged. Her smallish breasts moved beneath the flat knit wool. Her big, dark brown eyes in her pale ivory face moved sideways to watch Curtis. "Paris isn't all that fascinating when one's on one's own."

Curtis let the remark die away for a long moment. "Did your visit to the Trocadéro go well?"

She nodded somberly. "Spooky place, isn't it?"

"I've never been inside the inner vaults."

"Mausoleum." She drawled the word.

Curtis knew she was working herself up to something, but he didn't know her well enough to know exactly what she had in mind. He finished his drink, but held his hand around it to keep her from offering a refill. There was a—an aura around her—a field of force. Not the usual tension beautiful women created, nor the special atmosphere that surrounds a woman who is not only beautiful but rich. There was something radarlike about the lines of force she emitted, as if with those great dark eyes she was sending signals into the night, to return bearing messages.

The daughter, Curtis reminded himself. He cleared his throat. "Leila picked up her March money," he said then.

She nodded again, absentmindedly, as if her thoughts had already been on her daughter and Curtis's words had simply fitted in with them. "You still don't know where she lives?" she asked then.

"No. I've never followed her."

He refrained from telling Mrs. Irish that some of Louch's best men had tried to follow Leila without success. No need to worry her with that kind of information. Louch's men followed all sorts of people, often merely to fill some tiny gap in Louch's files and nothing more.

"But you must have some idea where she lives."

"None."

Netta sighed. "Then it's no good trying to seduce it out of you."

Curtis laughed. "You don't play fair."

She smiled at him, slowly, her dark-rouged mouth growing fuller. Her absolutely blank face looked alive for an instant. She stood and smoothed down her clinging black dress, took Curtis's drink and made him a new one. When she returned with it she sat down next to him. He could feel her warmth.

He set the drink on the glass-topped table and turned toward her as she turned toward him. Her eyes regarded him gravely. They kissed once, only their lips touching. Her mouth was soft. Curtis felt her arms go around him as her lips parted.

Kissing her, he got that same tingling shock of discovery he always got exploring a woman for the first time. Part mystery, entering the dark cave of her, part anticipation and, for Curtis, part wariness. He'd been married twice, still wasn't divorced from Birgit who'd gone back to live in Denmark. His lengthier experiences with women didn't turn out well. But there was no possibility at all that there would be any length to this one. Curtis cupped his hand over her breast. He felt the nipple stiffen beneath the fine black wool.

"Well," he said after a while.

She got to her feet and took his hand. They went into one of the bedrooms whose windows also faced out onto the Place Vendôme. As Curtis sat down on the edge of the bed, he couldn't help noting that this was an unused room with a smallish bed. Surely in the other bedroom . . . ?

She was adjusting the thin voile curtains so that the Paris night, still dripping, gave them the faint light of lamps on the streets below, four stories down. Then she turned and came to him.

She stood before him a moment and he drew her

to him, burying his face against the soft dress. He could feel her thighs where they flowed together. She trembled very slightly, and only for a moment. He reached up and pulled her knit dress down over her shoulders. She stepped back. It fell straight down her body and lay like a puddle of ink at her feet, her high-heeled black calf shoes half-buried in the fabric.

She was, as he suspected, wearing nothing under the dress but the shoes. He kissed the mound of dark curly hair and ran his hands up her flanks to her buttocks. She stepped out of her shoes and, with one sweep of a foot, brushed them and the dress to one side. Then she knelt in front of him.

In the darkness, as she undressed him, Curtis could only see her eyes, wide and black and as grave as the painted eyes of a Picasso. They gave away nothing, those eyes, nor did they miss anything. When he was naked she stood up and pulled his head against her body, burying her long, thin fingers in his hair, locking him in place against her ivory flesh as if forever.

It was that, more than anything else, that finally pushed Curtis over the edge. As she took him prisoner in that fashion, he felt his erection grow immense, swelling almost painfully.

She was on top of him now, pushing him down on his back. She was all over him, biting softly, kissing. He tasted her as they rolled over. He entered her slowly at first, then fully. She brought her pelvis up to meet the thrust, her great eyes staring up at him, her mouth pressed shut for a moment, then opening as she gasped. For a long time they rocked back and forth, in and out. Then she began to twist under him.

They were on their sides for a while and then she mounted him and brought her knees up until they pressed against his forearms. She shifted the tempo, slowing it. Her eyelids started to flutter. The great dark irises rolled upward. Her movements became excruciatingly slow. She began to contract around him like a great velvet clamp.

He was out of control. Someone was screaming softly, helplessly. His orgasm came in two separate jolts, separated by an eternity in which she pressed the soft part of her palm into her mouth and bit down. Her face contorted. He could feel her body shaking as he came again.

Then silence. In the Place Vendôme a car honked twice, snippily, like a small terrier. She took her hand away from her mouth and looked at the blood where her teeth had made four small punctures in her pale skin.

At eleven o'clock the telephone rang. Curtis awoke instantly. She had fallen asleep on top of him. After a moment, she slid sideways, her long arm reaching in the direction of the ringing. He picked up the phone and handed it to her.

"*Oui?*" Her eyes were closed. She seemed drugged. "*Oui, c'est Madame Irish.*" A pause.

"What?"

Those immense eyes sprang wide open, staring down at Curtis. "Leila!" she said in a high, hoarse voice. "My God, baby."

Curtis wriggled out from under her. Her face was transfixed, eyes wide. "But how did you know I was in P—?"

Curtis padded barefoot to the window and pulled the curtain back a few inches. The streets were still wet. Behind him he could hear a very faint, tinny voice talking over the telephone. The words were impossible to understand.

Netta Irish sat up on the side of the bed. "But when can I—?"

Curtis frowned. The Paris *Herald-Tribune*, in its "People" column, had carried a very brief item some days ago that Oscar Ferguson had found and bought some Matisse sketches from the owner of a country inn near Saint-Paul-de-Vence "for the Minton Irish Collection." But that clue alone wouldn't have placed Netta Irish in Paris, where her long-silent, long-hidden daughter could break the silence of—how long?

"Certainly, baby. Of course," Netta was saying. "At Senlis?"

Her hoarse voice showed no surprise, but Curtis's eyebrows went up. Long-lost Leila was well informed, if nothing else. "How marvelous!" Netta exclaimed. "It'll be like old times. We'll have a picnic under the—"

The disembodied voice, filtered through the telephone receiver, lisped faintly but insistently, as if arriving after a tortuous trip from intergalactic space, tired but sure of itself, stating, never asking.

"Tomorrow, then?"

Curtis turned back to watch her. She still looked like a haughty showgirl of a superior sort, expressionless, sleek, her narrow waist swelling to two small but lovely mounds, her long legs crossed negligently. Only her face seemed alive, as she listened to the tinny voice over the wire.

"Yes, baby, of course, just off Route N–330. You remember. But let me drive you. I'll have the car pick you up tomorrow morning at—"

The voice began again, stronger, more mechanical. "All right, baby. Yes, I underst—

"Good night, darling. See you in the m—"

The line went dead.

Netta listened for a long moment, then hung up. She replaced the telephone on the bedside table with slow, thoughtful movements. Then she plumped up a pillow and lay back on it, her upper trunk raised so that she could watch Curtis across the length of her naked body and the rumpled bed linens.

"Do you believe what just happened?" she asked then.

"The only thing that puzzles me is why."

"She says she saw me in the car yesterday, driving down the Champs-Elysées."

"Believable," Curtis muttered in an unconvinced tone.

"I don't remember being on the Champs yesterday."

They watched each other across the darkness with a kind of brooding air, as if each of them were engrossed in their own private thoughts. "How did she know you were going to Senlis?"

Netta shook her head. "Leila knows the place. She only mentioned that it might be nice to visit it . . ." Her voice died away as she continued thinking. Curtis imagined she was playing over the startling conversation in her mind.

"Well," he said then, "the good thing is that she's reestablished contact." Netta nodded.

"And she's well?" Curtis asked then.

She blinked. "What? Well? She didn't say."

"She seemed to be doing a lot of talking."

"Mm." After a long moment, Netta's thoughts reached some sort of conclusion. She looked at Curtis as if seeing him for the first time. "What are you doing over there?" she asked, patting the bed beside her.

"Freezing."

He settled in bed next to her and they held each other loosely. "She plans to show up at Senlis for lunch," Netta said then.

"Would you like me to be there?"

Her great eyes swung sideways to watch him. "I'd adore it. Oscar wouldn't."

"And that means . . . ?"

"That means I'll see it through alone and come back to town tomorrow night."

"Without Oscar."

She smiled. "I'll be at your apartment no later than nine."

"You know where it is?"

"I know the address."

"But when you get out of the car on Rue Washington at Number 26, you have to go through a long archway into a rear courtyard," Curtis told her. "There are several attached houses around a small park. It's a little enclave called the Cité Odiot. You pass the first two entrances. At the third, you'll see my name on the bell downstairs."

"Sounds charming. Isolated from the world."

"Quiet. No traffic noise."

"Quite like the Ritz," she said, laughing. "My God, Curtis, I can't tell you how relieved I am to be seeing her. It's so good to know she's all right. Really all right."

Curtis stared up at the high ceiling of the room. Below, in the Place Vendôme, the lights of a car swung in a small arc that cast a moving shadow on the ornate plasterwork of the ceiling. There were several things he could tell Netta Irish about her daughter's telephone call. He decided not to say any of them.

12

The main office of UBCO, on Fifth Avenue in the midtown area of Manhattan, is a tall, anonymous building of thick aluminum mullions and giant plates of glass, quite unlike the attractive original main office on Wall Street, which had been torn down some years before.

Bill Elston's department, Internal Security, occupied part of the thirteenth floor. It was typical both of UBCO and of Elston that, first, there actually was a floor labeled 13 and, second, that someone didn't mind having his department located there.

Elston usually reached his desk by half-past eight in the morning, not because he was an especially early riser but because he had people all over the world who worked in varying time zones. It seemed best, especially for Elston's people in Europe, Africa and Asia, if he got in early, read their telexes, took their calls and responded at once with decisions.

The inner life of an international bank is like no other organism. It is infinitely more susceptible to dangerous upsets than, say, the inner workings of an international oil company. Banks are not the hulking monoliths they seem, buying and selling the world and everyone in it. Although the business of banking is business, banks are far more sensitive to trouble than most businesses.

It was chiefly a matter of public image, as Bill Elston kept telling himself on mornings like this one. The top management of a steel company could

stand trial for price fixing, the chief executive of an
aerospace company could go to jail for bribing public
officials, the newest product of a pharmaceutical concern could be found to have lethal side effects. None
of this mattered in the end. The steel company kept
selling steel, the aerospace executive retired at full
salary and the drug company withdrew its dangerous
product with a brief apology and a few heart-balm
payments to the families of victims. Life went on for
such businesses.

But let this happen to a bank, Elston knew, and
all hell broke loose. Small depositors lined up to
withdraw their savings . . . in cash. Big commercial
customers reviewed their lending programs and
sought financing from the banks which were not making ugly headlines. And the IRS, scenting blood,
could be depended on to start circling the wounded
bank like a school of sharks, making terrifying rushes
at its soft underbelly.

It was Elston's job to anticipate trouble and make
sure it didn't happen or, failing that, didn't get reported to the public at large. In this work he depended on people like Curtis, his Internal Security
(Eur.).

The meeting in Paris with the trade commission
of Czechoslovakia was to have been a touchy propo-
sition at best. A major five-year funding request based
on the Czechs' own ambitious plans for increasing
tourism had produced an agenda made up entirely
of sore points.

Almost alone in Eastern Europe, Czech officials
were as secretive, suspicious and quick to take offense
as the Soviets would be. More so, Elston reminded
himself, since they knew themselves to be under the
direct scrutiny of the Russians. And ever more so, he
knew, because Czech tourism was in bad shape.

The local brand of bureaucratic paranoia made
casual visits to the country impossible. Czech greed
complicated matters, since the only way a Western

visitor could get a visa was if he contracted in advance to spend a certain amount of hard currency within the borders of Czechoslovakia. It wasn't put that crudely, of course, but the demand was still there.

And now, to have the meeting mysteriously postponed—three days had already passed—because the chief minister had somehow dropped off the map of Paris, was to complicate the whole project almost out of existence.

On his arrival this morning, Elston had fully expected to find a long coded telex from Curtis, who was easily his most resourceful agent in the field. If anyone could locate a missing Czech, it was Curtis.

Elston grinned. The blank Czech, he thought. Then the grin disappeared.

Why hadn't Curtis dug up anything? His contacts were good in Paris, as they were in London and Frankfurt and Basel and Milan . . . anywhere, in fact, where banking was a major concern. And Paris was where he made his home base. Surely in three days he should have developed the necessary information?

Like UBCO's other field agents, Curtis's business was information. He was good at collecting it. Elston knew just enough about him to understand what made Curtis good. He'd begun in armed forces intelligence. Something had soured him on the work— Elston had never pried enough to find out what it was—and Curtis had quit to become an itinerant kind of travel writer. He'd been hired by the Paris office, originally.

The rest of Curtis was blank pages.

Elston didn't really object to this. He judged his people by results, not past history. But he had the feeling that Curtis went to some pains to keep his history blank, not because monsters lurked there but out of an intense need for privacy. He'd been married twice, that much was known, and was currently separated or divorced.

Any other employer would have made it his business to pierce the veils. But Curtis was too valuable to rile that way.

He was perfectly capable, Elston knew, of quitting if his privacy was too deeply invaded. A prickly type, Curtis, but absolutely professional at what he did for—

The telephone rang. "Miss James here to see you."

Elston paused and checked his appointment calendar. Lee James had a nine o'clock with him and it still lacked fifteen minutes. "Show her in."

He sat back and tried to put the Czech problem to one side. Lee James represented a separate problem entirely, and in some ways a more potentially troublesome one.

Elston was well aware that banks were one of the last outposts of male chauvinist piggery, in that not many women rose much higher in the hierarchy than assistant vice-president, usually managing some small department that had little contact with the public. Because they had long been run entirely by men, who were now ensconced in the highest echelons of management, banks tended to believe that what the public wanted of a bank was to see a man in charge.

Whether there was any truth to this, or only the warped reflection of what the all-male senior officer corps wanted to see in its mirror, the fact remained that even if a woman reached the rank of full vice-president in a bank as big as UBCO—and two had— she was still usually nothing more than a glorified department chief. As for the rank, UBCO had, at last count, nearly three hundred vice-presidents, including Elston.

Elston employed a few women as secretaries. Lee James was no secretary. She had graduated fourth in her class at Yale Law School and spent her next three years as an assistant district attorney in the Bronx.

She had then gone on to make headlines as the first
woman agent ever hired by the FBI, creating an additional set of headlines when she resigned after a
year, claiming that she was being used as "nothing
more than a secretary."

Elston had seen a chance to camouflage his own
all-male department with a woman whose qualifica-
tions could stand up to any questions the bank's
board of directors might throw at Elston. She became
Internal Security's token woman.

When she came in, Bill Elston nodded pleasantly
and indicated a chair. "You're early."

"Is that all right?" Lee James asked in her low
voice.

She was not at all what Elston had first expected
of a brilliant law student and former enforcement
officer. Lee James stood about five-five, he judged. She
had a slight figure, but a good one, with narrow
shoulders and a long neck.

There was a trick to her appearance, however, that
made her look much taller. Elston watched her sit
down. Perhaps it was her head, which seemed smaller
than it should be, emphasized by pale blond hair cut
short, unwaved, and combed from a side part like a
man's.

There was no mistaking her for a mannish woman,
even with the deep tone of her voice. She was too
pretty for that, and her gestures were always feminine.
A man, seating himself now, would either have
hunched forward nervously, hands on knees, or
lounged back negligently, arm cocked over the back
of the chair. Lee James merely crossed her legs and
looked at him.

Elston blinked. He realized she had asked him a
question. "No, quite all right," he responded hastily.
"Just as well we get a head start on the day. What
did you want to see me about?"

"I've been here six months," she said then. She had
dark gray eyes almost the color of her pupils, which

gave her an intent, questing look. Elston wondered how criminals had felt, up against that pair of eyes.

"Yes." Elston paused. Then: "I see. The probation period."

"It's nearly over."

Elston glanced at his calendar again. "This week, I think."

He watched her for a moment. She seemed somehow older than she was. He knew a lot more about Lee James than she'd entered on her application form. He'd had her thoroughly checked before hiring her. The background was a small town in upstate New York where her father ran a hardware store. One brother was killed in Vietnam; another was a schoolteacher.

She was not yet thirty, Elston recalled. She was, in fact, twenty-eight, but she seemed much more mature. Perhaps it was because she didn't smile, at least not in his presence. She seemed to have no sense of humor, according to what some of the men in his department had told him. And, indeed, as of this week her probation period would come to an end and Elston would have to decide whether to let her go or give her a permanent assignment.

"There's no question about it," he said then, under the pressure of those dark gray eyes. "Your work has been eminently acceptable. I don't have to wait till the end of the week to tell you that." He paused again. He hadn't planned on having this conversation today. It was typical of Lee James that she took one by surprise, like a good courtroom lawyer on cross-examination, but in a way that one couldn't quite complain about.

"No question," he repeated. "You have a permanent place with UBCO," he went on, trying to choose his words carefully. "The only question—" He paused again.

"Is where?" Lee James suggested.

"Exactly. I mean, where is here, in Internal Security, but where where really is, I—" He stopped himself because he suspected he was babbling. "You've seen how we work," he said then. "Where do you think you'd fit in best?"

"Is it going to be that easy?"

"What?"

"If I tell you where I'd like to work, will you give me the assignment?" She gestured once with her small, neat hands. "Just like that?"

He produced a smile and hoped to get an answering one from her, but she remained grave and watchful. "Not quite. But I would like your thoughts."

She sat perfectly still for a long moment. "Overseas," she said then.

"A field agent?"

Elston tried to keep the note of surprise out of his voice. The work wasn't especially hazardous, but it always held the potential of danger. Curtis, for instance, had been in and out of some close scrapes. He'd even been shot once, in Basel. Elston's man in Hong Kong had gotten in a mess with the local authorities and UBCO had had to fire him. Elston didn't feel that he asked his agents to do hazardous work, but he knew that to produce the kind of information UBCO needed, they often had to . . . um . . . cut corners.

"It's not the sort of work," he began carefully, "that I—" He stopped, not knowing how to phrase his thoughts acceptably.

"That you'd pictured for a woman," Lee James finished for him. She still hadn't moved an inch from the position she'd taken when she first sat in the chair. The posture wasn't stiff, Elston saw, merely in utter repose.

"Something like that," he agreed lamely.

"It's investigative work," she said. "I've done quite a bit of that kind of thing. I know how to develop material discreetly. I don't have the contacts of a more experienced agent, someone like Curtis, for instance. But if you assigned me to him, I think I could generate my own contacts in six months or so."

"You don't know him, do you?"

"Just from his reports."

"A loner. Totally." Elston paused. "A very private guy. He doesn't, uh, share. The idea of an assistant would rub him entirely the wrong way."

She was silent for a while. Then: "His area of responsibility is quite large. England and Western Europe. A tremendous work load."

"He's never complained. Nor have I had any reason to suspect he's spread too thin," Elston added.

"I'm sure." The dark gray eyes flicked sideways for an instant and Elston found himself relieved for a moment of their scrutiny. Then her glance swung back to him. "With the proper orientation from Curtis," Lee James said then in her low voice, "I could relieve him of some of the pressure."

"I told you. He has no use for an assistant."

"What I had in mind, eventually, was that his area could be split. He could continue handling the high-volume countries. I could relieve him of, say, Spain and Portugal. Italy and Greece. Yugoslavia."

Elston realized his mouth was open. He shut it. Cool customer. Cool, but she made sense. The only problem was that Curtis would never have the time or the inclination to break her in. Anyway, if Elston sent her out of New York, what would become of his highly visible token woman?

"The trouble is," he began heavily, "that Curtis has no time to do training work, not a spare second."

"And even if he did," Lee James suggested, "he'd balk at a woman."

"That's not it. He'd just balk. And quit."

For the first time, her head moved in a faint up-and-down gesture. "What if you gave me time off and I spent my vacation in Paris? Naturally I'd look him up. And then . . ."

The silence in the room grew. "You'd charm him

off the branch and into your cage," Elston finished. "Not Curtis. He's not that kind of bird."

"If I fail," Lee James told him, "we'll just drop the whole thing. You can give me whatever assignment you like. But if I succeed," she sat forward suddenly, a movement so spare and quick that Elston blinked, "if I succeed, he'll think the whole thing was his idea."

Now the silence between them was far vaster than before. Elston realized he was in the presence of someone with a much stronger character than he had suspected. She was determined, resourceful and not shy. Being an administrator, he tended to protect all bets, come down on both sides of a question, move by indirection when possible. She was playing right into his character and they both knew it. She was saying: I know what I want; here's how you can give it to me without taking any administrative heat for it.

He cleared his throat. "How about a week's leave? Can you do it in a week?"

"Do it, or fail," she agreed.

"Then you've got a week. Starting now."

She stood up in one fast move and suddenly looked very tall. "Thank you. A week's just right. If I fail, I'll be back here in New York so fast nobody will really have lost sight of me."

The visible token woman. Elston got to his feet and held out his hand. They shook. She turned quickly and left so fast that the door had already swung shut behind her before Elston realized she was gone.

Remarkable woman. He sat down and glanced at his desk clock. Five minutes to nine. She hadn't once smiled, nor showed him any more of her legs than what would normally be visible. They were good legs, what he could see of them, and her rather pert face, topped by the pale hair, would have looked quite winning with a smile. But she'd done none of these things. She'd argued her case like a man.

Elston sighed heavily. He realized, too late, that he had been in the presence of a New Woman. Had her right here in his office and let her escape. He smiled faintly.

Then, the smile broadened to an evil grin as he pictured how Curtis would react to the arrival in his life of UBCO's New Woman.

13

North of Saratoga Springs and Glens Falls, the pale spring light began to fail in the late afternoon. As the tan Volkswagen convertible rattled northward along U.S. 87 toward the Canadian border, the driver glanced at his wristwatch. Four-thirty. He flipped on his parking lights and kept the speedometer needle at sixty-five miles per hour.

Slumped beside him, long legs folded in uncomfortable ways to fit into the VW's space, Nick Brown sat on the small of his back, eyes closed, and pretended to sleep. He didn't know Holland that well, just another classmate at Williams College. But Holland had a car and a girl in Montreal. And this was the Easter vacation coming up.

As for Nick, he was on a hopeless mission, but it beat sitting around Williams with all the credits for a B.A. but unable to bring himself to start work on his thesis. When you're stuck on dead center the only thing left is to blast off.

And he had reason for getting out of town. Two days before, after such a long silence, he'd gotten word of Leila. Not from Leila herself, of course. The letter had come from Jamie, a friend of Nick's who had magically prolonged his official junior year abroad into a whole way of life, backpacking through most of Europe these past years, following the sun and the best available grass, smoking, dealing, eternally getting his thing together.

"Spotted Leila in Paris," the note had reported.

"Part of the scene at the American Express office, from which all blessings flow. She didn't see me. Just as well."

Thinking about the letter, Nick felt certain he was right to be getting out of Williamstown. Between the lines of Jamie's letter, he could read things that upset him.

"Weird group she hangs in with. Arabs. You never told me she was into street rumbles and kif and that heavy Muslim number."

Eyes closed, Nick tried to picture Leila and the Arabs. What bothered him most was that the writer of the letter wasn't much better than a street hustler himself these days. That was what was so alarming. The people with Leila had to be real heavies if Jamie considered them so.

Not that Nick saw himself as Leila's guardian angel, no way. She'd made that very clear when they split. But there was no one else in his life. He knew it was crazy to keep worrying about someone who had no thought for him. Never mind. He still had to find her.

Nick had withdrawn all the money he had in the Williamstown bank, five hundred dollars. He knew he could always phone his mother or a brother for more money, but he wanted no one to know what he was planning or why he wouldn't be home for Easter.

The tan VW had left Williamstown at noon, speeding out of Massachusetts and into New York along State 2 to Troy and Cohoes, north of Albany. There Holland had picked up the superhighway direct to Montreal. His girl was holding dinner for him, an elastic sort of arrangement.

But Nick had to be at Montreal airport no later than 7:00 P.M. Otherwise there was no way his five hundred dollars would get him to Paris.

They shot through Plattsburgh at about five-thirty and Nick caught a glimpse of Lake Champlain through distant trees. Tension had started building.

The car was all right, but Holland was certainly no speed merchant. It was the timetable that left no room for delay. The only way Nick could qualify for the youth fare to Paris was via a Montreal flight. If he'd flown out of Boston, for example, they would have charged him at least a hundred dollars more, leaving him nothing to live on in Paris.

And nothing to pay whatever it would cost him to find Leila.

He hadn't many ideas of where to begin, except to ask questions of the people hanging around the American Express office in the Rue Scribe. If that didn't work, he had no alternative plan. But, as he slouched in the front seat of the VW now, faking slumber, he felt pretty optimistic about his chances.

Young people usually knew. They noticed each other. They weren't like older people, for whom one kid was pretty much like another. The young people hanging around at American Express would remember Leila. Whether they would know where Nick could find her . . . that was something he wasn't as sure about.

Another unsure quantity was his French. He'd taken two years of it in military school, but that meant nothing. Even the fact that he'd been to Europe before meant little. His last visit had been cut short by a skiing accident. When his photo showed up in an Italian scandal magazine, his father had brought him home fast enough to make his head spin.

Eyes still closed, he grinned slightly. No contact, no address, no language, no clue, no lead, not even a hint. What a way to spend five hundred bucks.

"You awake?" Holland demanded.

"Yum."

"How's about spelling me at the wheel?"

"Right."

"We'll change at the border." Holland nodded his head to indicate the international checkpoint looming ahead at Champlain. Once through the guard post, he pulled over to the side of the highway and Nick got behind the wheel.

Although it was late March, patches of snow still covered the ground. Nick's eyes swung to either side as he drove, keeping the VW's speed at seventy. Funny to think of a member of the Brown family breezing through the United States–Canada checkpoint in such a public way.

This whole border, especially to the west of here in little Canadian towns like Guelph and Hamilton, was part of the heroin trail. Nobody in Nick's family had ever spoken of it, of course. No one ever would. But the literature on the subject was extensive.

The stuff came through via Corsican routes from the Mediterranean to small Quebec seaports like Havre St. Pierre and Baie Comeau, where the Corsicans and the Quebecois spoke the same language, more or less. It moved quickly on back roads by private car to Montreal, a city well organized by the mob, where it was cut a few times and repackaged.

Then it moved by "mule" over the border into upper New York State and the feudal fiefdom of the family that had once been under the control of Stefano Magaddino, whose *sotto-capo* in those far-off days had been a hustling young roughneck who'd become Nick's father.

The "mules" were private people, usually unaffiliated, always with cover stories for their movements across the border. It was possible, given so many miles of international boundary, to send the mules through in many guises: workmen, farmers, tourists and the like.

Thinking about the heroin routes, Nick Brown realized he was moving in the wrong direction. The stuff always moved south, not north. To the south of this stretch of the Canadian border lay the target, the one market area that accounted for nearly half the heroin sold in the United States: the New York–

New Jersey megalopolis. Funny to find a Brown moving north on that well-worn trail.

Of course, he wasn't your average Brown. He wanted no part of the family's business. Oddly enough, his family respected the decision. Maybe they hoped, by staying clean, that he'd end up a U.S. senator. Nick smiled crookedly at the thought. Would that be a conflict of interest? Or simply the norm?

At six-thirty the signs along Canada 15 indicated he would easily make it to the airport if he only knew where the airport was. But just before he reached the St. Laurence River a sign diverted him left onto Provincial 3 and over the river where another road led directly to the airport at Dorval.

Outside the departures building, Holland got back behind the wheel. "Have a good one," he said, the VW already in motion.

Nick watched the small convertible roar off in a yammer of iron clanging. Whoever she was, Holland's friend had to be something. He didn't want to miss a moment with her.

Nick pulled the parka hood of his down-filled ski jacket up over his head. The beige hood hid his face from any sideways glance. He checked in for Air Canada 870, showed his passport and birth certificate and became perhaps the only passenger on that evening's 747 to pay in cash. He had credit cards he never used, a gift of his family.

Hoisting his shoulder bag, Nick Brown moved quickly out of the ticketing area and headed for the loading gate. Hooded or not, there was no point in showing himself too freely in any airport the size of Dorval. Most major airports—at least when it came to freight handling and the reconnaissance of passengers—were part of the mob's operation.

That was his reason for taking a regular scheduled flight at a legally approved fee. He knew he could have paid at least a third less by buying into a faked charter flight at the last moment. But he knew that a lot of the charter sharpies were mob-connected. Sometimes such a deal involved stolen ticket stock, another mob operation. And Nick wanted no one in the rackets to spot the Dominic Brown name on a Paris ticket.

That was also his reason for paying cash. Nick Brown wanted to be absolutely certain that no one in his family knew where he was going.

It wasn't that they violently disapproved of Leila, those of them who knew about her. Nor would any of them have stopped Nick from going to Paris if they knew in advance. His absence at Easter would be a cardinal family sin, of course, but no member of the Brown family needed to be told that sins were created not only to be avoided, but also to be committed. So that, with luck or cleverness, they could be forgiven.

No, it was the mission itself that would anger his family. Nick could imagine what his father or his brothers might say. "Stupid! With one phone call we could've spotted her for you!" But he didn't want Leila involved with his family, only with him.

As he slumped down in a curved plastic chair and waited for the boarding call, Nick Brown wondered if he'd find her in Paris.

And if he did, would she be happy to see him?

PART THREE
HOLY WEEK

14

It was entirely a matter of luck, and Louch knew it. His telephone had rung at ten-thirty in the morning. The telephone in his apartment, that is.

Normally Louch was out at that hour. This morning, he had in fact left before eight to meet an informer who worked nights. They had chatted at breakfast for a long time before Louch had drawn the interview to a close and headed for his office near the Quai des Orfèvres. But before he'd gone there, he remembered some notes he had left at his apartment.

It was typical of the way Louch ordered his life that his small apartment was easy to return to. It overlooked the narrow Rue de la Huchette where the tiny Rue de Chat Qui Pêche runs down toward the river. It took Louch only three minutes to walk from his apartment over the St. Michel bridge to his office on the Ile de la Cité. And this morning, after his breakfast on the Boulevard St. Germain, it took him scarcely a minute to reach his apartment again. Big, overweight men like Louch pay attention to such itineraries.

That was the luck of it. That he should be walking in the door of his apartment when, after calling him at various places all over Paris, one of his sergeants, in a fit of hopelessness, had tried telephoning the apartment one more time.

"Where?" Louch asked, taking out a pencil and his

pocket notebook. "Chennevières les Louvres? Where under God is that?"

The lucky sergeant explained that it was near the A-1 superhighway that led northeast out of Paris, past the old Le Bourget Airport and the new Charles de Gaulle Airport at Roissy.

"When?"

The sergeant reported that his office mate, the other sergeant, had been driving north from Roissy on surveillance of a dark blue Citroën when a Kawasaki motorcycle had roared past in the same direction "at one-fifty easily," the sergeant reported.

"And he recognized the girl?" Louch persisted.

"The girl and the boy we call Aziz."

"How long ago?"

"Ten minutes, sir."

"Get him back on the radio. Tell him to forget the Citroën and keep up with the Kawasaki."

"He has already done so, sir."

"Good. Get on the air. Have a radio car pick me up at once."

"Right away, sir."

Louch hung up and stared at the notebook page on which he had written "Chennevières les Louvres." He frowned and went to the bookcase where he kept maps and atlases. He found the town at last, in the northeast suburbs on the main road that led through Villeron to Senlis.

Downstairs, the police car was waiting. With no siren, the driver made his way out of town while Louch fiddled with the radio, trying to get headquarters to link him directly to his man in the field. They finally cleared a channel and let Louch speak.

"Parked in the cathedral garden, sir," the sergeant reported. "The boy has a camera. They are taking pictures of the cathedral."

"Nice work for a Moslem," Louch thought for a moment. "Have they seen you?"

"I don't think so."

Louch made a face. The girl had proved herself an expert at eluding surveillance. He doubted that she'd missed the sergeant's car. Perhaps that was the reason for the pious photography.

"Keep them in sight till I arrive," Louch said. "We'll use your car."

The police car dropped him twenty minutes later in Senlis, around the corner from the cathedral, in the old part of town which by now had become almost an open-air museum of archaeology, so ancient were the outbuildings of the cathedral. Of the Roman ruins little remained, but the cathedral's thirteenth-century spire could be seen for dozens of kilometers around. Louch paused to examine the west doorway of the church and its sculpture depicting the seasons of the year and the entombment of Christ.

Out of the corner of his eye he could see the gray Simca in which the sergeant was sitting. Across the lawn of the cathedral, a powerful Kawasaki was chained against a black iron pillar of the fence that surrounded the churchyard.

Louch waited inside the Simca, not bothering to make conversation with the sergeant. It is no crime to drive a motorcycle at high speeds once outside Paris proper, nor is it against the law to photograph famous landmarks of France. The excitement he'd felt had started to ebb away. So they were on an outing in Senlis. Why not?

He'd reacted to the phone call so vigorously because he'd had the panicky notion they were escaping Paris for good and he couldn't let that happen. But this leisurely visit wasn't part of any escape plan. The sergeant nudged him.

They were coming out the main door of the cathedral now, she with her frizzy yellow mop of tight ringlets and her immense dark glasses, he looking handsome in a short blue denim jacket of the sort cowboys wore. They took turns snapping photos of each other with their tiny pocket camera, then got on the Kawasaki and roared off at full speed.

"After them?" the sergeant asked.

Louch's big, placid face with its bulbous nose seemed to wrinkle with deep thought, as if trying to dredge up an almost unknown answer. And, in truth, it was no easy answer.

He could continue to waste his time and that of one of his sergeants on this obvious picnic outing, or he could get back to his desk and begin working on some of the very good leads his breakfast companion had given him this morning.

The day was cold, blustery, the last blast of March's chill and gloom. There wasn't even the excuse of a nice day in the country to keep him here in Senlis.

"Back to town," he ordered the sergeant.

The Simca came to life. The sergeant put it into a tight U turn and started back along the N-17 highway in a southwest direction.

As Louch settled back in his seat, he wondered if he'd guessed right. He felt as if he were swimming in ambivalence. The sight of the cathedral? Easter was almost at hand, a solemn, depressing time.

Not a favorite festival, Louch reminded himself. He wished that in his childhood, he or any other French child could have taken the holiday as lightly as the Protestants took it, for example, in America, with their silly rabbits and colored eggs.

But it began portentously with nearly six weeks of Lent and climaxed in that awful memorial of crucifixion, Good Friday. Plunged into such depths, the uplift of Easter Sunday never made it for Louch as a child. Christ had risen. Perhaps. But no one else.

Louch couldn't help thinking, as the Simca sped toward Paris, that he'd made a mistake. It was a premonition, as certain as Christ's at the Last Supper. Damn all cathedrals, all memories of childhood. Louch had put them aside forever with the religion they symbolized, but they still had the power to return.

He grabbed the driver's arm. "Turn around!"

"What?"

"Catch up with them."

The Simca made a left turn on two wheels and started back into Senlis. Louch sat forward, staring through the windshield. If only he could shake this heavy feeling on his shoulders.

And yet, it was his second piece of luck that morning.

15

The Duc de Clary was a perfect example of what the well-dressed spider monkey was wearing these days.

Netta had watched him with fascination ever since she'd arrived at the château. He was a tiny man of about sixty years with long arms and legs and a head the size of a large electric light bulb. One hundred watts, Netta decided, but not as bright. He moved in a series of lopes and scrambles, quite like the agile ape attached to an organ-grinder, except that he was dressed considerably better.

He had chosen for the day's exertions a three-piece suit of the palest mauve cashmere. Each jacket button, and all those on the vest, were executed in rhinestones so brilliant that as he moved he twinkled.

He had in addition worn a rhinestone earring—one—and sported on the little fingers of each hand identical rings which made the buttons and earring dim by comparison.

Oscar, looking like another species entirely, hulked in a corner of the great, high-ceilinged library, paging through a rare book. The duke and a young assistant, so airy that he seemed too ephemeral to be real, skipped this way and that, yipping to each other in the cabalistic language of their trade.

"Late sixteenth," the duke would call to his assistant.

The young man would make a notation in a large, leather-bound notebook. "School of?" he fluted back.

"Malmaison."

little antiques expert. "Just the furniture and

virtu as well," the duke explained. "The
the epergnes, the trays, the paperweights, the
ticks, the silver, the onyx, the chalcedony, the
d, the ebony, the statuettes, the inlaid nacre,
irons, all the small sculpture, the bronzes, the
rs, but not the brass caryatids or the ormolu
s. Of course, the—"

ther words," Oscar cut in rudely, "everything
paintings."

luke inclined his head sideways as if inspecting
eing proffered him. "Naturellement. In the
e of one as learned in art as you, cher maître,
s not dare vouchsafe an opinion on the paint-

s eyes felt as if they were going to cross. She
er before heard anyone use "vouchsafe" in a
. "Come to the point, Oscar. What does it all
?" she asked.

ut two million bucks." He handed her a slip

the paintings?"

contortions of his forehead deepened into a
y of anguish. "Christ, don't pin me down,

e to. Tom Sandweg wants an answer."

e three for the art. And five for the house
nds. That's eight, plus two for the junk. Ten
dollars. Will that get Sandweg off our backs?"
entioned double that."

he wants and what he gets are two different
life," Oscar said in a moody tone. "He's just
ve got this to sell."

buyers?"

orners of Oscar's mouth went down. "Got a
about that." He turned to the tiny antiques
Am I right that there can't be any one person
y the whole thing?"

In this fashion, Netta knew, they had cataloged
every antique and objet d'art in the château's rooms,
ending this morning with the library itself and its
hoard of extremely valuable rare books.

From time to time she had grown tired of the
theatrics of the little appraiser and his assistant, but
pacing alone through the rooms of this great tomb
of a house with its dull Watteaus and Greuzes was
as chilling an experience as spending a day in the
vaults at the Trocadéro.

As a matter of fact, a shipment now waited in the
entry hall, crated and labeled for the Trocadéro.
Netta had seen them this morning, four wooden crates
almost as tall as she was, in which some brass Vaincre
caryatids had been boxed.

Oscar was being at his most uncommunicative, so
it was almost impossible to get out of him why the
Vaincres were not to be cataloged with the rest of the
château's contents. "New York in September," he'd
grunted. "The Met."

After due reflection, Netta deciphered this to mean
that the caryatids were being loaned to the Metropolitan Museum in New York for a fall exhibition.
Until the Met picked them up, they would live in
their crates deep within the concrete fastnesses of
Trocadéro Tower.

Usually Oscar's moods of noncommunication bothered Netta. Not today. Today she found him childish,
outsized, awkward in a bearlike way. She realized she
was comparing him to Curtis, who had the neat, controlled size and movements of a tennis player, not
Oscar's big, fullback scale.

She studied Oscar for a long moment as he pored
over one of the rare books. Even his reading had an
elephantine intensity to it.

"Let's take a walk in the garden."

"Too raw outside," he grunted without looking up.

"Will they be finished by lunchtime? I've brought
some boxes from Fauchon and some wine."

She had his interest, finally. He glanced up. *"Le pique-nique?"*

"But of course."

"You're looking jolly this morning," he said then.

"Am I?"

"Full of beans."

"Beans, is it?"

He frowned, his square, sandy face looking puzzled. "What's up, Netta?"

"Nothing."

"Something." The frown deepened. "What'd you do with yourself last night?"

She gestured airily. "Nothing unusual."

"Then why this mood swing?" he demanded. "You've been smiling to yourself. You've been pleasant to everyone."

"What a picture you paint of the normal Netta." She wondered for a moment if her night with Curtis had done her that much good, or whether it was the imminent arrival of Leila. Or both. "Leila called me."

"What?"

"She'll be here any time now. We're all lunching together."

"Wha-a-at?"

He closed the book and replaced it in the shelf, got to his feet and walked slowly toward her. He really was a different species from the aging duke, Netta decided. The duke flitted and twitched. Oscar shambled.

"Called me up as if nothing had happened. As if we'd spoken a week ago or something."

"And invited herself down here?"

"N-no. I invited her." Netta paused. "I think. Is it important who invited who? The big thing is that we're seeing each other."

"Ran out of money, did she?"

"Oscar. Don't be so . . . so heavy."

"No excuse for the long silence?"

"None."

"How long has it been?"

"Over a year. More like eigh

"And for the price of a pho back. Just like that?"

Netta turned away. She stare for a moment, then called acrc *le Duc?"*

"Oui, jolie madame?"

"Can your assistant be spare

"Mais certainement, chère monkey man snapped his finger

"In the trunk of the car," N "you'll find some boxes fron chauffeur help you. Bring the

Netta turned back to Oscar eat in the garden, but the weat

He watched her for a long big, stubby fingers through I "Okay, Netta, she's your daug

"Have you been keeping a ru the duke.

"Of sorts. Educated guesse records."

Oscar towered over the litt He watched the duke delve mauve vest and produce a which he handed with great took the liberty of writing do hour ago. It could be off by you understand."

Oscar opened the folded finest of blue-line pencils wa by six zeros.

"Francs?" he barked.

"Yes."

Oscar's forehead contortec ment, then turned to Netta. he had another thought a

dappe stuff?"

"Th boxes, candle rosewc the an alabas: pilaste

"In but the

The a nut presen one do ings."

Nett had ne sentenc come tc

"Abc of pape

"An The cordure Netta."

"I ha

"Figu and gro million

"He i

"Wh facts of lucky w

"Any

The thought expert. who'd b

"Not quickly. The *cher maître* assured me speed was of the essence."

Oscar's face cleared. His brow unknotted. "But what's ten million dollars to the French government?"

The little duke cocked his head in the opposite direction. "Fifty million francs?"

"You know what I mean."

"But speed, *cher maître*. Speed is something of which my government knows nothing. They will take two years merely to consider the proposal."

"Two years in which the value of everything keeps rising."

The little man thought for a moment. It was an interesting exhibition, from Netta's viewpoint. He seemed to freeze and quiver slightly, his tiny eyes bulging, his glance locked on the middle distance. Then he smiled charmingly. "I see your point, *cher maître*."

At that moment, a darting movement outside the windows caught Netta's attention. She saw Leila and a boy arrive on a motorcycle, coasting in silently, engine turned off. They parked the bike on the gravel driveway near the Rolls, where the chauffeur and the duke's assistant were wrestling cartons from the trunk of the car.

Leila looked tiny, wild. Her hair! But the boy was almost criminally good-looking, Netta saw. They started in the direction of the topiary garden, snapping pictures along the way. Netta looked down at the floor again, feeling another surge of anger rise within her.

She never gave way to anger. But the sheer, cold nerve of the little bitch! A year and a half of silence. Then she took her sweet time saying hello.

No big, sentimental reunion scenes for Leila Darcy. Fine. Two could play it that way as easily as one.

Her daughter decided to make an entrance via the main doors. Standing in the library, listening, Netta could hear the two young people come in. They paused, called several hellos. Oscar looked up at Netta, who shook her head.

"One more picture, *chérie*," the boy was saying. His accent was thick and not French.

"Mother?" Leila called in a cool voice.

"In here," Netta said, matching her tone to her daughter's.

The two young people appeared in the library entrance. "There you are," Leila said. "Hello again."

Netta's glance swept past Oscar to fasten on her daughter. "Hello, Leila."

The girl dug into her mop of tight blond curls and scratched for an instant. "This is Raoul," she said, indicating the handsome boy with a thumb gesture.

"Of course it is," Netta purred. "Raoul is a perfect name for him." The two women stood motionless for a moment. "You remember Oscar," Netta said then. "And this gentleman is the Duc de Clary."

"*Enchanté, mademoiselle.*" The spidery little man danced to Leila and took her hand, bobbing his head over in a ritual sketch of a kiss. His glance lingered on Raoul. "*Sensationnel,*" the duke murmured and slipped away to continue his cataloging.

"And what else does Raoul do?" Netta asked.

"He studies art," her daughter said.

"I am a student of art," Raoul volunteered. His big, moist eyes flashed around the room. "*Magnifique,*" he said, rising on his toes several times and flashing the whites of his eyes. "I am an art student," he added helpfully.

No one spoke for a long moment. "Well, Mother," Leila said then, "you do expect an explanation from me, I imagine?"

Netta suppressed a smile. Leila had the nerve of a burglar. "Would you like to take a stroll, just the two of us?" she suggested. "We've got a box lunch laid on in a little while."

She closed the gap between them and, taking her daughter's arm, led the way out through some French windows into the same topiary garden where the young people had been snapping pictures. Walking in silence this way, Netta felt as if she had a stranger beside her. Leila seemed somehow smaller, in her tight jeans and track shoes, almost boylike. The down-filled jacket all of them were wearing this winter gave the girl an asexual shapelessness, and the Harpo Marx hair completed the transformation from the girl Netta had last seen a year and a half before, a brunette in a knee-length Saint Laurent dress, stockings and high-heeled shoes.

"How do you do that with your hair?" she asked suddenly. She had had no intention of mentioning Leila's appearance. The question had just popped out.

"Peroxide and then you sort of bake it."

"What?"

"In an oven. That's what kinks it up."

"How can you bear to bake your head?"

The girl shrugged. She had lost interest in the whole thing. "Thanks for the money," she said then. "It's been coming in right on time."

Netta let this pass. "Now that we're back in contact," she said after a moment, "let me have an address and phone number."

Leila nodded. "How long will you be in Paris?"

"Through Easter." Silence fell between them. They had stopped in a corner of the garden where the almost leafless shrubs had been pruned to resemble a row of ostriches, all craning their necks in the same direction. Netta wanted to know so many things, but she was afraid that asking about them would seal her daughter's lips.

"Who's the, uh, art student?"

"Raoul's a friend."

"Looks smashing. Sort of Bedouin-like."

The girl paused for an instant before replying. "He's Turkish," she said then.

Netta's big eyes took in the fact that this was a lie,

but she failed to see why a lie was necessary. "But Raoul isn't a Turkish name."

"His mother's French."

"His mother?" Netta's low, hoarse voice had gone up a notch. "I somehow got the idea that mothers don't count." A lame silence followed this. Then: "Are you . . . is your health all right?"

"Fine. You?"

"Tennis, when possible."

"And, when not . . . Oscar?"

For the third time that morning, Netta felt anger well up. She stood for a moment, staring down at the tips of her red-brown boots. Then her glance lifted to look directly into her daughter's eyes.

"Is that why you surfaced again after a year and a half?" she asked in a cracked voice. "To get in your girlish little barbs? Do you have any idea what it's like for me when I don't even know if y—" Netta stopped and took a breath. "Why did you call me? I've been in Paris half a dozen times this past eighteen months. Why now?"

Behind the dark lenses, Leila's eyes were hard to see. They didn't seem to waver during her mother's remarks, nor did they seem to register any real reaction. None that Netta could see, at any rate. When she spoke at last, Leila's voice was matter-of-fact. She might have been discussing a shopping list.

"I never intended to break off completely," she said coolly. "I always knew that, eventually, I'd get back in touch." She made a minimal gesture with one small hand, on which a variety of rather barbaric rings gleamed. "It's just taken longer than either of us expected."

Netta stood absolutely still. There had to be a way to get through to Leila, and anger wasn't it. "Do you think I'm that easy?" she asked then. "To believe such an answer?"

"It's the truth."

Netta was silent again. These children set such

great store by the truth. She took in a long breath of chill air and let it out slowly, glancing around the bare garden. "This is the only part of this place I ever liked," she said then. "This garden."

"So manicured," the girl responded.

"But in summer . . ."

"So regimented."

Netta looked around her. The bare branches had not yet begun to bud. The grass was brownish and patchy with winter mud. But in the summer . . . "Orderly," she said then. "I'm not a fan of nature in the raw."

"Fake nature." Leila's voice was small, but implacable. "Your generation thinks a lot of it."

"*My* ge—" Netta stopped. There was a twenty-year difference between them. She had never felt it so keenly. "There ought to be a way," she said then, choosing her words very carefully, "of being able to talk to one's mother without having to handle her as a category."

The girl's face remained unperturbed and blank. "Individuals really don't matter," she said then almost unwillingly. "I don't matter. You don't matter. Except as we stand for something larger. A group, a class. I can't tell you how much you stand for your generation."

Netta took in the words, trying to listen to what was behind them. As a little girl Leila had always been very animated. Her words had tumbled out headlong, bumping into each other, careless, free. Now she spoke in a strangely measured way, as if an immensely profound period of thought had preceded each syllable. She was . . . lecturing! . . . her own mother.

"I take it you don't have a great opinion of my generation?"

Leila's tiny face was impassive, a china doll that refused to break into either a frown or a smile. "Should we?"

"It comes," Netta told her, "with age. We all start by despising our elders. Then we get to be elders."

"And death stands near," the girl said in a curiously hollow voice. "And we compromise." She made one of her stingy gestures, indicating the bare winter garden. "Hoping we'll make it through another year."

"Do you really believe—?" Netta stopped herself. Of course the girl believed. When she'd been Leila's age, all the dark poets had attracted her, all the poems of sorrow and longing and hopelessness. "But let me tell you something, baby."

Leila's fuzzy head shook slowly from side to side. "Forget it."

"You don't wa—?"

"Save your breath," Leila said. Her voice had suddenly come alive, as if she was finally ready to communicate directly. "We're finished listening and believing."

"We?"

The girl turned toward the house. "Shall we go back?"

"Leila."

"Let's go."

Netta watched her move away. She followed, too slowly for her daughter, who went on ahead up the path, between the sculpture shrubbery. Netta watched her slight body slip between the hedges and out of sight within the house. Leila had always moved swiftly. As a little girl, she had skipped and danced and—

Netta stood still, her vision clouding. She turned her face away from the house, determined not to let anyone see her this way. Such a beautiful little girl, delicate, petite, a little sprite . . . She fumbled in the pocket of her red-brown leather coat and brought out a wisp of handkerchief. She blew her nose and then sniffed hard and pulled herself more erect as she walked back into the house.

As she strode in, tall, moving with her usual sureness, aware of her body's every shift and turn, she heard the faint lisp of a camera shutter. The young man called Raoul took the tiny pocket camera away from his face and gave her a big smile, his chin jutting, his teeth dazzling.

"Thank you, so much, madame," he said. Then he snapped some more pictures of her, standing by the crates.

16

Louch prided himself on his discretion. This was not the toadying deference the usual whey-faced public official, trembling in his corrupt shoes, paid to the wealthy and the powerful. Louch knew how much real power he himself controlled. No trembling for him.

No, his discretion was that of a thinking man, he often told himself, a man whose modest successes in life could be traced to his ability to place himself in the other person's shoes. That was the secret of all life, not just the strange life of one paid to ferret out other people's secrets.

Accordingly, Louch telephoned Curtis that night before presenting himself at 26 Rue Washington. He telephoned, first, because Curtis might not be available for a small talk and, second, because Curtis was after all, like Louch, a single man. He might have other plans for his evening.

"When do you want to come over?" Curtis asked.

Louch glanced at his watch. He'd driven back from Senlis well to the rear of the Kawasaki on which the girl and the boy called Aziz were riding. He'd had time to do things right. He'd assigned different autos all along the route, five changes of vehicle in all, plus two helicopter covers. Mission accomplished. A name for the girl and an address, not too far from her favorite restaurant, Mother's, in the old Marais section.

The premonition he'd had, brought on by the heavy

thoughts of Easter, had been a useful one. Having acted on it, the uneasy feeling should by now be exorcised. It wasn't.

Something heavy still hung over Louch. Damn all religious festivals, he thought. Damn all pagan feasts dressed in Christian trappings, old solstice orgies masquerading as resurrection myths. Why did they still have the power to haunt him? Or was he confusing the Easter chill with something else, for which he had yet to find a name? What meaning, for instance, did the holiday have for people like Aziz, with his talk of "shipments"?

"It's six o'clock," Louch said over the telephone. "What about seven?"

Curtis's reply came without hesitation. "What about right now?"

Louch produced one of his hearty chuckles. "I love working with you Americans."

"Is it work?" Curtis snapped back. "Not a social call, eh?"

"*Mezzo-mezzo.*"

"See you soon. Third entrance."

The line went dead. Louch stepped out of the pharmacy down the street from Number 26. He knew that, from the tunnel-like entrance to the inner courtyard of the Cité Odiot, he was almost invisible. He waited. After fifteen minutes he stirred ponderously and moved along the street, crossing it and walking into the arched entryway that led back to the small, parklike area where, free of Paris traffic noises, the residents of Cité Odiot lived in peace. He passed the first and second entrance and rang Curtis's bell at the third doorway, then moved with curious lightness up the broad stairway to the second-floor apartment.

There was no hesitation with Louch. Once he had made up his mind, no matter how peculiar or trying the thing would be, he launched at once into the doing of it. Yet this interview now would try the bonds of his friendship with Curtis more than Louch really wanted.

He liked Curtis. The man was amusing to be with because he was, in his own peculiarly American way, as professional as Louch. Professionals flocked together, whatever their line of work. It wasn't just that they shared similar experiences or spoke a kind of technical shorthand jargon, but rather that they trusted each other.

No, Louch thought as he mounted the stairs, it is not a matter of trust as it is of understanding.

One professional understood another, as fully as it is ever given to humans to see into their fellow beings. Brothers saw no deeper, nor lovers. The professional's insight was most profound because least clouded by emotion, by those dread mists of past hurts that wrapped themselves around family relationships and the choking toils of love.

Curtis had the door open as Louch arrived on the floor, breathing a bit heavily. "*Bonsoir, mon ami*," the Frenchman grunted.

"You'd better start losing some of that," Curtis said mercilessly, poking a finger into the Buddha-like pad of flab above Louch's belt.

He ushered Louch into the apartment. It was so different from Louch's own, as different as two bachelors could make their living quarters, and yet Louch felt at home the few times he'd been here.

He realized he had never invited Curtis to his own apartment in the Rue de la Huchette. In Paris, with the wealth of bars and restaurants, one usually entertained outside one's home. There was a very French feeling about one's home, especially if it were a modest place. A home told *too much* to an outsider, gave away too many clues.

Take this flat of Curtis's, Louch thought as he sat down with a whoof in an easy chair. Curtis had caused the walls to be stripped back to the original brick, then covered with plain plank bookcases on which everything in the room was kept, not just books: the radio, the tape recorder, the speakers, the phonograph, pictures, boxes, cigar lighter, ashtrays, glasses, bottles, all rested on shelves.

The remainder of the apartment, Louch knew, was just a bedroom and an office, monastic, white-walled, bare. But this living room, too, had been stripped. It was as if Curtis wanted nothing under his hand. It was all *filed* on the yards and yards of stout timber bookshelves that made up two of the room's walls.

The rest was furniture: a small sofa, the two easy chairs in which they now sat, a cocktail table with not even a newspaper on it, and some floor lamps of that aggressively modern Italian design that seem to have been robbed in advance from the operating room of a twenty-first-century hospital.

Louch watched Curtis for a moment and was aware that his confrere was watching him with almost the same cynical grin. "Drink?" the American asked.

"Some Lillet? No ice?"

Curtis got up and poured both of them small glasses of the sweet aperitif wine. He handed one to Louch. "Will you be smoking?"

"The thought may occur to me."

Curtis gave him an ashtray and lighter from a nearby shelf, then sat down opposite Louch and lifted his glass. "Chin-chin."

Louch nodded and sipped the pale, vermouthlike wine. He wondered if his apartment would tell Curtis as much as Curtis's told him. The American was pleasant enough but strangely cold between the ears, efficient in a way not even a German would understand.

People never gave Americans enough credit for what they really were, Louch decided. People thought of Americans as druggy teenagers or thick-necked tourists in Hawaiian shirts, forgetting the chill, singleminded efficiency that underlay the nation itself, the way it had spread itself ruthlessly from one coast to the other, and the way it had taken over Europe in only a generation. Not just the land mass, but the politicians, the businesses, the music, the clothing, the art, even the minds of the young.

Louch lifted his glass and watched the Lillet wine with a light behind it. "Curtis," he said then, "your Miss Irish."

His glance shifted instantly past the glass to Curtis's face, hoping the expression would tell him something. It did. Curtis's face showed mild confusion, nothing more. "Miss Irish?" he asked.

"The tiny girl with the great head of blond curls."

Curtis shook his head. "Leila Darcy," he said then. "Her mother remarried. But the girl is the child of a previous marriage. She's Leila Darcy," he repeated slowly, as if to a mental defective.

Louch grinned. Professionals understood each other too damned well. They understood that there was no point in pretending ignorance once it became clear that something was known. But he admired Curtis's manner of adjusting the balance in his direction by seeming to correct Louch and do him a favor in the bargain.

"Thank you," Louch said with dry sarcasm. "I am in your debt."

Curtis sipped his wine. "What'd you do, tail her to Senlis?"

"Oh?" Louch's thick eyebrows rose ponderously. "You knew she would be there?"

"I knew she was expected." Curtis thought for a moment. His pale blond hair was combed straight across his forehead, giving him the look of a . . . a . . . Louch struggled for the image. A new vicar in a small rural town? There was something inner-controlled about Curtis's slight body and casual dress. Yes, the new vicar, who played tennis. Louch found himself wondering if they had vicars in the States. England, yes. But . . . ?

"Her mother," Curtis was saying, "has been trying

to get in touch with the girl for some time. As you know, I've had the job of feeding her cash once a month, but it didn't help. Apparently she finally reestablished contact. Just goes to show you what regular amounts of salve will do when applied to a wound."

"Such salve heals all wounds."

"And now," Curtis said, suddenly taking the initiative, "you're here to tell me some very unpleasant stuff, read me the riot act and involve me in one of your Byzantine schemes."

Louch let a small moment of silence go by. Then: "Exactly."

Curtis produced a snorting laugh. "Louch, you keep trying to make a cop out of me."

"A hundred times, over the years, you have reminded me you are no detective," Louch kidded him. "And every time we work together on a case, I get fresh proof of your, ah, amateur standing."

"Unkind!" Curtis moaned. "I have damned well saved your ass more than once when you got in a bind."

"And I yours."

"Then try to keep me in a separate category from your official co-workers and cohorts. I'm only a kind of troubleshooter for my bank, Louch. Which is why sometimes my work degenerates to being an errand boy for some rich woman with a spoiled daughter."

"A rich and beautiful woman," Louch intoned.

"With a spoiled daughter who has somehow excited your interest."

"This girl's associates. This girl's activities. This girl's plans. All of it excites us. Not because she is perhaps an underground genius of crime. But solely because she has money and the terrorists need money."

Curtis nodded. "That young man you see with her now and then looks vaguely Arabic. That makes him some kind of terrorist?"

Louch held up his hand like a traffic cop. "We are

rapidly getting off on the wrong footing, Curtis. Let me tell this my way."

"Shoot."

"Let me ask a perhaps insulting question. Do you know much about the terror movements?"

Curtis shifted in his chair. He was wearing pale beige jeans of brushed denim, a heavy knit sweater and tan leather sneakers. He would easily have failed to pass the profile given airport guards to help them weed out potential troublemakers aboard a loading jet. Except, Louch noted, that his hair was not terribly long and certainly lacked the thickness of youth. In fact, Louch saw for the first time, the reason Curtis brushed it slightly forward was to minimize the gradual recession of his hairline.

"Go ahead."

With an if-you-insist gesture, Louch said, "It's a matter of mirror image. I believe there is a saying in the States, 'monkey see, monkey do'? Is there not?"

Curtis continued listening for a moment, as if Louch hadn't stopped. "Yes, I believe so," he admitted then.

"What we are faced with is a matter of reflections, echoes, but hideously distorted and amplified beyond all endurance. It is as if—" Louch hunched forward as he warmed to his thought, "as if our past had been tape-recorded and was now being played back to us on equipment so powerful and so warped that we are in danger of being deafened by it."

He sat back and lighted a Gitane, first offering one to Curtis, who refused. "Being French, you see," he went on then through clouds of Turkish tobacco smoke, "I have made an abstract study of my work, as well as the normal concrete studies one is forced to prepare each day. It is not enough for me to say, 'Eh, bien, now we fight the terrorists.' I have to know why there is terror."

Curtis shifted again in his chair, as if seeking a

more comfortable position. "Is this boring you so soon?" Louch pounced.

"Not at all. I enjoy listening to monomaniacs."

"You must be patient with us, Curtis." Louch puffed more smoke. "The philosophical base of terror is a tripod, the strongest foundation known to man."

"A tripod," Curtis repeated dutifully.

"Because it rests on three legs," Louch went on as if Curtis had asked him to explain the image. "First, the growing technologizing of our society." Louch frowned for a moment. Was there such a word? No matter.

"This first leg is composed of the absurd way in which urban society is automated and computerized, so that any lunatic with a hairpin can black out a city of millions. Any fiend with a vial of LSD can disable a whole province. It is so simple, these days, to bring vast segments of the populace to their knees by simply depriving them of the technological basis of society, even for a day or two. This is the first leg of the tripod."

"First leg."

Louch examined Curtis's face for signs that he was being made fun of. "Second leg," Louch continued, "consists of the racial memory of the Third World, which until recently was the colonial world. This world will never forget how it was colonized, by whom, with what tactics and strategy, and how it was kept that way for centuries. If we think that these Third World people lack heart, human feeling, if we picture them as cruel, insensitive, we are simply looking at a reflection in a distorted mirror of the oppression under which their grandfathers lived, tortured and enslaved by our grandfathers."

"Through a glass, darkly," Curtis quoted.

But Louch was in a hurry now. "Third leg, political. There is a point in the radical movement where leadership splits. One group wants to consolidate what has been gained and rule by oppressing dissidents. This is essentially the Bolshevik position, a posture of pragmatism which, as we have seen, works. The other position is the Trotskyite stance: remain pure, deepen the conflict, expose the grave contradictions of society until even the lowliest and least educated is radicalized to the point where the cry for revolution is universal."

"Third leg: deepen the conflict."

"Very good," Louch said, so caught up now that he was unaware of being mimicked for the purposes of gentle mockery. "And now you see how the tripod joins into one movement. With the technologizing of society, even a very ignorant terrorist can deepen the discomfort and disaster of daily life. And with no mercy, with the utter ruthlessness with which his own people were once enchained by merchant exploiters."

"But."

Louch frowned. "But?"

"But you were about to say 'but,' weren't you?"

Louch shook his head. "There is no but. Do you mean some ameliorating condition? Nothing like it. Oh, perhaps one thing."

Curtis nodded sagely. "There is always a 'but.'"

Louch examined his face again for signs of sarcasm. "It's a poor 'but,'" he said then. "Simply that everything costs so much these days. Even the modest equipment needed, let's say, to bomb a central powerhouse or kidnap a prime minister. So a lot of the terrorists' energy is dissipated in planning activities that merely raise money."

"Merely?" Curtis got up and replenished both their drinks. "I don't know a damned thing about the terror movements," he added, sitting down again, "but I'll bet raising money is mostly what they're into. After all, it deepens the conflict whether it's a direct political act or only a fund-raiser."

"I see you've grasped the essentials," Louch said.

"They're pretty intricate," Curtis said with a straight face, "but you make them very clear."

A pleased look suffused Louch. He sipped his new drink. Really it was such a pleasure discussing these arcane matters with another professional. He couldn't even talk at this sophisticated level with his own sergeants. He recognized a certain mockery in Curtis, but that was only the American style.

"*Alors*, you have the historical-political-technological base," Louch went on in a satisfied tone. "The tripod. But you don't have the essential psychological foundation yet."

"Tetrapod?" Curtis frowned. "Quadripod?"

The Frenchman shook his head in a kind of fatherly stop-kidding-me way. "The psychology, my good Curtis, is what the philosophical tripod rests upon."

Curtis slowly smoothed his thin, pale hair a bit farther down across his high forehead. "Can I hazard a guess?"

"Certainly."

Curtis lifted one finger toward the ceiling. "Awareness of mendacity."

"*Pardon?*"

"We live in strange new times," Curtis went on in a somber tone. "I don't say this has never happened before. I'm sure it has. But today the young people know us for what we are." He sipped his wine. "Liars."

Louch grinned broadly. "*Formidable*, Curtis."

"They are acutely aware that between their parents, their teachers and their politicians they have been spoon-fed such a mendacious view of life that it amounts, finally, to one great, global con job. Everything stands revealed as a lie: God, patriotism, work, art . . . even sex."

At that moment the doorbell rang once, a long peal as of an imperious summons. Louch watched Curtis sneak a look at his wristwatch. The man was expecting someone else. And, from the sudden look of annoyance on the American's face, this new arrival was both early and inconvenient.

"A lady caller?" Louch murmured.

"God only knows." Curtis got up. "Let me find out. I won't be a moment."

Louch made no effort to rise. The good chair and the Lillet, as well as the opportunity to lecture, had put him in a lazy, expansive mood. Curtis left the front door open as he made his way down the stairs on silent sneakers. Listening, Louch could hear murmurs. Another man, a low-pitched voice, in English. American accent.

Now footsteps. One pair of sharp heels, no sound from Curtis. He came in a moment later, a look of odd surprise on his face. Behind him in the doorway stood the other ma—No.

A woman. Good-looking, with short, pale blond hair quite like Curtis's. With his slight figure, too. And with his small-featured appearance, the pale, wide-set eyes, the faintly snub nose, the small, well-formed mouth, the face broad through the jaw, but with an almost delicate chin. Louch hauled himself to his feet. A sister, perhaps?

"Louch," Curtis said in a faintly disgusted voice, "say hello to a surprise visitor."

The woman watched him gravely. She extended her hand. "Lee James," she said in her low, man's voice.

Lee James accepted a glass of Lillet without knowing what it tasted like. She sat on the sofa, forming a triangle with the two men. They picked up their conversation almost as if strange women frequently dropped in unexpectedly. The theoretical discussion seemed to Lee to have no strong focus. It gave her time to sort things out.

First, and most important, Curtis had known who she was. He'd made a very thorough introduction of her to the Frenchman, even mentioning that she'd been with the Bronx DA and the FBI.

It was flattering—and quite alarming—that Curtis remembered so much about someone he'd never met. Normally, there would have been no reason to give the Frenchman so much of her background, unless it was to reassure him that he could talk freely in front of her. She was beginning to see, however, that Curtis didn't deal that much in expected normalities.

Her idea of appearing in person, without a warning telephone call, had been meant to take Curtis off guard. She was beginning to see that—like a vacuum —such a condition simply didn't exist in his nature.

Nor was she quite sure that he accepted her story, the unexpected week's vacation Bill Elston had given her, his suggestion that she look Curtis up and get his advice about hotels and places to visit. It was more likely, Lee saw now, that Curtis simply didn't want to discuss anything in front of the other man. Perhaps he believed she had come bearing confidential instructions from their mutual boss. In any event, he'd *seemed* to accept her openly. For now.

He was not an unknown quantity to Lee James. By reading his reports, she'd gotten some insight into the way his mind worked. He still, for example, used a cover identity of long standing. He filed a weekly column, "Travels with Curtis" which appeared in a few newspapers around the United States. A devious man, Curtis.

The other man—what had he called him, Louch? —was even more an unknown in the equation. French, of course, and obviously a cop. That wary placidity, that chill glint of eye, Lee James knew, could only belong to a cop and, what was more, one of the rare honest ones.

The gleam of honesty alone made Louch worth studying. He and Curtis seemed to be friends on a personal as well as a professional level. That made Louch someone fairly high up in one of the big networks, either the Sûreté Urbaine or the Police Judiciare.

Lee tried to remember which was which. The PJ was something like the FBI, working mostly on big, nationwide crimes. The Sûreté Urbaine was also national, but assigned to smaller crimes of a more local nature.

Lee James found men easier to understand, much simpler in their needs and responses, than women. Her sureness with men, she felt, had come from having both a younger and an older brother—and no mother. Lee's two brothers were quite different types.

Harold, the older, was the self-sufficient, inner-directed type, superficially like Louch here. He reacted slowly but surely. He hid everything until you asked. Then he hid nothing, left you in no doubt.

Her younger brother, Terry, had been a much different type. He had resembled Curtis in being physically slight, although not small, and possessed of a terrifying offbeat charm. With Terry, Lee recalled, you were always in doubt.

So was Terry. His enthusiasms sprang up suddenly, died within a few weeks. It had been his fate to conceive a quick enthusiasm for intelligence work during the Vietnam war. The CIA had recruited him out of S-2 and put him into the Golden Triangle on drug control.

He'd died in the Golden Triangle, not in combat.

Lee and Harold had never gotten proper information from either the Department of Defense or the home intelligence operative sent to interview them after the official report of Terry's death had finally arrived. Someday, Lee had promised herself, when she had the kind of contacts Curtis did, she would open up that unhealed wound and find out why the Reds had killed Terry.

". . . but there is no quantitative increase, Curtis," the Frenchman was saying with great assurance. "There is only better reportage. We have always had terrorism. It is only in the last ten years that we have been subjected to a—what do you people call it?—a 'media blitz' of statistics."

"Louch, you're using some typical, warped, Gallic definition of terror."

The heavyset man shrugged. "Terror," he said, seeming to relish the ululant rumble of the r's deep in his larynx, "is any warfare carried on against civilians."

The brick-walled room, with its miles of shelving, fell silent for a long moment. "Shit," Curtis said admiringly, "I have to hand you that one."

Louch made an air-churning, not-at-all-any-time gesture. "Which is why I state with utter confidence that we have always had terror, and always as much as we have now. Think of the Turks versus the Armenians or Greeks. Think of the Crusaders against the Saracens. Think of the American whites versus the American Indians."

Lee James had been sitting in her usual still-as-a-statue pose, legs crossed. She now uncrossed them. "Think of the French Catholics versus the Huguenots," she suggested quietly.

The Frenchman shook his head ponderously from side to side. "Do not make appeals to crude chauvinism. My point is still the same: we have always had terror. Even on the class level. What else does one call those ugly episodes of history in which private armies of thugs, paid for by industrialists, maim and kill unionists? Or where the legally constituted police forces do this same criminal work? But, of course, neither of you is old enough to recall such matters. The Republic Steel massacre, for example."

"Chicago, 1937," Curtis responded. "What's the name of this course, American history?"

"Very well. Let us consider Genghis Khan or an Attila the Hun. Let us muse over an Adolf Hitler. What is genocide but terror? And compared to such monsters of terror, what is a scattered rabble of disorganized Arabs?"

Lee James recrossed her legs. She sipped the sweetish wine and listened. The only thing she had found out about these two men as she sat here tonight was that both of them were pretending. Curtis she knew to be the most artful dodger on UBCO's payroll. But there were odd silences in Louch that worried her. Genghis Khan. Adolf Hitler. The Republic Steel massacre. Attila the Hun. Had he never heard of a man called Stalin?

". . . as to there being some sort of international conspiracy," Louch was going on at length, "we have a few clues, but nothing real to work with."

Curtis produced a Bronx cheer. "Surely you don't deny a tie-up between the Baader-Meinhof Gruppe and some of the Palestinian terror people? That was obvious at Entebbe."

"Perhaps."

"And what can you call it but a connection when

we know that Libya funds a lot of this and the Libyan government gives them staging areas and safe houses."

"Another probable."

"Then what more are you looking for in the way of linkages?" Curtis demanded.

Lee James watched the Frenchman rub the bulbous tip of his nose and take a sip of his Lillet. She had been waiting patiently to hear the one thing either of these men could now bring forward, Curtis to win his point or Louch to end-run him and come out ahead in the argument. But neither had.

"There is an ideological link," she said then.

Curtis's pale eyes flicked sideways at her so quickly that she almost missed the movement. He made a face. "That's too easy," he said then. "All these people paint themselves in Marxist tones of red. From what we can tell, it's mostly camouflage."

Louch's head was nodding in agreement. "If one were to search out ideological linkages," he went on heavily, "one would also have to poke into the death squads of Latin America and the secret police of governments like Chile and Iran, based on naked terror."

Lee James started to reply but a second flicker in Curtis's glance stopped her. The silences! She had to summon all her self-control to keep from shouting something. The silences were deafening! She found herself biting her lower lip. Slowly, she let it go.

"It's a mistake to ideologize the terror movement," the Frenchman was pontificating. "What people think of as their own motivation is not always so. A youngster in Milan, throwing a bomb at a police station, when captured will tell the world he is, let us say, a partisan of the extreme left or right. And he believes himself to be telling the truth. But he is deluding himself. And us."

"Come on, Louch," Curtis chivvied. "Are you riding that hobbyhorse again? The kid is only protesting the mendacity of the world?"

"No. He is reacting, first, to his own hormones."

Louch held up the thumb of his right hand. "Second, to the approval of his peers." He held up his index finger. "And third, to the models of behavior presented to him on the nightly television news by a press that makes much too much of violence." He was now holding three fingers aloft.

"And only fourth to the illegal party of which he's a member?" Curtis finished for him in a derisive tone. "Hard to believe."

The Frenchman shrugged again, a massive movement of his heavy shoulders. A silence fell over them. Curtis rather ostentatiously glanced at his wristwatch. "Enthralling as this has been," he said, getting to his feet, "and mindful as I am of my duties to a visitor from abroad," he smiled at Lee, "I'm going to have to ask both of you to beat it."

Louch stood up slowly. "A late visitor?"

"I'm putting each of you in charge of the other," Curtis said. "I don't want to find either one of you taking a plant outside my door to find out who comes and goes."

"That," Lee James murmured, getting up, "settles it." She turned to Louch. "Did you come by car? I'd like to get a lift to my hotel."

"More than a lift, young woman," Louch said. "You are not too tired from your flight, I hope, to share a light dinner with me? In that way Curtis can rest assured neither of us is spying on him."

In the awkward pause that followed this remark, Louch beamed on the two younger people. He liked Americans. They were refreshing to be with. "I want to thank you," he said abruptly, speaking from the heart as he seldom did, "for this little interval of . . . may one call it logic? I was depressed. Now I am elated."

"Nothing like the sound of your own voice," Curtis said, patting his shoulder. "Why should you be depressed?"

"The season." Louch churned the air with his

hands. "Easter is a different thing for people who live in a Catholic land."

"What could be depressing about Easter?"

"I am not expressing myself well," Louch admitted. "It is the season that started my mood. But it is something in my own mind. We all get these things, Curtis, even you sunny, even-tempered Americans."

"The feeling," Lee James asked, "that nothing's going right?"

Louch smiled at her. "And that nothing will ever go right."

"Ugh."

As he ushered them out the door, Curtis patted Lee James's shoulder as casually as he had Louch's. "Get a good night's sleep," he said, "and call me after lunch tomorrow. I'll have some ideas for you on hotels and such."

"But this is just a vacation for me. I don't want to cut in on your working day."

His pale eyes locked with hers. "One of the pleasant penalties of living in Paris is having to show it to vacationers."

A lot like Terry, Lee found herself thinking. Terry's abrupt stare. Terry's height and frame. Terry's coloring. Mine, too, for that matter. "That's exactly what I don't want you to have to do."

"I love it," Curtis said, giving her a slight, good-natured shove in the direction of the door. "Don't let Louch get drunk."

Louch touched Curtis's arm. "Always such a pleasure, my friend. You know I have no one else with whom to philosophize."

"Not even Vermeuil?"

"Not even le ministre himself," Louch agreed. "That gold-plated fake." He grew serious a moment. "I will call you tomorrow?"

"I know," Curtis said.

As she followed the heavyset Frenchman down the stairs, Lee James wondered who Curtis's later visitor might be. Not that she didn't expect Curtis to come fully equipped with a private life. Which he took some pains to keep private.

"She must be something special," Louch said as they paused in the little parklike courtyard outside.

Lee James glanced at him. He had the mind-reading knack, did he? "But we're not to lurk about," she warned him.

He drew a deep breath of night air, damp but fresh. "Mademoiselle," he said then, "it is a brief but educational walk to a small restaurant of some renown. Tell me," he said, linking his arm in hers and leading her away at a brisk pace, "in New York have you ever heard of Fouquet's?"

18

In the Eighth Arrondissement, halfway between the river and the rond-pont where the Avenue Franklin D. Roosevelt crosses the Champs-Elysées, lies the Rue Jean Goujon. It is an expensive quarter of large old houses and a few extremely modern new ones. In this neighborhood, for example, is the great restaurant, Ledoyen, its small manor house shaded by chestnut trees, and the offices of the newspaper *Le Figaro*.

On the Rue Jean Goujon, in the block between Rue Bayard and the Avenue Roosevelt, stands one of the newer apartment buildings, French only by virtue of being located in Paris. The same sort of high rise, with its blank, white marble face, high-speed elevators and secluded balconies, can be found in any large city from New York to Singapore. Like its counterparts in other lands, the building on Jean Goujon has as good a security system as closed-circuit television can make it, with a husky male concierge in attendance at the monitor screen off the main lobby.

If briefed in advance, an authorized visitor can get past the concierge without too much trouble. Tom Sandweg had been briefed.

He got out of the cab and rang the bell next to the plate-glass entrance. The concierge came out of his cubicle and stared sourly at him for a moment, then came to the intercom.

"Qu'est-ce que c'est?"

Tom bent to talk into the microphone. European

intercoms never seemed high enough in the wall for him. "M'sieur Amico, *Numéro Soixante-Trois.*"

The dour expression on the concierge's face deepened into great furrows of distrust. He buzzed the door open, however, and allowed Tom to advance into the lobby.

"Sandweg."

The look of distrust curdled into one of total disdain. Without any further amenities, the concierge left him standing there while he telephoned Apartment 63 and announced a "M'sieur Sedgewick."

Eventually, Tom arrived at the sixth floor and found George Brown waiting in the open doorway of Number 63. "Goombar Tom!" he boomed.

Inside, the apartment was severely modern, not at all the ambience Tom Sandweg had pictured for George Brown, even under his Parisian name of Amico. The front door led immediately into a small living room and dining area that ended in a wall of floor-to-ceiling glass doors which slid open onto a shallow terrace.

It was dusk. The Paris sky had changed from pale blue to pale pink to deep mauve. Brown put a drink in Tom's hand and led him out onto the terrace. "Nice, huh?"

Tom surveyed the view of backyards and buildings low enough not to obscure the view. "Great," he agreed, swallowing a slug of Scotch and water. "You Frenchmen really know how to live."

Brown banged him on the shoulder. "You said it, kid!"

Sandweg's glance moved to the left, where a building almost as tall as Brown's apartment house stood in its own grounds, an older building, obviously filled with offices. But what attracted his attention was the maze of antennas which the building supported. There were horizontal wires, vertical masts, cat's cradles, stacked arrays, microwave pickups, every conceivable kind of antenna.

king for money always listen patiently to
gs—produced another of his dazzling dis-
flawless dentition. "Okay, George, when
ep a secret from you?"
ever."

g put his glass aside. "The Wotan is Mach-3,
aded, with troposphere capacity." He
ill smiling, but thinking: That'll hold the
stard.
appeared to consider this description for a
Then he glanced slyly at Sandweg. "You
within the parameters of your mandate?"
without much humor.
u, George, anything."
he damned thing get up to Mach-3 in the
e?"
the whole secret. This mother skims in
the hilltops, below the radar screen. The
tratosphere missiles have to arc up and
n. That gives enemy radar time to spot and
ut the Wotan zooms in and hits before the
ven pick up a blip."
got up and made himself a second drink.
something mad about the whole conversa-
apon that would give his country at least a
th lead on the Soviets in kill power, and
ussing it with nothing more than a kind of
thug, a mob money manager. All because
t force that idiot woman, Netta, to unload
e daubs she and Ferguson had squirreled
e the Trocadéro. It was mad and it was
Not that using George Brown's cash was
him. Sandweg, and Minton Irish before
nade judicious use of mob money to meet
eed for cash flow. But to have to break se-
somebody who was really less than one
removed from towel boy in a Palermo

orge," he said then, turning back to face

"What gives there, George?"

Brown, heavyset, frowned in the growing darkness. "German embassy."

Tom laughed. "They don't miss a word of anything, do they?"

Brown guided him back inside. "Neither do we, Tommy." He indicated a deep, upholstered chair. "Rest the body, goombar." Brown then sank into a matching chair and stared moodily at the drink in his hand. "So congratulations are in order, huh?" he asked in a singularly noncongratulating tone.

Sandweg frowned. "About what?"

"I told you we don't miss nothing, Tommy, and I mean it. The German embassy is a bunch of amateurs compared to us."

"Then you know we got the Wotan contract. The Department of Defense just awarded it to our Jet-Tech subsidiary."

"Yeh'yeh'yeh." Brown's mind seemed to have wandered elsewhere. "I also know Jet-Tech has no cash."

Tom Sandweg's handsome face split slowly into a smile of great warmth and personal force, with a number of teeth in it. "What don't you bastards know?"

"Fuckin' little." George Brown brooded over his untouched drink for a while. "And, about IBI, I maybe know more than you do." He sat back in his chair and sipped his drink. "Minnie Irish was open with me, Tom. You know that. Not that he was a talker. But he let me in on a lot of IBI's things. The computer business, the oil tankers, that corn and wheat brokerage in Minneapolis. And I let IBI into the Caribbean casino business. Minnie and me, together, covered the whole casino market from Malta to Hong Kong. The only thing I couldn't show in was those nuclear fuel breeders in Oregon and the aeroframe stuff Jet-Tech does for Boeing and Douglas-McDonnell. Too sensitive, politically."

Sandweg finished his drink. "You told me once that

whatever you did for Minton Irish you'd do for me. That still go?"

"Absolutely." Brown sat forward. "But not for Jet-Tech."

"I beg your pardon?"

"I know what you want, Tommy. It don't take no crystal ball. Jet-Tech dug deep in its pockets for that Wotan contract. Your people must've transferred a few long green ones to Switzerland on that baby. How many senators did you piece off? Four or six?"

"You don't want to know," Sandweg said in a gloomy voice. "But it's peanuts to what we'll make on the damned Wotan."

"What's so special?"

Sandweg was about to reply, then stopped. If George Brown didn't know what made the Wotan special, then the information should be worth money to him now. Bargaining time.

"It's classified, George," he began. "I wish to hell it wasn't. But you know the way the Defense people operate."

The short, broad-shouldered man gave him a cold look. "I'm no fuckin' Commie spy, Tom. You don't have to watch your mouth with George Brown. In your whole goddamn life you're never gonna find a bigger patriot than George Brown. I donate to everything. You name it, Red Cross, Community Chest, cancer, the works. In my plants we have compulsory U.S. bond-buying on payroll deduction plan. No employee of mine gets away without at least a twenty-five-dollar bond a month. There is nobody you know who contributes more to the American way of life. At church. In the community. In the industries where I'm active. To political parties. Candidates. Newspapers. Radio and TV stations. I mean, it's no idle, fuckin' boast when I take the Pledge of Allegiance to the flag. To me, it's alive. I never forget that what I got America gave me. What I am, America made me. So don't give me that shit-eating 'classified' crap."

Tom Sandweg managed [...] than embarrassed. He no[...] right, George. But you do[...] of my mandate."

Brown blinked once, tw[...] sunlight. "Talk sense, will [...]

"It's need-to-know sec[...] who's involved in the W[...] anybody who was helping [...] cash needs—would have a [...] tell him."

The heavyset man laug[...] throw up, Tommy. Is t[...] play?"

"Not at all."

"Parameters of your ma[...] a disbelieving tone. "My, [...] ment. "How much cash?" [...]

"Chicken feed. Twenty [...]

Brown stuck his tongue[...] duced a sharp, tearing no[...] night, Tom Sandweg."

"I thought you were the [...]

"I am," Brown agreed, [...] who wants it and what for. [...]

"Naturally, if you com[...] what Wotan's all about." [...]

Brown laughed softly, i[...] remind me of the guy v[...] back again in the easy c[...] "Guy cups his hands toge[...] and asks his friend, 'Wl[...] friend says, on a wild gue[...] The first guy takes ano[...] 'What color?' " Brown [...] "You're asking me to b[...] sale."

Tom, who had listene[...] was the third time he'd l[...]

people a[...] such thi[...] plays of [...] could I k[...]

"Like [...]

Sandw[...] MIRV-h[...] paused, [...] guinea b[...]

Brown[...] moment. [...] sure tha[...] he teased[...]

"For y[...]

"Does [...] troposph[...]

"That [...] right ov[...] old-style [...] come do[...] destroy. [...] Russkies[...]

Sandw[...] He foun[...] tion. A v[...] twelve-m[...] he was d[...] high-clas[...] he could [...] some of [...] away in [...] maddeni[...] repellen[...] him, ha[...] a sudde[...] curity w[...] generati[...] brothel [...]

"But, [...]

the squat man, "my telling you this commits you. That's the way it has to be."

"Has?" Brown's voice had gone cold. "You guys kill me, Tom. You come with your hand out and you tell me what has to be. If I live to be a thousand, I will never understand WASP types. Never."

"I don't make the rules."

"Shit you WASPs don't."

Brown got up suddenly and moved to the open doorway that led out onto the terrace. Night had fallen. With the death of the sun, the air had gotten chilly and damp. Brown snapped on a lamp.

"Why don't Jet-Tech get the money from its own bank?" he demanded then. "They bank with UBCO, right? And last I heard UBCO had a few spare bucks lying around, right?"

Sandweg had begun to regret having made this appointment with Brown. He'd done it in a moment of near panic. Funny how people like Brown believed that if one were white, Protestant and Anglo-Saxon, one never panicked.

But, earlier this evening, when Oscar Ferguson had reported that the château at Senlis, with its contents, wouldn't bring any more than half the cash Sandweg needed—if a buyer could be found—the panic had begun to set in. Delays. Ifs. And Jet-Tech's cash position was already stretched too far to yield another inch of flexibility.

The lush Wotan contract, $1.5 billion, plus allowable cost overruns, was Tom Sandweg's baby, the first fruit of his stewardship of IBI since the death of Minton Irish, the first really big deal he could bring to his board of directors and say, "Make me your permanent chief executive, and I'll keep creating deals like this one."

Getting the contract had cost a bit more than the usual advance payments to government officials because there had been so much publicity lately about defense contractor bribery that a costly new layer of intermediaries and Swiss dummy structures had had to be established.

More than that, winning the contract had been the result of a process of premeditated, well-rehearsed lies told to the various senators in those Sunbelt states where Jet-Tech would be assembling Wotan hardware.

There was no secret to producing a missile that could come in at levels below the radar scan. The secret was to bring the Wotan in at speeds three times that of sound.

In the troposphere, the oxygen content was still rich enough to support life . . . and combustion. The alloys in a Mach-3 missile had to be able either to withstand this fatal combination of high heat and rich atmosphere, or in some arcane metallurgical way to burn away at a controlled rate of ablation that still brought the bombs on target in operable condition.

Jet-Tech's metallurgists had yet to solve the problem either way.

So even a highly paid WASP executive had a right to panic when it looked as if the momentum of the deal was about to grind to a halt from lack of cash, leading to inevitable attention by the press and from those congressmen whose states contained no Jet-Tech factories.

The Wotan technology wouldn't stand really close inspection at this point. Once it was under way, snoopers could be turned away or conned off by the usual appeals to national security. But until the machinery began rolling, the contract was a fragile tissue of lies, half-truths and pious hopes.

In the half darkness now, Sandweg watched Brown for a moment without speaking. The heavyset man turned away to glance out the window wall at the night. Sandweg stared with loathing at the fat back of Brown's neck.

And Jet-Tech wasn't the only IBI subsidiary that

needed Sandweg's attention in Europe. He was overdue in Frankfurt for talks with the West German
intermediary who was brokering a secret grain deal.
The broker supposedly represented vague "Third
World" nations, underfed millions of people, which
made the IBI sale of grain morally acceptable. Only
afterward was the German company to resell to a
Rumanian dummy representing the Soviets.

And here I am, Tom Sandweg told himself bitterly,
killing time being polite to this Mafia superpatriot
who only wants to squeeze additional details out of
me.

"What about it?" Brown insisted. "Why don't Jet-
Tech hit UBCO for the front money?"

"There are four development loans outstanding
now with UBCO."

"They turned you down, huh?"

"No. We haven't asked them yet."

Brown nodded. "Shit, you haven't. And what
UBCO won't do, none of the smaller banks will,
either. What's the scam? Something not kosher with
Jet-Tech?" His eyes narrowed. "Or with the contract?"

"Nothing like that," Sandweg said soothingly.

"Yeah?"

"George, this isn't big money we're looking for.
Just start-up cash. Normally," Tom went on with
practiced ease, giving it the full increment of WASP
sauvity, "we'd simply pull it out of daily arbitrage
flow. But the exchange rate's unfavorable at the moment, so we're looking for new dollars."

The stocky man's eyes seemed to glaze slightly, but
whether because he was impressed or bored, Sandweg
couldn't tell. Brown seemed to think about it for a
much longer time than he really needed. "Give me
twenty-four hours," he said then. "You're not the only
people with a cash scarcity. I got a dozen takers
knocking on my door at the moment. Where you
gonna be tomorrow night, Paris?"

"Frankfurt."

Brown's head, on his thick neck, swiveled from left to right. "Stay handy, Tom. If I can bust my hump finding cash for you, you can keep your ass in one place for twenty-four hours, capeesh?"

"Will you be staying in Paris?"

Brown eyed him glumly. "I asked you first."

"George," Tom Sandweg said in a reproachful tone, trying to reestablish some kind of superiority, "don't we trust each other anymore?"

19

Murray Olenick was barely thirty-five years of age, almost a millionaire, good-looking in the new Hairy Beast way, with his pick of Manhattan's most attractive career women. It was only fair that Murray had remained a bachelor so that he could spread around as much of himself as possible.

At the moment, however, Murray Olenick was perspiring profusely enough to reactivate the ballsy perfume with which he'd doused himself this morning after the shower that concluded his prebreakfast tennis game at the athletic club.

From the club, where Murray was one of the few Jews to gain membership—as well as acceptance—in recent years, he had been taken by limo across Central Park South to his office in an all-glass high rise not far from the United Nations enclave.

He had put in an easy morning with a few clients —Murray was a corporate tax adviser—before repairing to lunch with one of them at his favorite hangout, a lushly decorated restaurant in the east sixties, called Le Bird, where other socially acceptable Mafia consultants often ate and drank.

Murray Olenick was not a crook. He'd been second in his class at Fordham Law School, a brilliant young man who chose not to take the bar exam but to pursue tax law instead. In the sense of committing acts contrary to or prohibited by law, Murray was innocent of wrongdoing. In helping clients like George

Brown with their multifaceted business operations, Murray also remained within the law.

Yet when the preliminary telephone call reached him amid the potted greenery of Le Bird, Murray Olenick began to sweat like an embezzler with his hand in the till.

The call was from Paris. It could not be completed until Murray was back in his office, which meant that he would have to cancel dessert, repeal the coffee and cognac and leave his guest to finish lunch alone. It was not the suavest exit Murray Olenick had ever made. He knew that his favorite waiter, who was gay, turned very pouty at last-second rush-rush-rush. It simply didn't go with the ambience.

Nevertheless, at 2:00 P.M., Murray was back in his office waiting for George Brown's second call.

"Good boy, Mur. I want you to find me twenty mill."

"When?"

"Now. Cash."

"Mr. Brown, it's impossible."

There was a pause filled with faint, ethereal beeping. "This is a lousy connection, Mur. Did you hear me ask you to find the cash now?"

"Mr. Br—" Murray Olenick stopped. His lower lip was trembling. Brown was being so damned unfair. "Look," he began, hating the faint tremor in his voice.

"You look," Brown cut in. "Get on the pipe to Sally. Between the two of you, it shouldn't take too long."

"I'll tr—"

The line went dead.

Murray listened to faint, high-register organ notes across the far spaces of the Atlantic. After a while, he replaced the telephone in its cradle and stared at it for a long time.

He rarely did business with Sally Fish, only when Mr. Brown forced him to. Salvatore Fischetti was

Brown's majordomo, his private secretary, valet, driver, butler and bodyguard. He was a short, bald, sawed-off, dese-and-dose type where Murray Olenick was tall and tan, tennis year round, skiing all winter, thick head of glossy black hair, luxuriant Guards mustache and cultured way of speaking.

The notion that Murray had to work something out with Sally Fish was repellent. And the idea that anybody like Sally could help him find a fast twenty million dollars was even more degrading to contemplate.

Murray Olenick canceled his afternoon appointments and returned to the club, where he hid away in the second hottest steam room, worrying about how unfair life could be, until almost four in the afternoon, when finally, as he knew he would, he telephoned Sally Fish.

The farm was less than fifty miles from the city, across the Hudson River near the town of Warwick, New York, where farms of modest size, fifty or one hundred acres, are usually devoted to dairying, apple orchards or onion fields.

In point of fact, Faraway Farms raised horses. This was not a tax scheme designed by someone like Murray Olenick to run rings around the IRS. Faraway Farms actually raised horses, some for show and many more to race. It also ran rings around the IRS.

The main house was three stories, Early American, white clapboard, twelve-light windows. Each story grew smaller in size until the top one, which had once been an attic. This level was now one large room which Sally Fish used as an office from which to run Faraway Farms and other matters.

The road outside was quite far from the house, easily half a mile. Both utility and telephone wires for the house went underground the whole distance. Nevertheless, it was possible to see, at the road, that the incoming phone line was unusually thick. Half a dozen trunk lines lay beneath the armored insulation.

Sally Fish was using one of the trunk lines at the moment. He sat like a gross gnome, hunched over the long table at which he conducted most of the business of Faraway Farms. He had already dialed through to Paris and was waiting patiently for the last shush-click that preceded the start of ringing.

In the parlance of his trade, Sally's profession was that of *cuscinetto*. In Italian dictionaries, the word translates to "pillow," but in Sally's world a truer definition would be "buffer," not so much in the sense of taking up the shock of a collision, the way an auto bumper would, but more in the sense of an impermeable intermediary, a solid wall through which one had to negotiate in order to reach George Brown.

Sally was Mr. Brown's *cuscinetto* on this side of the Atlantic. In Europe, however, a squint-eyed Mick named Neil (for Cornelius) Groark handled the job. Sally Fish hated the bastard, who wasn't even a Catholic, but one of those left-handed Irish Protestants. Why Mr. Brown trusted the treacherous son of a bitch was a mystery, at least to Sally. It wasn't as if Neil Groark knew Europe that well. He'd been born and raised in the South Bronx.

Sally puffed at the stub of a Montecristo Imperiale tucked in the corner of his wide mouth. He rubbed his bald head and stared out the windows at the March wind bending white birches sideways, willows just beginning to show faint blurs of green. The boss was not going to like this telephone call. But in a lifetime of serving him, Sally had learned to live with the angers of George Brown.

"Hello?"

"*Si, padrone.*"

"Let's go."

Sally placed the telephone he was using into a foam rubber enclosure contained in a gray metal box. The rubber enfolded the telephone and cradled it like a baby in deep pillows. Then Sally picked up another telephone from a hook on the side of the gray box. "How's Paris doing?" he asked.

Sally didn't pretend to understand how the gray box worked, but he knew George Brown had one in his Paris apartment and had done exactly the same thing at his end of the telephone call. Their voices were now being scrambled as they flew across transatlantic cables or satellite microwave relay channels.

Anybody tapping in had to set his scrambler to the same pattern, or the voices were gibberish, like monkeys chattering. The scrambler setting was changed according to a simple formula that depended on the number of the day in that month. This was now March 28. If one divided 28 by 3, whatever the two numbers were to the right of the decimal point were the setting for the scrambler. Simple formula. It had taken Sally Fish six months to master, but now he would never forget it.

Sally also knew that these scrambler conversations had to be short. If an eavesdropper had time to try a lot of different scrambler settings, eventually he'd get the right one.

"Problems, boss. There's a kinda pause in shipments."

"White?"

"White don't exist. We're moving brown into the pipeline but it'll take a couple weeks."

"Whad'y'tell Murray about the twenty mill?"

Sally paused for an instant. Murray Olenick was also a buffer for George Brown. He stood between the boss and the legitimate business world. *Il cuscinetto bianco*, Sally called him privately, the "white" buffer. Murray could never be told even one syllable of the things handled by Sally, *il cuscinetto nero*.

"I'm working on it."

"Keep it that way. Ten-four."

"Boss," Sally's voice went up anxiously. "Don't hang up. Boss, they lost track of Nicky."

"They what?"

"He lammed outa Williamstown. They lost him."

"You fuckin' better find the kid."

"Look, boss, he's a big boy. If he—"

"Find him, *stronzo*, or you're a dead man. Ten-four."

Sally replaced the gray-box telephone, retrieved the original instrument from its foamy cradle and hung it up. He sat there for a moment, frowning. He puffed and no smoke came from his cigar. Scowling, he relit it.

That was the trouble with short conversations. There was never any time to explain, just unload and get spattered. Not that he took George Brown's threat personally. Nicky was something special to the old man, the thorn in his side whose pain was excruciating and necessary, but if anybody died, it wouldn't be Sally Fish.

Sally produced three fat rings of cigar smoke. His first job was to get the cash flowing again. The stalled shipments of Number Four White were backed up all the way to Marseilles and Ankara. The Mexishit took a while to come in from Culiacán, on the Pacific Coast.

And it was moving in a costly direction, brokered by families who loved to tack on a stiff tariff just for the privilege of shifting the stuff through their territory—Arizona, New Mexico, Texas—before it reached families more closely affiliated with George Brown. The brown, which started out being half the price of white, reached the East Coast at almost the same price, thanks to all these friendly hands.

And then it still had to be recut and rebagged before it hit the streets and the cash started flowing again. A tough moment to go looking for $20 million.

That problem should have had his close attention, Sally Fish knew. But after all, a man didn't survive this long in George Brown's family as the "black" buffer without knowing his true priorities. In this case, the first thing Sally had to do was find fall guys on whom to blame Nick Brown's disappearance. He had to have them strung up and talking freely by the time the boss returned.

The cash could wait.

20

Curtis had put away the Lillet the moment Louch and Lee James left his apartment. He didn't care for the sweet wine and really kept it on hand only for French visitors.

After going to the window to watch Louch and the girl cross his courtyard and disappear through the arched passage to the Rue Washington, Curtis went back into his kitchen. He filled a tall glass of ice cubes half with Johnnie Walker Red and half with Perrier.

He sat down in the same chair where he had listened to Louch's thoroughly exhaustive discourse on terrorism. He sipped and thought.

Some of the same stuff he'd heard from Louch before, but without the ideological trimmings. The fact that he had launched into it tonight in such detail meant that Louch had established a connection between terror underground and Leila Darcy . . . or hoped to get Curtis to help him establish one.

Nothing unusual there. But the arrival of Lee James was something else.

She'd had an impeccable cover story, of course. Something about having checked into a hotel, but wanting a less expensive one. And Bill Elston had told her the resident authority on Paris life was Curtis, so naturally, she had come to him for advice.

Curtis grimaced as he sipped his Scotch and water. The only part of her story that rang true was Elston. He'd undoubtedly sent her. But why?

And her arrival had been so badly timed. Louch

had been about to uncork something—a favor or two and some confidential information—to which Lee James's arrival had put an end.

When she called him tomorrow, he'd damned well get to the bottom of it. All this and the missing Czech minister *and* Netta Irish. What right did Lee James have to breeze right in and overcomplicate his life?

Vacation, indeed. Why was an attractive young woman, alone in Paris on her first evening in town, knocked out by the jet flight, reporting to Curtis as if he were running some sort of UBCO message center? It didn't ring true.

They didn't even know each other. He'd seen the memo everyone had gotten six months ago when Lee James had been hired, a standard interoffice memo. Since then her name had surfaced only once, when she'd asked Elston a question about something in one of Curtis's reports, a question that showed she was cleverer than the normal rookie.

What was Elston trying to pull, sending her here?

Curtis finished his drink and made another. He supposed he was overreacting. His job wasn't that great, was it, that there was a driving urge to protect it? Getting paranoid about Lee wasn't his style.

He sat down in the same chair and continued drinking. His style, he decided, was no style. What he would do was always unpredictable, even to him. And because of this he could seldom be outguessed.

His style was to have the mother of the tiny terrorist tot coming here at any moment while the pursuer of her daughter breathed heavily down his neck and supercool New York females dropped in like mysterious birds of passage. It was a goddamned Marx Brothers movie.

He was halfway through his second Johnnie Walker and Perrier when his downstairs doorbell rang twice. He sighed, put aside the glass, opened his front door and started down the stairs to the street entrance.

She looked angry, even from a distance, her pale

ivory face flushed along the cheekbones, her dark red lips sulky, her huge eyes avoiding his glance. She wore tall, red-brown boots with heels so high that she towered over him as he stood there in his sneakers.

Saying nothing, she mounted the stairs at a rapid pace, heels making the sound of .22-caliber-pistol shots. In the leather coat and slave-driver boots, she seemed to Curtis to lack only a whip. He ushered her into his flat and closed the door behind them.

"Damned, insolent little bitch," she spat out. "Get me a drink."

Curtis brought her a replica of the kind he'd been drinking. She downed half of it on the first swallow, then collapsed slowly, like a Grecian column in an earth tremor, into the easy chair in which Curtis had been sitting. She extended her long legs before her, ankles crossed.

"Take off my boots," she ordered.

Curtis sat down in the chair Louch had used. He lifted his glass to her. "So nice to see you again. Lovely of you to drop in," he went on in a tone of mock politeness. "Inclement weather we've been having, isn't it? Do you think," he continued, quoting the feed line of an old vaudeville joke, "that the rain will hurt the rhubarb?"

She stared at him insolently. Her lips twitched. Then she managed a small, tight smile. "Not," she said slowly, providing the correct punch line, "if it's in cans."

"That kid really gets to you, doesn't she?"

Netta finished off her drink. "She is my one and my only. That makes her a very sharp knife in my heart."

"I don't have kids," Curtis said. "Neither wife wanted them. Nor did I, for that matter. Is there ever any good from them?"

Netta considered the question. "When they're small, they're adorable. You just can't get enough of

them. Leila was the most darling little girl you'd—"
She choked off suddenly. "Another, please?" she asked
then, lifting her empty glass.

He brought her a second drink and freshened his
own. She stared at the drink. "I suppose some adorable children grow up to be adorable adults. There's
no law against it. But Leila's gotten to be the coldest,
most calculating, heartless, self-centered, demanding,
egomaniacal—"

"Hey."

Netta stopped. "I'm sorry." She flexed her ankles.
"Please take off my boots?"

"In a minute. Now that you've started saying
'please.'"

"Boots don't turn you on, eh?" She held her glass
before her face and watched him from behind it, eyes
wary. "They were Minnie's thing."

"Minnie?"

"Late, lamented husband." She sipped her drink.
"I gather that was what sent his first wife into suicide
and his second to the loony bin. He was Mr. S-M.
He liked it both ways. Give pain and receive it."

"Charming."

"Do you know his favorite idea of fun?" She waited
for Curtis's response and, when she got none, continued anyway. "He and I were in that tacky Mirabelle
in London one night. We were, I believe the phrase
is, engaged. The room was filled with people. He
somehow got his hand in under my dress and began
plucking out pubic hairs . . . one by one."

"And you?"

"It was a nightmare. I couldn't scream or jump.
He knew that, the evil toad. All I could do was get
up and go to the ladies' room and stay there for great
periods of time. Everyone in the room must have
thought I had terribly weak kidneys."

"It wasn't something he did in the privacy of your
boudoir."

"Of course not. The torture was that one couldn't

respond properly in public. In private he had other charades."

Curtis watched her take another sip of her drink and wondered whether she had consciously dedicated herself to proving that money can't buy happiness. In any event, he wasn't interested in the sex life of dead men.

"In private," she continued, her voice growing suddenly hoarse, "he played slave. That was where the boots came in. He liked to lick dirty leather. He made one wear them for days on end until things were very ripe when one took them off."

"This was when you were . . . uh . . . courting?"

She shook her head. "After the marriage. He had a thing for body secretions and wastes." She stopped and decided to change the subject. "How was your day?"

"Tremendous." Curtis paused. "And the work at the château?"

"Finished tomorrow. Please take off my boots, like a dear?" She smiled in a more relaxed way. "I promise I've only had them on today."

Curtis knelt in front of her and removed the boots. She flexed her long, narrow feet. "Oh, God. Heaven."

"Too tight?"

She finished her drink. "My whole life has gotten too tight. My only child thinks of me as a specimen under glass. Oscar has always been a surly boor, but it's increasingly more difficult for me to overlook it. I seem to spend my time in hotels, in transit lounges, on strange tennis courts and beaches. I don't have any friends, not really. And now I've begun to hop into bed with perfectly charming men who are, after all, strangers."

She ran her fingers over his head and patted his hair into place. "You have to do something about your hair, darling. It's too straight and formal this way." She cupped her hand under his chin and tilted his head an inch up. "But you're not really a stranger.

I'm telling you all my most intimate secrets. Are you going to be my first new friend?"

When he said nothing, she extended her legs around him and locked her ankles behind his head, drawing him in toward her. "It's funny about mothers and daughters," she murmured, head back. "She's blond and has this smashing, dark brute called Raoul. I'm dark and my weakness is blonds . . . like you."

Curtis felt cradled between her legs, enfolded in her smell which closed over him like a drugged mist. Her immense eyes regarded him with utter gravity, the eyes of a surgeon about to open up a patient on the operating table. There was a complicity between them, an atmosphere of shared lust, she to open him, he to surrender himself.

It was true, he found himself thinking. There is a pact between the victim and the killer. For an instant he pictured her last husband, humiliating himself in unspeakable ways before her cold, dark beauty. There was that . . . implacable . . . air of cruelty about her. His glance was locked in hers. Her eyes seemed to suck him dry.

"You're a hypnotist," he heard himself saying.

Her head shook slowly from side to side. "It's in your own mind," she told him. Her thighs pressed around him.

A great wave of heat seemed to flow over Curtis. He was going down, drowning.

Not my style, he was thinking. Heavy relationships stirred up the banked, hidden fires. It was a mistake to move that deeply into the raunchier regions of sex, those uncharted places where anything has a license to happen.

Not my style at all, he thought, breathing her in like the bouquet of a funerary wreath.

Then he stopped thinking.

21

They had eaten well at a place called La Ferme just outside Senlis, a rural restaurant with a roaring fire in an open hearth where the owner grilled spitted chickens laced with marjoram leaves, as well as the thick veal steak Oscar Ferguson mulishly insisted on ordering off the menu.

Oscar was the only one drinking hard liquor—four whiskies before dinner—but he also kept up with the wine the Duc de Clary and his assistant ordered, a Beaujolais of the previous autumn, very light and clear. Altogether, the three diners put away an equal number of bottles, as well as a few after-dinner cognacs.

Despite the good food and the drinking, there had been no loud-voiced jollity. Oscar seemed wrapped in some private shroud of his own weaving, gloomy and taciturn. The duke and his assistant, who enjoyed each other immensely, had started on a note of chatter and joking which Oscar's dour mood soon chilled.

They returned to the château well after eleven o'clock, carrying two more bottles of the Beaujolais and some odds and ends of food for the two night watchmen.

With the barest nod, Oscar retired to the master bedroom. The two antiques experts went upstairs to try one of the large beds in the guest wing. The guards, who had been observing the antics of the duke and his young man for the past two days, exchanged their usual eyebrow-lifting looks as they plucked out wine corks and began drinking.

Ever since Minton Irish had given it up as a part-time residence, the château had been protected by an array of brilliant sodium-vapor lamps which flooded the perimeter of the main house with yellow light of an almost daytime intensity.

The same lighting system, but with the lamps spaced farther apart, covered the main gate and the road leading back to the château. All these high-intensity lamps were controlled from inside the house by a master panel which switched them on auto-matically at a preset time each evening and turned them off at daybreak. There was a manual override which could be used, as now, when people slept over-night at the château and found the day-bright glare through the windows disconcerting. Oscar had or-dered the lights switched off. After all, the system was designed only for those times when the château was untenanted.

As a result, the two guards used flashlights when they made their rounds. They left the main entrance of the château every hour on the hour. One turned to the left and made a casual loop of the property in that direction, the other turned right and followed a mirror-image route.

They would meet at the main gate on highway N–330 after about thirty-five minutes and stroll back to the château together. This gave them time for a cup of coffee or a few marcs before it was time to re-peat their routine.

Over the years, as is only natural, the routine had softened quite a bit. In order to get a little sleep, they took turns with the outside surveillance. At eleven o'clock, for example, one man would remain asleep in the château while the other did both tours at a faster pace. He would return for his nap, when, at midnight, his partner did the honors. Naturally, this lax version of the routine was not followed with Oscar Ferguson in the house. Both men worked.

At one in the morning, sleepy from their unaccustomed exertions, the two guards left the main entrance of the house and turned in opposite directions. They moved through the moonless dark at a leisurely pace, flashlight beams shifting lethargically along the paths ahead of them. In a few minutes they were too far apart to see each other's beams. It was 1:07 A.M.

The van was a dark gray Renault with rear doors. It paused for a moment at the main gate while someone got out and attended to the lock.

Then the van proceeded without lights down the private road to the main entrance of the château. It curved away from the broad steps and backed up to them so quietly, and with such little engine effort, that its progress went unheard.

Two figures opened the rear doors of the van and disappeared inside. One let out a ramp which bridged the distance from the rear of the van to the top of the entrance stairs. Slowly, moving on the noiseless casters of a large wooden dolly, a crate about as high as the figures was pushed out of the van, along the ramp and up to the front doors of the château.

The lock was picked and the wooden crate was gently wheeled inside. The two guards had been gone about ten minutes at this point.

Less than five minutes later, the two figures inside the château appeared again in the uncertain dark, pushing a crate out of the house, up the ramp and back into the van.

The doors to the château were closed, the ramp drawn into the van and the van's rear doors locked.

The two figures silently drove the van back along the inner road to the gate. The night watchmen had been gone between fifteen and twenty minutes by now. Their itineraries had both reached the point farthest from the château. Both were on their way back now, walking toward their usual rendezvous at the main gate.

The dark gray Renault van moved out through the gate, paused while the lock was closed, then sped off into the night along Route N–330, taking the northwest direction away from Paris.

It had been out of sight less than five minutes when the two guards met and walked slowly back up the private road to the château. One sat at the kitchen table and cradled his head in his arms. He yawned convulsively. The other checked the second of the two Beaujolais bottles and found an inch of wine remaining. He held it up silently to his partner, who shook his head. It was now 1:30 A.M.

The man put the bottle to his lips, tilted it up and swallowed the last of the wine.

Then he began yawning, too. It was another slow night.

22

By half-past one in the morning, Louch was beginning to droop, but Lee James had not yet begun to feel tired. Her internal clock was still set at New York City time.

They had already finished a leisurely dinner at Fouquet's by eleven o'clock and, after his fifth cognac, Lee James had given Louch his graceful exit pass. He "must have a heavy day tomorrow" and wasn't to "put himself out" on her account.

This and the cognac had the effect, as one who knew Louch better could have predicted, of steeling the stubborn streak in him. He did have a heavy day in the morning, putting into high gear the surveillance of the Leila Darcy girl, now that her address was known. Instead of taking Lee James to her hotel and bidding her good night, however, he invited her to Mother's.

It is possible to give Louch the benefit of the doubt —all of his superiors did—and say that by going to Mother's he was combining business and pleasure, entertaining the attractive blond American woman and perhaps—who knew in this sort of work?—getting a new line on the machinations of the kinky-headed Leila and her various confreres.

By half-past midnight, Louch was—as Curtis had warned Lee—quite drunk. She could not be expected to know this, since a man Louch's size can absorb a great many cognacs and still function well enough. But even a stranger like Lee became aware that

Louch had been drinking when, brushing her knee under the table, he glanced up guiltily at her.

"It's not what you think, ma'amselle."

Lee swung her knees out of range. "It never is," she said, not on a pejorative note, but merely as an observation.

"*Pas du tout.* I am not, what you call, 'cooping a feel,' Miss James."

"Your command of slang is tremendous," she said. "But the verb is 'to cop.'"

He frowned. "Ah! To cop. To cop a key of horse," he added as an aid to memory. "But I merely wanted to disconnect the contact microphone," he added. His frown deepened. "*Merde alors.* Someone has already done so."

He sighed unhappily. Then his face brightened. "But I am given to understand that your cops also coop, *n'est-ce pas?*"

"They sometimes park a squad car in an alleyway and take a nap," she explained. "That is 'cooping.'"

Louch nodded with great seriousness and his lips moved silently as he repeated the word, adding it to his vocabulary. He signaled the waiter and Lee James was not surprised to see that, despite the packed, noisy room, the waiter instantly abandoned a nearby table to take Louch's order.

"They say alcohol's a depressive," Lee James remarked, "but it's snapped you out of that mood you said you were in."

"Not a mood of depression. More of a . . . a premonition of things to come."

"Bad things?"

Louch looked serious for a moment. "One learns to trust premonitions." Then he smiled broadly at her and at the waiter hovering over him.

"*Un cognac. Et pour la jeune fille . . . ?*"

"Campari-soda."

Louch looked hurt. "Curtis warned you not to let *me* get drunk. He did not forbid *you* to drink."

A curious silence fell between them which the noise in the room could not cover. He eyed her for a long moment. Then, matter-of-factly: "You are sent to replace him, eh?"

Lee blinked. "Nothing of the sort. I've got a few vacation days in Paris and—"

"Of course," Louch cut in, waving his hand like a traffic cop. "I understand. And Curtis is an admirable guide to Paris. But unfortunately, dear Miss James, you have picked a holiday weekend."

"What?"

"Yes. Tomorrow is Good Friday. Some places close at noon. And nothing is open Saturday but a few pharmacies and grocers and restaurants, of course. The next day is Easter Sunday, followed by Easter Monday, also a holiday. Paris, Miss James, is somewhat closed down."

Again they watched each other without speaking. Louch knew he understood people very well, even this advanced kind of American female person. There was no way an intelligent, educated, well-organized, cold-headed type like this one, he told himself, would blindly take off for Paris on a weekend when banks, galleries and even some museums were shut tight.

"Of course, there is still much of the exterior to see in Paris," he added then, trumping this ace in case she tried to play it. "Even shut tight, this is a marvelous city in which to stroll."

Still she said nothing. Her glance, locked in his, shifted slightly to gaze past him. Louch waited patiently to see how clever she really was. "Why do I know that man?" Lee James asked then.

Louch frowned. The one tactical thrust for which there was no parry: changing the subject. He turned slowly to look at the man she meant. "You know him?"

"I've seen his face."

"On an FBI bulletin, perhaps?" Louch asked. "You know him?"

The Frenchman shook his big head. He had seen the man the other night, arriving in a Fleetwood with George Brown. It was this man with the close-set eyes who had met with the terrorist daughter of the idle rich and her little coterie of hoodlums. It was this man who had disconnected the contact microphone before beginning his conversation.

He was a man in his forties, whose dark blue suit was American tailored, as was his white-on-white shirt and pale ecru tie. In his narrow head, his dark eyes seemed to be set unnaturally close because of the squeezed space they occupied.

Louch had not had the time to do his homework on that face. Otherwise, he would by now have found it in the photo files of his own department, or perhaps in files on loan from Interpol. Instead he had been chasing Kawasakis.

"No," Louch said with real sadness in his voice, "I don't know his name."

"And that pretty woman with him?"

Louch eyed the tiny, dark-haired woman with the glitter on her long eyelashes. She sat with her attractive legs tucked up under her, like a small child at grown-up tea. She was facing the entrance, and watching it, as if expecting someone to arrive. The black dress she was wearing was V-cut down the front to show almost exactly one-half of each swelling white breast.

"A princess," Louch responded finally.

"Obviously."

"Perhaps one may call her a queen."

"Really?"

"The Queen of Blackmailers," Louch said.

"This is thrilling," Lee James said in a voice that almost matched her words. "Nothing Curtis could show me would be this exciting."

Louch watched the waiter deliver their drinks. He picked up his cognac and leaned back in his chair to hold the glass against a light. He sipped and found that they had given him the best cognac in the house. He smiled broadly.

"Curtis is a good man," he said then in an expansive way. "He and I have worked together, off and on, for years. A very discreet, intelligent man, a good colleague, a friend. But we are not in the same business." He leaned forward and captured one of her small, neat hands. "In the business of gathering intelligence," he went on, "we French invented the game, Miss James. From the time of Richelieu and Louis Quatorze, we created the whole bloody thing. And to this day we still do it best."

"So I've heard."

"So you have not heard." He patted her hand rapidly, as if dabbing away a mistake scribbled in fast-drying ink. "In the eyes of the world, we are perceived as a nation of sexual perverts and drunkards who"—Louch finished off his cognac and wiped his mouth with the back of his hand—"are a mean, small-spirited people, niggling, parochial, tradition-bound and therefore . . . *naturellement* . . . we do poorly in police and intelligence work."

Lee James considered this mock diatribe for a moment. Louch could almost hear the gears in her brain whirring and clicking through a series of permutations. "Some of your police work is as bad as the worst of our own," she said then.

Louch paused to admire the neat, diplomatic balance of the statement. "You refer to corrupt agents and operatives. I quite agree. The Frenchman is a human being. All humans are corruptible. Some French can therefore be corrupted."

The young woman produced her first smile. "That's a lovely syllogism," she said, "but it has what's called an undistributed middle."

"*Pardon?*"

"Not all humans are corruptible."

Louch threw both hands out sideways, palms up.

"Next you will be telling me not all French are human," he teased.

He watched her start to say something, then think better of it. In the interim, Louch signaled for another cognac.

He squeezed her hand. "I am a man of all worlds," he told her. "France, other nations, the upper world and the underworld. I know. Miss James, *I know*."

Had she returned the pressure slightly, he wondered, or was it only an illusion? He fixed her with his stare. "It matters not at all. We go our way. We know our superior worth. We take lessons from no one."

This rather grandiose thought left a dead space between them for a long moment, which Louch finally sought to fill. "We have been tested, as a people, far beyond the normal experience of other peoples. You Americans, for example, have never been occupied by an enemy force."

"Never."

"This is a test of such stringency that it amounts to a national dissection . . . a racial autopsy." Louch listened to the sound of the phrase for a moment and found it good. "Our Maquis, for example, our Underground, were forced to function under conditions of soul-shattering fear. We—"

"Surely, the Italian *partigiani*—"

"Don't talk to me of Italians," Louch cut in brusquely. "The Italian experience is entirely different. The *partigiani* were in existence long before the Germans took control of their country. The Italian underground had been institutionalized for fifteen years under Mussolini."

"Against Mussolini."

"Against, against." Louch shook his fingers about, as if repelling a swarm of gnats. "If you quibble over words, Miss James, you will never appreciate the point of what I am trying to tell you. *Alors*, I myself was in a Maquis cell both here in Paris and, later, in the south. And we had not only the German occupation to worry about, but our own Vichy government coalition. Because there will always be a few Trotskyite positions which hold—"

"Do you mean Trotskyist?"

Louch's cheeks had gone red in two patches over his cheekbones. "You make me sorry I ever took the time to educate you, young woman."

"But don't the Trotskyites call themselves Trotskyists?"

He stared at her. "Very well, then, Trotskyist." He swallowed the drop of cognac left in his glass. "You are being deliberately provoking."

"Not deliberately," she assured him.

"There is a certain grain to the behavior of you American women." He looked around for the waiter. "This is not a good evening for me. I had wanted to talk to Curtis and you materialized. I had wanted to educate you and you turn obdurate. I order more cognac but it doesn't arrive. And now I stand accused of terminological inaccuracies." He sighed deeply.

"It's not only important what a group calls itself, but what other groups call it. Don't you agree?"

"A certain abrasiveness," Louch mused. "You look smooth enough, you young American beauties. You look soft enough. But you are in reality like a piece of grit one cannot get out of one's eye."

The waiter brought his cognac and left. In the doorway of Mother's the captain was talking to a tall, skinny young man in one of those balloonlike, down-filled jackets that made everyone, in Louch's opinion, look like the famous Michelin cartoon man made of rubber tires.

The young man in the jacket stared around the room, eyes darting. He dug into the pocket of his jeans and produced something small, folded and green which he handed to the captain, who stopped all talk and led the newcomer at once to a small corner table.

In the background, the jukebox started throwing out great waves of Aretha Franklin sound, half gospel, half sexual moan. Louch saw Lee James glance with circumspection at her wristwatch. "I bore you," Louch said then.

"Not at all."

Louch checked his own watch and found that it was nearly two in the morning. The cognac had begun to prop him up. A few more drinks and he was good till daybreak.

"What makes our work so superior," he went on grandly, "is our lack of illusions. Think of how far your own police and intelligence might have gone, what great forward strides they would have made, had your country not been blinded—that is the only word—by the myth of Communism."

Lee removed her hand from his. Louch didn't seem to notice as he waved his half-full glass in a stately gesture. "Is your paranoia so great, I ask, as to assume that alone in the West, the United States is the sole arena of Communist activity? *Pas du tout.* All capitalist nations are ripe for Marxist movements. Capitalism has within itself the seeds of its own destruction. . . ." His voice died out a moment.

When he spoke again, it was as if his words were arriving by radio signal from a fringe station. The volume rose and fell erratically, its ups and downs having no connection with what he was saying.

"But this peculiarly American *folie* infects your entire national life, my dear girl. The British, the Italians, the Germans . . . all are aware of the left within their national borders. But it is a left that is treated as a part of life. And no nation understands this with more clarity than the land where supreme clarity of thought is the preeminent quality of life. I refer," he belched softly, "to France."

"Naturally," Lee James said.

Louch seemed to listen to the deadpan note in her voice, but went on almost at once, voice fading out and in at odd intervals. ". . . blinders, turning your best people, your statesmen, your intelligence agents, your military leaders, into children groping blindly in a self-imposed darkness, prattling endlessly of the invisible specter of a mythical enemy."

"Mythical?" she asked after a moment. Her voice had gone dead cold.

"Well, then, not mythical," Louch admitted. "But entirely overblown. One can be sensibly concerned without being violently paranoid, am I not right?"

"Concerned?" Lee James wanted to know. "We have been locked in a war with them. Don't you think 'concern' is too weak a word?"

"A war? Do you refer to Vietnam?"

"And Korea before it. And the Cold War in between. And what would you call the half-dozen near blowups we've managed to avoid in places like the Middle East and Cuba and Chile and—"

"Avoid or provoke?" Louch snapped, suddenly sounding much less lazy.

He watched her warily. She had seemed one thing and now she had become another. "I had no idea I was talking with a True Believer, Miss James." His tone had lost its easy quality. "I had been led to believe that Americans had finally stopped looking each night for Reds under their beds."

"It's easy enough for you French," Lee James began, her low voice rising slightly. "You lammed out of Vietnam as soon as the going got tough and dumped the whole mess in our laps. It's not as easy for us. I lost a brother there."

Louch's mouth opened to crush her with a riposte so telling that it would have destroyed her, intellectually. Instead he held back his words. One wins no arguments about imperialist wars with the sisters of men killed in those insane frolics.

Instead, with an important frown, Louch put down

his glass and pushed it carefully away from him, as if renouncing the cognac in perpetual memory of the dead brother. "I had no idea, my dear," he said in a soft, gruff voice. "I am most terribly sorry. I was there, you know. When the Americans were."

"Were you? In combat?"

Louch shook his heavy head. "Intelligence. The heroin routes from the Golden Triangle."

On the jukebox, the nasal Streisand voice nagged at a '40's tune, inflating it with a self-pitying whine its words never had. Lee James's face seemed to pale slightly but she said nothing, nor did she move. Instead her eyes swung slowly across the room, taking in the jukebox, the tiny woman with the glitter, the lanky young man in his goosedown jacket. Then her glance came to rest on Louch.

"Where in the Triangle?" she asked casually. "What year?"

Louch wondered if she always asked questions with such casual intensity. He shrugged. "Many places, many years. But most of all a little border town on the Mekong called Ban Xien."

Her dark gray eyes looked almost black. "Ban Xien? What year?"

"Seventy-one and two."

"Interpol?"

"No. Our Bureau des Stupéfiants."

"Did you liase with U.S. Army Intelligence?"

Louch smiled at "liase." He hadn't heard it in some years now. "They called themselves S-2," he said. "We always harbored the suspicion they were CIA."

She started to ask something else, then seemed to realize she had begun to sound like a professional interrogator. She sat back in her chair. Some of the color returned to her face. Louch waited for her next question. But she seemed to have stopped, drawing back almost warily, the way a forest creature instinctively retreats from the edge of a pit trap.

Very smooth, Louch thought. What did the Americans call it? Good moves. No wonder they'd sent her to take over Curtis's job. She was infinitely shrewder than Curtis. This one was a tigress, smooth, fast, patient, and, oh, so cold between the ears.

What had excited her about Ban Xien and the Mekong border between Laos and Burma? Many other border towns were opium entrepôts. At Muong Sing, farther from the frontier, there was a processing plant that reduced the gum opium to morphine base. Several factories at Houei Sai on the Thailand border had the capacity for turning out Number Four White Injectible on the spot.

But Ban Xien was only a crossover station, a collection of holding warehouses where the stuff remained for a day or less before smuggler platoons moved it across the frontier, or one of the Air America planes flew it out of the country in a CIA pouch.

Louch's remembrance stopped as suddenly as if it had run full tilt into a stone wall. He stared at Lee James. Behind his eyes, in the immense photo file stored there, he saw a face like hers on the body of a dead man.

Louch had run across the corpse, one of several, in the forest near a camouflaged Air America landing strip close to Vieng Pou Kha. All the bodies wore the suntan summer uniform of the American Army. The shirt epaulets on this one showed where single bars had once been pinned. He'd been forced into a kneeling position like the rest of them and shot in the back of the head. Standard execution.

Her brother?

"Mr. Louch?"

"Pardon?"

"Are you all right?"

He nodded unsteadily. The whole thing with the murdered men had ended in chaos. But chaos was everywhere in those days. Louch had had the bodies brought in. He'd forced the base surgeon to retrieve the bullet lodged in each man's skull. Louch had had no idea why he'd ordered the examination except that the entry holes had been big. Only two calibers in common use out there could have made such a hole: the 9 mm handguns of Luger design favored by Red intelligence and the .45 Colt automatic used by Allied troops and the CIA.

The slugs had been from a .45. The Americans had been killed by their own people.

Louch smiled slightly at the woman sitting across from him. "It was a bad time," he said then. "I am most sorry about your brother, Miss James."

Her face had become a noncommittal mask. She was giving away even less than usual now, Louch noted, but that would have been a paradox, since when one begins with nothing, there is no way of doubling it.

His glance wavered. The German who palled around with Aziz had come in. The good-looking Aziz, he of the white teeth, was not with him, nor was the frizzy little yellow bird, but the other one was, an ugly Bedouin Louch had recently identified as one called Khefte.

The captain halted them for only a moment. Mother's was not as full anymore. It was well past two-thirty. The captain led the two young men to a table near the one in the ski jacket. By a nod of his head, he brought the first one up out of his seat and over to the new table.

Louch watched the three young men confer. Then the German, who used the name Bert, made room for the man in the jacket. The three of them now ordered beers and talked softly. Louch found himself torn between duty and pleasure. He would have given a lot to be across the street in Room Number 7, listening to what the three were saying.

"Can you bear with me for a moment, Miss James?" Louch had gotten slowly to his feet with the unsteady majesty of a set of fire ladders ascending skyward.

"This will not take long. Then I will see you to your hotel."

He was leading her out of Mother's. No check was tendered him. The street outside was deserted as Louch started to guide her across to the *hôtel d'accommodation.*

"It's on the first floor front," he was saying, "Room Seven."

Lee James stood still on the sidewalk and Louch found she could not be budged. "It's not what you think, *chère ma'moiselle.*"

"It's exactly what I think."

"No, no. Upstairs, in Room Seven, I have a means for amplifying my—"

"It's a little late," Lee James cut in.

"You misunderstand. My apparatus is the finest in P—"

"I can get myself to the hotel. Thanks, anyway."

He watched her disappear into a taxi in a swirl of tight wool skirt around longish legs. *Merde,* he'd done abominably. Louch produced a short, bitter bark of self-disgust and trotted across the street. Room 7 was vacant. He fiddled with the wires and hearing-aid headphone until he had tuned in on the table where the three were talking.

Lighting a cigarette, Louch paced back and forth, dangling a wire. He showed no signs of being drunk now as he moved through the darkened room to the window that overlooked the Rue de la Grande Truanderie. The three young men had apparently settled something and were getting ready to leave.

They had been talking an incredible mixture of French and English as they faded out of range of the contact microphone. A few moments later, Louch observed them leaving Mother's. They turned to their right and headed in the general direction of the gigantic hole sunk in what had once been the belly button of Paris.

Louch pulled out his pocket binoculars. The three

had paused for a moment and the one in the goose-down jacket seemed to grow reluctant. While they argued, Louch stepped to the connection box and plugged into the table where the Principessa Carloni and the American thug had been sitting. Louch made an "ach" sound of dismay. The bastard had disconnected the microphone at this table, too.

This was always the trouble with technological advances, Louch told himself severely. What the mind of man can devise, the mind of another man can undo.

At one end of the Rue de la Grande Truanderie a long Mercedes turned in from the Boulevard de Sebastopol. Louch saw the tiny Principessa Carloni stop it and get in. The sedan moved slowly past Mother's and turned the corner at the excavation called "The Hole."

Louch watched Bert and Khefte grab the young man in the jacket and hustle him along the street. He went unwillingly, in Louch's view, but without a real struggle.

They bundled him into a dark gray Renault van with rear doors and drove away.

Through his binoculars, Louch got the license number of the van, knowing in his heart of hearts that it would do him no good at all. He stood there, feeling again the heavy load of certainty that something was going wrong.

Damn Easter.

PART FOUR

GOOD FRIDAY: MORNING

23

The Sogegarde routine varied slightly from run to run but, basically, it consisted of a lead auto, moving a few hundred meters in advance of an unmarked truck, which in turn was followed by another auto as a kind of rearguard.

The Trocadéro, along with many other Paris facilities of a banking nature, would close promptly at noon today, not to open again until Tuesday morning. That deadline, and the heavy nature of the load being transported, had made it necessary to send the convoy out early. It arrived at the gate to the château on Route N–330 precisely at eight in the morning.

A house guard walked to the entrance and inspected the driver's credentials, unlocked the gate and let the three vehicles onto the property. The guard cars pulled off the road and let the truck proceed to the château, where it made a half turn in the courtyard and backed cautiously up to the steps that led into the entry hall.

Four men got out of the truck and opened it up with much banging of heavy steel drop doors. Oscar Ferguson's head, sandy hair sticking up in clumps at odd angles, poked out of a second-story window.

"What in Christ's name is g—" He stopped as he saw the truckmen begin to lay heavy sisal carpeting over the marble stairs. "Be ri' down," Oscar mumbled.

A moment later, blinking in the chill morning light, he appeared in the open entrance of the château, tying the belt of a ratty dressing gown. "Lemme see your papers," he grunted.

When no one responded, he raised his voice: "*Montrez-moi vos* fucking *papiers.*"

One of the truckmen produced a sheaf of papers fastened to a clipboard. Oscar paged slowly through. There was a covering contract from the New York moving company which was supervising the whole arrangement. There was a form from Sogegarde concerning transfer to its Trocadéro Tower of four crates destined to be picked up in May for transport by sea routes to the Metropolitan Museum in New York. A copy of the Met's original request to Oscar for the four Vaincre caryatids, together with his response, was included. There were forms from three insurance companies, covering the caryatids in storage, on display and in transit. And, finally, there was an affidavit attesting that the crates did, in fact, contain the aforementioned works of art.

Oscar went back into the château and stood by while the four heavy wooden crates were carried, two men to a crate, with exquisite care down the sisal matting and into the truck, where they were muffled in old quilts and strapped to keep them motionless during the trip back to town.

The truckers moved as carefully as if the crates themselves were the valuable objects, as if their orders were that no nick or scratch be allowed to appear on the rough pine boards. By nine-thirty all four crates had been stowed like rare eggs. The truck was sealed shut by three immense Chubb padlocks with bolts of vanadium steel.

Oscar signed all the forms, grumbled something about making goddamned sure they didn't race back to town at goddamned high speeds, and returned to his bed. The truckmen exchanged glances with each other and with the château guards.

"*Quel type, celui-là!*"

"*Une merde qui marche comme un homme.*"

Nevertheless, the truck maintained a steady speed of only fifty kilometers an hour on its way back through late-morning highway traffic into Paris. At thirty miles an hour, the three-vehicle cortege constituted a menace to traffic. It arrived at 11:30 at the Avenue Poincaré entrance to the curious reinforced-concrete tower hidden behind the respectably ordinary triangular building operated by Sogegarde.

In half an hour, all four crates were transferred on dollies to a section of the Trocadéro known as Racine-12. The nomenclature within the tower had been devised during World War I. For patriotic reasons, each floor carried the name of a great French man of letters or the arts.

On each floor, the circular space was divided into twelve segments, based on the principle of a clock face. Racine-12 was on the fourth floor in the most northerly position, a giant wedge of space like a slice of pie.

But within each wedge, spaces were boxed off by walls of steel and required additional nomenclature. For example, Racine-12 was the repository for much of the Minton Irish Collection, using up spaces A, B, C, D and E. Other clients used F and G. Since the crates were to rest temporarily in the Trocadéro Tower, they were assigned to Racine-12-H.

By noon on Good Friday, all four crates were in place in Space H and machined-steel doors of case-hardened rods had been slid shut and locked.

Easter weekend was about to begin.

24

The garret room was freezing. They had taken away his down-filled parka before tying him into the chair. That had been Bert's idea. The other one, who spoke no English at all, the Arab one, had wanted to tie him up a different way.

When he'd gotten Jamie's letter, Nick Brown had been prepared for Arabs, and even for the kind of heavy scene these Arabs lived with. But he hadn't been prepared for what the Arab had wanted to do to him.

The Arab had already knotted Nick's ankles together and his wrists, behind the back. Now he was planning to bend Nick backward like a bow, arching him against the natural curve of his own backbone. Then he planned to tie a slipknot around his neck and attach the other end of the cord to his feet.

If Nick struggled to get free, he would choke himself to death, slowly. Even if he only moved an inch or two to relieve the agony in his back, the noose would cut off his air.

Dominic Brown knew all about the technique. It had been invented in Sicily.

But Bert had intervened. He was older by five years and he pointed out—or so Nick translated his gestures and words to the Arab—that they didn't really know if the American was an enemy. Perhaps he was exactly what he had spent half the night swearing he was, a school friend of Leila's.

"In either event," Bert had told Nick as he was

three afternoon flights back to Milan. Or
a plane from Milan south to the new air-
t' Eufemia, not far from her villa.

world of needful financial transactions and
btropical warmth awaited her if only these
ar Americans would finish their business,
decision and let her be off.

n't quite sure where she stood with George
ce their conversation in her apartment high
an last year. He had been looking for some-
general and she had asked for a very spe-
which he'd so far refused to produce.

hadn't agreed, but he remained interested
ort of deal. The Princess was too much of a
oman—and far too Italian—not to have
hat George Brown's delaying tactics were
he purpose of learning how much material
bject she already had. As proof that Brown
interested in a deal, however, the man called
ad, in fact, sold her an imitation leather
containing some interesting, but not essen-
rmation.

dn't even known Brown was in Paris until
, when his peculiar associate, Groark, with
ezed-in head and narrow-set eyes, had asked
eet Brown last night in that dreadfully noisy
led Mother's.

had never appeared. Today's meeting was
1 to remedy that but, in truth, if George
hadn't been the influential man he was, the
would already have left for Basel.

elationship to the powerful of this world, she
now, was a strange and shifting one. There
 any people who considered her a very powerful
by which they betrayed the fact that they con-
oney with power.

rincipessa Carloni was not in business for
Only for money. Or so she repeatedly told
There were so many times over the past three

knotting him into the chair, his English precise and
low-pitched, almost soothing, "we cannot have you
running around Paris. Enemy or friend is a thing of
the past. As of now, the entire world is an enemy."

In a way, Nick thought as he sat immobilized, although this was a more humane form of restraint, it
left him in an even more hopeless position. Each
hand was now tied separately, as was each leg. They
couldn't help each other by flexing and relaxing.
Slowly, as the hours passed, all feeling left them.

And the weird thing was that nobody even knew
he was in Paris. Nobody would be coming to rescue
him. Even if some passerby stumbled into this cheap
top-floor garret and released him, what could he tell
the police? Once they'd gotten him in the van, Bert
had hit him on the back of the head with something
hard like a wrench.

He'd done it very scientifically, the way he'd tied the
knots, the way he'd taped his mouth. Bert was a professional, and more than that, a German professional.

So all Nick had to remember now was a sore spot
where the back of his head joined his neck. For all he
knew, the apartment wasn't even in Paris. The sun
had come up, but it had failed to warm him. Hours of
daylight had passed.

Trying to think logically, Nick Brown decided that
the room really wasn't as cold as he thought it was.
It was the obstruction to his blood circulation that
was making him feel chilled. Good. One problem
solved.

What a dumb idea, sneaking out of Williams. The
guy who'd given him a lift, Holland, was the only
human being on the face of the earth who knew Nick
Brown had gone to Montreal airport. But even Holland didn't know where Nick was heading. He had
been careful never to mention Paris.

And as for Holland, he was shacked up till Monday
with his Canadian girlfriend. Nick Brown wouldn't be

missed at Williams till late Monday afternoon. The police would ask if anyone knew—

What police? The family of George Brown didn't resort to police. Shit, no. They would put out "the word." And days later the answer would trickle back: disappeared.

It didn't matter, anyway. With his circulation cut off this way, and no food or water, Nick figured he would pass out some time this evening. The rest would be in the lap of the gods. Today was Friday. The way Bert had talked—not in so many words, but by a certain tone of voice—he and the Arab weren't planning on coming back to this room.

Ever.

He dozed for a few minutes. When he awoke, his mood had changed. Damned near found Leila, he told himself. Hit it right on the button my first night in town. And wasn't it clever as hell to slip a sawbuck to the maître d'? Stroke of genius. Otherwise how could he ever have met up with Bert and Sabu, or whatever his name was?

Clever Nick. First time at bat and hits a homer.

La Principessa Claudia Ca
on the narrow terrace of t
the Rue Jean Goujon own
Her immense dark glasses
face as she surveyed the q
antennas bristling from th
man embassy.

Behind her, in the livin
sliding glass doors, the stra
and his boss were conferri
culated not to reach her ea
of holding this private confe
had, with quite a bit of grac
ordering people around, "s
cess might like to take the su

In fact, the Princess wa
thinned-out whiteness of Pa
hot yellow heat of Calabria's
kept her villa.

Her business in Paris had e
hoard of documents, photogr
the Trocadéro. That and the
Cemetery had been her total
was planning to leave town t
dred thousand Swiss francs ric

Swissair had a flight at ten
that got into Basel an hour la
her funds in the morning, have
banker, get herself to Zurich a

any one o
even catch
port at Sa
A whole
glorious s
two pecu
make thei
She wa
Brown si
above M
thing ver
cific thin
He sti
in some
business
noticed
also for
on the s
was still
Groark
portfoli
tial, inf
She h
yesterda
his squ
her to
place ca
Brow
arrange
Brown
Princes
Her
mused
were m
woma
fused
La
power
hersel

decades since the war when she could—all by herself, standing exactly 151 centimeters high in her bare feet on the face of this earth!—have affected the outcome of millions of lives. Oh, yes.

She smiled bitterly in the general direction of the radio antennas. Oh, yes, there had been information that would have brought down prime ministers, toppled governments, bankrupted giant corporations, impeached presidents. None of these things had she caused to happen.

She nodded sharply. She was not the kind of woman to use her information merely to flex her muscles, push around giants, affect the course of history. Her nose wrinkled as she thought of it. The idea had never appealed to her.

So she sold the information, and in almost every case to those it affected most poignantly, the guilty parties. It was up to them, then, to engineer their cover-up, safe in the knowledge that Principessa Carloni sold prime goods only one time. Run-of-the-mill sellers of information were nothing but common blackmailers. They could never be relied upon not to keep an extra copy of whatever they were selling . . . against a rainy day.

The Princess's tiny shoulders lifted slightly in a shrug. Naturally, she kept photostats of everything she sold. But she kept them safely locked away in the Trocadéro, not for purposes of resale. Simply as a life insurance policy. The best.

A woman alone in the world and disinterested in power, such a woman needed to maintain peer relationships with powerful people, and also needed a photostat file in the Trocadéro. Both.

She glanced at her watch. After 1:00 P.M. and she was hungry and neither of these two American *pezzi di novanti* would even think to offer her coffee and a biscuit, any more than they remembered to light her cigarette. The thought triggered her need and she lit one herself now, sending a sharp plume of smoke into the damp April air.

From the fact that George Brown had stalled her so long, she had the feeling that what she wanted he was not prepared to sell or trade. Perhaps he was too involved himself.

The rest of the documents, more or less, reposed in her vault at the Trocadéro, affidavits from CIA bureau chiefs, long dead, letters from Batista to his bankers in Lugano, interoffice memoranda stolen from the U.S. Joint Chiefs of Staff files, decoded operational telexes and cablegrams from Allen Dulles, two extremely important scribbled notes from Bobby to Jack Kennedy, pages from Eisenhower's private notes —the contents of the folder Groark had given her— the affidavits of three Dallas police, now dead, of Phil "The Stick" Kovolick, once Lansky's right hand before he ended up in a fifty-five-gallon drum in Hallandale, Florida, and a cassette apparently taped by Murray Chotiner a week before he'd been run down by a truck.

She wasn't sure how much of this material George Brown knew she had. Some she had hinted about. About some she had reserved comment. But she had felt herself forced by circumstances to disclose a bit of what she had. Otherwise her offer for the rest of the information would not have carried much weight or respect. She would not have seemed . . . serious.

None of this material explaining the Mafia murder of Kennedy had she sought in the beginning. She was not, she told herself now, the kind of person to let *una idèa fissa* take over her mind and send her off on quests for Holy Grails. No. The information had come to her in bits and pieces over the years since Batista and Lansky had first realized that Castro might win control of their island.

Crusades were not her style. Nor obsessions. Many things came to the Principessa Carloni. Over the years, like a magpie, she had picked up bits of this and pieces of that which she stored away, often without having a clear idea when or how they might become useful.

She had in her files right now, for example, a similar collection of odds and ends relating to the manner in which a number of Italian, German and French politicians—including Vermeuil of the police —had come to depend heavily on payoffs from the heroin and cocaine traffic in their countries. In another file at the Trocadéro, she had most of the jigsaw puzzle pieces that explained—

"Princess."

George Brown stood in the doorway behind her, his squat body filling the space completely. She turned to look at him. When she had come to this apartment half an hour ago and seen him for the first time since Milan, she had noticed something strangely different about him, a kind of preoccupation that had taken over the front of his mind, forming a screen through which he dealt with everyday matters.

It was undoubtedly a personal matter, the Princess decided, perhaps a family matter. But, knowing George Brown, the problem could not have been one of long standing. He was, of all men, the kind who would leap in and solve a personal matter with brutal speed. Any Sicilian would.

"Are you well, *caro*?" she asked.

He frowned. "Why'd y'ask?"

"You look . . . *molto preoccupato*."

His frown blackened and he turned to glare at Neil Groark through the glass door. "You hear that, Neely? She has ears like a cat."

"Wha'd I say?" Groark complained.

Brown turned back to the Princess and forced his forehead smooth. "How much did you hear, Princess?"

"Of your conversation? Nothing."

"Then who told you?"

She paused for a moment. Obviously this was a delicate moment in which she could make a serious mistake or, if clever, discover something wonderfully useful. Or she could be smart, she cautioned herself, and not play games with a man like George Brown.

"*Caro*, I have heard nothing."

She closed the gap between them and lightly touched the lapel of his dark blue blazer with her long fingernails painted a caramel color. "When I say to you that you look *preoccupato*, this is the evidence of my eyes, nothing more."

She had pushed her great sunglasses up on top of her hair, but she was too old a hand at telling both truths and lies to let her eyes widen with convincing sincerity. She trusted George Brown to read her right. For once, she was telling the absolute truth.

After a long moment of fierce eye contact, he nodded once. "It's my youngest," he said then. "The crazy bastard's run away."

La Principessa Claudia Carloni stood stock-still. Somewhere in the pit of her stomach a vibration began, a kind of chilly radiation, as of a pebble thrown in an icebound pond. Ripples radiated outward, slithering across her shoulder blades. It was the sensation that a big-game hunter gets when the wild animal pauses to feed right in the cross hairs of his telescopic sight.

Dominic Brown had run away? Successfully eluded the entire network of spies and informers under the command of the Brown family? The thorn in his father's side, the baffling child, the one George Brown wanted most to impress, to win over? Gone?

The Princess patted George Brown's chest comfortingly. "He'll turn up soon."

"It's been two-three days. I'd give my right arm, Princess. My right arm."

She smiled in a reassuring way, but it was a concealed smile of triumph. La Principessa Claudia Carloni was not flying to Basel.

The abortive meeting last night, at which George Brown had failed to appear, had served a purpose after all. The idiot Groark, who probably knew what Nicky Brown looked like even better than she did, had been facing away from the door last night at Mother's. But the Princess had been looking directly at Nicky as he came in, a handsome boy who closely resembled his photo last year in *Oggi*. She had seen him meet the other two boys and leave with them.

"If there is anything I can do to help, *caro*?"

"I got everybody turned out on this one, all over the world."

"Perhaps . . . as you know, I have my own contacts."

George Brown took a deep breath. His tiny, piggish eyes looked moist. "Princess, you give me Nicky, and anything I got is yours."

Including, she thought to herself, your right arm.

26

At one minute after noon on Good Friday, the closing bells rang inside the Trocadéro. Workmen on various floors checked wall and door locks. There were no alarm switches to set manually, since these were controlled from a center inside the building that shielded the Trocadéro from the eyes of Paris. But there were many locks to secure . . . dozens.

The workmen filed slowly down to the ground level, known as Voltaire. The duty officer checked each of them off his roster as they filed past him and descended a kind of vertical tunnel that ran down through the reinforced concrete floor of the tower.

Iron rungs had been set in the sides of the chimney-like opening. When the last man had gone down, the duty officer lowered himself into the aperture and swung a large circular cover down over the top, a round of cross-braced steel nearly two inches thick and several feet across, something like a hinged manhole cover. A red rubber gasket ran around the inside of the rim, quite like the sealing ring in a mason jar.

The duty officer swung two levers and locked them in place with a single turnscrew. Then he climbed down the iron rungs and into a narrow corridor that led beneath the tower to the triangular building around it. These walls, too, were reinforced concrete.

The corridor was peculiarly small, oppressively so, as if, having been built at the time of the First World War, it was designed for a shorter, narrower race of human beings. The tunnel measured scarcely two feet across. From concrete floor to concrete ceiling, there was not even five feet of space. All the men filed through in slumped-over postures, like miners in some new, exploratory vein deep beneath the earth.

What added to the oppressiveness of the tunnel, aside from its squeezed-in feeling, was that the only light came from the far end, some fifty or more feet away. Overhead, where one might have expected a line of small electric lamps connected by a conduit tube, there was nothing, no source of light at all, just a few tiny air vents.

When the last of the men on duty had crept through to the outside and straightened up to his full height, the duty officer emerged. He turned and swung shut a thick steel door which had an inner gasket of red rubber. He fastened it firmly in place with three levers secured by three combination locks.

Before they had left the tower, the men had locked, from the inside, the ground-floor doors through which during a normal day paintings and sculpture were moved by dolly. The only way into the tower now was the minelike tunnel and shaft through which they had just passed.

The duty officer checked his wristwatch, then reached for a large, cast-iron wheel to one side of the locked tunnel door. He gave the wheel a tug and started it turning slowly in a counter clockwise movement.

From behind the locked steel door a sound began, grew louder and louder despite the thick door through which it could be heard. It was the sound of rushing water, tons of it, flooding the tunnel. The men had already walked away, but the duty officer remained, checking his watch. It took exactly eleven minutes to fill the tunnel to its ceiling.

When he finished the job and swung the valve wheel shut, the duty officer was alone. The men had already gone to their dressing room and changed into street clothes. By the time he got to his own locker, he and the *chef de la sécurité*, M. Hardy, would be the last human beings in Trocadéro Tower or the triangular building that surrounded it.

Together, they would double-check the proximity alarms, the sound sensor network, the smoke detectors, the electric-ray relays and the automatic television cameras. This was normal procedure. They did it every evening at the close of the day's business. The procedure was no different for a long weekend like the one coming up.

The alarms fed information to various parts of the city, day or night. One set of monitors was only a block away in the Sixteenth Arrondissement police station on Rue du Bouquet de Longchamp. Another monitor array was installed at the Société Générale's command headquarters in another part of Paris, a message center open twenty-four hours a day to handle incoming information from all over the world.

Before they locked themselves out of the building, M. Hardy and the duty officer of the day activated a gas-discharge system—a maze of ducts throughout the eight floors of the tower, from Voltaire all the way to Lully, at the top.

When tripped by an intruder, the ducts spewed forth thousands of cubic meters of a mixture of carbon dioxide and nitrogen—inert gases that could not harm sculpture, paintings or documents stored in the vaults. But these gases soon altered and displaced the normal mixture of the air, thinning out its oxygen content until, finally, the intruder suffocated to death, or scrambled out of the Trocadéro.

It had been one of M. Hardy's hopes, when he had been promoted to *chef de la sécurité* several years ago, after serving for ten years as assistant to the former chief, that the bank and its subsidiary would find enough funds in the budget to keep two men on duty all night, every night, and especially over weekends. To date his suggestion had not been acted upon and

M. Hardy was too much of a career politician to press the matter much further.

In his view, however, it would have made excellent sense to have men on duty, not in the tower but in the surrounding triangle, to keep an eye on everything, "if only," as he put it, "in case of a false alarm, caused by an intruding insect or draft of chill air."

His plan would have made even better sense over such a long weekend as this one, extending from noon Friday until Tuesday morning. But he had given up promoting the idea. There was no sense calling attention to oneself as someone who wanted to spend money on something which the Trocadéro had done without for decades.

After all, in leaving this place unattended—as they did all of their bank offices—unguarded except by alarm systems, the general managers must, in M. Hardy's view, know what they were doing.

In any case, as it turned out, it wouldn't have mattered much either way.

27

In his office on the Ile de la Cité, Louch was spending the lunch hour alone at his desk, without food. His sergeants had gone for their usual leisurely meal, taking perhaps a bit more time today since, although the office remained open, it was Good Friday.

Louch's big head throbbed with a slow beat, the inexorable tempo of his own blood pushing its way with difficulty through constricted capillaries in his head. Cognac always did this to him. A lot of cognac did an even more thorough job, producing a hangover headache that defied aspirin and even his headache compound that also contained codeine.

The office lay in blessed silence, however. The headache had been muted a bit by the third codeine tablet, enough so that Louch could try to focus his thoughts on devising a plan.

It would be no good, he knew, to place any of his regular agents on the trail of the yellow-curled girl. She was too good for them. What he needed was a young operative, street-wise, who could look scruffy and barely out of his teens. It would help if the operative were dark-skinned, perhaps an Algerian, perhaps with some knowledge of Arabic and, certainly, one who also spoke English.

From the very cellar of his lungs, a sigh surged upward through Louch, a sigh of such profundity that it became a celebration of utter failure, a hymn to defeat. There was no such agent, not in any of the various police systems on which Louch could call for help. No such young operative existed.

He sighed again, a smaller version of the ur-sigh he had first produced, and ran his fingers backward through his graying locks from his receding hairline to the back of his head.

Louch winced. Each hair hurt. He stared down at the sheet of paper crisscrossed by pale graph lines, the normal paper on which he drafted memoranda and plans.

Young women were giving him trouble, he decided. The one with the frizzy hair was only one example. That one last night, Lee James, was in a different way even more troubling to him. The frizzy blonde could be fitted into a known category. The cool American with the dark gray eyes—of a grayness found mostly inside the apertures of gun muzzles—was something unknown and troublesome to Louch.

It was not, he told himself now, that he was beginning to close off to new experiences, new data, new types of people. No, Louch prided himself on remaining open, spongelike in his receptivity to new information. For this, after all, was his primary weapon, an up-to-the-moment awareness of the world around him.

This weapon he trusted. But although he knew better, he had still not learned to trust his premonitions. The heavy sense of doom that had hung over him since the cathedral at Senlis he could now attribute to a monumental hangover. But what else could he do about it? Louch wondered. It was so vague, this feeling of uneasiness. What was it, after all, but his rebellious reaction to a holiday that had always depressed him, whose "happy ending" he detested, even as the core miracle of the Christian faith. The good man dies for us all. Sorrow. But, wait! He lives! And did one's spirit soar with him? No longer. Never again.

Louch started to run his finger through his hair

again, but decided not to. He still had to finish his talk with Curtis. There was a way of using Curtis against the tiny blonde. Later today, when the cognac let him alone, Louch would put his mind to it and call Curtis. And, by the way, he would get Curtis's ideas about his confrere, Lee James.

Louch grimaced. Why did the woman bother him so?

The odd points of their conversation. Louch never drank so much that he couldn't remember what had been said. The peculiar things she seemed to pick up. The Vietnam experience. That funny business about the Trotskyites. Her bristling defense of anti-Red paranoia.

He let his big, slightly bulging eyes close, the lids descending heavily. The room was now dark as well as quiet. Peace seemed to descend upon him like a welcome mantle of softest wool, blotting out everything of reality but the pain in his head. In this dark and silent cocoon, Louch tried to free his mind of all problems, all—

Ring!

Louch literally jumped an inch from the seat of his chair. His eyes flew open. He stared at the telephone and flinched when it rang again. Gritting his teeth against a third ring, he snatched the telephone from its cradle.

"Louch here." His voice sounded rusty. He cleared his throat. "Louch here."

"Louch, have you heard?" It was the rather high, terribly superior voice of Vermeuil, the politician to whom Louch reported, an emaciated dilettante with powerful connections. The only reason they got along at all, he and Louch, was that Vermeuil was too busy playing politics to supervise closely the small bureau of which Louch was in charge.

"Heard what?" Louch asked.

"You mean they hav—?"

Ring!

The second telephone on Louch's desk exploded with noise. He winced at the second ring. "Excuse me," he muttered. "I am alone here. The other phone."

He picked it up with his left hand and held it to his left ear. "Louch here. Hello?"

"Mr. Louch, Gravelines of Associated Press. Can you—"

"Excuse me. I am on another call. Hold on."

Louch put down the phone with his left hand. "Vermeuil," he began, "can you tell me wh—?"

Ring!

"*Merde!* The telephone in the outside office is ringing."

"Let it ring," Vermeuil snapped in his affected, pseudoaristocratic way. "And hang up on the other call."

"It's Associated Press."

"I myself hung up on Reuters. Has anything arrived by messenger in the last hour?"

"No. I'd—" Louch stopped himself. He'd been wrapped in his cocoon of hangover pain. Something could well have been delivered to one of the sergeants who sat like statues in their office next door.

"Look for it," Vermeuil ordered. "It will save us both a great deal of time."

Louch got to his feet. He stared down at the two unattended telephones lying on the desk. Carefully, gently, he hung up on the Associated Press. Then he moved with a certain ponderous speed into the sergeants' office, where one phone continued ringing.

He found an envelope in the in box of the sergeant nearest the door to the outer corridor. After lunch, perhaps, the large, beige-colored envelope would move to this sergeant's out box, from which, in time, it would be picked up by the second sergeant, who might have brought it to Louch by the close of the day.

It was not addressed to Louch by name, but rather

to his special bureau. He carried it back into his own office and picked up the phone.

"A beige envelope? No return address?" he asked Vermeuil. "What the hell is it, a letter bomb?"

"Open it."

"Just like that?"

"Open it!" Vermeuil shouted in Louch's ear.

Louch held the telephone away from him. His head was pounding miserably again, with a thump like a steam hammer driving piles deep into hard earth. "Just like that? Open it?"

"Open it, fool!"

So the bastard was angry, Louch thought, but why with me? He shoved his thick thumbnail under the flat of the envelope and managed to crack open the frail bond of cheap mucilage there. He spread the envelope to peer inside and found a single sheet of paper on which something was typed.

In the other room, both of the sergeants' telephones were ringing. Now the second phone on Louch's desk started again. He closed his eyes. Dear Jesus, brain-shattering!

"Louch, read the manifesto."

"So that's what it is," he muttered, extracting the paper from the envelope. All around him the air trembled and shook with the sound of telephone bells. Premonitions of doom shook him mightily.

Louch felt as if he were going mad.

28

On the Avenue Raymond Poincaré, as it radiates from its beginnings at the Place du Trocadéro, Numbers 13 and 15 are instructive buildings.

Not so much for what they can tell us of architecture and design—since both of them, like most of the buildings in the block, are five floors in height, fairly narrow and attractive in the less ornate style of the late nineteenth century—but for what they reveal about the blind whimsy by which chance distributes its favors. Just as some people are born pretty or talented while others must make do with far less, so, too, does this rather cruel whimsy make some nations strong while others must scrape along.

At Number 15, the embassy of Bahrain represents a land which, on the surface, chance has blessed with nothing. No scenery. Nor could its population—a few inbred families at the top of a pyramid with no middle—be said to have enriched the world's art, science or philosophy. But under its surface Bahrain has oil.

At Number 13, the embassy of Uganda represents a hard-pressed group of tribes who hate each other and must make do with what chance has thrown them: traces of copper and tungsten, coffee plantations and grazing land for cattle. A small, landlocked squeeze of a nation, between Lakes Albert and Victoria, Uganda attracts few tourists except to Murchison Falls and, occasionally, the airport at Entebbe. As money-makers, all of this adds up in a year to less than a day of Bahrain's oil.

So Uganda makes do.

In the classic pattern, it tries to be of service to its more powerful friends by being all things, all odd jobs, all alliances, any loyalty. Name your mixture.

The garret atop the Bahrain embassy at Number 15 has a few windows which face Avenue Poincaré. Someone standing behind the fine-mesh curtains can look directly across at the fifth floor of the triangular Sogegarde Building that hides Trocadéro Tower. But no one stands behind that curtain. The garret is used only for storage.

At Number 13, at 1:00 P.M. on Good Friday, no one was standing behind the curtain of the garret window, but two young men were sitting farther back at a long table.

It had been improvised by placing a wooden flush door over two wooden carpenter's horses. A telephone sat on this table. Beneath it lay two ordinary 12-volt storage batteries, the kind found in automobiles. One, the backup spare, was neatly covered by a sheet of plastic. The other was connected to a small device beside it on the floor: a converter which could change the 12 volts of direct current from the battery to several other voltages.

At the moment, the converter was only bypassing the current, unchanged, to a 12-volt, 23-channel CB radio transceiver that sat on top of the table, next to a small FM transmitter with a range of perhaps a kilometer. The transmitter operated at a frequency near the bottom of the dial, around 88 megahertz. A small hand microphone had been jacked into its control panel. A second, standby transmitter, smaller in size, sat on the floor near the auto batteries.

The two young men sitting out of range of the windows contrasted with each other at almost every point. One was dark and good-looking, with bright teeth and a frequent smile. Called Raoul by his girl, Dris by the rest and bearing the code name Aziz in Louch's files, the young man still exuded what had first made Louch notice him, charisma.

The second young man, a bit older, had an awkwardly long torso and a plain face under dirty blond hair. In his small-featured face, his mouth never smiled, nor did his hazel eyes betray any other kind of emotion. Thanks to help from the West German police, Louch had an identification of him as one Bertolt Kron. It was Bert who had assembled the electronic equipment and hooked it up. It was he who knew how to operate it. But it was Dris, through his organizational contacts, who had secured the all-important garret at Number 13.

The young men were different in other, more subtle ways, as well. Dris was a relative newcomer to the work, having been chosen for this assignment mainly because he had demonstrated great courage and cunning in the Athens airport affair. The organization he represented had the unofficial backing of three Arab states, heavy with oil.

Bert, on the other hand, represented no nation. He had been in the movement since he was fourteen and had drawn this assignment because he had already won a reputation for dogged, error-free, generally successful work.

In a war, there are rear-echelon generals and front-line soldiers. One group plans. The other dies. The chief difference between Dris and Bert was that, while they were both prepared to die, one was determined not to.

There had been delicate and prolonged negotiations by the nations Dris represented, primarily because Uganda was afraid the base in its garret would be uncovered. The fear was unreasonably exaggerated, because the embassy was Ugandan soil and under international protocol could not be searched. But since the Ugandans were not told *why* a communications base was needed in the garret, they feared the worst, something so heinous that even the French police could claw their way through diplomatic red tape and, eventually, search the place.

So a combination of tactics had been used. The bait was a new three-year oil contract with Uganda at favorable prices. The balm was a promise that the communications base at Number 13 would be removed within three days at the latest, long before the *flics* could get official backing for a search.

As binder to the arrangement, the three-year oil contract had been written so that a commission of one dollar on every barrel had been allocated to Idi Amin, Uganda's leader, the payments to be made directly into his personal account in Zurich. If anything effectively cemented the agreement, this did.

Dris had picked the Ugandan embassy for the very best reasons. Its proximity to Trocadéro Tower, of course. The vulnerability of Uganda to pressure. The embassy's immunity, at least for a few days, from search and entry. And, best of all, the fact that it was not an Arab nation.

Bert, who had seen a few more corners of the world, had his doubts. His plans had called for control from a much greater distance, using equipment of such sophistication that it would have had to have been stolen from U.S. Army arsenals.

But the technical demands of such a conversion were a bit beyond Bert. He had found an Arab expert to do it but, at almost the last moment, before the man could board a flight to Paris from his homeland, a dangerous eye disease, normally in remission, had flared up and killed him.

In everything, Bert knew, there is order. Even in the overthrow of order there must be order. On this team, Dris was the leader. Bert, as the technical person, had equal rank. But he did not assume the power of making yes-no decisions about the fate of the work.

He could tell Dris, as he had so many times over the past months, that from the technical viewpoint, the work could easily fail. From the human viewpoint, as well. He could tell him, again and again, that the original plan, using the original equipment, was still the best plan, that waiting for another technician to implement it was the soundest strategy.

But Dris had the final say and Dris was in love.

Bert had no doubts about Leila. If anything, she was less given to show, to oratory, to flamboyance than even Bert himself. In that sense, she was a counter-weight to Dris, whose mind still dealt in rallying cries.

But, down deep, both of them were the children of wealth, she much more so than Dris. Bert had thought often about this. His own father had been a steel puddler killed in an accident at the plant. His mother still worked in a bakery. They had both known what an aching muscle was, what it felt like to be so brutal-ized by fatigue at the end of a day that even wages didn't rebuild self-esteem.

To Dris and his woman, all this was an intellectual exercise. For Bert it was bred in his blood. For them, it was the smashing what they hated, the ruling class. For him, the elevation of what he loved, the working class.

Bert understood the danger of we-them divisions. He had studied his Mao. He knew that when the earth blossomed forth, it produced many different flowers. He had also learned his Lenin, unlike so many in the cadres now for whom Lenin was both old-fashioned and reactionary. Bert knew that to achieve solidarity even doubtful temporary alliances were useful. Even alliances with the ranks of the hated oppressors. After all, finally, one pruned the flowers.

He glanced at Dris now, who had been carelessly switching back and forth through the CB channels, listening a moment, moving on. For Dris, the trans-ceiver was a toy. Nothing was coming in over any of its channels yet, not even the police channels.

Bert stood up and moved toward the window, then thought better of it and carefully sidestepped the opening. On a folding chair in the corner, a small Grundig portable black-and-white television set had been plugged into the wall. A digital electric clock sat next to it.

The clock showed the time to be 13:00. Bert snapped on the television set.

29

She had roused him several times during the night, Curtis remembered. But he had fallen asleep again at first light and now the smell of fresh coffee was waking him. He glanced at the electric clock on his bedside table and saw that it was just past 1:00 P.M.

He sniffed the air. She wasn't making instant coffee. It smelled like the expensive dark roast ground coffee that he kept in the freezer and used on special occasions.

Curtis sat up in bed and contemplated the chaos around him, linens on and off the bed, blanket on the floor, pieces of clothing flung here and there. Well, he supposed, undoubtedly this was a special occasion.

"Netta?"

"Just a second," she called from the kitchen. "This fucking toaster."

"You have to force the slices up or they burn."

"That has already happened."

He sank back down under the single sheet that covered him, folded his fingers together across his chest and stared at the ceiling. What was happening to him?

Why this hideous note of domesticity? What gave her the right to fool around in his kitchen? In his life? Last night she had been as demanding as if she had bought him at auction. Now the housewife bit. He already knew he didn't understand women very well, neither what he gave to them nor took from them. But it had begun to dawn on him that more experiences didn't clear up ambiguities. The more women he knew, the less he knew about women.

What was she, after all, but an extremely attractive woman whose sexual tastes had been too broadly opened up by her late husband? She might have disliked what she'd been used for, but her husband had stirred something inside her that, once sparked, still burned. Curtis wondered if she demanded the same services of people like Oscar Ferguson.

Still, last night hadn't been Curtis's first experience with a woman who knew exactly what turned her on and wasn't shy about asking for it. Most of the younger women around Paris these days, whatever their nationality, had heard the news about open orgasms openly arrived at.

Lying there, arranged somewhat like a corpse on a mortuary table, Curtis decided that Netta was lovely, but too much for him. He'd have to start disengaging.

On that cue, she appeared, carrying a tray on which rested his small espresso pot, one cup, sugar and two pieces of toast from which the crusts had been removed.

She was wearing only a smile. She did something— took a breath, perhaps?—that made her small, neat breasts seem to rise up like a greeting. The narrow ray of sunlight that had penetrated into the room raked slowly across her ivory skin as she moved toward him.

"Out of bed," she told him, "sit in the easy chair."

"Mm?"

"Nobody can eat breakfast properly in bed."

He stared at her with something like awe. "You know," he said, getting out of bed and reaching for his robe, "you're the first person who's ever agreed with me on that."

She took the robe away from him and chucked it across the room, then stood there, heels together, like a slightly more indecent version of the usual French farce maid. Her black hair had been brushed, Curtis saw as he sat down naked in the armchair, and she had applied a touch of lipstick.

She put the tray on the end table beside him and poured a thin stream of hot black coffee into the cup. "Sugar?"

"Mm."

She added sugar, spooned the coffee and handed him the cup in its saucer. "I hope you like lightly buttered toast," she said, getting into bed and occupying exactly the same space from which she had ousted him. "You've left the sheets very cosy," she said, snuggling down into the bed linens. "Thoughtful man."

He sipped the coffee and found that it was just about the way he liked it, as was the toast. Watching her, he began his breakfast in silence. She had pulled a sheet part way over her and was sitting up in bed with her arms folded over her knees, her great eyes fixed firmly on him.

"Aren't you having any?" he asked then.

"I don't eat breakfast."

He munched toast for a moment. "What d'we have between us, four marriages?"

"Two and two?"

"We're highly trained for this act, then." He finished his coffee and poured some more. "Specialists in domesticity." He lifted the coffeepot in her direction. "Coffee?"

She shook her head. "Is that what they call this scene? Domestic?"

"Yep." He put the cup away and sat back in the easy chair. "What was it you told me last night?"

Her big eyes widened even more for an instant. "Darling, I told you a hundred things last night."

"No, something about not having friends. Of my being your friend."

She nodded. "You really are some kind of detective. I was feeling very low. Leila . . ." She faltered. "It was not seeing her and then, when I did see her, of being kept at arm's length. No, worse. Of being treated like a stranger." She frowned. "It's not that I define myself in terms of Leila. I'm really not what anybody would call a professional mother."

Curtis smiled. "Not my idea, either."

"But, then, how does one define oneself?" she asked. "I don't do any work, not really. What I do for the foundation is make-work. Oscar does it and I sign the papers. So I can't define myself in terms of, say, being in the world of art."

"But in that world," Curtis told her, "you could be considered quite a power. If you wanted."

"I don't," she said quickly. "But, Curtis, do you see what I mean? I am a professional at only one thing, possibly because my family prepared me only for that."

"Marrying money?" He tried to say it as gently as possible.

Her smile was lopsided. "You really don't leave me in doubt, do you, darling?" She shrugged. "But that's my only profession. I do very well at it. But if you stop to analyze it—and I've had a lot of time to do that recently—you don't find any great difference between being a professional wife and being a call girl."

He thought about it for a while. "There has to be some difference."

"Dearest Curtis, how much candor can one take this early in the day?"

The telephone rang. By reflex, and because it was at her elbow, Netta reached for it and had it off the hook before she realized what she'd done. Silently, she held it up to Curtis. He stood up and came over to the bed.

"Hello?"

"Curtis, it's Lee James."

"Oh."

"Am I calling too early?"

"No."

"You said to call you about lunchtime."

"Did I?"

"Are you all right?"

"Sure."

"You sound . . . funny. Look," she went on in a rush, "I know you have things to do. I'm at my hotel looking at TV to brush up on my French."

"Mm." Curtis watched with utter dismay as Netta began to play with him. "Lee, there is no television this early in the day."

"There's a man reading something."

"Impos—" Curtis stopped. Electric flashes were radiating outward from his groin.

"Curtis?"

He stood there, unable to speak.

"Curtis, turn on your television."

"Mm?"

"I don't believe this," she said, her voice going from low register to high. "My French isn't that good, but—"

He reached over and snapped on the television. "Curtis," Lee James asked, "please tell me if I'm right about what he's saying?"

The image of an announcer came on the screen. ". . . *la Tour de Trocadéro*," he was saying, as he continued reading from a sheet in his hand.

"Curtis, is he saying what I think he's saying?"

"Mm."

"Curtis! Answer me!"

30

Bill Elston usually got home to his apartment on Beekman Place in New York City about six o'clock. His wife was out of town, however, so there was no reason to rush home. Instead, it being the last day of the business week, Elston spent an extra hour at his desk setting up his work for the week to follow.

The Easter weather was brisk in Manhattan. Elston walked home and let himself into the apartment as the mantel clock was chiming seven. He dropped the mail on the semicircular hall table, hung up his coat and, on his way to the bar in the living room, turned on the television set.

Cronkite's voice came on in midsentence, announcing new casualties in a flare-up of Middle East border fighting. Bill Elston opened the tiny bar refrigerator. He snapped three ice cubes out of their square plastic cups into a glass and covered them with vodka. Then he opened the dry vermouth and poured a tiny amount into the bottle cap. From this he let one drop fall into his glass.

The CBS Washington man was posed in front of the White House, reciting what the president had done that day. Elston sat down opposite the TV and, with the tip of his little finger, made the ice cubes swirl around for a minute or so. Then he sat back, sipped and sighed.

At seven-twenty he got up during a commercial in which someone named Aunt Ruth was telling her tiny nephew why she used Vaseline on her hands. Elston popped another ice cube into his drink and sat down at the TV again.

At seven-twenty-one, Cronkite held a single sheet of paper in his hand, as he sometimes did. But Elston noted that he was reading from the paper, not looking up into the camera at the TelePrompTer which normally flashed words to him.

"This just in from Paris." Cronkite's normally placid face creased suddenly as he scanned ahead in his copy.

"A terrorist group has planted a powerful explosive charge in France's leading art repository. Irreplaceable and priceless works will be destroyed unless a ransom is paid, reportedly in excess of ten million doll—"

Elston was at the telephone, dialing the 011 international access code. Then he dialed 33, the code for France, followed by Curtis's number.

31

Khefte felt anger a lot of the time. The German and the "Movie Star," as he called Dris, left to him the menial work. It was the Movie Star, the one his American woman called Raoul, who did the glamorous things. It was the German, Bert, who arranged technical matters. But the risky work, ah, that was left to Khefte.

The Movie Star professed Islam. But he was not trustworthy. He was too full of smiles. Driving the dark gray Renault van along the Champs-Elysées, Khefte shook his head angrily.

He who smiles, lies.

Khefte had just finished what was perhaps the riskiest part of the work, and he was still quivering a little inside.

The manifesto demand had been run off on a copying machine yesterday. A dozen, in addressed envelopes, had been given to a messenger service at one hour before noon today. These were the copies to be delivered to the banks, the police and the press.

But Bert had warned: "The bourgeoisie is adept at the suppression of information. Do we not know this from our own lives?"

So Khefte had been assigned the dangerous work of scattering additional copies of the leaflet, some in English, where they would be sure to be seen, along a route where tourists might be expected to find the one-sheet manifesto, lying on the sidewalk or a public bench.

Because only speed would keep him from being caught, Bert had devised a route down the Champs, starting in the Porte Maillot area, in the Air France terminal there and some of the shops in the same building. Then Khefte was to drive rapidly along the Avenue de la Grande Armée direct to the Arc de Triomphe and continue dropping leaflets from the van as it moved with traffic. This would keep him fairly distant from the Trocadéro.

The instructions were clean. Finish the job. Leave the van. Forget it. Write it off. Then, if possible, move in with a walkie-talkie to an observation point near the Trocadéro, in the Passy Cemetery for example, or the Palais de Chaillot.

Khefte hated getting instructions.

It was bad enough to take them from a straw-haired, light-eyed one like Bert. Ah, but Bert was all right. His heart was good. Worse was to take instructions from one who called himself a brother, Dris, or Raoul, as the woman called him.

In what book was it written, Khefte asked himself as he negotiated the curve around the Rond Point, that because one is a Movie Star, pleasing to the eye and with flashing teeth, one has the privilege of ordering others around?

He finished his run in the shadow of the obelisk at the Place de la Concorde and turned right toward the river, picking up traffic along the Quai des Tuileries. After the Louvre the van swung left on the Rue du Pont Neuf. Khefte was in familiar territory now, near "The Hole," where he knew all the streets and where friends could hide him, if necessary.

The Movie Star and Bert, who knew many parts of Paris as well as Khefte knew the Marais quarter, were already safely ensconced in their hideaway. Only Khefte was out on the streets where any passing *flic* might make trouble for him, merely because he didn't like the dark coffee color of Khefte's skin.

It wasn't fair. He had told this to Bert. "Nothing

is fair in life, my brother," Bert had said in Arabic. His accent was good, even better than Dris's. "Life is a struggle. And only through struggle does one define a life."

Khefte didn't pretend to understand Bert. But he knew Dris and Bert had taken from him any initiative whatsoever. It wasn't right. Khefte came from a tribe where the only proof of manhood was how mercilessly one could dispatch an enemy.

This was life, never mind how Bert "defined" it. And Khefte grew even angrier at the thought that his own comrades were trying to change a way of life that had sustained him, his family, his tribe and his people for thousands of years.

A traffic light stopped him at Rue Rambuteau. Khefte sat behind the wheel, fuming. He had run all the risks and now he was demoted to a passive watcher from the outside, one they didn't really need to complete the rest of the work.

But they had left a loose end. Perhaps the Movie Star, whose blood was watered down by the French blood of his mother, had forgotten. It was hard to believe that Bert, with his German toughness, had overlooked it. But there *was* a loose end.

The American boy tied to the chair.

He would live for days, Khefte judged. He looked to be in good shape, slim, no fat on him. He would linger. And if he were found, he would talk.

What would the American be able to tell them? Ah, but it didn't matter. A loose end exists . . . to be snipped off.

His face set now, Khefte wheeled the van around a corner and began driving back to the deserted garret in which they had tied up the American. It wouldn't take long, but it had to be done with style.

And then there would be no loose end.

32

AUX ENNEMIS . . . LES BANQUES ET LES CORPORA-
TIONS AVIDES . . .
LES ZIONISTES QUI LES CONTRÔLENT . . .
LES GOUVERNEMENTS CORROMPUS QUI LES SER-
VENT . . .
VOUS QUI DONNEZ TANT D'IMPORTANCE AUX GRI-
BOUILLAGES MAIS QUI CONSIDÉREZ LA VIE HU-
MAINE SANS VALEUR . . .
VOUS QUI DÉPENSEZ DES MILLIONS POUR ABRITER DES
OEUVRES D'ART MAIS QUI REFUSEZ UN TOIT AUX
PAUVRES . . .
VOUS QUI AVEZ EXTRAIT DE NOTRE PROPRE CHAIR CES
INUTILES TRÉSORS DE DÉCADENCE . . .
VOICI NOTRE JUGEMENT DÉFINITIF:

The police technician stopped studying the typewritten document for a moment to answer the telephone. "*Oui*, M. Vermeuil," he said. "Yes, I understand. With the utmost speed, M. Vermeuil."

He put down the telephone when Vermeuil finally
ended the conversation, his third call in the past half
hour.

But the fact was, the technician told himself now,
that all the damned ransom notes delivered at noon
by the messenger service were from the same run of
the same package of paper.

He slid the typewritten sheet up a bit on the opal
glass insert set into his table. Beneath the glass a
powerful fluorescent light shone upward. He swung

the big magnifying lens over the paper again and
stared at the words.

The technician smiled grimly. These Arab terrorists wrote a pretty good French. For none of them was
it their mother tongue unless, of course, one of them
came from, say, Algeria or Tunisia or Lebanon. If so,
he would have been taught French from the day he
entered school. The thought never crossed the technician's mind, now or later, that anyone capable of
blowing up the Trocadéro could be native French.

He pulled over a long pad of lined paper and
scribbled a note in pencil on it. His responsibility was
not the text of the note but its manufacture. A
colleague next door was handling the text. But it
didn't hurt, with one's superiors, to show that one
wasn't the usual blindered bureaucrat who only saw
what was on his own plate.

The technician returned to his study of the text.

À MOINS QUE 25,000,000 DE FRANCS SUISSES, EN
BILLETS DE VALEURS DIFFÉRENTES, NE SOIENT DÉ-
POSÉS AVANT MIDI LE LUNDI DE PÂQUES DANS LE
COFFRE 73 À LA POSTE CENTRALE DE BENGHAZI,
LYBIE, LES RICHESSES DE LA TOUR TROCADÉRO À
L'ÉTAGE DE RACINE, UNE PARTIE DE CELLES DE
DIDEROT AU-DESSUS ET DE POUSSIN EN DESSOUS,
SERONT DÉTRUITES.

40 KGS. DE K-7 (FORCE MILITAIRE) SONT POSÉS,
ET DES APPAREILS SPÉCIAUX TRÉS SENSIBLES FERONT
ÉCLATER LA CHARGE SI QUELQU'UN S'APPROCHE.

UN MÉCANISME DE PRÉCISION À BASE DE QUARTZ
FERA SAUTER LA BOMBE K-7 À MIDI LE LUNDI DE
PÂQUES.

CE DÉTONATEUR NE PEUT-ÊTRE RENDU INOFFENSIF
QUE PAR UN SIGNAL, ABSOLUMENT SECRÈT, DONNÉ
PAR RADIO SUR UNE CERTAINE LONGUEUR D'ONDES.

Foolproof, the police technician thought. But very
sophisticated. He found himself wondering where

such equipment could be found. Once again his pencil went to the lined pad of paper and he scribbled another note. "Check recent break-ins at arsenals and other military entrepôts."

Tracking down such devices as proximity sensors and timing mechanisms would be a NATO job, since the instruments could as easily be American or German as French. He continued reading the ransom note.

> LE PRIX DEMANDÉ EST MODESTE. C'EST NOTRE
> ARGENT EXTIRPÉ DE NOTRE PROPRE LABEUR. MAIN-
> TENANT, IL SERVIRA À FINANCER NOTRE COMBAT
> SANS RELACHE CONTRE VOUS . . . LES ENNEMIS.
> C'EST NOTRE DERNIER CONTACT.
> PEUPLE, EN AVANT!

Eh, bien, the technician thought. What a gift for rhetoric these little Arab pederasts had. Clearly one of them had gone to French schools, at least until finishing the secondary grades.

He peered through the lens at the typewriter type. It was an elite-sized face common to several European makes. Olivetti and Adler used a face almost identical to this one.

He scribbled another note to have a high-resolution enlargement made of several letters, including a slightly worn *E* and an *N* that seemed to have a broken serif.

The paper was a common brand of dual-purpose white sometimes called "Type 4024" produced for use in the Rank-Xerox copying process or on offset presses of the Multilith type. The grain ran the long way.

The door from the other room opened and his colleague entered, carrying a second sheet of paper. "*Alors,* they have turned loose an English version along the Champs-Elysées."

The new sheet was placed over the light source and examined through the magnifier. "It's more or less the same," the colleague mused. "My English isn't perfect, of course."

"Does Louch know?"

"I telephoned him."

"And Vermeuil?"

"Please, spare me."

They laughed without mirth and bent over the illuminated leaflet, heads together as they read its text through the lens.

> TO THE ENEMY . . . THE GREEDY BANKS AND CORPORATIONS . . . THE ZIONISTS WHO CONTROL THEM . . . THE CORRUPT GOVERNMENTS WHO SERVE THEM:
> YOU WHO PUT SO HIGH A VALUE ON DAUBS OF PAINT, BUT HOLD HUMAN LIFE SO CHEAP . . . YOU, WHO SPEND MILLIONS TO SHELTER WORKS OF ART BUT BEGRUDGE THE POOR A ROOF OVER THEIR HEADS . . . YOU WHO HAVE DISTILLED OF OUR FLESH THESE USELESS TREASURES OF DECADENCE . . . WE NOW RENDER THE FINAL ACCOUNTING.
> UNLESS SF 25,000,000 IN MIXED DENOMINATIONS ARE DELIVERED BEFORE NOON, EASTER MONDAY, TO BOX 73, CENTRAL POST OFFICE, BENGHAZI, LIBYA, THE CONTENTS OF TROCADÉRO TOWER, FLOOR RACINE AND PORTIONS OF DIDEROT ABOVE AND POUSSIN BELOW, WILL BE DESTROYED.
> 40 KILOS OF K-7 (MILITARY STRENGTH) ARE EMPLACED. SENSITIVE DEVICES WILL EXPLODE THE CHARGE WHEN ANYONE COMES NEAR. A QUARTZ-CONTROLLED MECHANISM DETONATES THE K-7 AT NOON, EASTER MONDAY. THIS DETONATOR CAN BE DEACTIVATED ONLY BY A RADIO SIGNAL OF SECRET PATTERN AND WAVELENGTH.
> THE PRICE IS CHEAP. IT IS OUR MONEY, STOLEN FROM OUR OWN TOIL. NOW IT FINANCES OUR UNENDING STRUGGLE AGAINST YOU . . . THE ENEMY.
> NO FURTHER CONTACT. FORWARD THE PEOPLE!

This version too was signed with three sets of initials. It was these initials, rather than the cant and rhetoric of the note, which had impressed the two technicians:

SN

BMG

PLS

The technician whose laboratory this was reached the end of his reading and sighed heavily. "Bad business."

"All that art," his colleague said in a wistful voice. "One in the eye for Western civilization, eh?"

"Do these people care?" the other asked, indicating the list of initials. "They hope and pray they will destroy such a heritage."

"But why?"

"Because," he said in a somber voice, "it isn't theirs."

33

Curtis got to the Trocadéro well ahead of the press and television people. That is, he got as close to the Sogegarde Building as he could.

A cordon of police and army units surrounded the entire block. All traffic was halted on Kléber and Poincaré. Barricades of official cars and motorcycles closed off these avenues as well as the Rue de Longchamp, behind the building.

The curved thoroughfare that ran around the Place du Trocadéro was clear of traffic. Private cars and buses had been shunted away from the area. French motorists, who never dared touch their auto horns except in an emergency, were beginning to honk pettishly. Traffic police, already peeved by the horn-tooting, were waving vehicles directly through, past the Palais de Chaillot, into Avenue Wilson.

A kind of command post had been set up at the head of the triangular block facing the Place du Trocadéro, directly in front of the Café Kléber, next to the Métro station kiosk. This entrance, too, had been blocked. Passengers trying to come up these stairs from the subway were forced to descend again and emerge some distance away, via the exit at the Palais de Chaillot.

It was a mess, Curtis reflected as he stood there sorting it out, of the kind police everywhere took a perverse pleasure in creating.

When three or four security cops ran to the corner of Wilson to help untangle a particularly untidy jam-up, Curtis walked at a leisurely pace across the empty street to the command post. There was no reason for him to think he would not be shooed away. But the temporary shortage of police there, and the calmness of his approach, at least guaranteed that no one would let off a burst of submachine gun fire at him.

The command post itself was a communications truck whose back and side doors opened to give access to an array of telephones and radio equipment. The instant Curtis got within a few yards of it, a young cop raised his Browning automatic riot carbine to a port arms position.

Curtis had already dug out his wallet. He flipped it open to display the card, with his photo on it, that ten years before had given him access to the stacks at Low Memorial Library of Columbia University.

"M'sieur Hardy, s'il vous plaît," he told the young cop.

The policeman stared for a moment at the college card photo and then at Curtis. He swung half right and indicated Hardy with a nod of his head.

"Curtis," the little gray-mustached man whispered, obviously in need of a friend. His pince-nez had a precarious clawhold on the bridge of his nose. "It's incredible, Curtis. And we are totally paralyzed."

"How is that?"

"Because we have no idea of the sensitivity of these so-called sensors they speak of in the note. There are sensors and sensors. These are amateurs, Curtis. If they were professionals . . ." He let the thought die away.

The fitful horn-blowing subsided as the jam-up at Avenue Wilson began to clear. It was then that Curtis realized how silent this quarter of Paris had become. Without traffic noise it was quiet enough. But he noticed that the police, the civilians at the command post, even a new detachment of soldiers which had just driven up, were all conversing in whispers.

"Sonic sensors?" he asked the little *chef de la sécurité*.

"How can we be sure? There are also devices that react to changes in temperature. To air currents. To the vibrations of a footfall. Perhaps these are only electric-eye sensors. Or perhaps," he added in a murmur of concentrated misery, "they are a combination of many kinds."

Curtis nodded. "But the warning, the whatever-you-call-it, ransom manifesto, only says, 'when anyone comes near' the device. This would indicate a proximity-type of sensor. You'd have a safety radius of, say, twenty meters."

"*You* say," Hardy snapped. He lowered his voice at once. "You say and perhaps I would agree. But how do we *know*?"

"Is Louch around?"

"Nowhere." Hardy's response had heavy overtones of the usual never-there-when-you-need-one complaint.

"Has anyone figured out," Curtis whispered, "what forty kilos of K–7 will do?"

"Their note warns us that they have it at the very center of the Tower, on the fourth floor, Racine. The entire structure is as airtight as the casing of a gigantic bomb. At the very least, forty kilos would reduce the center to rubble and blow out exterior sections of the wall."

"And start fires."

"And start fires," Hardy echoed in hushed despair.

Curtis paused. His next question would touch Hardy's sorest point. But he was sure the little man had already had to answer it several times in the past half hour. "Any idea how they smuggled in the stuff?"

Hardy's face went grayer than usual. "That is the devilish part of it, Curtis. Shipments come and shipments go. The forty kilos could have been there for weeks. Perhaps months."

A captain of police bore down on them. His long

face was split in the middle by an extremely well-brushed mustache. He eyed both Hardy and Curtis with a sour expression. "Who is that one?" he demanded of Hardy.

"M. Curtis, of the UBCO bank."

The captain's dark eyes flashed. "We do not need the Americans in this."

There hung in the air the distinct aura of a get-rid-of-him order. Hardy watched the man stride off, leather and gold flashing in the pale April sun. "I cannot leave it in their hands," he murmured to Curtis. "My job . . ." He almost sobbed. "My job hangs by a thread. But if I leave this to the *flics*, they will storm the place and everything will go up in one great bonfire."

"Surely the parent company can control the police."

"The Société? To a point, Curtis. But you know how sensitive the police are about terrorist activity these days. No one has forgotten the Daoud affair. They have made many mistakes by trying to play civilian games of politics."

"So this time they'll play it their way?"

"Smash and grab," Hardy muttered disconsolately.

"Then only Louch can help you. He's a reasonable man. He has the rank. And the terror movements are his job."

"Then where is he?" Hardy wailed in a miserable undertone.

The two men stood there for a moment, chewing over their own private thoughts. Curtis knew where his first loyalties lay. If the explosive was emplaced on Racine, the Minton Irish Collection was in danger of being atomized.

In the confused three-way conversation at his apartment only fifteen minutes before, that much had become clear. It had been another of those Marx Brothers movie scenes to which Curtis did not want to become accustomed: Netta Irish naked in his bed, Bill Elston on the long-distance phone asking questions only Netta could answer. There had been a lot of hand-over-the-phone moments while he quizzed her, then relayed information he really wasn't supposed to know to Elston.

"Get Oscar Ferguson," Elston had snapped. "Have him give you a ball-park estimate of the value in there." And hung up.

Standing outside the Café Kléber, staring unhappily at the command center truck with its gaggle of telephones and headsets, Hardy finally stirred. "If only," he mused in a near-whisper, "if only I had the courage to let myself into the outer building. I could examine my monitor systems. They could tell me something."

"Don't they feed into your central message center, too?"

"I can get no one here on the telephone," the little gray man admitted. "They are simply not answering."

"Then what about the local police station?"

Hardy stared at him a moment. His face seemed to regain some of its color. "*Alors*, let us go."

34

At night, the Rue de la Grande Truanderie was accustomed to cars as lengthy as the rented bittersweet chocolate Mercedes 600 that now turned slowly into the street. But this was not yet two in the afternoon.

"*Lentamente*, Nico," the tiny woman in the sable coat said.

Her chauffeur slowed the car to a crawl. The Princess knew how much Nico liked the 600 model. It was a machine geared for anything, for the steady 160-kph speed of the *autostrade* superhighways, and for the snail's pace of a parade past reviewing stands.

This trip was neither. The Princess had a visual memory, as acute in its own way as Louch's. She was trying to remember last night, sometime after two in the morning, when she had finally left the peculiar Mr. Groark to his own devices in Mother's and had been driven back to her hotel.

"*Ricordi i tre ragazzi?*"

"*Si. Anche un furgoncino grigio. Marca Renault.*"

The Princess nodded enthusiastically. She remembered the three boys, of course, but only Nico would remember a gray Renault van. Leaning forward to speak to him through the glass partition which had been pushed open, she asked, "Is it a common make, this van?"

"I don't know."

"You didn't notice the license?"

Without taking his hands from the wheel, Nico managed to lift his shoulders, his chin and his lower lip in an orchestrated what-do-you-expect-of-me gesture.

"But you would know it again?" she persisted.

"Perhaps."

"Go back and forth on these streets for a while, then."

At "The Hole," Nico swung left and left again on the Rue Rambuteau. The heavy Mercedes moved with ponderous slowness past sex shops and boutiques, closed now but whether because of Good Friday or only because they didn't normally open until evening, the Princess had no idea.

They crossed the Boulevard de Sébastopol. Ahead loomed the peculiar outlines of the new Pompidou art center which still looked unfinished this long after it had officially opened. The inner part seemed to hang from an exterior grid of scaffolding that was permanent. The Princess frowned at it as the brown Mercedes turned right on Rue St. Martin and traversed the entire front (or was it the side?) of the museum (center?) with its orange and blue exterior ducts.

As is common in the older parts of European cities, they now found they could not get back to where they had started from. There were no more right-turn streets for several blocks. Looking for a place to turn, the Princess was distracted, but Nico wasn't.

"*Guarda*," he said, braking the Mercedes to a smooth halt, "*il furgoncino grigio*."

The gray van was parked at the rear of a dead-end called the Impasse St. Fiacre. Its right wheels had been run up onto the sidewalk to leave room on the street for other vehicles to come and go. Nico backed up the big Mercedes and turned slowly into the impasse. The car was moving so gradually now that the speedometer needle didn't even flicker.

Without warning, Nico pulled the sedan up onto the pavement. "*Ma, che cosa?*" the Princess demanded impatiently.

"*Guarda.*"

A dark-skinned young man was getting into the van. Of the two who had been with Dominic Brown last night, one had been a blondish young man with an expressionless face and the other had been this ugly boy, who now started the van, turned it around at a sharp angle in the narrow street and drove past the Mercedes. He quickly disappeared around the corner of Rue St. Martin.

"*Presto*, Nico!"

"No good," her chauffeur said gloomily. "By the time I back out of this hole, he will be long gone."

The Princess threw herself back in the voluminous rear seat. She bounced up and down twice like an enraged infant and smote the dark brown glove-leather upholstery several blows. "I cannot believe we were this close and missed!" she cried out.

"*Paziènza, Signora.*"

"Don't babble of patience! Do you have any idea what it was worth to find out where that boy lived?"

Nico shrugged again, complexly, with shoulders, arms, chin and lower lip. "He came out of Number 22," he said then, in his own good time.

"*Stupidoggine! Cretino!*" There was an explosion of sable fur as the tiny woman flew out of the car and dashed for the entrance of Number 22. Nico managed to get to the door ahead of her.

"*Piano, Signora.*" He held up a cautioning hand. "Let me go first. What are we looking for?"

A smile flitted across her small, perfect mouth. The glitter on her eyelids sparkled. "We are looking for a right arm," she said, "made of solid gold."

35

Since ten minutes past one o'clock, Vermeuil had been making a hell of the Sixteenth Arrondissement police station for anyone who got in his way.

He had almost kicked out of his chair the officer who normally monitored the screens that indicated what was happening at the Trocadéro. Vermeuil, who had only a little more flesh on him than a skeleton, lowered his lanky frame into the chair to glare at the small television screens as if trying to force information to appear on the cathode-ray tubes. From time to time he scribbled on a pad, dashed off a frantic telephone call or covered his protruding eyes with his hand, as if overcome with unutterable grief.

That was how Louch had found him at 1:20 P.M., a figure out of an etching by Kollwitz, emaciated, elongated and in total despair. "Anything on the monitors?" Louch asked.

Vermeuil whirled in the swivel chair. "I want you to know," he began in his high, aristocratic honk, "that I not only hold you personally responsible for this, but I am even now initiating an investigation into the performance of your whole bureau for the past five years. Lack of performance, I should say."

The room tilted slightly, as Louch perceived it. He sat down suddenly in a wooden chair across from Vermeuil and stared into that death's head. The man resembled the oceanist Cousteau, but without a gram of human feeling anywhere in his skull-like face.

"Lack of performance," Louch repeated, trying to get an aggrieved note in his voice.

"In five years, these Bedouins have taken over France," Vermeuil spit out. "In five years, you—*you*!—have handed it to them on a platter."

"But that's nonsense, Vermeuil."

"I know what I am talking about," the skinny man said in his superior way, as if he had been studying the matter for a long time now, rather than thinking of it in hectic fits and starts for only the past half hour.

In fact, Louch thought, watching him, he's been perfectly content to let me run the bureau without supervision. He's been content because his real job is not law enforcement but the aggrandizement of his personal fortune. I have made it possible, Louch told himself, for this pederast son of a pederast to grow rich and even more socially prominent without having once to worry about police work.

"I have taken it all off your shoulders, eh, Vermeuil?" he burst out. "And the moment you feel a bit of the weight, you panic."

He made his voice lower and more soothing. "But there is no reason for panic," he went on reassuringly. "We know who we're dealing with here. They simply aren't good enough for the job."

"Really?" Vermeuil's voice went up half an octave, more in anger at being patronized by Louch than with concern for the problem. "Have you seen the initials on the ransom demand?"

"SN," Louch repeated, "BMG and PLS."

"These are not amateurs," Vermeuil warned him.

"*Septembre Noir* is hardly even a movement anymore," Louch said. "The Black September cadres have mostly been absorbed in the Palestine Liberation Squadron."

"Yes, yes," his superior said. "The PLS indicates that."

"And what is the PLS?" Louch demanded. "A shell

of its old self. It has quarreled with the PLO. It is no longer welcome in any Arab land except Libya."

"Where there is money and equipment for all," Vermeuil added nastily.

"But not for fringe groups like the PLS."

"Don't talk nonsense," the thin man exploded. "With these groups, only results count. The group that succeeds is the group that gets the most support from Qaddafi and the Libyan treasury. And what do you call ransoming the Trocadéro? It's *merde* in our eye, Louch. Before the entire world."

"Please. Let's be sensible."

"Louch, you are an idiot." Vermeuil's paper-thin lips worked themselves into a silent frenzy for a moment, then burst out in words again. "France, center of culture, of romance, of art. France, world capital of the humanities. Paris, the umbilicus of the art world. And . . . we . . . can't . . . even . . . protect . . . our . . . heritage," he said, spitting each word out like a piece of a broken tooth.

"It's not that bad," Louch muttered.

"It's worse! I notice you don't even have the courage to discuss the BMG signature."

"The Baader-Meinhof Gruppe is out of business," Louch said wearily. "It's been leaderless for more than a year. In West Germany it doesn't even exist."

"No? But in Paris, under your protection, it flourishes."

"Exaggerations will not help."

"Nothing will help." Vermeuil swung around on the chair and nodded to the monitor screens. "There isn't a sign of anything wrong here. Nothing has been disturbed. Nothing is out of place. It's a tomb in there. *And you've buried me in it!*" he suddenly shouted.

Louch blinked at the ferocity of the attack. He shook his head sadly, as if witnessing the demise of someone cherished.

"Vermeuil," he said at last in the soothing tone

that hadn't worked before, "whatever happens, you cannot lose. We will work this thing out successfully, but even if the worst should happen, I take it all on myself. You are in the clear. Understand? I am promising that I will specifically exonerate you. I will lie. I will tell the press that I concealed things from you. You will not be blamed. That is a promise."

"Yes?" The skull face looked interested.

"Yes. Now stop screaming. Let's get to work."

Vermeuil's bony body seemed to relax slightly. "Well, then." The aristocratic yelp came down an octave to a more conversational tone. "What's our first move?"

Louch looked at him, trying to conceal his feeling that this apparition of bone and skin was the man-sized roach predicted by Kafka. Vermeuil didn't have the slightest idea of police work. He was a rich man who'd bought himself a sinecure office through which to make even more money. France was full of fakers like this.

Some of them had their own business connections with the Arabs, or with the oil companies who had financed their rise through the corridors of government power. Louch didn't know if Vermeuil was one who owed his start to oil money or Arab money. But he was certainly part of a government which had long ago dedicated itself to pacifying the Arabs in the name of oil, to selling them fighter planes and nuclear reactors, to giving their assassins first-class tickets out of the country on demand.

It was a policy about which Louch had no feeling one way or the other. Being French, he wanted what was best for France. Being himself a part of the bureaucracy, he understood how a policy handed down from on high frequently ended up in embarrassing events that angered other governments . . . or stung them to make noises of annoyance, anyway.

But, being something of an observer, Louch also knew that his country's pro-Arab policy had gained it

no better oil contracts than any other nation of Western Europe. The Dutch, who spurned the Arabs, paid
no more for their oil, and got all they needed.

"Louch, stop staring at me."

"Sorry. Our first move," Louch repeated then, in a
quiet voice, "our first move is to verify the threat."

"Verify?" Vermeuil looked puzzled. He rapped his
knuckles on a copy of the typewritten ransom mani-
fest. "This thing was delivered almost simultaneously
to all the news agencies, the television, the Sûreté,
the Police Judiciaire, all the big banks, the newspapers, even the *Herald-Tribune* and other foreign
newspapers. It exists, Louch."

The heavyset man shoved back in his chair, looking more Buddha-like than before. "The pieces of
paper exist, Vermeuil. I have to find out if the forty
kilos of K–7 exist and, if so, where they are placed
and how they will be detonated."

"There is a timing device that—"

"I know what it says on the piece of paper." Louch
heard the contempt in his voice. He tried to repair
his tone as he went on: "It is difficult to set up a
detonation-timing schedule over more than twelve
hours. Twenty-four hours is a possibility, but beyond
that requires special equipment."

"Why?"

Louch started to explain the twelve-hour nature of
a clock mechanism and the digital kind that could
handle a twenty-four-hour range. Then he despaired
of getting the idea across to this scarecrow. "Just believe me, Vermeuil."

"They say it's quartz-controlled."

"Quartz-controlled what?" Louch burst out. "I am
trying to suggest that it is Friday afternoon and a
device set to go off Monday noon is something I will
have to verify."

Someone rapped discreetly at the closed door of the
monitor room. "Go away!" Louch shouted. Then, to
his superior: "In short, we have to see for ourselves

if this piece of paper represents a real threat or a hoax."

The thought of a hoax had obviously never crossed Vermeuil's mind before. It did so now, almost visibly, like a tiny bug crawling sideways behind his eyes. "You mean . . . with luck . . . this could be a false alarm?"

Louch rubbed the bulbous tip of his long nose. "You want my opinion? It's real. But I'm not paid for opinions, only for certainties."

Vermeuil's face fell. "Then—?"

"I would suggest, M. le Ministre, that while I dig into this, you begin rounding up the money."

"The ransom?"

"It will not be easy over the long weekend." Louch thought for a moment. "But perhaps the Swiss don't celebrate Easter Monday. If so—"

Again the knocking at the door. "What is it?" Louch bellowed.

The door swung open diffidently. The small gray Hardy stood there, with Curtis behind him in his usual costume of sweater and sneakers. Louch produced a truly leonine growl, accompanied by a frown that would have caused cardiac arrest in a charging elephant. "What in the name of sweet Christ do you two want?"

"To look at my monitors," Hardy said in a miffed tone.

"And to hold your tiny hand," Curtis added sweetly, in English.

Louch indicated the television screens with a thumb gesture. "There's nothing out of the ordinary there." He paused. "M. Vermeuil, this is Hardy, of Sogegarde, and Curtis, who represents one of the banks whose clients use the Trocadéro."

The men shook hands briefly, Hardy's glance not leaving the cathode tubes. "Vermeuil," Curtis mused. "I remember the name now. Weren't you—?"

"You really have no business here," Louch cut in

heavily in English. "Do you understand what I am saying?"

Curtis nodded. "Is the bomb planted on Racine?"

"Probably."

"It's the Irish Collection."

Vermeuil leaned forward. "I beg pardon?"

"Not the country of Ireland. The Minton Irish Collection of paintings and sculpture," Curtis explained.

"Worth how much?"

"I'm getting an approximate figure."

Hardy let out a gasp of annoyance. "The sensors show absolute normality inside the Trocadéro."

"I'll need dossiers on all your employees," Louch told him. "And I want your log for the past week."

Hardy spluttered. His pince-nez finally gave up their nasty clutch on his nose and fell the length of the thin cord by which they were attached to his lapel. "I beg your pardon, Louch," the little man said in an aggrieved tone. "I beg your pardon in the extreme. But this has nothing to do with any Sogegarde employee. That much I swear to."

Louch's heavy head was swinging from side to side. "Nevertheless, all the dossiers, within the hour."

"But they're inside the building."

Louch thought for a moment. His glance wandered from face to face. Vermeuil seemed already to have lost interest, now that he'd been assured Louch would take the blame. Hardy looked hostile, since his own internal security had been called into question. Louch's glance rested finally on Curtis, who looked faintly amused.

"Are you thinking what I am thinking?" Louch asked him.

Curtis's small-featured face went blank. He gave a nervous brush to the sandy hair that had fallen over his forehead. "I'm thinking there's no other way to authenticate the note."

Louch let out a heavy sigh. "It's a job for a very small squad. Two, three men. Volunteers, of course."

Vermeuil frowned. "What job?"

Louch kept his voice absolutely flat. "We've got to go in."

PART FIVE

GOOD FRIDAY: AFTERNOON

36

Her suite at the Ritz seemed chilly to Netta. She had asked Room Service to set up drinks and canapés in the long living room, with its line of windows overlooking Place Vendôme. She had hoped the availability of food and booze would keep Oscar calm.

He'd arrived with Tom Sandweg, at two o'clock. The men had apparently run into each other in the lobby and come upstairs without speaking. Tom produced a proper greeting, giving Netta a brief hug and a peck on both cheeks. Oscar stood in the doorway of the living room, fists jammed into the pockets of a particularly grubby beige sports jacket he'd worn on the Riviera all the month before.

Netta stared back at him. She knew she was looking particularly good at the moment, in a floor-length djellabah of a gauzy off-white wool, very thin, with vertical streaks of gold and brown at random intervals.

"Where the hell were you last night?" Oscar demanded.

"What happened to 'hello'?" Netta responded.

"We don't keep Oscar around for good manners," Tom said in a curiously bitchy tone.

He made himself a Scotch and Perrier and stood by the windows looking pensively down at the street. The afternoon sun, still wintry pale, seemed to frame his handsome face, with its deftly gray sideburns, and make it stand out brightly from the rest of the room.

"I still want an answer." Oscar remained in the

doorway, as though he would turn on his heel and leave if Netta gave him the wrong response.

"I was here," she said then. "I had them turn off the phone calls. When they told you at the switchboard there was no answer, I'm afraid it was a little white lie I demanded of them."

"Bullshit." Oscar strode heavily into the room, upended the whisky bottle in a glass and filled it halfway. Carelessly, he flipped an ice cube into the glass, making whisky splash on the lovely patina of the credenza.

"And where were you," Tom asked suddenly, "while they were arranging to blow the Irish Collection to smithereens?"

Oscar gave him the pained look one gives a dog who has just peed on the rug. "Back off, Sandweg. You have no connection with this."

"I'm a trustee of the foundation."

"That makes you just another spear carrier, sonny boy." Oscar drained half his drink. "When are you pencil pushers going to understand that you have no control over the foundation or the Collection? Just go back to doing whatever it is you do over at IBI. Bribes and kickbacks, or whatever you're in charge of."

"It's amusing," Sandweg said, "to hear a loud-mouthed parasite like you, who never lifted anything heavier than an Alka-Seltzer, talking about pencil pushers." He came back and sat down on the sofa. "Can the chitchat, Oscar. Let's get to the point. What's the value of the stuff in that goddamned concrete tower of yours?"

If Netta had expected Oscar to blow up, she was disappointed. He seemed remarkably calm, as a matter of fact. He stood stock-still for a moment, as if considering Sandweg's insults, and then downed the rest of his drink before sitting in an upholstered chair by the window. The April sun came from behind him.

Netta recognized that he had put the rest of them in the position of being interrogated.

"And, Oscar," she began, "let's not—"

"Right," Tom Sandweg cut in, "let's not have your usual ten minutes of toe dancing. We have already heard you on the topic of how impossible it is to evaluate the collection. Spare us the crap."

Once again, Oscar seemed to take the whole matter with massive calmness. "You rich folks," he said then, more to himself. "You do turn snotty when the chips are down."

"Come on, Oscar." Netta refilled his drink and sat beside Tom on the sofa. The room *was* cold. She shivered slightly. "Be a good boy. How much could we lose if . . . if the bomb went off?"

He ignored the fresh drink, a novelty in itself. Instead, he folded thick arms over his chest and stared at her. "Netta, that information is for your ears only. This leech sitting there with his tongue hanging out is wondering how much of the Collection he can hock to bail out a company he ran into bankruptcy. I know the way these guys operate, Netta. He's not above planting the bomb himself, just to force our hand."

Outside the windows, Paris was strangely quiet, Netta thought. Everyone had already left for the long Easter weekend. She wished she had, too. It would have been pleasant to take Curtis away, perhaps to Rambouillet or Compiègne. They could have found a little country inn . . .

"Don't be difficult, Oscar," she said then. "Tom has agreed that if we sell the château, he'll find the rest of what he needs elsewhere."

"The arithmetic is fascinating," Oscar mused. "I can squeeze ten million out of the château. But this bloodsucker needs twenty million. So, all of a sudden, somebody plants a bomb in Racine-12 and what's the ransom demand? The Swiss equivalent of ten million bucks. Fa-sci-nating."

Tom Sandweg sighed. "Netta, if it'll help matters,

I'll leave. Then perhaps he'll give you an estimate."

She ignored the offer. Something had begun to bother her, and she couldn't be sure exactly what it was. "Oscar," she said then, trying to get her thoughts in order, "Oscar, you're taking this whole thing too calmly."

"What do you want me to do, wet my pants?"

"The Minton Irish Collection," she told him, "is almost the whole of the Minton Irish Foundation. And most of the collection is in the Trocadéro at this moment. In other words—"

"In other words," Sandweg interrupted, "your meal ticket's in mortal danger, Oscar. But it doesn't seem to bother you."

Netta frowned. "Tom, I wish you'd let me deal with this."

"Sorry."

"But he's right," she went on. "You are the chief executive of the foundation. I'm listed as chairman of the board of trustees, but it's not a salaried position. I know," she went on in a softer tone, "that tomorrow morning you could get an equally good job at a museum somewhere. I know you've had offers from universities. But, Oscar, it's only natural for you to show a little more concern. It's only human. Some of those paintings are part of everybody's heritage."

He sat there in silence for a long moment, a faint smile at the corners of his mouth, his sandy hair mussed up, his broad, freckled face almost totally at rest.

"Human," he said then, in a dour sort of croak.

"I'm sorry if I offended you," Netta offered. "I'm quite upset by this ransom threat. I know you are, too."

"Human," he repeated. "That's rich, coming from you two. On the mortuary slab, the undertaker isn't going to drain half a pint of real blood out of either of you."

The chilly silence in the room seemed to Netta to be intensified by the silence outside. Paris seemed to be holding its breath.

She shook her head as if to clear it. It was nonsense, wasn't it? Oscar was behaving abominably, as always, and the threat to the paintings was real. But why did this feeling suddenly close over her like a shroud, like a strangler's knotted cord, making her shudder with a premonition of . . .

Of what? Something she couldn't put a name to, something heavy and deadly, a feeling that she was at the center of a dark and tragic thing the world was watching with fascination and . . . and blood lust.

"Blood?" Tom Sandweg asked then in his offhand way.

No one spoke. "You're talking of bleeding us?" he went on then in an almost conversational tone. "How long have you had this job with the foundation? You've made your bundle, Oscar. Don't take that insufferable tone of righteousness. You've profited very well from all this."

By way of answer, Oscar pursed his lips and produced a rude noise.

"My trade is corporate finance," Sandweg continued matter-of-factly. "But that doesn't mean I don't know the tricks of other trades. I can imagine what happens to the man who buys and sells art for Minton Irish. I can picture the under-the-counter commissions, the gifts, the substantial 'inducements,' if that's the word, to favor one dealer or gallery over another."

Oscar nodded. "Your mind would take that approach."

"You were giving me the business about bribes and kickbacks? It takes one to know one, Oscar. I've done my share of paying on the sly. And you've done your share of raking it in."

The burly man laughed softly, not real mirth but not far from it. "Are you expecting me to deny it? One of the first things Minton Irish told me was that he expected me to supplement my income that way. If I've taken gifts from time to time, he always knew it."

"And is no longer around to confirm." Tom Sandweg stared into his untouched drink. "Neat."

Netta stirred restlessly. "We're wasting time," she said. "There is a time bomb—literally—and there are things we have to do to keep it from exploding."

Oscar produced the same rude noise. "What things?"

"Evaluate everything."

"Does it make any difference to these terrorists if the Irish Collection is worth ten cents or a billion dollars?"

"It makes a difference to us," Netta responded. "We have—"

"Any minute now," Tom cut in on her, "they'll be calling us for an evaluation. They have to. They'll do that with everybody who admits to having anything stored in the Trocadéro. They have to determine whether the ransom is worth paying. It's just that cold-blooded. And they also want to find out who will help them pony up the ransom cash."

"Them?" Oscar growled. "Them who?"

"The French. The Trocadéro is a subsidiary of a national bank. Eventually, whoever asks us for an evaluation will be speaking with the full force of the French government."

Oscar's beefy face set in lines of rejection. Netta studied him for a moment. "Come on," she said then. "You must have some sort of figure in the back of your head. It doesn't have to be accurate."

The sandy-haired man got to his feet so abruptly that the heavy easy chair shoved back a foot with a screech of wood on varnished floor. "I don't have a figure, Netta. I don't even carry around an inventory list, would you believe? But because we were there only a few days ago, looking at the stuff, I have a rough idea of which pieces are the biggies."

He started for the door. "Oscar?"

"I'll reconstruct a list and try to work out some prices. But only for you," he added, pointing a stubby finger at Netta. "This high-minded jackal isn't to know. If I don't have your promise on that, you won't get anything out of me."

He turned and left. In the silence, they could hear him clumping heavily through the suite to the outer door. A moment later he slammed it firmly behind him. Now the silence was complete again. Netta shivered.

Tom Sandweg took the first sip of his drink. "Christ."

"He's behaving impossibly. He seems to be in shock, or something."

Tom stared at her curiously. "You think so?"

"Of all of us, Tom, he's the one who really appreciates the value of the collection. I don't mean the dollar value. The . . . cultural value. The emotional value."

"Yes?"

"How can you doubt it?" she countered. "Art is his whole life. It's all he knows and, in his field, Oscar knows almost everything."

"Knowing isn't feeling."

"Tom!"

"He's an insensitive, nasty son of a bitch," Sandweg said then. "There is no sign in him that he cares any more about that art than about an ashtray of cigarette butts."

She shook her head quickly. "No, you're wrong. It's because he feels it so deeply that he seems . . . shut off, turned off. It's his way of handling the shock."

"If you say so."

"I know him better than you do," she said. "He distrusts emotional displays. He's very . . . very Scotch, if you know what I mean."

Sandweg smiled crookedly into his drink. "He behaves this way all the time. What's his excuse when there is no bomb threat?"

Netta hugged her arms, trying to fight off the chill that had entered her. "I agreed he was being impossible."

"So are you," Sandweg countered. "Whatever possessed you to start an affair with that lunatic?"

She was silent for a moment. "It's a long story."

"It's a long affair. It must have started soon after you married Minnie."

"Soon enough."

"But you see what a false position it puts me in," he told her. "Right now I should be forcing an emergency meeting of the foundation's trustees. I should be demanding Oscar's head."

"Why? What's it got to do with this bomb thing?"

Sandweg was watching her without speaking. "In any event," Netta said then, feeling that she was saying more than she'd planned to, "the thing between Oscar and me is over."

"So I gather."

"From what?"

"From the fact that he no longer knows where you are at night." Sandweg accompanied this with a small grin, just a baring of teeth, nothing more. "Does that mean I can start trying to get him canned?"

"Tom." She gestured in a fluttery way, moving her hands as if batting off a swarm of moths. She hated women who played the fluttery game, but sometimes it was the only game left. "None of what you say hangs together. Oscar being my lover doesn't qualify or disqualify him as curator. And what this Trocadéro business has to do with it doesn't make sense, either."

"Just that it brings his total incompetence to a head."

"He? Incompetent? That's not so."

"I despair of making you see what's really bothering me." He took another careful sip of his drink.

"This is a big, cold, cruel world. It looks very complex sometimes because it's full of people trying to overcomplicate it."

He put down the drink and stared at her for a moment. "The lead bank for IBI is UBCO, in New York. Lately we have been presenting something of an uneven profile to UBCO. First Minnie dies and the board refuses to name a successor. I'm only in an acting position, remember, not a permanent one. Second, one of our big subsidiaries, Jet-Tech, gets so far on the hook with UBCO that the bank won't extend another nickel of credit. If you were UBCO, you'd look at the entire spread of IBI as one entity. You'd see a ship that's sprung a leak and nobody's at the helm. You'd know it was a ship still worth billions. You'd know that part of its assets were related to the largest private art collection in the world. You'd be reassured by its physical assets and also collateral like the Minton Irish Collection. And then . . ."

The silence seemed to wrap the two of them in something clammy. Netta cleared her throat. "You've made your point, Tom."

"Good."

"I don't know if you're right, or—"

"I'm right," he interrupted. "Or close enough."

Netta picked up his drink and sipped from it. "Are you hungry?" she asked then. "I've had them send up all these canapés, or whatever the Ritz thinks they are. And you've taken away my appetite completely."

He shook his head. "You should have made up a doggy bag for Oscar."

She laughed. "You really want to get rid of him."

He didn't answer, but sat thinking for a long moment. "Netta," he began then in a distracted tone, "what's Racine-12?"

"It's . . . the section of the Trocadéro where we keep the Collection. You were with us the other day. Wasn't that what the guard called it?"

Tom nodded. "I remember now." He sat in silence for a long time. Then he leaned forward and began playing with the bite-sized canapés, moving them around with the tip of his index finger, like checkers on a board. After a moment, he started to say something, then stopped and continued pushing the circles of bread, with their nameless toppings of yellow and brown paste squeezed from a tube in starry shapes.

"What is it, Tom?"

"Racine-12 is where the Collection is," he said slowly, "but who says that's where the bomb is?"

"Who?" She stared at him. "Isn't that what—"

"What Oscar said," Tom cut in. "Yes."

37

At eight o'clock in the evening, peace had settled over Faraway Farms in Warwick, New York. The horses were bedded down in their stalls. The stables were locked up for the night. The staff, most of whom lived away from the farm, had gone home.

Sally Fish sat in his office at the very top of the old white clapboard house. A small color television set was reproducing a rerun in black and white of *I Love Lucy*. Sally had been watching this particular episode for almost fifteen years now. He loved it.

Hunched gnomelike in an armchair rocker, Sally held an aluminum TV dinner in his lap. He had defrosted it in a microwave oven but hadn't warmed it much. If he heated it hot-hot, his thinking went, then two things happened: he burned himself holding it and the food got cold anyway as he watched TV and ate. This way, no problems. The food was cool to begin with.

The telephone rang at 8:05. Sally put down the TV dinner and answered. "It's me," George Brown said. "Let's go."

Sally Fish put the telephone into the foam-rubber cradle of the scrambler box. Then he picked up the scrambler phone. "What's shaking, boss?"

"Any word on Nicky?"

"I nailed that lamebrain Rocco. He's the *stronzo* who was keeping an eye on the kid up in Massa—"

"Fuck that. What about the kid?"

"No news yet."

"Christ!" A moment's silence over the transatlantic circuits. "Find Murray fast. Tell him to unload all files on the Cuban matter. Immediately."

"Huh?"

"It all goes. There's a dame over here who's too close for comfort, capeesh?"

"What dame? We can take care of h—"

"I don't want none of that," Brown cautioned him. "I just want the files clean. Today. Tonight. No later. I'm taking care of the dame my own way." The heavy voice paused for an instant. "Get back to me tomorrow morning and tell me Nicky is okay. Otherwise, Sally, nobody's life ain't gonna be worth living. Ten-four."

"Ten-four, *padrone*."

Frowning, Sally Fish replaced the telephones and turned back to look at the television. In this episode, where Desi had to impersonate a Carmen Miranda kind of female singer, the funny part was coming up in just a minute. Damn it.

Sally turned down the sound on the television and started dialing Murray Olenick's numbers. Funny to think of George Brown worried by some dame. Who would she be, some reporter or something? And, for Christ's sake, why was the Cuban thing surfacing now, after all these years? It had all happened when they could keep the truth hidden. If it busted loose now . . . well, times were different. It could blow a lot of shit sky-high.

He tracked Murray down to the apartment of one of his girlfriends. He passed along the message and got a squawk of protest in his ear.

"It'll take days!" Murray complained.

"He wants everything dumped by tonight, the latest."

"But it's sealed. I don't even have the lock combination."

"Sealed in what?"

"Sort of a footlocker. Army footlocker."

"Wood or metal?"

"Wood."

"Okay," Sally said. "Load it in your car and drive it up here. Tonight."

"You're insane."

"Tonight," Sally repeated. "It's an hour's drive. You can be back in the sack with that *tzotzkileh* of yours by midnight."

"Be reasonable. What do you want it up there for?"

"Up here," Sally Fish said, "we will have us a nice big bonfire. Footlocker, files and all."

He hung up and reached for the TV knob, turning up the sound just as Desi, in drag, began his number. Sally Fish sat back with a contented sigh and ate some more cold TV dinner.

38

Vermeuil had gone with Louch and Hardy to the Avenue Kléber entrance of the triangular building to make sure they got through the tight ring of police and soldiers.

"And Curtis?" Louch asked at the last moment.

"He has no status in this," Vermeuil's high voice was stiff with official distaste.

"That may be," Louch said, "or it may not be. I want him with me."

"It's irregular."

Louch stooped and picked up a smeared copy of the ransom manifesto from the gutter. He handed it to Vermeuil with a deadpan look. "So is this."

Vermeuil frowned and stepped aside to let Curtis follow the two Frenchmen to the doorway of the building. Vermeuil stared at them for a moment, then turned and walked away. Hardy bent over the locks and opened the outer door.

They were inside the first television-covered area. The red light on the camera over the door lit up. Hardy moved to the inner door and used two keys in two different locks. He stood back and spoke into the microphone.

"Hardy is here. Open up, please."

Louch glanced at Curtis. "Tragedy has unhinged his mind," he murmured. Then, to Hardy: "There is no one inside, dear man."

"Our voiceprints are on a computer," Hardy explained. "The apparatus compares my new print with the name I announce. It then decides if I am who I say I am."

He was. The door swung open. The three men advanced into the second surveillance area. This time the routine was exactly the opposite. Hardy spoke into the microphone first and then, when the door buzzed, used two keys to open it.

They were in the third area now, where the person one had come to see normally stood behind bulletproof glass to identify a new arrival face to face. Hardy tiptoed to a box on the wall behind the guard's desk. He opened the box with a key and pressed a switch. Light flooded down on them from recessed lamps in the ceiling high overhead.

Hardy motioned them closer to him. He whispered in their ears: "Step where I step. The electric-eye alarms have not been turned off."

Moving with great slowness and stepping silently on the balls of his feet, the little gray-faced man tiptoed along a corridor. Louch followed Hardy and Curtis followed Louch. Once inside the security office, Hardy carefully closed the door, flicked on the lights and began switching a series of controls to one side of the television monitor screens.

"All right," he said at length. Sitting at the monitor console, he switched on more cameras. "They operate on infrared radiation, like a sniperscope, but they watch only the ground floors."

Louch made a clucking noise. "Can I use this telephone?" he murmured.

Hardy nodded. Louch dialed a number. "Louch here. Keep this line open from now on. Do you have a Noctron unit?" He listened. "It does not have to be mounted on a weapon, no." A pause. "Bring it to the Kléber door. Curtis will take it from you." Another pause. "The American, yes."

He laid the telephone down on the desk. "It's a kind of sniperscope. Can you retrace your steps?"

"I think so." Curtis looked at Hardy. "Will you pass me through?"

"No need. The doors remain open. The alarms are turned off."

Curtis looked surprised. "A first for the Trocadéro," he murmured under his breath. He started to leave.

"Wait." Louch turned to Hardy. "Somewhere in the building, are there rags?"

The gray-faced man looked up from his screens. "What? Rags?"

"Rags. Cleaning rags. Mop rags."

"Of course. In the supply room. Why?"

Louch turned back to Curtis. "Get the Noctron," he whispered.

Curtis moved back along the corridor. He let himself out through the middle surveillance room and, at the outer one, carefully opened the door to the Avenue Kléber. A grave sergeant of police was crossing the street toward him, carrying a small dark blue fiberboard suitcase. "M. Curtis?"

"Yes. The Noctron?" He took it and returned to Hardy's office. "Louch, how does this work?" He had unsnapped the clasps and was staring down into the blue velours interior of the suitcase, in which lay what seemed to be a small but bulky prism telescope, resembling in design one-half of a pair of hefty binoculars. "Does it plug in?"

"Battery-operated." Louch stared at the television screens. "Found anything?"

"Nothing," Hardy whispered.

"Nor will you." Louch sighed heavily. "It's all upstairs, probably on Racine. Is there an elevator?"

"I couldn't let you use th—"

"Quite right," Louch agreed hastily. "Too much noise. A stairway, then?"

"Several."

"First the rags, then the stairway."

Hardy got up and started from the room. "And some string," Louch whispered after him. The heavy-

hole, on a plate beside a sandwich of red
frowned. Raw cucumbers? Raw meat?
ch were real barbarians, when it came to

the Princess cooed. *"Poverino,* do you
"

Brown managed to free his face from the
breasts for a moment. "Just tell me who
ly." His voice was hoarse.

of your father, *caro."*

of alarm that crossed the boy's face was
ven to Nico. "Not a friend," the Princess
noothly and quickly, "so much as a . . .
tagonist."

erican wriggled weakly out of her embrace.
ull length on the bed, clad only in his
he managed to prop his head up on one
tare at the Princess. He swallowed several
ld I have some—"

Subito!" the Princess cried out to Nico.

t the water run in the bathroom, Nico
the boy croaking a volley of questions in
ly part of which Nico understood, things
e he was and why he had been rescued
e going to tell his father where he was.
ou don't want me to, *carissimo ragazzo,"*
ing as Nico brought in the glass of water.
" Nick gulped some, then slowly sipped.
. That Arab kid really wanted me dead.
ack, you know. He came back and—"

" The Princess made moves that threat-
orison him against her breasts again. "You
o talk about it anymore."

me here to find Leila, and if I d—"

rcy."

woman had been sitting on the bed, her
under her like a tailor. Now, slowly, she
er legs to the floor and got to her feet,

set man stared glumly at Curtis. "You don't mind
being pulled into this?"

"Should I mind?"

"I have a reason."

"How reassuring."

Louch shook his head. "Since we may both go up
in one grand poof . . ." He grinned at Curtis. "You
have met Vermeuil."

"Poisonous."

"In order to have a free hand with this, to do it my
way," Louch muttered keeping his voice down, "I
had to promise that cadaverous piece of offal that I
would take full responsibility, full guilt. I would exonerate him in advance, even if I had to tell the press
I lied to him. You understand what I have agreed
to?"

Curtis's smile had curdled at the corners. "Everything is your fault, even the terror group. And, especially the bomb, if they detonate it."

"Correct."

"Which is why you don't want one of your own
men with you," Curtis went on. "He wouldn't be in
on the charade."

"More than that, I wouldn't want him tarred with
the same brush that will destroy my good name. So
I picked you, old friend." Louch produced a mag-
nificently evil grin. "Of course, there is a bright side."

"The hell there is."

"Oh, yes. If we are somehow successful," Louch
told him in an undertone, *"la gloire* is all ours."

"No, Vermeuil's. If you pull this off, only he gets
the credit."

"But your bank and its customers, they will thank
you."

"I couldn't care less," Curtis told him.

Louch rubbed the bulbous tip of his nose. "You
can back out," he said then. "This is purely volun-
tary."

"Back out of what?" Curtis demanded in a whisper. "What's your plan?"

"The rags we wrap around our feet and tie with string. So far you follow me?"

"Keep talking."

"Because we have no way of knowing what kind of sensors protect the K–7, we cannot use flashlights. They may trigger a photoelectric cell. For the same reasons, microwave detection of the radar kind is prohibited. Also the magnetometer type of metal detector."

"Go on."

"With the Noctron we ascend to Racine. The Noctron sees in the dark under its own infrared emissions."

"And?"

"And we . . ." Louch gestured weakly. "We reconnoiter."

"And then?"

Hardy returned carrying a bundle of rags and a ball of string. "And then," Louch told him "for the contents of this mad place, for the art heritage of Western civilization and for our own lives . . ."

"Yes?"

"We shoot craps."

cumber,
meat. Ni
These Fr
food.

"Carin
feel bette

Domin
overhang
you are,

"A frie

The l
apparent
went on
business

The
Sprawle
underwe
hand a
times. "

"Acq

As h
could h
English
about
and wa

"Not
she was

"Tha
"My th
He can

"Sh-s
ened to
don't b

"But

"Leil

"Lei

The
legs cr
extend

The hotel was a small, ine
Wagram not far from t
third-floor bedroom had
days ago. Standing in the
street, he had a clear view
thentic kosher restaurants,

Nico was, in fact, standi
ing with curiosity the on
that sat next to some hi
Strange food these French a

Behind him the murmu
and down the scale of rea
the young American's hea
stroked his face and patted

Despite everything, Nico
for hours in a cold room,
of the Arabs to make hi
nasty little throat-to-heel
fact that the Princess's brea
pressed against the boy's e
tively strangling him, still

Young, and lucky. Left
and he would have strang
When they'd started to
Arab's apartment, Nico h
garret. It was the America
choice. Five more minutes,

Nico watched through t
as the man behind the co

moving as if in a trance, eyes unfocused. She joined Nico at the window.

"Do you think his father can locate this hotel?" she asked her driver in Italian. "You have lived here three days now. Isn't it possible . . . ?"

"It is possible," Nico agreed. "Shall I move to another hotel?"

"Take the boy with you. I have given him a tranquilizer. I shall give him another tablet and then leave. When you have relocated in a new hotel, call me at the George V. But speak only to me. Do not leave a message."

"*D'accordo, Signora.*"

"Darling boy," the Princess told Dominic Brown, "am I right that you do not wish your father to know you are here in Paris?"

"Definitely," he said in his hoarse croak.

"Then you will have to go with Nico to a new place. Just for tonight. Meanwhile," she added, "I will find Miss Darcy for you. Yes! Her mother is here, you know, here in Paris."

"She wouldn't know where Leila is."

The Princess stared at the lanky young man for a long moment. Nico, who was standing beside her, could feel the waves, the vibrations, the signals. American men go for the young ones, he thought, with the silicone breasts. But if this *ragazzone* here had a week with someone like the Princess, it would spoil him forever for young flesh.

Nico himself was carefully immune to her charms. He had to be. His job depended on it. And, although he'd once had fantasies about his employer, after years of suppressing the urge, he'd tamed it. But he could see the way the boy was beginning to react, first to being fussed over and then to being fondled and given little nudges, a breast here, a thigh there. He was falling for it, Nico saw, and he envied the poor bastard.

The Princess was digging in her tiny handbag. She

came up with a ten-milligram, blue-green tablet of Valium, the second she had given Dominic Brown. "This will make you feel much, much better, *caro*."

"I don't really need—"

"I know best, lovely boy." She popped the pill in his mouth and held the glass of water to his lips. He swallowed dutifully.

"Good. Now, stay with Nico and do what he says." She eyed the American thoughtfully. "You speak Italian, of course."

"Not a word."

"Incredible." The Princess turned to Nico and in rapid Milanese dialect, she spat out a quick series of orders. "He's groggy. But if he gives you trouble, cool him off with a tap on the skull. Otherwise, be nice to him, understand?"

"*Ho capito, Signora.*"

"I want him where I can lay hands on him instantly, Nico," she went on in dialect Italian. "If you do this properly, you get a bonus that will make you leave me, it's so much money. You'll be able to buy your own garage, you ravisher of automobiles."

"With respect, *Signora*, it's not autos I hope to ravish."

She patted his cheek and, as she started out of the room, dipped an instant like a feeding bird to peck a kiss at the boy's cheek. "Be a good boy, *caro*," she told him in English.

She squeezed his hand. There was a moment of confusion in the boy's mind. And then he kissed her hand. Nico kept an absolutely straight face.

"You are among friends who love you," the Princess said and turned to leave.

Nico watched her flit out of the room. He double-locked the door behind her. Friends, he thought, who in the end will sell you, little boy, for enough money to pay off the national debt of Italy.

40

In the absence of any advice from Curtis, Lee James was still living in the hotel suggested by a woman friend of hers as being clean and cheap and "totally at the center of excitement," as the friend had put it. This turned out to be in the area of the Café Flore, Le Drugstore and the Brasserie Lipp.

It didn't take Lee James long to realize that in the ten years since her friend had lived in Paris, the excitement center had moved somewhere else. For those people who needed to know where everything was, this area would probably now be known as "where it used to be."

In any event, the hotel was still clean, but no longer cheap. When the telephone rang in Lee James's room at five-thirty, she had showered, redressed and was making up her face, preparatory to trying to find Curtis, who seemed to have disappeared off the face of the earth.

She snatched up the telephone, thinking it was Curtis calling. "Miss Lee James?" an American voice asked.

"Yes. Speaking."

"One moment please."

"Lee, Bill Elston. Can you hear me?"

"Perfectly."

"What the hell is going on?"

"It's a news blackout here," she told her boss in New York. "Nothing in the papers. The original statement has been read once again over television. I can't find Curtis anywhere. Or Louch."

"Who's Louch?"

"A contact of Curtis's. He's the man in charge of terrorism."

"Huh?" Elston decided to let it go. "I just watched the eleven o'clock news. Big roundup. The wire services estimate fifteen private collections are stored in that place. Nobody wants to hazard a guess, but the total value is in the billions. Have you gotten hold of Oscar Ferguson?"

"Tried everywhere. Phone calls. Personal visits. He's in hiding."

"He's at the Ritz," Elston said. "Check Mrs. Irish's suite." He paused. "Lee, this thing may be blacked out in Paris, but it's stirred up a tremendous storm in New York and London and even in Moscow. It's such a threat to culture that the Reds are busy disclaiming any connection with the terrorists."

"You know a lot more than I do." She sat down and stared at herself in the mirror. Her face looked washed out because she had yet to put on lipstick. She wondered whether it was her responsibility to—

"Mr. Elston," she said then, "have you assigned me to this or what?"

"It's Curtis's bailiwick. But where is he?"

"I . . . that's the point. I made it my business to get to know this Louch in person."

"Who?"

"I told you, the terrorist man. Met him at Curtis's last night. Something about him." She stopped.

"Speak up," Elston urged her.

"Something struck a sour note. He's the man the French have put in charge of keeping an eye on terrorist groups. But I think he's a plant."

"A what?"

"I think the Communists planted him as far back as World War Two." Even in her ears, the words sounded silly. "I don't mean it that way. He was in the French Underground. Then he went into police work. He's definitely some sort of left-wing type. If this business is left in his hands, he'll sell out for twenty-five million Swiss francs and that'll be that."

At his end of the conversation, Elston was silent for a moment. "Lee," he said then, "what alternative do we have?"

"Get inside and defuse the thing."

"I assume it's being tried."

"That's my point, Mr. Elston. If it's Louch who's trying, the attempt is doomed in advance."

"That's hardly our business." His voice had hardened slightly. She saw she'd taken a step too far. "Our business is only to make sure our client's property is safe. If it takes ten million bucks, that's what it takes."

"I understand," she said quickly. She didn't understand. Gaping holes seemed to have opened up around her. She thought she knew Elston well enough to report her suspicions to him. But he didn't seem interested.

"And another thing, Lee, don't get mixed up in French politics," he added. "I don't understand it and neither will you."

"But this man is not on our side," she said, aware that she should have dropped the matter. "It's hard to explain why I f—"

"Lee," her boss cut in. "Going over there was your idea. You're there to show Curtis you can be a help to him. Which means a help to me. Now, drop this whole Louch business and find Oscar Ferguson. I have to have a rough estimate of the Minton Irish property in that place."

Lee found it almost impossible not to ask the next question. What she wanted to say was, "What business is that of UBCO's?" But she'd already stepped out into some sort of jungle without a map. With great effort what she finally managed to say was, "Okay, I'm on my way."

"Good." Elston sounded relieved. "Call me anytime tonight. We have a situation here. I don't care if you have to wake me up. Just get back to me."

"Will do."

"So long."

The line went dead. Lee sat and stared at herself in the mirror. Why couldn't she learn to keep her mouth shut? Why was it so hard? Louch was some sort of undercover Red. He used Stalinist terms. He spouted Marx. He talked of accommodating the left. Worst of all, he'd probably been mixed up with them in the Golden Triangle drug traffic. It was ironic, wasn't it, that out of the blue, dropped in her lap, was this man who could probably tell her something about her brother Terry's death? If she could make him talk. If she could believe him.

If she could keep from being fired in the meantime.

Lee James opened her lips and applied lipstick. She blotted it with tissue and examined the results. A lopsided downturn of one corner of her mouth was the only sign that she found her position ridiculous, untenable and confusing.

Curtis would know what to do, if only she could find him and get some advice. But Louch was his friend. Maybe even . . .

No, there was nothing else between them, nothing political. Because, if that was the case, the best thing she could do would be to take the next plane back to New York.

41

"I don't know," Hardy whispered, wringing the words from deep inside him. "You ask too much of me, Louch. I simply do not know."

He and Louch and Curtis were standing at the very base of the circular tower, looking at a narrow steel door fastened by levers. An edge of bright red rubber gasket showed all the way around the door. Staring at it, the little gray-faced man seemed to bristle with fear, like a hedgehog, the pince-nez on his nose vibrating visibly.

Curtis watched both men, aware that if they guessed wrong now, at the very beginning of the affair, it would be instant disaster. Hardy was determined to make Louch responsible, while Louch, by asking the same questions over and over again, kept trying to include Hardy in the decision making.

"It's your damned tower," the heavyset man repeated in a sullen murmur. "If I can't count on you for accurate information, I might as well pack up and leave."

"I simply do not have that information," Hardy insisted, quivering now with rage as well as fear, and with the effort of trying to suppress both.

"But you do know the water is pumped in," Curtis whispered.

Both Frenchmen turned on him as if he had uttered a malediction. "Yes," Hardy admitted then. "Such a quantity of water is needed to flood the tunnel quickly that it must be pumped in."

"And you," Curtis looked at Louch, "are afraid that if you open the drain valves, you'll start a pump and the vibration . . ."

Louch threw his hands up and out at his side. "Correct."

"But surely, down here in the subbasement, imbedded in concrete and rock, the vibrations wouldn't reach any sensors they have upstairs."

Hardy produced his own version of Louch's throwaway-hands gesture. "Perhaps, yes. Perhaps, no."

"Is it possible the tunnel drains by gravity alone?" Curtis asked.

"Possible," Hardy muttered. "But only in an emergency."

Curtis was staring at the steel door. "Is there a master switch for this place that shuts off everything, electricity, alarms, the works?"

"Yes."

"Suppose you pull that switch. Then you open the valve wheel. If the tunnel is going to drain by gravity, it will. But in any event, with the switch pulled, no pump will go on."

Louch nodded. "*Vite.* The switch."

Glasses rocking precariously on his nose, Hardy ran off. Curtis and Louch stood there eyeing each other. They seemed dressed for the same costume ball, their feet swathed in rags, as if they had agreed to come as a tramp act. The lights suddenly went out. They waited in total darkness.

Louch switched on a flashlight. By its light, stumbling here and there, Hardy returned to them. "It is done."

Holding the flashlight between his teeth, Louch reached up and gently eased the valve wheel in a counterclockwise turn of an inch or two. They listened but nothing happened. He carefully turned the wheel a few more inches.

"There," Curtis murmured. "I hear something."

The three men stood listening to a faint shushing

sound from behind the steel door and beneath their feet. "I am afraid to open it any farther," Louch said in an undertone. "At this rate the tunnel will take hours to drain."

Curtis smiled somewhat grimly. "With what we've got ahead of us," he whispered dryly, "I'm not in any hurry to start."

42

Dris set fire to a fresh cigarette from the butt of his previous one. Bert watched him but said nothing.

The room was thick with the sweetish smell of Turkish tobacco. Bert didn't smoke, of course, nor drink. But he had been in the movement long enough to have learned not to tell other people they were smoking too much. On such tiny silences was solidarity founded.

He had propped his feet up on the folding wooden chair which held the small television set. Nothing had been broadcast now for hours, but from his vantage point in the Ugandan embassy across the street from the Trocadéro, Bert knew the cordon around the triangular building had been drawn even tighter.

He watched Dris click back and forth through the CB radio channels with nervous restlessness. Both of them were waiting for a report from Khefte, who should long ago have taken up an observation post covering the Kléber entrance to the Trocadéro. The electric clock read 17:10.

Bert listened to the mixture of police and army radio traffic that had taken over some of the CB channels. From what one of the embassy people had hold him, the *flics* had a command post at the Place du Trocadéro end of the block and another in the Sixteenth Arrondissement police station down the street.

The Ugandan embassy employees were frightened, no question of that. They had not yet had to face up to a house-to-house search by the police, but Bert wondered just how well they would brazen it out. They were within their rights in turning the police away. Everything hung on that. But the ability to say no and the nerve to carry it off properly were two different things.

"*Merde!*" Dris yelped. "I am going to break radio silence."

Bert lowered his feet from the chair. He sat up straighter and watched the Tunisian, with his handsome face and bright-bright teeth. "You know," Bert began in his most casual, reasonable tone, as if discussing the weather, "the moment we break silence they begin to triangulate the signal."

"I don't care. We take chances. It will be just another chance we take." Dris's voice sounded high and tense. His big eyes stared here and there, the whites muddy. "If I get off the air fast, they can't find us."

"Not the first time," Bert agreed calmly. "But you'll be tempted again. Piece by piece they'll locate the signal."

The Arab shrugged. "And then? They can't come into the embassy. So what good does it do them?"

"What good does it do us to break radio silence?"

Dris considered this for a moment. "I can't stand being out of touch."

"There is nothing you have to transmit," Bert pointed out in the same reasonable tone. "Nothing has changed."

"Perhaps they have begun to search the Trocadéro."

Bert gave this difference of opinion the benefit of deep consideration. "You may be right," he said then, on the principle that he couldn't keep contradicting Dris without getting him angry enough to lose control. It was better to concede this minor point. "If I were the police," he went on, "I would first have to determine if this were a hoax. So you may very well be right."

The rare conciliatory note seemed to calm Dris. He stopped playing with the CB radio and sat back, inhaling cigarette smoke and letting it out in big plumes. The room had begun to stink not only of smoke, but of sweat.

Bert could smell the difference between this acrid perspiration and the normal kind. He had been trained to detect the smell. As a matter of fact he had been trained to detect many such clues. His instructors had even pointed out to him the validity of inspecting the stool passed by members of a team.

"It isn't enough to watch and listen to them," his instructors had pointed out. "How and how much they void tells the tale." It would be possible, for instance, by this method to detect an infiltrating agent. Unlike a dedicated fighter for freedom, used to the iron rations of the people whose cause he advances, the agent would have a full belly. His next two stools would tell a remarkable tale about him, if one were alert enough to examine them.

Bert closed his eyes. He found himself wondering now and then whether a lot of his training wasn't just that . . . shit. It was a case of the training cadre working mostly to justify its luxurious existence.

They lived well, the instructors, while training one to work on an empty belly for the greater good of mankind. When Bert took charge of such training— and he never for a moment doubted that one day he might—he would make sure these all-knowing instructors took their turn in the field, practicing some of the iron regimen they preached to expendables, like him.

And yet, expendable or not, Bert and his team were expected to be self-sustaining, even to the money it cost to mount such affairs as this one. To Bert came the responsibility of finding the thousands of francs this was costing. To Bert fell the necessity of making deals with a strange, back-street world of "sponsors."

"Old Louch isn't that smart," Dris said then.

Bert opened his eyes and tried to remember what they'd been talking about. That was the trouble working with someone, like Dris, who had an emotional attachment that was warping his judgment. Instead of keeping his mind clear, he would be worrying about the American woman, Leila.

"What about Louch?" Bert asked.

"He isn't smart enough to go see whether it's a hoax or not."

"Have no illusions," Bert assured him. "Louch is no fool."

"Leila spotted him in Senlis, you know."

"I know."

"And only a great fool would let himself be spotted."

Bert shrugged negligently. It wasn't the time in Dris's life to introduce him to the kind of double and triple ploys that were commonplace in this work. "Louch is all right," he said then. "He's conflicted, like the rest of the old guard. But his instincts are all right."

"What do you mean, old guard? He's a Fascist swine," Dris said.

Bert gazed at the dark, handsome young man for a long time. Finally he stirred and said, "Right. A Fascist swine. Absolutely." And let the whole matter drop.

In a few minutes, Bert realized this had been an error. Dris was fidgeting again, playing with the CB radio, lighting a new cigarette. There was a kind of innate paranoia in the Muslim petite bourgeoisie, probably exacerbated by Dris's French blood as well. They grew up in comfort, but never the kind of lascivious luxury of the ruling classes in their lands.

And, always, beneath them, was the plight of the exploited classes to which they could be demoted without an instant's warning. It made them naturally jumpy, wary of alliances, of teamwork, especially with whites.

Bert grimaced. He knew better than that. Dris and Khefte would kill to protect their perception of themselves as white. Well, perhaps not white as Bert was white, but of the Caucasian race as opposed to the blacks which, eons ago, their people had enslaved and sold at market. He had to be more careful in the way he thought, Bert cautioned himself. An error like that, if voiced aloud, could explode everything.

As it was, he had a better working relationship with Khefte, the darker of the two. And this would always be so, no matter where Bert was assigned. The alliance between himself and Khefte was a working-class understanding. Different as their origins were, they came out of the same stratum of society. Dris did not. He did, of course. But he thought he didn't. Self-deception.

Khefte could be expected to understand the concept of Leninist solidarity, of alliances with any useful force, at least temporarily. Bert was especially good at forging such alliances. He had a natural graveness of demeanor that went over well with even the most corrupt and ruthless elements of the ruling class. They trusted him to be as corrupt as they, to "stay bought" as the Americans put it. Bert arrived out of the shadows, made his deals, used his temporary allies to the advantage of the cause, then retreated into the shadows again. Not an easy life, but a deeply satisfying one. A commando life, but a survivor like Bert was always adept at the carefully calculated risk.

Bert watched Dris's fingers play with the jack of the microphone cord. In another moment, he would be switching on the FM transmitter "just to pass the time." And from there it was only a step to going on the air.

Bert stood up. "Take a break," he suggested.

Dris blinked. He got to his feet. "A break where?"

"Walk. Exercise. Slip downstairs and talk to that

fellow, the liaison man from the embassy. Zada. You remember the one?"

"He's a craven idiot."

"He's not used to tension, as we are."

Dris walked to the window and glanced out at the street. "It's almost night. What are they doing, do you think?"

"I don't know." Bert quickly sat down in the chair Dris had vacated. "We have done our planning well. We have carried out every detail. The rest is in the hands of Allah."

He glanced sideways at Dris to see how this went down. In his experience, even the most atheist of Arabs still allowed a corner of superstition to live in his heart.

"Allah?" the dark young man asked. "What do you know of Allah?"

"Only of the Prophet's wisdom. Of accepting the will of Allah."

"Don't talk rot." Dris's black eyes burned as he stared at Bert. "My people accepted all of it. For thousands of years we left it in His hands. And where are we today? In the hands of our sheikhs. Without owning even a square millimeter of the riches of our land, knowing only that riches always go to the sheikhs and, after much pain, we die as poor as we were born."

Bert let the echoes of this outburst die away. Then: "To be as rich as a sheikh? Before Monday is over, you will have your wish, Dris. With ten million dollars one can do much. Is that what you want?"

The black eyes hooded. Dris's big chin jutted out. "Huh! That's an insult. You know the money is for all our work, not for one of us."

Bert had surreptitiously coiled the microphone cord. He tucked it in his hip pocket now. "Dris, my brother, have you ever watched the white trails in the sky left by the jet fighters?"

"Many times."

"To have our own jet fighters . . ." Bert nodded wistfully. "That would be something."

"We will."

"When the Shah of Iran buys an F-16 fighter from the Americans," Bert said then, "do you have any idea what he pays?"

Dris shook his head.

"Twenty million dollars, my brother." Bert let it sink in. "With all of our work and Allah's will, this whole plan will raise enough money to buy half of one jet fighter."

Dris stared at him for a moment, then sat down in the chair in front of the television. "It isn't fair," he said then.

"No. Fairness doesn't enter into it. Never forget that." Bert relaxed. Dris was . . . defused. "The system is everything. Big enough to swallow you and me and every work of art stored in the Trocadéro and never once belch. We have to understand that and yet keep fighting."

"The system is . . ." Dris repeated dully.

"It is the immovable object."

"And we?"

"Are the irresistible force."

43

When he arrived in Netta's suite at the Ritz for dinner alone with her, Oscar brought along an armful of foreign papers he'd picked up at Le Drugstore on the Champs-Elysées near the Arc de Triomphe. He dumped them on the coffee table in the living room, next to the tray on which stood a bucket of ice and the fixings for drinks.

Netta leafed through some of the English and German papers, tabloids mostly, to find that "Trocadéro" was on every front page.

So far none of the press had connected the Minton Irish Collection with the case, but it wasn't for lack of trying. All afternoon the telephone had been ringing with calls from wire services and New York newspapers. Finally, Netta had asked the switchboard to take messages.

"You're sure that bastard Sandweg won't be here?" Oscar grunted, making himself a stiff drink. From the veined look of his eyeballs, and the smell of his breath, this would not be his first of the day.

"He thinks you won't be back with a report until first thing in the morning. Asked me out to dinner, as a matter of fact. Some American business associate of his. Boredom Central."

She had changed from the striped wool djellabah into a kind of peignoir, then thought better of it and changed again, this time into a shirt, tennis sweater and thick wool skirt over low-heeled walking shoes. Sitting there across from Oscar now, she missed the ringing of the telephones. She had kept answering all afternoon on the chance that one of the calls would be from Curtis. Now there was no way he could get through to her. She stood up. "I'll be right back, Oscar."

She walked into the small bedroom, the one in which she and Curtis—it seemed a long time ago—had begun their affair. If that was what it was. She picked up the telephone and listened until the switchboard plugged in. "You're holding my calls and taking messages?"

"*Oui, madame.*"

"If a Mr. Curtis calls, put him through to the suite."

"*Oui, madame.*"

"Only Mr. Curtis."

She returned to the living room and saw that Oscar was flipping through a folder of notes and other papers. He looked puffy and petulant, much put upon. What had she ever seen in him?

But that was never the question. He'd been the one to see something in her. He had made it his business to close the gap between them within less than a year. By which time she'd found out what Minton Irish was really like, in and out of bed, and was ready for something normal, if that was the word, in sex.

Oscar supplied it. Or rather reconfirmed that it existed, that somewhere men and women pleasured each other instead of arranging elaborate fantasies of humiliation and punishment.

She sat down on the sofa again and watched him, wondering if he even knew she'd come back into the room. He was in a strange mood today. Where once he'd followed her with hawk's eyes, fiercely possessive, now he seemed distracted and somehow under attack, busy defending himself against assaults that were invisible.

It had to be his feelings about the Collection. He'd lived with these paintings and sculptures for so long,

even as a student. He'd chosen some of the art himself and convinced Minnie to buy it. To him these
were living things, parts of him as connected as arms
and legs. Of them all, Oscar would feel this ransom
threat most keenly.

"They'll be safe," she said then, wanting to reassure
him. "The ransom will be paid. They'll make it,
Oscar."

He glanced up blankly, frowned, then made his
forehead smooth again. "Hope so." He delved back
into his folder of notes again.

Hope so. Netta considered the two monosyllables.
On matters of art, Oscar could expound for hours,
lavishing polysyllabic preciseness like a pastry chef
decorating a wedding cake, meanings within meanings spurting endlessly. But with this dagger at his
heart he had retreated almost to silence, like a
wounded animal.

Netta felt sorry for him. As for the paintings . . .
it was dizzying to understand that so much of her
net worth was tied up in them. If they were destroyed
she would lose a tremendous amount of money, despite the insurance. The world would lose a great
chunk of its cultural heritage but she, as if by sur-
gery, would lose everything of hers that had been
Minton Irish's.

There was a breath-stealing vertigo in such a vision.
For an instant she felt as if chains were about to be
stricken off. The feeling was almost worth the loss of
so much money.

Free. The death of the paintings freed her of Irish's
hold. She could begin her life again.

This kind of disloyal, anticultural feeling she could
confide in no one, not Tom Sandweg, least of all
Oscar. It could be confided to Curtis, but where was
he? He would know how to help her handle all of
this . . . ambivalence.

"Oscar," she said then, "do you remember Curtis?"

He didn't answer for a while, then looked up slowly. "The UBCO guy? What about him?"

"Don't you think he could help us with this?"

Again the pained frown, again the deliberate effort to smooth it away. "Help how?"

Help me, Netta said silently. Instead, she pointed to Oscar's folder of notes. "What's the verdict?"

He finished his drink. "It's hard to talk about this," he began then.

"I know that. And I appreciate what you're doing. It must kill you to have to review everything and set a price on it. As if . . . well, as if everything were already gone and you were reporting it to the coroner or something."

"More likely the insurance people," he said in a gruff voice. "Not," he went on, holding up his hand for silence, "that we'd ever collect the true value. Insurance doesn't work that way. As a matter of fact, I expect the insurance people will try to invoke one of their famous escape clauses."

"I don't understand."

"All insurance policies have them, clauses that say the protection is not in effect for losses caused by acts of God, civil insurrection, atomic warfare and the like. They'll try to argue that this is some sort of unforeseen bolt from the blue which invalidates the coverage. But our lawyers can beat that back. The whole intent of the plot is to ransom the paintings. It's exactly as if they were kidnapped or, in other words, stolen. And we're covered for that."

Netta watched and listened, aware that Oscar had lost his usual truculent tone. He shuffled his notes. "Ready?"

"Please."

"I've organized this by artist. For example, we have three small Rembrandts, five Holbeins, and so forth. But we have some quite special pieces. We have the Lucas Cranach *Serpent*, the third panel that completes his *Adam* and his *Eve*. There is really no way to put a price on it." He stopped, thought, scribbled a note, then looked up.

"Two big Titians," he went on, "two Caravaggios the Vatican has been asking for, several very good Turners, mostly seascapes, acres of Watteau and Delacroix and David—drugs on the market, along with Greuze—and half a dozen Inness landscapes the Art Institute in Chicago has a standing offer for. I haven't even mentioned our El Greco, or the Goya oils, or the Velázquez. Yards and yards of this sort of thing, mostly bought by Minnie's father. It's standard stuff, except for the Cranach, but it's only the beginning. When we get to the things Minnie bought, we're in an area of extremely hot stuff."

"Hot?"

"Well," he leafed through his notes, "how else would you describe the fact that we are sitting on more Schiele and Klimt than you'd find anywhere in Vienna? We have what amounts to a corner on them and we control the reproduction rights as well. The same could be said for our prewar Picassos and English Pre-Raphaelites. The other day I was looking through the Klees and early Gauguins. Do you have any idea how hot all this could be? We have dozens of Vuillards and Signacs and other late Impressionists. There are popularity trends that govern what brings unusually high prices. Sitting in Racine-12 we have stuff that would blow the art auction world sky-high."

He frowned again and this time couldn't quite erase the creases. "I didn't mean that the way it sounds. Like a cheap pun. But, Netta, the point is this: no insurance company will take my evaluation of these newer items. There is no way I can convince them of what they'd bring if we auctioned some of them tomorrow."

They were silent for a moment. "Oscar," she said then, "that's the second time you've pinpointed Racine-12."

He glanced up at her. "What?"

"This afternoon you said it, and again just now. Maybe we're being unduly pessimistic. Maybe the bomb is planted somewhere else."

"Did I—?" He stopped. "Yes," he said then, "of course. Maybe it's in another part of the Trocadéro. You're right."

Without waiting for an answer, he launched into a report on prices.

Netta watched him, feeling that same light-headed dizziness again. Nothing was what it seemed. The great Irish Collection could not bring, in insurance, what it was worth. Its loss would slash deeply into her fortune. And yet she still felt ambivalent about it. What was worse, she was beginning to suspect that Oscar didn't care about it, either.

44

Just off the Boulevard St. Germain, the restaurant called le Petit Zinc has an unpretentious exterior and an expensive menu. Although it lies in Louch's neighborhood and his apartment is only a few blocks away, he himself never frequented the place. He was well-paid, as government servants go, but being an honest cop, he could ill afford le Petit Zinc.

George Brown could. He liked the atmosphere of small tables jammed together, the open stairway leading to the second story, the general noisiness that made it hard to eavesdrop on one's neighboring table, and prices that kept out all but the affluent. Whether or not the food was any good didn't really concern George Brown. What did was the fact that of all the many Paris restaurants, in this one he could be fairly certain not to run into anyone he knew.

It also gave him a certain pleasure, as tonight, to introduce a visiting American to a place he'd probably never heard of before. "Like it?" he asked Tom Sandweg as they finished their second perfectly made, extra-dry martinis.

"Bit of home."

"But damned few Americans." Brown hesitated for a moment. He had bad news for Sandweg about the money he wanted to borrow. Not that he couldn't have it, just that it would take more time.

Normally Brown had no feelings one way or the other about delivering bad news. He'd had plenty of it to dish out over the years. But his own head was in disarray at the moment. The business with Nicky had him spooked.

It wasn't so much the fact of the kid lamming out of college. What the hell, boys will be boys. But the ease with which he'd slipped past the hidden guardians whose only business was to keep track of Nicky . . . that bothered George Brown a great deal.

Then, as the days passed and no sign of Nicky had been brought forward, he'd begun to fear that his youngest son had been kidnapped by experts who'd eluded the watchers or paid them off. Either reason was particularly bad news for George Brown.

So, as he sat sipping his icy martini, his mind was too full of conflicting thoughts, his heart too crammed with strange passions, to put in order what he had to tell Tom Sandweg. He sighed heavily.

"That bad?" Sandweg asked.

Brown laughed unhappily. "You think you got problems, Tommy."

"I do."

Brown's dark, flat eyes shifted sideways. "Like what?"

"Well, not the twenty million I was looking for." Sandweg smiled reassuringly, his handsome face in shadow, his glance fixed on the rim of his martini glass. "As I mentioned, I've found a way to raise half of it."

"Good boy. Because I was gonna have to tell y—"

"It's the Trocadéro business."

Brown's face, normally impassive, suddenly seemed to go a shade deader, as if a blank wall had abruptly concealed. His glance moved slowly up from the same glass Sandweg was watching, inching its way higher until it fastened on the other man's face. "What about the Trocadéro?" he asked with great care.

Tom shrugged. "Most of Minnie Irish's paintings are stored there."

"So?"

"So this bomb threat hits us rather heavily."

"Bomb th—?" George Brown stopped talking. His glance moved down to his left wrist. He consulted the watch there, pressed a button in its side and stared at the red numbers displayed on its face. "Oh, yeah," he said then.

"What?"

"The bomb threat," Brown said. "I didn't know you stashed Minnie's stuff in there." He flagged a waiter. "One more round." He stared after the waiter's retreating back. "What section?"

"I believe it's Racine-12."

Brown folded his hands together on the table in front of him. "But you're insured for it."

"I don't think you understand, George. The stuff is priceless. If it's destroyed . . . if the rest of the art in the Trocadéro goes up with it . . ." He gestured strangely, shaping a kind of mushroom of disaster. "I don't have to tell you how hard it'd be to keep the wraps on this."

"Rough."

"And, no matter how Minnie hedged, the Collection is part of the estate and the estate controls twenty-eight percent of IBI and there is no amount of insurance money in the world . . ." His voice died away as he was assailed by new thoughts. "Do I have to tell you," Tom went on then, "how chancy and partial any insurance settlement is? Especially if they can claim it was an exempt act of violence. You know their escape hatches."

Brown's head, set so close to his shoulders that his neck was almost invisible, had been nodding for some time now. He continued to nod in the silence that followed, as if he were reciting prayers for the dead.

"I guess I should've known," he said then. "It never occurred to me you kept the stuff in Europe."

"I have nothing to say about it. We have a curator, a real pig-headed bastard named Ferguson." The new drinks arrived and Sandweg sipped his slowly. "If it'd been up to me, George, you know my attitude about

frozen assets. Thaw 'em and sell 'em. Money does nobody any good locked up in a jail like the Trocadéro."

Brown's head kept on bobbing out of sheer momentum. "Racine-12, huh?" he said then, more to himself
than his dinner companion. Suddenly he stopped
nodding and picked up a menu. "What looks good to
you tonight, buddy?"

"A little cyanide soufflé?"

Brown's laugh had a strange ring to it. "Plenty of
time for suicide after you've tried everything else."

The peculiarity of the remark made it lie on the
table between them quite as if Brown had suddenly
spilled a deep, staining wine. He looked vaguely
flustered for an instant. "You know," he amplified
then, "you try a little harder. There are ways of making an insurance company toe the line, Tommy. I
can give you some advice there."

"Insurance?" Sandweg wigwagged a let's-not-rush-
things sentiment. "We haven't reached that point yet,
George. The government's going to raise the ransom
they're asking, you can be sure of that."

Brown's glance was on the open menu in his hands.
He found himself wondering if, after all, it had been
such a good idea. When Groark had come to him at
first and told him about the Arab group that needed
front money for its wild scheme, it had seemed to
George Brown like an easy shot. The investment was
a tiny price to pay for destroying the Principessa's
documents. The Arabs were going to try their luck
anyway, but they didn't mind a little advice and a
little cash from Groark.

"The only thing," he told Tom Sandweg then, in
an oddly reluctant tone, "is can you be sure of the
people who planted the bomb?"

"In what way?"

"Like, you pay the ransom but they blow the stuff
anyway."

Slowly, his glance lifted from the menu to Tom
Sandweg's eyes. He recognized the look on the man's

face now. It made George Brown feel as if he were some kind of hospital intern giving the family bad news.

Bad news seemed to be in the air.

45

Curtis had the feeling he and Louch had died and were making their way in utter darkness, without benefit of a guide, from one ring of outer hell to another.

The Noctron told them very little. It covered an area roughly a meter wide, bathing it in invisible radiation which it made visible as one peered through the eyepiece. By focusing, Curtis could range forward and back along this narrow, yard-wide tunnel of vision, but, God, it consumed time, hours of it.

Hours of it. They crept, step by step up the triangular iron rungs of the spiral stairways that connected the floors, placing each rag-shrouded foot with the kind of terrifying care a surgeon must use for every scalpel stroke.

Both were carrying flashlights and the temptation was great to flick on a light, just for an eye blink of reality, just for the reassurance. But neither did. They had finished Poussin. The fourth floor, Racine, was next.

At each floor, they stood silently in the stairwell and Curtis, first, made a slow sweep of the blackness using the Noctron. Without comment—neither of them had yet spoken a word—he handed the monocular to Louch, first finding his hands in the dark, then pressing the instrument into his fingers, making sure he had a firm grip on it.

Louch then made his own sweep of the floor, moving from side to side with slow precision, racking the lens in and out to focus on things near and far.

They had found nothing.

Perhaps it was the silence, Curtis mused. Perhaps it was the total blackness. But most probably it was lack of communication that gave him the desolate feeling of isolation that the drowning man feels in midocean, the climber feels trapped on a glacier face.

It would do me a world of good, Curtis thought now, if I knew Louch was as lost and frightened and desolate as I am.

There was no way of knowing. They communicated—if one could call it that—by touches. Several times they traced letters in the palm of a hand to spell out a word. Any way they tried, it was unsatisfactory.

Curtis had once—in another life, as part of a biology experiment in college—volunteered for something similar. Dressed in bathing trunks, equipped with goggles and a snorkel, he entered a small indoor pool. All the lights were extinguished. His instructions were to assume a version of the dead man's float, legs dangling downward, face in the water, trunk rising and sinking as air filled and emptied from his lungs.

At first there was the feeling of being a jellyfish, appendages floating. Then there was no feeling. Zero weight. No sound. No light. Only the faint up-and-down of the lungs, only the lisp of water at the edge of the pool.

After an hour, he was lifted out. After some of these sessions he lost the use of his legs for a few moments.

Eventually, he was interviewed, tested, analyzed, given batteries of psychological tests, sketches to draw, Rorschachs to interpret.

The sense of alienation from reality built up over a period of weeks. Finally, he was excused from further experiments. The lab people thanked him. He forgot all about it.

* * *

Except in dreams. And now, again.

They were climbing the spiral stairs once more. Poussin had proved empty of whatever it was they were hoping to find. The great concrete silo of the tower was their amniotic sac. They were floating upward in viscous fluid, like squid, cuttlefish, circling tensely, cut off from reality.

Two steps from the floor level of Racine, they stopped. Louch pressed the Noctron into Curtis's hand. The touch of the cool, leather-bound instrument was a brief instant of reality, but not enough.

What were they hoping to find? Curtis wondered. What did they expect to see through the infrared monocular? To hear? The ticking of a time bomb? But quartz-controlled mechanisms didn't tick.

It was a dream again, a dream of madness. Louch held onto his hand a moment longer and began tracing letters in his palm. E . . . x . . . t . . . r . . . a . . . c . . . a . . . r . . . e.

Wasn't that what the crazies always did, took extra care? With everything. Curtis lifted the Noctron to his eye. Somewhere inside its electronic heart, with its cathode-ray tube and myriad of transistor circuits, it produced a very faint whine, as of a mosquito, faraway and never closing the distance.

Extra care. Because this was Racine, this floor? Because the ransom note had more or less pinpointed Racine? What the hell else had they been taking but extra care? The live thing in his hand, squeezed to his eye, pressed against the bone over the socket of his eye, transmitted its thin noise into his brain.

Racine was laid out in the same pattern as the others. The stairway came up through the center of the round area. Each of the twelve segments, behind their walls of tooled-steel rods, radiated from the center like spokes of a wheel. Somewhere in the 360 degrees around them could be 40 kilos, 88 pounds, of K–7, military strength, enough explosive to—

Curtis stopped. His body froze.

A drop of sweat that had begun at his hairline ran slowly down his forehead and into the eyebrow over his left eye, to which the ocular of the sniperscope was pressed.

He moved the Noctron back half an inch in its circuit. Trying not to tremble, he slowly turned the knurled ring and sent the zoom lens deeper into the darkness, increasing its telescopic power.

He took a breath and held it, as if the instrument through which he was sighting were a rifle. One hand started to shake. He tried to relax the muscles.

He adjusted the finer focus. The direction was 12 o'clock, due north. He was looking at Racine-12.

Just inside the vertical bars were a series of boxlike shapes. He judged them to be about five feet high. They seemed to have rough surfaces.

Crates. He was looking at four wooden crates.

And sitting on one of them . . .

He twisted the zoom control until he had maximum magnification. Then he turned the fine focus by a slight touch.

Sitting on one of the crates . . .

Curtis cleared his throat with a tiny sound.

Beside him he could feel Louch flinch at the noise. He reached out for Louch's shoulder and patted it gently, as if to reassure him.

Then, with the same hand, he reached into his hip pocket and pulled out a flashlight. Using the Noctron as an aiming device, he sighted the flashlight in the direction of Racine-12.

He flicked on the light.

Louch gasped.

The thin illumination was almost blinding, after such darkness. By its light they both saw her turn slightly to face them.

She was wearing skinny jeans and a tank top. Her frizzed yellow hair looked like a traveling cloud. Her eyes, with their big irises, stared into the blackness, lemurlike.

"Leila," Curtis said. "What kind of horseshit is this?"

She stood up on the crate with a dancer's ease, her arms outstretched to either side, hands dangling from her wrists. In the flashlight's beam she struck a pose, head cocked to one side, as if, nailed to a cross, she was drooping elegantly in her deadly passion.

46

It had turned into a strange evening for Netta. Oscar had finally disclosed his estimate of what was stored in the Trocadéro, a figure that had already escaped Netta's mind, and then he had proceeded to finish the whisky. She'd put him to sleep in the big bedroom. The television was on, but no further word had come through about the Trocadéro. She switched off the set at ten o'clock.

Because she'd stopped all telephone calls, except from Curtis, she jumped up eagerly when the bell rang some time later. But it was the door, not the telephone. She opened it and found a young woman with short blond hair looking somewhat too steadily at her.

"Mrs. Irish?" Netta nodded. "I'm Lee James, of UBCO. I work with Mr. Curtis. I know it's late, but this is an emergency. May I come in a moment?"

Netta stepped back and the younger woman entered. She had a purposeful stride, but she stopped short in the entrance foyer under the downward glare of a recessed ceiling spotlight that turned her hair almost platinum in color. Her pretty face, small-featured, broad through the jaw, resembled Curtis's.

"Is this about the Trocadéro business?" Netta asked.

"I have to get in touch with Mr. Ferguson. My New York office is asking for an estimate of what's in jeopardy from this bomb threat."

"No reason why I couldn't—" Netta stopped herself. "How did you get up here?"

"It wasn't easy. They wouldn't telephone you. Then I mentioned Curtis's name and they gave me your room number and said I could pick up the house phone and call you. But I decided it would be faster to—"

"Do you have something to identify yourself?" Netta cut in. She had taken a quick dislike to this brusque creature.

Lee James opened her handbag and brought out her wallet. She went through it for a while, then laid down on the foyer table a business card and her passport. Netta barely glanced at the card. She opened the passport and saw that Leora James had been born barely eight years before Leila. She closed the passport with a snapping sound and dropped it to the table.

The two women eyed each other. "What is it, Miss James?"

"If I could get an estimate of value."

"I'll see."

Netta turned on her heel and walked into the living room. She hadn't invited Lee James in, but the younger woman followed her. Netta bent over the folder Oscar had been fussing with all evening. What gave UBCO the right to know such things, she wondered.

"I'm afraid I don't have it," she said then, straightening up.

"Oh?" The slight upturn in Lee James's voice indicated a willingness to be convinced. Her glance shifted from the folder to the empty Johnnie Walker Red bottle, then up to Netta's face.

"I really don't see that it's UBCO's business anyway."

From the bedroom, faint but unmistakable, came the sound of Oscar's drunken snore.

They were watching each other warily. Netta saw

that the young woman had very little makeup on, other than lipstick. She was beginning to detest her. She felt angry with herself for letting her in.

"Curtis . . ." Lee James let the word die away.

"Yes?"

The younger woman paused and looked to be at a loss for words. "I seem to have gotten off on the wrong foot with you, Mrs. Irish."

"It does seem that way."

"I'm sorry. I should have telephoned."

"Yes."

Lee James turned to go. "Please forgive me. I'll get out of your way." She started for the doorway, then stopped as she got there. "Will it be all right if Curtis touches base with you on this?"

"I'll see." Netta watched her turn to go again. This young woman knew where Curtis was. Worked with him. "Will—?" She stopped for a moment. "Will you be seeing him later?"

Netta hated herself the moment the words were out. She just wasn't functioning well tonight. First letting Lee James in, then blurting out that business about Curtis. She was astute enough to—

"Do you want me to give him a message?" Lee James asked.

"No."

Netta tried to calm herself. All right, she knew something. The fact that Curtis's name at the desk downstairs had been an open-sesame password would have told her Curtis played a special role in Netta's life. Damn her. Meddling little snip.

"Then I'll say good night, Mrs. Irish. I'm sorry I butted in this way."

"That's—" Netta stopped herself again. She'd been about to forgive her. But she couldn't let her leave, could she? She'd offered to take Curtis a message. Why not?

"Miss James," she said, "don't go."

Lee stopped in midstride. She had scooped up her

passport and tucked it into her bag. Now she pivoted to face the older woman. Netta wondered how well she played tennis, this well-coordinated young woman with the absolutely deadpan face.

"What is it, Mrs. Irish?"

"I'm not being very hospitable." Netta produced something she hoped was a smile. "This whole business has upset me more, I suppose, than I realize."

Lee James took two long strides closer to her. "It's a shocker," she agreed. "It's got New York turned on its ear. London, too."

Netta led the way back into the living room. "Can I offer you a drink, Miss James?" She sat down and waved her into another chair.

Again the dark gray, gun-muzzle eyes took in the empty Scotch bottle. "No, thanks. I really am imposing on you, Mrs. Irish."

Netta found it hard to get her thoughts together. She wanted to ask this woman a dozen things about Curtis, about the Trocadéro business. In the silence, Netta could hear again Oscar's heavy snore from the bedroom. If she heard it, too, Lee James didn't react to it.

"I suppose Curtis is at the Trocadéro," Netta said at last.

"They've got it tightly ringed. I was over there to look at it. I couldn't even get close. You'd think they'd planted an A-bomb, the way the area's been cordoned off. I saw them going from house to house, asking people to evacuate."

"That bad?"

"It could be. The shops are all closed for the long weekend anyway, but a lot of the people who live there are moving out. There are some embassies, too. They're staying. They wouldn't even let the police inside the door."

Netta saw that she seemed to have settled in for a nice long chat.

Since she didn't seem the gabby type, Netta reminded herself not to drop her own guard. Lee James "worked" with Curtis? But there was no substitute for the real Curtis. The fact that Netta desperately needed to talk to Curtis didn't mean she could open up to his surrogate.

"So you don't think he's there," Netta said then, unable to keep Curtis out of the conversation.

"I don't know how good his contacts are at the Trocadéro."

"Good," Netta assured her.

Lee James produced her first smile of the evening, not a dazzling one but with a certain warmth. "You know Curtis a lot better than I do," she admitted. "I only got to Paris yesterday."

"But I thought you wor—"

"I do. But he's only been a name on a report until now. Last night at his apartment was the first time I'd set eyes on him."

Netta relaxed in the easy chair and tried to loosen up the muscles that had tightened across her breast and abdomen. So the woman had been in the flat last evening. Netta found herself smiling at the idea of Curtis having to shoo her out before his late date arrived.

"Have you known him long?" Lee James asked.

"A year or so. He's been most helpful." Netta found herself wishing she hadn't let Oscar finish all the whisky. There was something insistent about Lee James, a kind of prodding that Netta felt, rather than actually saw or heard. She was already regretting her invitation to sit down.

"I think he's overworked," the woman was saying.

"Really?"

"He's got a tremendous area to cover."

Netta got to her feet. It had been a mistake to chat with this woman. She knew very little about Curtis. "I'm sorry about the value estimate," Netta said then. "Mr. Ferguson gave me one, but I seem to have misplaced it."

Lee James stood up. "Do you think . . . in the morning . . . ?"

"Most likely."

They stood there eyeing each other again, for all the world like antagonists, Netta thought. It didn't occur to her that, while she disliked the woman because of her brash youth and good looks, Lee James perhaps resented Netta's money and position, none of it earned. Netta never saw herself that way. She felt, at all times and in both marriages, that she had worked quite hard for the money.

"Then I'll be leaving," Lee James said.

"Yes."

The telephone rang. Netta controlled her sudden desire to snatch at it. The call had to be from Curtis. She moved languidly toward the telephone. "Excuse me a moment," she told Lee James. Then, into the phone: "Hello?"

"Netta," Curtis began, "can you come down here?"

"Where's here?"

"The Trocadéro."

"It's awfully late."

"I'll . . . explain when you get here."

"Your Miss James is here," Netta said then.

"Bring her with you."

"Right away."

The line went dead. In the silence, Oscar snored loudly again from the other room.

PART SIX

HOLY
SATURDAY

47

It was midnight when Louch stripped the rags from his feet and hurried back down the spiral staircases to have Hardy switch on the Trocadéro circuits. Curtis stood next to the vertical bars protecting Racine-12. He held the flashlight so that its beam hit the concrete ceiling over his head, bathing the scene in a low-key, indirect light.

"You recognize me?" he asked then.

The girl didn't speak. Her eyes seemed to peer out of cavernous sockets under the mop of wild yellow curls. She had swung around to face Curtis and her bare feet were dangling over the edge of the crate.

"I'm the guy who brought your cash to American Express every month," he went on, trying for a casual tone.

He and Louch had already made a mental inventory of the situation. Three of the crates were unopened. The fourth, the one on which the girl was sitting, seemed to have a false panel in its side, a plank wide enough for a small person, hidden inside, to squeeze through.

Beside her on top of the crate was a battery operated AM-FM radio and a leather-covered detonator box, its plunger handle raised. Wires led from the detonator through the open plank in the crate to what was apparently the 40 kilos of K–7 hidden inside.

"So," Curtis said then, still trying for the light touch. "You are the *appareils spéciaux très sensibles*

mentioned in the ransom note. We'd imagined some
terribly sophisticated sensing equipment."

He couldn't be sure but this seemed to draw a
faintly malicious grin from her. Curtis tried an answering smile. "And are you also the, ah, *mécanisme
de précision à base de quartz?* Or is that asking too
much of a normal ninety-five-pound girl?"

Dangling, her bare toes seemed to curl contentedly,
as if in appreciation of her importance. She dug her
hand into her frizzy hair and scratched for a moment
or two. "You're sitting right on top," Curtis told her.
"The eyes of the world are on you. Or will be, as soon
as we tell them who's planning to destroy this place."

Slowly, she pulled her legs up and under her in a
kind of lotus seat position. Her eyes seemed fixed in
the half-darkness on a point slightly to one side of
Curtis.

"The only drawback," Curtis went on in the same
bantering tone, "is that you're going to have to blow
yourself up with it."

He stood silently for a moment, wondering if he
should abandon the soft touch and start hammering.
Probably better to play Mr. Light. Then Louch could
play Mr. Heavy and they could whipsaw her between
them for a while. She didn't look strong enough to
withstand more than five minutes of really skillful
interrogation.

"Which is the flaw in the scheme," he said then.
"Because you'll never convince anybody that an
attractive, intelligent, rich young woman is going to
say bye-bye to the world and all its pleasures at the
tender age of twenty." He saw her blink and wondered if he had hit something worth digging further
into.

"Nobody will believe it," he continued. "It's the
one thing you didn't count on, Leila: credibility gap."

In the silence of the immense, circular area, with
its walled-off sections and its dimly seen vistas of

wrapped and crated works of art, her voice came with more force than it should have.

"Better believe it," she said then.

One small hand rested lightly on the plunger of the detonator box. Curtis retreated into silence. The standoff was a classic one: he didn't believe her but he couldn't afford to test her. At the same time, if he pressured her far enough to push the plunger, the whole ransom scheme went up in smoke and her accomplices got nothing. Double standoff.

The only way of testing her with any safety lay in ideology. If he could keep her talking, he could at least measure the degree of her commitment. "Are you that concerned about the starving millions of the Third World," he asked her, "so concerned you'd lay down your life for them?"

"What's your name?" she asked.

"Curtis."

"Curtis." She seemed to consider the name as a word, devoid of any other identification but perhaps having secret vibrations. "Curtis," she said, stressing the sibilant. "It's the hiss of a snake."

"The snake that tempted Eve."

"Hissing snake." Her voice had dropped to a murmur. Curtis wondered if she'd been taking drugs.

"The serpent of self-knowledge," he responded.

"Sss."

"The snake that brought your cash every month, regular as clockwork."

"Do I owe you for that?" Her voice sounded cold.

"Not a damned thing."

"Then why mention it?"

"A rich young woman." He let the phrase echo slightly in the dark concrete chamber. "Who will inherit even more, much more than ten million dollars. Such a woman could feed starving millions . . . if she really felt for them."

"Typical liberal pap." Her voice had gone even colder. "Do-good social-democrat Band-Aid on an open chancre, running with pus."

"Oh, Christ," he moaned.

Curtis turned away from her and played the flashlight here and there for a while. "Save me from hackneyed double-talk. I thought the New Left didn't need all that old-fashioned rhetoric." He swung the light beam back until it rested on the detonator plunger.

"What'd you have in mind, Curtis? Soup kitchens?"

He'd hoped to keep her talking ideology, but there were limits to his ability to follow her rapid shifts.

"Is that what I should do with Minton Irish's money?" she demanded.

"It's your mother's money now. Irish is out of the picture."

"That only changes the face on the body. There is an endless supply of greedy faces." She sat quietly for a moment. "Get that thing out of my eyes."

Curtis swung the beam of the flashlight toward the ceiling again. "Your stepfather's greed lies all around you," Curtis said then. "He sank it into preserving our cultural heritage."

"Saving it for himself. And to evade taxes."

"Right," Curtis agreed. "For the rottenest of reasons. But here it all is. Nobody has the right to destroy it."

She jerked a thumb over her shoulder at the packages and cases behind her. "Sometimes, you talk real shit. You read the manifesto. The money to buy this stuff was squeezed out of the poor people drop by drop."

"Oh, it's worse than that." Curtis leaned against the bars. "Think of how the rich first squeezed this art out of the artists. Paid them off in pennies. Kept them in poverty so they'd have to produce. Think of how they've traded up all this art from pennies to the millions it's now worth. If you want to feel concern, Leila, try—"

"Elitist art doesn't interest me."

"What does?"

"Justice," she said.

"Or revenge?" Curtis was watching her closely now. "I had no idea you knew your stepfather well enough to hate him."

"Did you know him?"

"Not at all."

"Then shut up about him."

"Leila, can I ask you something different?" When she said nothing, he went on: "What's going to happen to you if the ransom's paid? I think I understand how this is supposed to work. When it's paid you get a message over that little radio, right? So you don't shove the plunger down. You let us unlock the gate and defuse the charge. Then what? Are we supposed to give you a police escort to the airport, or a dinner at Maxim's?"

"When the ransom's paid I don't expect any special treatment." Her voice seemed to warm up slightly as she talked. "I didn't do anything more criminal than sneak into the Trocadéro. How much time can they give me? A year? Two?"

"Terrorist conspiracy? Try fifteen years."

"No way. We have powerful friends, Curtis."

"I'm aware that strange things happen to Arab terrorists in France, or rather, don't happen. What makes you think they'll treat you as leniently?"

"That's our business."

"You fascinate me, Leila."

"Really?"

"I find you intriguing. This whole setup hangs on your shoulders. One way you go up with a bang. The other way you go to jail. Either way, you take the fall for the rest of them. I know you're smart enough to have figured out you're the patsy. Yet it doesn't seem to bother you."

"Not for a minute."

He watched the cold set of her face, locked into herself and her dream. So far he hadn't opened even a thin seam.

He'd been flattering her intelligence, but it was obvious that he was dealing with a tiny mind. Not dumb, just purposefully restricted to a tiny area of thought. He found himself wondering what could have happened to her in only twenty years to produce such a blindered view of life.

In his experience, those who purposely narrowed their view this way were the hardest to deal with, the last to crack. They had already discounted most of the motivations that had an effect on other people. It was a process of self-hypnosis, with a little help, Curtis was sure, from her friends in the movement.

"You've steeled yourself for the struggle," he said then. "You've become a real robot."

"In this kind of work, it's not a bad way to be."

Curtis propped up the flashlight to shine on the ceiling. He began pacing the floor in front of the wall of bars. "And ten million dollars will buy a lot of continuing struggle," he said then. "It will certainly help you expose the rottenness of the system. It will absolutely allow starving people to take control of their own destinies."

She sat without speaking, still in the lotus seat, like a temple idol, unmoving, eyes fixed on the middle distance.

"But if they don't pay the ransom . . ." Curtis let the thought die away slowly. "You'll simply die. That'll be it. You'll die. Some expensive paintings will die. And the Third World won't be an inch closer to freedom."

"They'll pay."

"Maybe not."

"They'll pay." He thought he heard a faint wobble in her voice. "They always do."

All hell broke loose. Lights went on with a wild flare. Elevators began grinding upward through the walls. Alarm bells went off in crazy sequence. To one side, two doors slid open and Louch appeared with a uniformed police officer behind him.

"Sorry. The alarms are finally registering the fact that there are intruders in the Trocadéro." He came to the bars and stared at the girl as if she were an animal in a zoo. "So that's what it's all about. No sensors. No timer. No fail-safe devices. We are dealing with the Bedouin mentality here, Curtis, the real peasant mind. Just one girl."

"Willing to die."

The heavyset detective, his head bent down, looked through the bars at the label of the crate on which the girl was sitting. "Ah!" he said in a sharp tone. "They're in transit to New York. That is why they remained unopened." He nodded somberly. "Clever, clever, clever." He glanced up at Leila's eyes. "Is she on something?" he asked Curtis, as if the girl couldn't hear.

"I doubt it."

"Then we are in worse shape than I feared. There is nothing to wear off. She is high on ideology." He snatched up the flashlight, switched it off and stood motionless for a second, brooding. *"Merde!"* he snapped, smashing the flashlight down onto the concrete floor. The lens shattered.

Leila smiled.

48

Lying on the garret floor of the Ugandan embassy, Bert had fallen asleep in the early hours of Saturday, before dawn. He rarely dreamed, although he had been told often enough that this only meant he was suppressing his dreams. This time he was alone on a sand beach which extended as far as the eye could see. Passive surf, of the Mediterranean kind, rolled up softly from his right as he walked this alien shore. A hot sun poured over him and turned the white spume of the surf almost blinding. He felt alone in a land not his.

". . . all is darkness where you are," Dris's voice was saying. "But, my beloved, my soul calls to your soul."

Bert came awake and jumped to his feet in a single movement. He lunged across the room and dove past Dris for the microphone cord. With one sharp pull, he yanked the jack out of the FM transmitter.

Then he stood, glowering down at Dris. "How long?"

"Just now."

Bert switched off the transmitter. Crafty Arab thief, stealing the cord from his pocket while he was asleep. Not to be trusted, never again. "How much went over the air?" he demanded harshly.

"Ten words. Twenty."

"Fool."

"They won't notice."

"You think the world is made of fools?" Bert pocketed the microphone and cord. There had to be a way of immobilizing Dris. He felt in the right hand pocket of his jeans, where he kept the tiny Browning .25 automatic, as flat as a wallet. It carried a shell in the chamber and a clip of six in the butt. The gun was inaccurate, except at point-blank range, because it was only four inches long, with a barrel half that length. But if he dared threaten Dris with it, of course, the treacherous Bedouin would be his enemy to the death.

Instead, he'd have to continue to reason with him and try to stay a jump ahead of his flamboyant taste for radioing his girlfriend. "Dris," he told him, "I have explained often enough that they can trace such a signal, have I not?"

Dris shrugged. He had an air of not being bothered by mundane details. "Triangulation."

"You remember triangulation," Bert said in his reasonable tone. "Brother Dris, you remember driving around in the little VW with the loop antenna? How we moved around and around the Trocadéro? Till we located what we wanted on the fourth floor, the one they call Racine?"

"I remember, of course," the handsome young man said on a note of huffiness. "Silly business. Just a kind of whining sound."

"But we found what we were searching for, and very quickly, too."

"I remember clearly," Dris said in a haughty voice. "It was a . . . a folder in a file." He nodded, satisfied with himself. "Someone had put it inside the Trocadéro."

"Someone who didn't know what it was." Bert watched Dris's big brown eyes. The significance of the operation they had carried out—to locate where the K-7 was to be placed—did Dris recognize its meaning now?

"Just as we found the location of what we wanted,"

Bert said, an edge to his otherwise solicitous voice, "so the police can find us if we keep broadcasting."

Dris ran fingers through his thick black hair. "I cannot live that way," he complained. "I am not a technician like you. I am a patriot, a man of action."

"Who will lead the police to us unless he stops going on the air."

"That's nonsense."

Something clicked against the glass of the rear window.

Dris's eyes flared wide, muddy white showing all around the irises. Bert had the Browning in his hand.

It looked more like a toy than a toy gun would, since most of it was trigger guard. It almost disappeared in Bert's hand as he pointed at the rear window. Again the clicking sound, twice, then three times. Bert moved to one side, in case bullets began to pour through the glass.

Instead, Khefte's head appeared in the window, grinning from ear to ear. He motioned for them to unlock the casement. Bert pocketed the tiny gun and let him in. "Khefte, my brother, did they see you?"

The dark young man, still grinning at his exploit, shook his head. "There is a way, over the roofs. One comes in from the Place du Mexico. There is a passageway off the Avenue D'Eylau to the rear of one of the houses there. No *flics* patrol there. There is no barrier."

Bert went to the rear window and stared out of it. "And you came up the roofs on this side, on the Poincaré side?"

"My brother, it was easy," Khefte assured him proudly.

"But it took you this long to find it," Bert kept his voice soft and friendly. "And all this time we waited to hear from you at the lookout post."

"They wouldn't let me stay there. The *flics* swarm like locusts." Khefte's eyes swung in arcs as if gazing at clouds of insects. "*Flics*, soldiers, plainclothesmen . . . we have them jumping like fleas, my brother."

"With luck," Bert told him, "'when the bomb goes off, we can kill a few of them."

"*If* it goes off," Dris remarked in the same haughty voice he had used before. "Remember, when they pay the ransom, all of this ends."

"Really?" Bert grinned at him.

The handsome young man stared hard. "Our arrangement has always been that. We cannot ask Leila to make the ultimate sacrifice if the ransom is paid."

"That," Bert told him, "is one arrangement."

"The only arrangement!" Dris shouted.

Bert said nothing. He only smiled.

49

It wasn't until seven in the morning that Leila finally replied to her mother. Netta's voice, normally hoarse, had reached a point near inaudibility. Curtis had been with her some of the time and Lee James had taken over when Curtis had to leave Racine to confer with Louch in Hardy's office on the ground floor.

There had been one break, and only one, at about five in the morning. The good-looking boyfriend had called Leila on the radio. Curtis had alerted Louch's radio squad, but the transmission had been cut off almost at once. Curtis hadn't learned if they'd gotten a fix on the signal.

In a way, Curtis supposed as he stood outside the cage of iron bars and stared at Leila, it was lucky he was here when the girl decided to speak. He was, at least, something like a friend of the family, at least of Netta's. Lee James had gone downstairs. Only Curtis and Netta were there when Leila finally spoke.

"I never thought I'd ever call a woman a cunt," was the way she broke her dogged silence.

Netta had been sitting in a folding chair. "Baby," she croaked, voice ragged from hours of pleading, "I just want to hear your side of it."

"Since when did you start listening to me?"

Leila's voice was smooth, wide-awake. She had a small bottle of no-sleep tablets, the sort that supply about as much caffeine as a cup of coffee.

The caffeine tablets had given Louch some heart. As he had confided to Curtis: "If she was on something stronger, Benzedrine or another speed capsule, she would eventually begin to suffer delusions of grandeur."

Remembering this, Curtis smiled crookedly. What a thin straw to clutch at. Leila had every right to delusions of grandeur, sitting there with her hand never farther than a few inches from the detonator plunger. From time to time she let her fingers rest on the handle, as now.

"I'm listening," Netta assured her, standing up and holding the bars. "We all are, baby."

"Stop calling me baby."

Netta's head, held erect for so long on her slender neck, seemed to droop now, but with fatigue or despair, Curtis couldn't tell. Outwardly she hadn't changed all that much.

Like her daughter, she had the knack of looking untouched, unmussed by the passage of endless hours of tension. Neither she nor Leila looked any different now than they had around midnight, when Curtis had ushered Netta into Racine. Nor, for that matter, did Leila show any outward sign that she had been nailed into the crate no later than Thursday night and hadn't emerged from it until Friday at about 1:00 P.M.

Probably something hereditary, Curtis decided, something in the bones of the body that kept them looking cool and unscorched through the endless passageways of hell. A thermometer, placed between mother and daughter, would have had a hard time registering normal body heat.

"Leila, tell me what you want."

"Nothing you can give me."

"What haven't I given you over the years?" Netta asked. "Was there anything you wanted that you didn't get?"

Leila dug her fingers in her mop of yellow fuzz and scratched vigorously. "Will you stop that?" Netta snapped.

"What?" Her daughter's voice sounded cool in its utter disbelief.

"It's bad for your scalp. So is whatever you're doing to your hair to make it kink up."

"I don't believe this."

"Baby—" Netta stopped herself. "Leila, I'm sorry. You're right. This is no time to be—" She stopped again. "Look, if there is anything I can do, with whatever money I can raise, that will let you stop all this and walk out of here with me, tell me."

"With your money?"

"You're asking—" Netta stopped. "They," she changed the wording, "are asking for ten million dollars. Leila, walk out of here and I'll give ten million to whatever cause you say."

"That's too gross for words."

"I'm serious."

"No, you're trying to trick me. With what you've done to get that money, throwing it away so easily? It's not to be believed."

"What I've done?" Netta asked in her ragged voice. "Your father earned that money, Leila. And your stepfather."

"And all you had to do was put out for it."

Netta stared at her blankly, then sank back in the folding chair. "Is that how you saw it?"

"Is there another way?" Leila had been squatting in the lotus position for what seemed like hours now. Effortlessly, with the muscles of the very young, she stretched her legs in front of her and wiggled her toes.

"You're a whore," she said then in her chilly, matter-of-fact voice. "Maybe a high-class whore, I wouldn't know."

"Leila!"

"Marriage doesn't make a woman a whore," the young woman went on. "What she does in the marriage makes the difference."

"You really don't know what you're talking about."

"There's damned little I don't know about you," Leila assured her. "Or that kinky second husband. Whatever gave you the idea you could stage those little scenes, the two of you, with nobody in the house knowing what was going on?"

Netta glanced sideways at Curtis with the look of someone who has just waded breast-deep into quicksand.

"I suppose," Leila went on in the same cold-blooded way, "you're going to tell me it wasn't your idea. He made you do it."

Netta shook her head, but said nothing.

"The whore never takes responsibility," Leila said. "She's only a pet animal. She does what she's fed to do." Her eyes, in their hollows, looked only mildly interested, almost as if the words were coming from someone else.

"It's a role nobody has to play anymore," the young woman continued then. "We're going to make certain of that."

Netta groaned as she got to her feet. "How do you intend to do that? What can you buy with ten million dollars?"

"Not much," Leila admitted. "We know that. We know that other things have to be corrected first. By correcting them, we correct things like the games men play with women."

"You don't know," Netta told her. "You have no idea what it was like when your father died. You haven't known a troubled day in your life. Never lacked clothes or shelter or schooling. And now, it seems, you've had too much schooling. Where did these ideas come from?"

Leila gestured easily with the hand that wasn't playing with the detonator plunger. "Not from a teacher. From watching."

"Watching me?"

"Among others."

Netta glanced at Curtis again. "Can you leave us alone for a while?"

He shook his head. "I'm here in lieu of a squad of cops. It's Louch's idea of delicacy."

Netta looked away. "They're afraid I'll upset her, is that it?" She laughed softly, a hoarse, choking sound. "It doesn't matter what she does to me."

"No, it doesn't," Curtis agreed almost cheerfully. "She's holding all the cards."

Leila wiggled her toes one more time, then resumed the lotus seat. She glanced at her wristwatch and popped another caffeine tablet in her mouth. From the thermos bottle standing next to her, she swallowed some water. The angle at which she held the bottle told Curtis it was almost empty.

"Can I bring you some more water?" he asked.

"Fuck off, Curtis." She grinned impishly. "And slip me a Jones? You're as bad as the cops."

"Just doing my bit for the art treasures of Western civilization." He yawned. "Oof. How long do you expect to stay awake, Leila?"

"Even if I doze off, there's no way they could get in without waking me up. So I'd have plenty of time to push the plunger."

"Yes, you would. You're a real Attila the Hun, you are. Does that good-looking boyfriend of yours know how much woman he's got?"

"He knows."

"Enough woman to blow herself up if she has to?"

"He knows."

"Stop that," Netta said. "She's not blowing herself up. If I have to handcuff myself to these bars to stop her."

"That wouldn't stop me."

Curtis gestured at Leila. "She's made of sterner stuff."

"Don't tell me what she's made of!" Netta snapped, her voice rising. "I made her. She's my flesh. And she's not destroying herself. That's final." Her voice had reached the last crags of understandability. Curtis had to strain to make out her words, which seemed to be forcing themselves thinly through narrow slits in vast walls. Each word seemed physically ejected, with a tearing sound.

"I *will* do," Leila said coldly, "what I *have* to do."

"You dumb kid," her mother croaked. "Dumb, spoiled, self-centered little kid." Her voice was giving out completely now.

"Whore." The word came from Leila with a kind of inexorable roundness.

"Stop it!"

"Whore."

"Leila!"

Finally, the young woman's face showed something. Curtis watched her lips move, as if choking back words. Then it all came out. "Get out of here!" she shrieked. Her right hand grasped the detonator plunger. "The first creep who comes back in here, we all go!"

50

La Principessa Claudia Carloni had been waiting a long time for the telephone call. When Nico hadn't called by midnight Friday, she assumed he and the American boy had had an accident on the road. When she heard nothing through the night, she was sure of it.

Thus, when Nico finally called at eight on Saturday morning, the Princess was no longer interested in chastising him. She simply was glad he was alive.

"Where are you?" she demanded.

"I took him to the big Jacques Borel place near De Gaulle Airport," Nico explained.

"And that took all night?"

"He kept falling asleep. He couldn't walk. It was very hard, Signora. And then, I got nervous about the Borel. It's too big. Too many Americans. So we are in the Novotel near Le Bourget."

"Why this passion for airports?" she demanded. "Never mind. You feel at ease in the new place?"

"I checked in here at two A.M., alone," Nico said. "Afterward, I carried him into the room. No one saw us. No one knows I am not alone."

"*Allora, caro,* sit there until I call you."

The Princess hung up and flashed the switchboard at her hotel, the George V. She gave the operator George Brown's telephone number at the apartment where she had met him yesterday. The phone rang just once and was immediately picked up.

"It's Principessa Carloni calling," she began in a high, here's-fun voice. "Any news of your Nicky?"

"Princess, if you called to make conversation, I—"

"Perhaps I can help," she cut in.

"What?"

"The thing I have been asking from you. It is available in Paris, is it not?"

Brown paused for a long moment. "Why don't we just forget that little item for now."

"But I thought you wanted your son."

This time the pause was longer. "Hold it. You're saying you know where Nicky is?"

"First the tape."

"God help you if this is some kind of gag."

"Can you have the tape by tomorrow?"

"Sunday? I don't know. What about Nicky?"

"He's well."

"Don't tell me you put the snatch on the kid?"

"All this is of his own will. He has asked me to be his intermediary. The tape?"

"Tomorrow noon." Brown was silent for a moment. "My place."

The Princess produced a rippling laugh she liked to think of as silvery. "We will meet, you and I," she said. "There is a decent café on the Place du Trocadéro, the Café Malakoff. Let's make it one o'clock."

The silence at Brown's end went on for quite a while now. She had been in bed when Nico's call came. Now she sat up and swung her small legs over the edge, pushing her feet into tiny feathered slippers. "Hello?"

"Yeah." George Brown's rumble had a puzzled quality to it. "Princess," he said then, "I guess you don't watch TV, huh?"

"What?"

"Or read the papers?" Brown jumped back to the original subject. "You sure want that tape bad. You gotta buyer for it?"

"No."

"I have to know who it is, Princess."

"No buyer. I have a lot of incomplete files, *caro*. When I can complete one, it becomes available for sale. I run a business. No one will buy a dossier that's missing key material. If I can complete this file, then it becomes a salable item, not before. Simply business, nothing more."

"It's a business people die from."

"It's a low-risk business for me. Everything I have is available on my death to my lawyers here and in Milan and Switzerland. I shudder to think what would happen in that event."

"Neat."

"Just business."

"And holding Nicky for ransom, that's just business, too?" His voice had gotten louder. "Sometimes, when you use the wrong fork to prod a guy, he don't react the way you'd expect, Princess. Sometimes he gets so angry, he upsets your plans."

"I know people like that," she agreed. "But you are not one of them. One P.M. tomorrow at the Malakoff."

"Not the Malakoff."

"Very well. The Drugstore at the Rond Point on the Champs-Elysées."

"You really like public places, huh?"

"Adore them. *Arrivederci*." She hung up and sat on the edge of the bed, frowning. At the same time her brain conjured with two different problems. One was his reluctance to meet near the Trocadéro which had something to do with something on television. The other was the fact that she simply had to stop frowning or the vertical lines between her eyes would deepen like twin furrows.

She snapped on the television set in her room, but the screen was blank. Then she called for an Italian newspaper to be brought up. In fifteen minutes the bellman brought her a copy of the *Corriere della Sera*, flown in from Milan.

She didn't have to search far to learn why Brown

was reluctant to meet near the Trocadéro. As her eyes
flicked back and forth over the ransom story, taking
in descriptive writing that relied heavily on phrases
like "heritage of civilized man" and "irreplaceable
masterpieces," it began to dawn on her that the bomb,
or whatever it was, had been planted on the floor
called Racine.

The entire hoard of la Principessa Claudia Carloni's
files, the information that made her a rich woman safe
from the violence of revenge or retaliation, was locked
away under a numbered account in Racine-12.

The furrows between her eyes bit deeper as the
Princess finished the story and started reading it all
over again, from the beginning.

51

Louch noted the two plainclothesmen as they entered Hardy's office in the Trocadéro and showed their identification to the officer on guard. He indicated Louch with a thumb gesture. Something in his indifference told Louch what the two men wanted.

They showed no emotion as they asked him to accompany them to Vermeuil's office, first making it clear that Louch was not in custody. He glanced at both of them in turn, trying to gauge what would happen if he refused to come. But there was no reason, at the moment, that he couldn't leave the Trocadéro, at least for a while.

Upstairs, in Racine-12, matters were at a queasy standstill. The girl had ordered everyone out. She sat in solitary splendor.

Louch had called for detailed architect's building plans. He was looking for possible secret passages, ways of sneaking onto Racine—he was open to desperate ideas by this time—and firing a tranquilizer dart into the girl. But none of the building plans were worth much. They dated from 1914 and 1915.

Grunting slightly, he got up from his desk and followed the two plainclothesmen out of the Trocadéro. In the five years Vermeuil had been his superior, Louch had never once been summoned to the ministry office. There had never been a need for it. Vermeuil had never taken that much interest in what Louch did, as long as it went smoothly and without publicity.

Outside the Trocadéro, Louch and the two men got in an unmarked car and sped off along Avenue Kléber.

Vermeuil's office was grand, lacking windows, but huge with a high ceiling decorated with gilded garlands of plaster grape leaves. He was not waiting for Louch behind his mastodon of a desk, with its three telephones and banked rows of buttons and switches. Instead, Vermeuil was leaning over a long side table on which perhaps a dozen newspapers were strewn.

"Wait outside," Vermeuil told the two plainclothes agents.

He watched them close the high double doors behind them. "Have you seen these?" he asked in his high, patrician honk. He flung his skeleton's hand in the direction of the newspapers.

Louch glanced at them. "Some. Not the German ones."

The telephone rang. Vermeuil whirled and stared at it for a moment before picking it up. "No," he said after a moment, "that's not enough. It's less than a quarter of the cash required for ransom."

He listened again. "Damn it," he burst out, his voice going higher with anxiety, "we must tap the Swiss with something harder than a kid glove. These fat little fondue dippers have the cash."

His skull's face swiveled to glare at Louch as he listened. "There are three contingency funds from which the Treasury can allocate—" He stopped. "To hell with that. All the Swiss must do is honor a simple letter of cred—"

"I see." His voice crumbled. "I see. Well, try again." He slammed down the phone and, almost at once, picked it up again. "Get me Charette at the Société Général."

Bony fingers drummed on the tabletop as he waited. His eyes seemed to glow balefully as he stared at Louch without seeing him. "Charette? Vermeuil here.

They tell me the Swiss—" He paused. "I am not panicking. You will simply have to assemble the ransom in other currencies, deutschemarks, guilders, what-have-you. The Swiss can send a courier to Benghazi by Sunday night, carrying Swiss francs. What?"

He was motionless for an instant. Then he crashed the phone into its cradle. "He hung up on me!"

"I am sorry, M. le Ministre."

"Oh? Sorry? What about those newspapers?"

"Sorry for that, too."

Vermeuil picked up a London paper. "Allow me, from the editorial page."

He scanned the paper for a moment then read aloud: "The entire civilized world awaits the outcome of this tragic affair. The eyes of every nation to which Western art is a heritage of almost incalculable value is fixed upon the government of France. And the nations of Western Europe, plagued by terrorist tactics, are wondering how well France will acquit itself in this desperate hour. What accommodations will it consider with these hooligans? What loyalty will it pay to the antiterrorist agreements among E.E.C. countries? And, finally, what precautions will it take to safeguard this precious hoard, the heart and soul of all we hold dear in our common heritage? Our commiseration, our encouragement, our assistance, if asked, all these we offer France in this dark hour. But we offer more: the unblinking vigilance with which we will observe every move the French make. At one and the same time we wish them well, and woe betide any weakening of resolve, any craven compromise, any sign that they do not take their responsibility with the greatest of gravity."

He looked up at Louch. "You fumbler!" he barked.

"I beg your pardon?"

"The girl should have been shot between the eyes the moment she was discovered." Vermeuil's narrow face contorted. "Too late now. That's not why you're here, Louch."

"I should be back at the Trocadéro."

"To continue messing it up?" Vermeuil snarled. "Tell me something. There isn't a journalist within two city blocks of the Trocadéro. And yet in New York, in Rome, in Frankfurt, they know everything that happens. The Amsterdam papers have not only told the world about that horrid little worm of a girl with her hand on the detonator, they've also got her name."

"I don't understand how."

"Don't you? So has Copenhagen. The New York *Daily News* also knows that Leila Darcy is the step-daughter of the man whose paintings are stored there around her forty-kilo bomb. Can you explain how they know that?"

"No, I can't."

"I can."

Vermeuil took a long, shuddering breath of air, meant to calm himself. Instead the quavering intake made him shake harder with repressed rage. "There is only one way the press and television can know these things as soon as we do."

"A leak," Louch said. "I understand. But from whom?"

"That was what I asked myself," Vermeuil assured him. "I thought of Hardy, but he's too cowardly to try such a thing. Besides, Sogegarde pays him well for his discretion and silence. I thought of one of our lower-ranking officers, but few of them know anything they could sell to the press."

Louch saw what was coming. He was prepared to explain to an amateur like Vermeuil how the press worked, the fact that it could monitor the police radio as well as anyone else, cadge meaningless bits of information from cops on the corner and put everything together like a jigsaw puzzle. But he wasn't prepared for the force with which Vermeuil delivered the blow.

"Then," his superior shouted, "I thought of the one man who combines access to information with a motive for selling it. You, you *swine!*"

His bony hand flailed out at Louch's face, trying to deliver an insulting backhand slap. Louch's face went dead as Vermeuil's hand missed him by millimeters. His slightly bulbous eyes hooded. "Be careful, M. le Ministre," he said in a grave voice.

"I would sack you this instant, but I want you as scapegoat for the entire fiasco." Vermeuil's face looked as gray as cigar ash. "The moment it comes to a conclusion, you will be thrown to the wolves, Louch. None of us will protect you."

"We'll see."

"No way out!" Vermeuil screamed in his face.

"We'll see."

"Dirty, conniving Judas. You've been selling the story over the counter like a butcher sells tripe." Spittle was fizzing through Vermeuil's thin lips. He picked up a German newspaper and waved it in Louch's face. The headline was bold with black ink. Louch's German wasn't that good, but the headline seemed to pose a question: WILL THE FRENCH SELL OUT TO THE ARABS AGAIN?

Louch turned and started for the door. "You're not dismissed yet, Louch."

The heavyset man kept on going. At the double door he opened both, which had the effect of silencing Vermeuil. Then he turned in the doorway and nodded gravely. "M. le Ministre," Louch said.

He left his superior, shaking with the effort of repressing his voice. Louch's footfalls echoed along the corridor. He passed the two plainclothes agents who eyed him but let him pass. Outside, in the courtyard where police and civilian cars were parked, Louch surveyed the place. Thirty years of this dirty work. Thirty years.

He didn't want to owe Vermeuil anything, not even

a ride back to the Trocadéro. Nor the police, for that matter. He would find a cab.

Moving slowly, with the caution of a man who had just been shot somewhere in the abdominal region, Louch began walking.

PART SEVEN

EASTER SUNDAY

52

Glancing at her watch, Lee James saw that it was now 5:00 A.M., which made it Easter Sunday. But nothing she knew had less of a holiday air about it than the operations center Louch had set up in Hardy's office. A uniformed police officer sat by the door, trying to stay awake. Louch himself, sprawled across his desk as if dropped from a great height, was asleep. Curtis and Netta Irish stood at the window that faced out on the Avenue Kléber. They hadn't spoken in some time.

Louch had wanted to assign a policewoman the job of keeping track of the tall brunette. But Curtis had suggested that a countrywoman of Mrs. Irish's would be a more soothing companion. The job had been given to Lee James.

Watching the sleeping Louch, Lee could imagine his reluctance to allow her in here. But he needed Mrs. Irish in one piece, emotionally speaking, until he could decide what to do with her.

Up above, on Racine, the young woman with the fuzzy hair still demanded to be left alone. Lee James had been watching her on a closed-circuit television Louch had managed to activate without Leila's knowledge.

Leila's behavior bothered Lee James. Not the obvious part of it, playing games of revenge and destruction. It was the ease with which Leila fitted into her role that bothered Lee.

One thing Lee James remembered from the time when she was twenty years old was a tremendous impatience. It seemed to her that she was always waiting for something to happen, and finding the hours and days unbearable. When she'd been twenty, time crawled.

But not for Leila Darcy. With the amount of caffeine she was popping, she should now be climbing walls. Nobody her age could be expected to sit tight this long and yet, there she was, motionless for hours, then stretching a bit. Once in a while she would stand up and stretch her arms. That was it.

"I don't know," Netta Irish murmured.

Lee James watched her out of the corner of her eyes, not wanting to seem to eavesdrop. ". . . got to be found," Curtis was saying in an undertone.

"I just don't know. He passed out in my suite at the Ritz. That was the last I saw of him." Curtis muttered something. "Friday night," Netta Irish replied. "He could be anywhere now."

" . . . need him for further verification of . . ."

". . . folder he left in the suite . . ."

"Is it an inventory?" Curtis asked with sudden clarity.

"I don't know."

Louch shivered and came awake. *"Qu'est-ce que c'est?"*

Curtis looked over at him. "Sorry. Go back to sleep."

Louch straightened up and glanced at his watch. He turned to the officer at the door. "No calls?"

The man shook his head. Louch grunted as he pulled himself up on his feet. "We are in isolation," he said, to no one in particular. "It's as if the world has washed its hands of us. That accursed scarecrow of a political bastard."

"What?" Curtis asked.

"Nothing."

Louch stretched and yawned. He stared at the television monitor and saw the tiny figure of Leila Darcy, squatting in the lotus position. "Miserable creature," he mumbled. "Deliver me from true believers." He turned to look at Lee James. "Except for you, of course."

She watched him for a long moment before replying. "Is that supposed to be insulting?"

"Of course. *Regardez-là!*" Louch pointed at the television screen.

Everyone watched as Leila slowly rose to her feet and stretched her arms out, head dangling on her neck.

"The Little Jesus of the Trocadéro," Louch muttered.

"That will be the next phase of it," Curtis predicted. "As soon as the Third World people get their operation rolling, we'll be accused of martyring this little lady. Her lonely passion will be likened to—"

"Not by Moslems," Louch interrupted. He yawned again and rubbed his face vigorously. "She is the martyr," he said, rolling the r's deep in his throat for dramatic emphasis. "But it is I who am being crucified."

"*Pauvre petit,*" Curtis mocked him.

"No, in truth after all these years, nailed to the cross and left to dry in the wind."

"By Vermeuil?"

"By who else?" Louch made a throwing-away gesture with his hands, as if disposing of garbage. "Enough."

"I'm sorry." Curtis thought for a moment. "You've been in long enough to retire. Won't he—?"

"No. The sack." Louch gave him a hurt look. "Do I really look like a man ready to retire?"

"N-no."

Louch slapped the slight bulge of flab about his belt. "I had hoped to be a *flic* for another fifteen years. Never mind." He saw that Lee James was staring at him. "Yes," he told her, "old enough to be your father. Old enough to avoid getting caught in traps like this Trocadéro business. Old enough, but not wise enough."

"That's not what I was staring at," she told him.

"I thought it was the picture before you of an aging civil servant thrown to the political wolves. Enough to wring a tear even from your cool, cool eye, Miss James."

She frowned in annoyance. "I was looking at those drawings on your desk. Architect's plans for this building?"

"Yes." Louch stepped away from the desk. "Look at them to your heart's content." He walked to the window and stood with Netta and Curtis.

"I'm going after Ferguson," Curtis said then. "We still don't really know what there is upstairs."

"I'll go with you," Netta suggested. "If he left that folder in my suite . . ." She stopped and glanced up at the television screen. "I won't be long," she said, as if to the electronic image of her daughter. "I'd like to bathe and change. Do—" She stopped. "D-do you think," she fumbled, "I ought to bring back a change of clothing for Leila?"

Louch cocked his head to look at her. "Surely you don't wear the same size?"

"I could stop at a boutique somewhere and—"

"On Easter Sunday, madame?"

Netta passed the back of her hand across her eyes. "I . . . forgot."

"But you won't be gone long?" Louch cautioned her. "If we need you, I want to know you're here."

"Certainly."

"You, too, Curtis."

"We'll be back in an hour or so."

"*Au revoir*, then."

"*Au revoir*."

Lee James noticed that Curtis had hold of Mrs. Irish's elbow, as if to guide her on their way out. It could have been simple courtesy. It could have been something else. She saw that Louch had noticed it, too, and she was prepared to talk him out of any suspicions he might have. But she didn't get the chance to defend UBCO's honor. The heavyset Frenchman said nothing at all. He simply turned and stared out the window at the Avenue Kléber, lying in darkness beyond the alarm-wired plate glass.

"M. Louch," Lee James said at length.

"*Dites-moi.*"

"There seem to be two sets of plans."

His back remained turned to her. "Yes, I managed to locate a second set. The first was circa 1914. It was of no use. On the second set someone has at least penciled in the various wiring ducts and conduits for alarm systems."

"Is that what these are?" she asked, pointing to some vertical channels drawn on the side elevation cutaway view of the tower itself.

He turned slowly and came over to the desk, moving as if he hurt inside. "Those." He thought for a while. "Those are air-conditioning ducts. That is, they don't deliver cold air but exhaust used air. There exists an automatic system for using these ducts to flood the tower with a gas that suffocates an intruder."

"Poison?"

"Not really. A nitrogen-carbon-dioxide mixture. It replaces the oxygen."

She nodded. "Is this the place where they keep it, these little sketched cylinders?"

"I believe so. Hardy would be more positive." Louch's bulbous nose twitched. "If Hardy were here. But, you see, only Louch has been left out for the buzzards to peck at. Even Hardy is smart enough to stay away from here."

Her dark gray eyes lifted slowly from the plans to his face. He felt as he had before, facing those twin gun muzzles, that some natural force of nature was held in tight leash behind such eyes.

"This is going to sound insulting," she said then, "but I have to ask you: are you really interested in getting that girl out of there and disconnecting the K-7 from the detonator?"

"I have been insulted by experts, Miss James. You hardly sting." Louch produced a tremendous frowning glare. "What in the hell kind of question is that?"

"Because there's a way of doing it."

"What way?"

"I have to know we're on the same side. As far as I'm concerned," she said with the kind of offhand voice that Leila Darcy used, "you're some kind of left-wing agent."

Louch's mouth opened. The bar of color across his cheekbones went bright red. But he managed to close his mouth and even smile, although tightly. "Let me understand you, then," he began in a reasonable voice. "As an agent of international communism, I want those pictures blown up?"

"Yes. No. It's a lot more devious than that. These Third World terror groups are all Marxist-oriented. You might be unhappy about those pictures being in danger, but you want the ransom paid. That way, your friends get their money and you keep the pictures intact."

"Clever of me," Louch muttered.

"My way, we can keep the money and the pictures."

"Clever of you," he said. "Enough of this, Miss James. Speak your piece or shut up about it."

"These ducts."

"You want to release the gas and suffocate the girl? I thought of that."

"Did you?" Lee James asked. "Then why didn't you try it?"

"With her mother standing here?" Louch's long, heavy finger tapped the sketch of gas canisters. "By Sunday night, if nothing else works, I am prepared to kill the girl. The only problem is that this affair has already produced endless reams of unfavorable publicity for France. Killing the girl would give our enemies even more to talk about."

"But save the art, and the ransom money."

"Always the practical American, eh, Miss James?"

"Have you heard of G/S gas, Gamma/Sopor?"

He thought for a moment. "You were using it in Vietnam, as I recall. If you didn't know to which side a village owed its loyalty, you would shell it or bomb it with this stuff. But it was called something else. The GIs called it . . . ah . . . 'sleepytime gas'? Something like that."

"Fast-acting soporific. No residual effect. Wears off in a few hours."

"Sleepytime gas," Louch said. "Through the ducts to Racine-12. Yes. But there isn't a canister of G/S in all of Paris."

"Where's the nearest U.S. Army detachment?"

Louch's bulging eyes stared at her. Then his heavy lids came halfway down as if, in a poker game, he had just been dealt his fourth ace.

"Miss James, whatever I said about you, or thought about you . . ."

"Yes?"

"I now take back." He grabbed her hand. "Let's go."

53

The night clerk at the Ritz handed Netta her messages. There were three from Tom Sandweg and a letter from New York. Nothing from Oscar Ferguson. Curtis escorted her to her suite.

She stood in the door of the big bedroom and looked around. "He passed out on this bed, snoring. Your Miss James was in the other room. Then you called me to the Trocadéro. It seems like a week ago."

"And the folder?"

She turned and went back in the living room. "This is it," she said, lifting it from a pile of magazines where the maid had neatened things. She watched Curtis leaf through it. "I'm going to bathe. It won't take long."

The folder held slips of paper with penciled memoranda, printed forms bearing the carbon copy of receipts, several telegrams and letters of transmittal. As he leafed through the collection, Curtis could hear the shower running in the other room.

After a while he was able to recognize Oscar Ferguson's slanted, angular handwriting, a series of leaning peaks like the edge of a ripsaw blade. It was in this handwriting, finally, that a list had been drawn up with dollar figures added to it.

Curtis sat down and recopied the list in neat printing. It began with names like Cranach, Holbein, Hals, Tintoretto, and a group of French and English artists. By the time it got down to Impressionists, the dollar amount on the right-hand side had exceeded eighty million. When Curtis turned over the sheet and began wading through moderns like Braque and Miró, the right-hand column had soared up over two hundred million. At which point Netta came to the door.

She held a bath towel to her face in such a way that she failed to cover the rest of her. "Curtis?"

"I know. You want me to dry your back."

She managed a smile. Her face, without makeup, looked wan in the oddly dark way of people whose normal complexion is faintly olive. There were slight circles under her eyes. Otherwise, Curtis noted, she seemed untouched. The idea of touching her crossed his mind. They really owed it to Louch to get back as soon as they could. But, still . . .

He got to his feet and took the towel from her. Then he moved around behind her and slowly patted her back dry. He rubbed the towel over her creamy buttocks. My God, he thought as he sank to his knees, men really are animals.

But as he kissed her, she took a step away from him. "I wonder," she asked him, "how on earth I managed to raise a puritan daughter."

"Is that bothering you?" Curtis sat back on his haunches and watched her move slowly out of his reach. "Those were just words to hurt you."

"They did."

She had draped herself in the towel and was staring at him, as if he were something dangerous, about to spring forward and attack her. "But she has it dead right," Netta said then. "My relations with men."

Curtis shook his head. "You don't remember what Oscar Wilde said?"

"I probably never knew." She smiled in a haunted way. "I'm really quite ignorant, Curtis."

"Something . . . something . . . 'children start by loving their parents,'" he quoted. "'After a while they judge them. Rarely, if ever, do they forgive them.'"

"I didn't hate my parents."

"Leila doesn't hate you."

She thought for a moment. "I do hate my parents." She had begun to redry her breasts again, slowly, not seeming to notice what she was doing. "They didn't—" She stopped. "No, they did. They trained me for only one thing. There was no fall-back position. I was pretty and so it was all decided. I was trained to marry well."

Curtis got to his feet and went back to the coffee table where the folder lay. "There are lots of fall-back positions for that. Junior League, church work, pet charities, travel, all those ladies who subsidize theater and ballet and the arts."

"Yes, I'm one of those." She laughed softly. "Unskilled labor. Excess energy. Oh, and don't forget child-rearing. Another position of safe retreat."

"With unforeseen results." Curtis lifted the telephone message slips. "I'm wondering," he said, "can you do me a favor? Call the telephone operator? Oscar may have made some outgoing calls and there'd be a record of them."

She nodded, her great eyes searching his face for a moment. "You're really not all that interested in the plight of one rich bitch, are you?"

"Netta."

"Oh, forget it," she said. "I'm not fishing for pretty speeches."

She picked up the telephone and asked for the operator. "Madame Irish here," she began briskly. "As you know, I've been out of the suite overnight. But M. Ferguson was here, at least yesterday morning. Do you have a record of the telephone calls he charged to my account?"

She watched Curtis for a long moment of silence. "One moment," she told the operator. Then, to Curtis: "Take these down, will you?" She waited for him to find a pencil. "Yes, go ahead, operator."

There were four telephone calls in all, two to New York numbers, one to Teheran and one in Paris. "Oh, really?" Netta said at last, after Curtis had written down the numbers. "Thank you." She hung up. "The Paris number is for Air France reservations, the operator says." They eyed each other rather bleakly.

"Oscar," Curtis said, "has split. I'll give all this to Louch. Let him develop a flight and a departure time. And find out who belongs to these New York and Teheran numbers."

"Oscar? To leave in the middle of all this?" She pulled the towel more tightly over her as if warding off a chill. "Curtis, is everybody around me going crazy?"

"Just Oscar, maybe. And Leila."

"Did I do something to deserve this? You heard the things that girl called me." She thought for a moment. "Such hatred."

"Not hatred."

"What would you call it, then?"

Outside the long row of windows overlooking the Place Vendôme, a motorcycle with a faulty muffler roared past. Curtis sorted through his feelings and decided it was plain-speaking time. "Clear vision?" he suggested. "Lucid thinking?"

The moment he said it, her face fell. Her huge, dark eyes began to mist over. Why were these great beauties so damned easy to insult? he wondered. Did their egos have no armor at all?

"That's what you think of me?" Netta asked in a thin voice. "What she thinks?"

"She has the same perception of you that you have of yourself."

"I?"

"You told me Minton Irish gave you a hard time. He set up scenes in which you gave him one. That sort of thing doesn't go unnoticed by a young girl, sneaking around corners."

"You both see me the same way," she insisted. "A fuck machine. You wind me up and I act out your fantasy for you like any competent whore."

Curtis nodded. "There's a lot of that. Beautiful women play that role, even with men they've never met. Men who've seen them across a room or in a movie."

"That doesn't explain why my daughter—"

"Yes, it does. She sees you reflected in men's eyes. She's old enough to envy you for the way men perceive you. She is never going to be a long-stemmed, dark-tressed American Beauty rose, that little girl. She is always going to be a teeny-tiny cutie pie. Men are not going to torture themselves because of her. She is never going to excite their dark, animal fantasies. And, by now, she knows it."

Suddenly, Netta collapsed on the sofa in a huddle of bath towel. She covered her face with her hands. From between her fingers a kind of painful mewing sound strained through. Curtis came over and put his arms around her.

"That's why Leila has latched onto more cosmic things," he told her. "She has moved far beyond individuals. She's into nations and peoples."

"And . . ." Her voice wavered badly. "And suicide," she sobbed.

Over her head, where the gesture went unnoticed by Netta, Curtis nodded once. Leila was one of Louch's true believers; she would kill for it, even kill herself. Instead, he only patted Netta's shoulder and said:

"I'm sure it won't come to that."

"Are you?" Her voice was small, wanting reassurance.

"I'm sure," he lied again.

". . . the moon of my life, as I am your sun," Dris was saying softly into the microphone. He was crooning it so gently that Khefte, who was dozing, failed to hear him.

Bert had gone out the rear window of the garret at Number 13 to check the route by which Khefte had reached them without being spotted by police. It would do well as a possible escape route, should one be needed. The moment Bert eased himself out onto the slates, Dris found a microphone and patched it into the FM transmitter.

". . . courage above all else," he was saying. "The courage to maintain total vigilance against—"

The sound was small, too small to alert Khefte. It was the noise the edge of Bert's hand made as it chopped into Dris's neck below his left ear. The handsome young man went down onto the floor in a tangle of arms and legs. Bert switched off the transmitter and stood over the prone body, eyeing it with a mixture of disappointment and concern.

Khefte came awake at the sound of the body hitting the floor. "What?"

"Dris. Broadcasting again. The second time."

"Is that bad, my brother?" Khefte asked. He didn't pretend to know about the mysteries of radio.

"Very bad. Do you have cord?"

Khefte nodded. "I will fix him the way I fixed the American."

Bert looked doubtful. "We don't have an extra chair."

"Not that way," Khefte went on eagerly; "I returned and tied him up again, the American in the skiing jacket." Quickly, eyes flashing, Khefte pantomimed a tight cord around his neck, running to his ankles. "He is dead, my brother," he concluded.

Bert sighed so softly he was sure Khefte hadn't heard him. They really gave him such untested material to work with in these groups. A potential leader like Dris who couldn't keep radio silence because he was in love and a bloodthirsty desert tribesman like Khefte who had now made quite sure that if they were caught, they would be in serious, nonpolitical trouble.

This would be the kind of trouble the police were not programmed to ignore. Nor could such a murder be excused as a political execution. Who knew who the American had been? Their situation here had been risky enough, but with certain safeguards. Now Khefte had moved them a significant step in a direction where no amount of protection would work.

Bert kept all of these thoughts off his rather flat, pale face, knowing how sensitive to such things a Bedouin like Khefte would be.

Granted, Bert told himself with a sternness steeled in many battles, we are front-line troops. We are expendable forces, prepared to die. To us the risk. To us the glory.

But when they put together a team of such undisciplined people, they were saying, in effect: "Since they're going to die anyway, why waste the best material?"

It angered Bert because he knew he was the best. He had proved it so often it no longer needed saying. Dris was designated group leader for political reasons, to front for the pan-Arab forces that had bribed Uganda into letting the embassy be used. But it was

Bert who put the mission together, the money, the equipment, the plan itself.

He took the cord from Khefte now and knotted Dris's wrists behind him, then his ankles, bending him back slightly to link wrists and ankles and keep him from being able to hobble around the room.

Nobody realized the kind of logistics that went into such an affair, certainly not Dris or blood-simple warriors like Khefte. Nobody knew, for example, how to finance such an affair.

These days, any blow struck for the freedom of oppressed peoples was costly. When he'd been a teenager disrupting movements of coal trains through the Ruhr, missions were simpler. Everything cost less: radio equipment, explosives, even a hotel for a night or a plain meal at the workingman's *lokal*.

But an affair like this one, in an expensive city like Paris, with months of effort emplacing themselves and working out schedules, was far too expensive for a simple liberation movement to finance.

"Khefte, my brother, a handkerchief, please?"

Khefte's headshake was scornful. "I don't have one."

Bert glanced around, then went into his electrician's toolbox and removed a roll of black tape. He sealed Dris's mouth with three long bands of the stuff.

Even this kit of tools and supplies, minimal stuff, had cost him a hundred francs. It would be abandoned when they left, so the cost of it could not be amortized over other missions. But everything else! The motorcycle rental for the Kawasaki. The rental of the Renault van. Of the garret where the dead American now lay, with three months' worth of rent paid on it. Even the two storage batteries, each of them as expensive as the tool kit. Thousands of francs going out week after week. And where was he supposed to get the money?

Dris had, it was true, found Leila for them. Her money helped with the daily living expenses. But she'd proved a mixed blessing, since she'd been the cause, as Bert saw it, of Dris's lovesick irresponsibility. A costly alliance.

It was just assumed, by people inside the movement as well as the reactionary newspapers and magazines on the outside, that here was a well-padded war chest from which disbursements were made on demand.

Bert smiled grimly. Moscow gold. Libyan dinars. But the facts were otherwise: like true behind-the-lines guerrillas, they were trained to live off the land on funds they had stolen or schemed or lied or cheated to secure. The dynamics of coalition encouraged this approach. Solidarity demanded it.

So, in addition to the rest of the work, it was up to Bert to develop "sponsors," sources of cash, people or interests who could be trusted because their requirements paralleled Bert's.

It didn't matter who these sponsors were or what promises he made to get their money. Only the money mattered.

This was one reason he no longer answered to the established Left. This and a growing conviction among the revolutionary cadres that the parliamentary Left, whatever it called itself in Russia or France or Italy, was a sellout. Berlinguer, in Italy, with his wife and children who went to church every Sunday in a chauffeur-driven car provided by the party. What sort of street leader would he be? Or George Marchais, with his natty white turtlenecks and upper-class hunting jackets. Did he present a model of unrelenting class struggle? Or just another sellout to bourgeois culture?

Bert's glance was still locked on Dris's prostrate body, curled slightly like a slaughtered sheep, gutted and skinned but still bearing the kink of life.

The fat-cat established Left would be the first to mislead the people, Bert told himself. Give a strutting actor like Dris a little power and he would make endless accommodations to keep it. Give Khefte and his clan a guarantee of food and the right to slaughter their enemies, to bugger their little soft-assed boys and gobble their sheep's eyes and sweets of sickening honey and sesame, to listen to the quibbling, quarter-tone whining of flutes and voices while a female shoved her pelvis this way and that . . . give Khefte all this and what inside-out betrayals would he not stage?

Dris was coming to. He whimpered for a moment with pain, then realized he was bound hand and foot. His big eyes opened slowly, already aware of what had happened. His big jaw worked from side to side against the electrical tape across his mouth, but it held firm.

Bert sidled to the window that looked out over Avenue Poincaré. "Khefte," he called softly. "See, oh, my brother, what the lovesick madness of Dris has brought?"

The dark-faced young man joined him at the window as a police truck, with a loop antenna on its roof, rolled past, the antenna rotating in a slow circle. "What is this?"

"Radio locater truck," Bert said. "We can only hope I stopped him before he betrayed our position."

"But all is lost," Khefte said.

"Perhaps not." Bert left the window for a small closet in one corner of the room. "Bring to me the extra battery," he called to Khefte.

The dark young man hefted the standby storage battery under the table and carried it to the closet. Bert had unlocked the closet door to disclose a transmitter unlike the FM one or the other used for CB broadcasts. This was an obviously military piece of equipment, small, ugly, with a minimum of dials and meters, its metal body painted olive drab in baked-on crackle enamel.

Bert picked up the digital clock that had been sitting next to the television receiver. He fastened two wires to the back of the clock and ran them to the transmitter. Then he attached leads from the transmitter to the twelve-volt auto battery. He checked the face of the digital clock against his wristwatch.

"Half-past two," he mused aloud. "In less than twenty-four hours, they will pay the ransom into the post office at Benghazi, my brother."

Khefte's grin was broad with pride. "It will be," he intoned.

Bert peered at the alarm setting on the electric clock. "Too soon," he muttered. "I can only connect it after midnight. If this mooncalf has not betrayed our position in nine and a half hours, we can set this clock for twelve noon and leave by the rooftops."

"My own escape route." Khefte's smile grew wider.

"Leaving Dris to face them."

Khefte burst into a loud giggle. "We will be miles away by twelve noon tomorrow."

"Miles and miles, my brother," Bert assured him.

"And they will have Dris to play with." Khefte kicked Dris in the leg, not hard, but with a kind of mindless contempt, as if kicking a ball of dust out of his path. "And the girl?"

Bert's face was as solemn as Khefte's was distorted with glee. "The girl, oh, my brother," he intoned, "will pay the supreme price for freedom."

Trussed, Dris managed to kick sideways in a spasm that uttered more of a protest than words alone could have managed. Bert glanced somberly down at him. "You think that unfair, Dris?"

Khefte brought back his foot and gave the prostrate young man a sharp kick in the ribs that left him unable to breathe for a moment.

"Such was not our understanding?" Bert went on, interrogating the speechless one. "But Khefte and I have a different understanding."

"The moment the ransom is paid," Khefte said, his voice bubbling up in a fount of pure joy, "everything ascends to heaven in a great cloud of smoke."

"The girl included," Bert added in a grave voice. "She has served her purpose well. The police are spending every moment trying to get her to relent. We have focused all their attention on the bait, not the trap. What will they not promise her? What bribes will they not lay before her? What threats and cajolery?"

Khefte's laughter sprayed spittle over Dris. "A joke of great richness, my brother," he said.

"Of rich complexity," Bert corrected him. "But never a joke."

"No," Khefte reversed himself at once.

"In the service of mankind," Bert told him solemnly, "there are no jokes."

55

La Principessa Claudia Carloni badly missed the dark, chocolate-colored Mercedes 600 and the comforting presence of Nico. But this Sunday he was better occupied keeping the Brown boy quiet in a place where the boy's father wouldn't find him.

The father arrived promptly at 1:00 P.M. From her seat on a bench amid the curved plot of grass that surrounded the Rond Point, the Princess watched a black limousine deposit George Brown at the entrance to Le Drugstore. The narrow-faced man with the squinty eyes, whom she knew as Mr. Groark, remained in the back seat of the car as it drove away up the Avenue Matignon.

Behind her immense sunglasses, the Princess's eyes squinted slightly to follow the progress of the limousine. It stopped at the next corner and Groark leaped out onto the sidewalk. Then the car sped away along the Rue Ponthieu. Groark disappeared in the same direction, walking.

The Princess supposed that Groark would double back to the Rond Point via the Rue Jean Mermoz, to be available if George Brown needed help with one small, defenseless woman. Her mouth set in a firm, thin line as she got to her feet and crossed the Rond Point to Le Drugstore.

Things were moving too fast. This business at the Trocadéro had been a real blow. Her only hope of keeping such powerful monsters as George Brown at bay was the cache of secrets she kept in Racine-12.

And yet there was nothing she could do to protect her hoard, not even complain to the police. All she could hope was that rich owners of art stored in the Trocadéro would pressure the government to pay the ransom.

But Brown would know nothing of this, she reflected as she stepped inside the chrome-and-glass interior of Le Drugstore, with its sections for food, periodicals, gifts, cosmetics and even, in one corner, drugs. Brown would have no idea her treasure chest of valuable documents lay within a few yards of where an insane little girl sat with her hand on a detonator.

The Princess's command of English was good, but she was still wondering about the headline in a London tabloid that had referred to the girl as an "heiroist." Sometimes the English brand of humor escaped her entirely.

"Over here, Princess."

The stocky man was wearing sunglasses easily as impenetrable as hers. He had gotten up from a table by the window and was holding a chair for her. She sat down with her back to the pale sunlight streaming in through the glass, leaving him to stare into it. Obviously he wanted to be able to spot Groark, if necessary.

"You're looking great," he told her.

"*Forse*. And you, dear man? How do you look?" She gave him a fetching smile. "Do you look like a man who is carrying a cassette with him?"

Even before she had finished speaking, Brown's hands were out in front of him, palms toward her, wigwagging from side to side, an all-points negative. "Princess, you gotta know better'n that."

"I know a man could have left New York last night and brought it to you this morning."

"A man could," he assured her. "A man did. But this man," carefully he bunched together the fingers of his right hand and tapped himself slowly in the area of his heart, "is not carrying such an item on him."

"Then the mean-eyed one, Signore Groark, he has it?"

"Huh?"

"The one who is hanging around outside now, waiting for a signal?"

George Brown threw back his head on his thick neck and laughed happily. "Oh, baby, are you good." Still smiling, he snapped his fingers for a waitress. "What'll it be, Princess?"

"*Café noir, s'il vous plaît.*"

"Make it two," Brown said in the automatic tone of a man who isn't quite sure what he's ordered and doesn't care.

"Lemme ask you something, Princess," George Brown began then in the same affable tone with which he had complimented her before. "Here you sit, a small bundle of nothing, trying to hold a gun to my head by keeping Nicky under wraps, and are you worried? Do you have a care in the world? You gotta excuse me, Princess, but that . . . is balls."

"Not so, *caro*. I am the most feminine of women. A man who has my heart can twist me around like a feather boa." She waited while the black coffee was delivered to the table. Then: "But I am also a very secure woman. As you know. My business inventory is also my life insurance policy."

She tasted the bitter coffee and wrinkled her nose. Nobody understood coffee. They could use the same *macchinetta* as the Italians, the same brand of coffee, everything the same, but it wasn't a decent drink unless it was made in Italy by Italians.

Brown had already drained half his coffee in one gulp. "I admire your confidence, Princess," he said then. "You must have the stuff stashed in Fort Knox."

"It is in a safe place."

He spent a lot longer sipping the second half of his coffee. To the Princess, experienced in reading faces,

George Brown showed very little. Just as she had trained herself to read such signs, he had trained himself to avoid giving any signals. It was a case, she thought bitterly, of having an X-ray machine, but being faced by a wall of lead.

The next step was his, she warned herself. If she pushed him now, he would turn ugly. Besides, pushing too hard would be a confession of positional weakness. No, the next move had to come from Brown. She had to sit there like a small Gibraltar, serene in her security, as if nothing on earth was threatening her cache of secrets in the Trocadéro.

A minute passed. Two. The Princess had reason to understand, to the depths of her soul, how long a minute could be. But she was determined not to break the silence first.

Finally George Brown sighed, a thick, rheumy sound filled with chest rumbles. "It's a damned shame," he said then.

"Pardon?"

"You heard me." He pushed his sunglasses up onto his forehead and his small eyes narrowed against the light as he stared at her. "You're a handsome woman, Princess," he said then, "and you got about an hour to live."

Around them, the few Easter holiday tourists at nearby tables continued their conversations as if nothing had happened. A waitress passed nearby, retreated. Beyond Brown's heavyset face, a tall woman bought a German newspaper at the periodical counter.

"What does that mean?" the Princess asked at last.

"You got an hour to produce Nicky. Here. Here at this place, alive and well. Or you don't leave here alive."

"That's insane."

"Take a look behind you."

She turned and found herself looking through the plate-glass window into Groark's narrow-set eyes beneath the pulled-down brim of a suede hat. He had both hands in the pockets of his trench coat.

"He wouldn't dare," she said, turning back to Brown. "This is a public place."

Brown turned his hands palms up and moved them apart and together several times, as if testing for rain. "You know how these things work, Princess. A shot. Confusion. Groark beats it. I go out the side door and into my car. It takes thirty seconds. Less."

She shook her head vehemently. "The well-known poker bluff," she told him in a voice she was keeping steady. She had no idea how long she could maintain its firmness. "The man of respect, the international business executive, George Brown, mixed up in a common street shooting? Impossible."

"You put the stakes so high, there's nothing I wouldn't do to win the pot, Princess."

"I have told you. Nicky is alive and well. The safety of your son is not at stake. And, to tell you the truth, he doesn't even want to come back to you." Her voice continued to hold up well enough. "It was his idea, running away. Don't forget that."

The heavyset man leaned forward suddenly, almost as if to hit her, then relaxed and settled back in his chair. "One hour," he said then.

She could feel the lack of air in her lungs. The newspapers were full of such killings, with confused stories from witnesses and, in the end, no arrests, no solutions. Had she pushed him too hard? He had the reputation of being—

"No," she burst out, "a bluff is a bluff. If you kill me, how could you find your son? He wants to remain lost. Without me, you will never find him."

Brown produced a very faint, almost embarrassed frown, as if catching her in a grammatical error. "Prin-cess," he drawled. "Come on. You think we haven't had a tail on that chauffeur of yours? You think we can't put our mitts on Nicky any time we want? But maybe you got it set up with the kid as a hostage to be killed by your flunky. So, I don't take the chance. Instead, I make you my hostage. Standoffs make for an easier life."

"You mistake me, Don Bruno," she said in a hurt undertone. "I do not order murders,"

"Great. So get on the phone and order Nicky brought here."

"And you then hand over the tape to me?"

"No way," he brayed in a voice that attracted a few looks from nearby diners. "Forget it, Princess. It's one-on-one. You give me Nicky, I give you your life."

The Princess considered her position. She didn't quite believe that he knew Nicky's whereabouts. Brown could have had her hotel watched. He could have seen her leave it today without the limousine and driver. The rest he could have guessed without knowing where Nico was hiding his son. She took in a long breath that made her nostrils flare. Her lungs seemed starved for oxygen. What to do? What to believe? It was only a matter of her life.

The Princess settled back in her sable coat, wondering what it would be like to die in it.

She had had a good life. She had reached for the moon and caught it a number of times. From here on everything would be downhill anyway, her figure, her face, her ability to attract men. She had always known that someday she would cross paths with someone for whom one particular secret meant so much he would kill first and face the consequences of the killing later. Maybe today was the day.

The siren song of suicide. Every pretty woman who looks in the mirror knows the music. Die now, while the world still looks upon you with favor, while men still smile at your beauty. Die now?

She had chosen a high-risk business because it suited her style and because she had hedged the risk by relying on the safety of the Trocadéro.

Now that safety was breached. Like everything else nowadays, it proved false. Of all people, she should have known how hollow the facades of life were. She who dealt in the dirty reality behind the facades, should have known what life really was.

A part of her brain was busily calculating her chances of survival. The angle of the bullet would be slightly down. The window glass reached the floor, so there was no nearby place she could drop to or roll under.

However, if she stood up, the angle of entry became parallel to the floor. It would easily go through her and reach Brown. Was that her best chance?

Even in the midst of death, and her acceptance of it, she realized she wasn't ready yet. Suicide was only acceptable if one could take a few sons of bitches along with one. Her mouth curved in a gorgeous smile. Maybe there was some mileage left in it, yet.

"Don Bruno," she murmured, "this Cuban matter, is it of such consequence that you would risk everything to snuff it out, along with me?"

George Brown's stubby hands, fingers extended, palped his breast like two exploring spiders. "Princess, you're reading this wrong. Forget the Cuban stuff. Produce Nicky and we call it quits."

"How do I know that?"

He shrugged. "My word."

"Good enough," she lied with a smile. "But how do you know that what I have on the Cuban matter, even without your tape, won't be sold by me as soon as I am out of range of Signore Groark."

"It won't."

"Why not?"

Brown produced a peculiarly southern Italian sound, something like the bleat of a goat, a let's-stop-kidding-each-other sound. His smile matched hers in broadness. His teeth, in their perfect caps, shone in the pale spring sunlight.

And then she understood. She tried to keep it from showing on her face. She hoped to God it didn't show, her sudden understanding that he *knew* her cache of material was in the Trocadéro and that was why a bomb had been planted.

Her memory raced back over the past months to the meeting with Groark when he had handed over to her, for a sum that now seemed paltry, the imitation alligator portfolio containing a few pages of notes in Eisenhower's handwriting, notes about the Cuban situation and the CIA connection with a man whose name he persistently spelled Lanky.

The portfolio had been thin. But nowadays what did that mean? It had contained—what?—something electronic. Perhaps it emitted a signal, a beep, something. People had been able to trace it to the Trocadéro and somehow learn on which floor it reposed.

"Don Bruno," she began then, altering her smile somewhat, but keeping it pasted to her face, "why is it so important that the Americans never learn of the connection between Dallas and the Bay of Pigs?"

"You don't understand America, Princess. Leave that part to me."

"But surely, it no longer matters that your people had a private arrangement with Kennedy to provide air cover? Surely," she repeated, her voice almost cooing now, "everyone knows that your people were the real invaders at the Bay of Pigs? And that they died on the beaches because Kennedy betrayed his promise to you. These things have been in the air for over a decade now."

"Princess, you don't know America."

"Don Bruno, are you telling me that even now, this late, there is still some fire left in the people? That if they knew why you executed their president they would rise up and . . . and what? You *own* America, Don Bruno."

He nodded somberly. "Let's just leave that our little secret, okay?"

"But am I wrong? You even once put your own president in the White House, *è vero*? And when he was found out, still you survived. What can you possibly fear anymore?"

"Americans are funny." His voice had become uneasy or impatient, she couldn't tell which. "They swallow anything. Then, all of a sudden, they eat one turd too many and they start throwing up."

She smiled ironically. *"Molto gentile*, Don Bruno. Such language."

"We had it happen a couple of years ago," he brooded. "I won't take the risk of it happening again. The Cuban stuff disappears . . . forever."

"Never to reappear?"

"It can't. What do you think it would do to all those hardhat stumblebums back in the States if they found out who really owned them? Who really made things run? Who enforced the real discipline? And how much it cost them out of every paycheck?" He stopped and his mouth set in a tight line, as if unhappy he'd said even that little.

The Princess's brain clicked off possibilities. If she gave him Nicky, she might buy her life, for a while. But her treasure trove was about to be destroyed, thanks to this monster, so the rest of her life wasn't really worth living, anyway. She had seconds to decide.

"Very well," she said in a low voice. "You win."

His tense posture eased slightly. As it did, the Princess abruptly lunged sideways and fell forward on top of him. She threw her arms about him.

"Caro!" she cried, covering him with her body. *"Carino mio."* She began babbling in French, interspersed with tiny pecking kisses. Twisting to get away from her, Brown slid sideways off his seat onto the floor. The holiday lunchers smiled at them.

She glanced over her shoulder. Outside the window Groark crouched, peering inside, body locked in an anguish of indecision.

She rolled sideways, let go of Brown, continued rolling under a nearby table. Two women sitting at it jumped to their feet as a pot of tea spilled over their laps. The Princess's sunglasses flew across the floor.

She was three tables away now, on her knees, peering wildly about Le Drugstore. One false eyelash hung by a hair. She crawled toward the service kitchen, then jumped up and ran behind the counter.

Brown was on his feet, dusting himself. He stared after her for a moment, then ran out the side door and disappeared into a waiting black limousine. When she peered over the service counter, the Princess saw that Groark, too, had vanished.

People were laughing now. The two tea-drenched women were screaming for napkins. Oblivious, the Princess turned to a mirrored column and carefully, pursing her lips in concentration, pressed her loose eyelash back in place.

She surveyed her repaired face. Not bad. Now what?

56

The motorcycles pulled ahead of them through the streets near the Trocadéro and roared down Avenue Kléber, going the wrong way on a one-way street. Bored police and soldiers glanced at the cortege as it reached the entrance to the Trocadéro.

They had had a wild trip north out of the city beyond Compiègne, Louch and Lee James in a police car with motorcycle escort. The return trip had been much more sedate, with four canisters of Gamma/Sopor wrapped in quilts in the trunk of the car.

Louch had been silent. Until now, Lee noticed, he had seemed like a man in love with his own voice. Until now. As the police car braked carefully to a stop at the curb, Louch jumped out and summoned four uniformed officers each to carry one of the canisters inside.

They had an ugly look, the stainless-steel canisters, each the size of a two-liter wine bottle. Nozzles and valves sprouted from their flat tops. A brilliant fluorescent orange "G/S" was stenciled on each container.

Louch and Lee James followed the officers inside. They paused at the door of Hardy's office and gathered the architect's plans. Then they marched deep into the recesses of the Trocadéro.

Unshaded electric bulbs in the concrete ceilings gave them enough light to find their way to a shedlike metal structure nestling in one corner. Louch swung the door open and peered inside. A group of four red-painted and four green-painted canisters were

linked together by thin copper tubing which led upward to a junction box.

Above the junction a single copper tube ran upward out of the shed and into a rotary blower attached to the end of a duct. Louch frowned and
muttered something to one of the police, who set
down his canister and started to leave.

"*Vite!*" Louch barked.

The man burst into a run. He was back in a moment with a man in overalls, carrying a toolbox.
Gruffly, Louch explained what he wanted. Lee James's
French wasn't up to following the whole thing, but
as the man set to work, Louch's plan became obvious.

Four of the painted canisters were shut off at their
valves. The remaining four were removed. Using rubber tubing, the man linked the four stainless-steel
containers to the network of copper tubes leading to
the junction box. He bound each rubber joint with
wire and twisted it tight to seal it to the metal.

Louch sent him away with a thumb gesture. He
examined the modified arrangement and then glanced
up at Lee James. "Your sharp young eyes," he said in
English. "Anything wrong with this?"

"Not that I can tell."

"*Alors.*" Louch cleared the police out of the area
and led Lee James back to Hardy's office. He picked
up a telephone and dialed Hardy's home number.

"You amaze me," he began after a moment, without introducing himself. "I would have thought, on
a lovely Easter weekend like this, you without a care
in the world would have left Paris far behind you."

The sarcasm was apparent even to Lee, who didn't
get every word. "Hardy, *écoutez-moi*. I have to trip
your gas-release system. Which is the proper lever?"
Louch listened. "No, only on Racine." A pause. "But
that's madness. Why cannot one floor be isolated?"
He listened impatiently. "I see. Tell me, what can I
expect of four double liters? Will the concentration
be too low?"

Louch glanced at Lee James and put his hand over the telephone. "We should have gotten more G/S gas," he whispered. Then, into the phone: "Hardy, go back to your comfortable Easter Sunday dinner, you clod." He listened, then laughed grimly. "If you are even one-tenth as unhappy as I am, Hardy, then you have made me feel much better." He hung up.

He turned to the sergeant on duty at the door. "Is everyone out of the building?"

"Yes, sir."

"Seal the front entrance and come back on the double."

Louch was rummaging in Hardy's wall cabinets. He finally found a carton and took out three respirator-type face masks, the kind used by workmen sandblasting a building. "These are useless," he grunted. "What kind of fool can Hardy be? I need . . . I need . . ."

"Aqua-lungs," Lee James suggested.

"Exactly." He picked up the other telephone, the one connected directly to the Sixteenth Arrondissement police station. "Who is this? It's Louch here. I need Aqua-lung packs. Three of them. The scuba diving kind, with full tanks of oxygen. What? Shit to that. I don't care if it's Easter Sunday, have them here in fifteen minutes!" He slammed the phone down.

Staring at it, he suddenly looked sideways at Lee James and winked. "You are going to see how an old cop goes out with a big splash."

"You're not that old."

He smiled with mock broadness. "Precisely the correct thing to tell me. What's that?" He could hear voices coming closer from the direction of the entrance.

The sergeant appeared with Curtis and Netta Irish behind him. "Louch," Curtis said, "why is this monkey trying to keep us out of here?"

Louch produced an important frown. "We are about to—" He stopped himself. He was looking at

Netta, his bulging eyes half covered by heavy lids. "Madame Irish," he said then. "What do you think? Will your daughter receive you again? Has she, as you would say, cooled down?"

"I'd like to try."

Louch glanced up at the television monitor screen. The little girl with the head of yellow kinks was slumped forward, half asleep. As he watched, she came awake and slowly straightened up. Her reactions were fatigue-ridden, but still under control. Louch wondered what would happen if she fell asleep with her hand on the plunger. Would she let it go? Would her whole body relax? Might she fall over on top of it?

"We are about to introduce harmless sleep gas into the Trocadéro," he told Netta. "We believe it may work, although the concentration isn't very strong. Nevertheless, we hope it will overcome the caffeine your daughter has been using. What we can't guarantee is what happens at the moment of sleep. Or suppose there is a slight odor to the gas. We have been assured there is almost none, but that is a judgment based on outdoor use. Do you understand the problem?"

"You want me there with her?" Netta asked. "To ... distract her? To reassure her?"

"Exactly. She would not as readily suspect the use of gas if you were with her."

"Why not?" Netta countered. "She doesn't trust me any more than she'd trust a stranger."

Louch shook off the thought. "There is a profound difference between you and a stranger," he said. "This is especially true if she enters a semihallucinatory stage. We are playing a desperate game here. Many things could go wrong. I don't ask you to be there with her. No one has the right to ask that. But I suggest that you can be of great help to us if you were there."

"I don't see it," Curtis said flatly.

"We're dealing in imponderables. Emotions. I want to know we have done everything we could to disarm the girl's suspicions. Otherwise we stand the chance of—" He stopped.

"Of getting her so angry she blows the whole works," Curtis finished for him. "And takes Netta with her."

Lee James watched them as they stood silently for a long moment. So she was Netta, Lee thought. She wondered if Louch had caught the familiarity, too. But nothing got past Louch.

"Never mind," Netta said then. "I'll try it."

"Look," Curtis began.

She touched his arm. "That's all right. This is . . . work I can do." She turned to Louch. "Let's go."

"You are certain?"

"Let's go."

Curtis took her arm. "I'll take you up there."

She turned to him and smiled slightly. "That's good of you, Curtis." They started out of the room. "I suppose it's no worse than a general anesthetic?"

Their voices died away.

Louch looked up at the television screen. The girl was standing again, stretching. She shot her arms out at right angles to her body. "She's doing it again," he murmured.

"For her, the crucifixion's still on," Lee James said.

Louch's face was set in tired lines. "Let's see if we can engineer a resurrection."

PART EIGHT

EASTER MONDAY

57

The gloomy lighting in Hardy's security office hadn't really changed in what seemed to Lee James days. Louch had shuttered the windows looking out on the Avenue Kléber. He had locked all doors, including the one that led from the office to the rest of the triangular building and to the giant concrete tomb where Leila Darcy and her mother were the only living beings.

The electric clock, Lee saw, was showing a time quite different from that on her wristwatch, which indicated three minutes after 3:00 A.M.

"Louch," she said, "is the clock wrong, or am I?"

He and Curtis had been watching the television monitor screen. They both now checked their watches and the wall clock. "When we cut the electric current . . ." Louch let the rest of his thought die away.

Lee pulled over a chair, stood on it, reached behind the clock and reset it. Louch noticed this out of the corner of his eyes and murmured "*Merci*."

Netta Irish could be seen sitting quietly on a chair just outside the bars of Racine-12. There had been a moment, when she arrived upstairs, when Leila had seemed about to order her out again. But nothing had been said and Netta had settled herself for the long wait. For some time now she had tried to get Leila to talk, but the girl remained obstinately silent. Louch's plan required that the girl be talking, that some sort of conversation be going on, before he released the G/S gas.

"Eventually," Louch told Curtis, "she has to begin talking again."

"Why? She and her mother don't get along."

"Understood. But who else could I send in there? Would she talk to you?"

"Probably not."

"I understand it is the fashion in the States for daughters to war with their mothers. Something of the sort is not unknown in France. But, *enfin*, Curtis, *enfin et au fond* a girl will trust her parent or her lover over anyone else."

"Her lover is somewhere in Paris, with his handy-dandy FM transmitter."

Louch nodded with somber slowness. "The two times he has transmitted, we have been too slow to triangulate him fully. But we know he is not 'somewhere' in Paris. He is very clearly nearby."

"Then start combing the neighborhood."

Louch continued to nod with a funereal air about him, as if moving in time to some incantation or liturgy. "Vermeuil has cut me off from that."

"What?"

"The men surrounding the Trocadéro are all I can count on. In the cowardly depths of his wisdom, this bureaucratic turd has refused me any more personnel. I am to sink or swim with what I have. And, either way, old friend, I drown."

"But that's insane."

"It's politics. You haven't been reading the foreign press. Vermeuil's in a tight place. I am sure he will sack me, with prejudice. And in this way, Vermeuil backs up his contention that I am a madman run amok, on whom the entire affair can be blamed."

"Why does sacking you prove it?"

"He will say I gave out the story to the press. This is a departmental offense. If we take into account the fact that Vermeuil undoubtedly has my *dossier noir*, the case against me will be very telling."

Curtis went silent for a moment. On the monitor

screen, the girl had shifted position so that, still in the lotus seat, she was facing her mother. She stared impassively at her.

"Leila?" Netta asked.

But the girl looked away.

"Louch," Curtis said then, "how much of a *dossier noir* have you got? Of all people, you would be in a position to know."

"I have seen what purports to be my secret file," Louch said. "It's page after page of my record in the police, all favorable."

"But you don't believe it's the real file."

"Of course not."

"And what could there be in the real *dossier noir*?" Curtis persisted. "Your wartime work with the Maquis? Surely they don't hold that against you?"

"It was a Communist cell."

"A lot of them were. The best." Curtis turned to watch the heavyset Frenchman. "But it doesn't stop there," he went on. "Postwar popular front stuff, too?"

"Of course."

"And the Sûreté has ways of knowing how you vote," Curtis surmised. "It's a secret ballot, but still they find out, don't they?"

"Of course."

"And, you, you boob, have been voting Communist."

"Not always."

Curtis's glance shot past Louch to Lee James. "It's a lovely picture for Vermeuil. You infiltrate the police. You sabotage the antiterrorist bureau. You let these Arab Marxists run wild. My God, you're to blame for everything, including this Trocadéro caper." He paused. "Right, Lee?"

For the first time since she'd met him, Lee James understood what a formidable bastard Curtis was. She'd been a fool to think she could somehow wheedle her way into his confidence. "Why ask me?" she countered.

"Because you and Vermeuil seem to see eye to eye."

"That," she told him, "is a low blow." She was really talking to Louch now. "I know what I said before, but . . ." Her voice died away. Then: "But I don't feel that way anymore."

"Maybe you should," Curtis needled. "This fellow may be more dangerous than either of us realize. Vermeuil has his number."

"That's nonsense," she began. "He's—"

"Please," Louch interrupted. "He's trying to get you to defend me. But I don't need a defense. I'm here. I'm doing all I can. With luck, it may work. Let it rest at that." Then, in a *sotto voce* that still carried to Lee's ears, he muttered to Curtis: "What are you trying to do, you swine? Play Cupid?"

Curtis grinned at both of them. He started to say something, but the outside telephone rang. Louch picked it up. *"Oui?"* He began scribbling notes. *"Oui. Oui. D'accord. Merci."* He hung up and stared at his notes.

"The telephone numbers?" Curtis guessed.

"Yes. Your Mr. Ferguson called two art galleries in New York, one on Fifty-seventh Street and one on the Avenue du Madison." He gave the last word a strong French nasality. "And he called an international dealer in *objets d'art* in Teheran, the company that buys for the shah and his family."

Neither of them spoke for a moment. On the television screen, Netta Irish moved her chair until it was touching the bars of Racine-12. Her daughter watched this maneuver in utter silence, then looked away.

"Nothing wrong in that, I suppose," Curtis suggested then. "He calls people like that all the time."

"Not," Louch said, "before embarking on Air France Flight 184, nonstop to Teheran."

Curtis thought for a moment. "Is there a way of talking to Madame Irish?"

"No. And if there were, I wouldn't let you. Why?"

"She might know why Oscar did what he did."

"Leila," Netta's hoarse voice came from the monitor speaker.

Everyone looked at the screen. "Leila, this must be torture for you." The girl remained silent.

"I don't mean having to stay awake," Netta went on; "I mean, not knowing if you'll have to push down that thing or not." More silence. "Not knowing if you'll live or die." Her voice faltered. "I c-can't think of any agony worse than that."

Slowly, the girl stretched out her legs. They were quite close to each other, physically, Lee James saw. If the mother had been a trained cop, she could have made a lunge for the girl and pinioned her to the bars. But that, obviously, was not going to happen.

"Can't you?" Leila said then.

Her voice remained cool. There was no sign of fatigue in it. Just a kind of carefully distanced impersonality. I am not of you, the voice said. I make note of you, but nothing about you touches me.

"No, I can't," the mother admitted.

"But your own life is torture," the girl said, "all inside yourself. You're just whirling in your own little world of one, suffering and not knowing it."

She got to her feet and stretched her arms again, then made her head flop loosely from side to side to relieve tension in her neck. Standing, she stared impassively down on her mother's dark head.

"This is for something bigger than me," Leila told her. "Not just for me. For everybody. I don't call that suffering."

"And if you die," Netta asked in a hoarse voice, "won't you call that dying?"

"Call it whatever you want. If you insist on staying here, two of us will die. Is that what you want?"

The mother's head lifted. Her big dark eyes stared up at the girl with the yellow mop of hair. "Maybe."

"Is that why you came back here?"

"Something like that."

Leila sat down on the crate again. The detonator with its plunger was behind her. She stared at her toes and wiggled them for a moment. "Mother," she said at last, "you're really bizarre, you know that?"

"This whole thing is bizarre."

The girl hunched forward. She was within inches of her mother. "This past year or so, I've gotten into reality. Everything that went before was unreal. But when you get in touch with the real world, it's neat, like being born all over again."

"I don't understand any of that."

"I didn't think you would." The girl leaned back on her elbows. "But people your age are into it. You could be, too. Nobody's so far gone that they—"

"Okay," Louch snapped, "now."

He went to Hardy's console of dials, switches and meters. Touching each one in turn, he came at last to a switch covered by a band of metal that prevented someone from accidentally moving it. Louch tucked one long finger under the safety bar and flicked the switch. Immediately a red light glowed above it.

Three pairs of eyes swung to the wall clock. Three-thirty.

Lee James felt sickness at the pit of her stomach. This was all so damned do-or-die. If the G/S didn't do the trick—if the concentration wasn't strong enough—they really had no alternate plan. And if it didn't work, would the girl go peacefully to sleep?

"How long?" she heard herself ask in a hollow voice.

"Hardy couldn't give me an answer," Louch said. "Hours."

". . . but mainly, everybody will have enough to eat," Leila was saying. Her voice had droned on for a

long time now. She seemed to be making up for having
said almost nothing for so long.

Lee James felt as if she were in someone else's
nightmare, a spectator but a captive one. What gave
this girl the right to lecture all of them? They were
flies caught in sticky paper and Leila was God, hand-
ing down Her truth.

"It'll be warm where we all live," the girl was
telling her mother. "No one will ever hassle anybody
else. Does that sound so bad?"

Netta shook her head slowly, sleepily.

"There won't be money, Mother. Everything will
be free. So there won't be any crime or any jails.
There won't even be any cities. We'll all live with
green things around us and animals."

Netta's head sank against the bars of Racine-12.
Her daughter noticed this, but went on talking.
"Women will have children when they want to,
Mother. And if they don't want any, they won't have
any. And all the children will belong to everybody.
It'll be so great."

On the television screen, Lee James could see that
the mother's eyes were closed. Had the G/S started
to work on her? Or was it just fatigue?

"A child will have a thousand mothers," Leila was
saying. "A thousand fathers. No one will ever hurt a
child, Mother. No one will ever beat a child or rape
it or force it to work."

Louch glanced at Curtis. "The oldest fairy tale,"
he murmured.

"And we won't get sick because doctors will know
how to keep us well," the girl went on. "People won't
die from working hard, or not having enough to eat.
And no one will ever die in war again."

"Sing," Louch said. "Sing that song again, little
one."

Leila was leaning over her mother's head now,
almost as if she were telling her a story at bedtime.
Lee found herself mesmerized by the reversal of roles.

The mother was asleep. The daughter was soothing her with words.

"And no one will have to marry anyone if they don't want to. We'll all be the same, Mother. We'll live with people we love and only because we love them."

"Ah, God," Louch groaned. "She is piercing my heart, this tiny little mind."

"Don't be a cynic," Lee James told him.

"The oldest story known to man," he said. "It tells us we *are* good. We are here on this rock, hurtling through the void . . . for *something*. And this fairy tale still has the power to move us to tears." He looked at her face. "You are crying?"

Lee sniffed. "Don't be silly."

". . . and the air will be pure to breathe and the water will be sweet to drink. No animals will ever be killed, Mother, never again."

Leila was stroking her mother's hair through the bars of Racine-12. The tears were rolling freely down her cheeks.

The image on the monitor screen seemed to blur before Lee James's eyes and she rubbed at them with the back of her hand. It came away damp.

"Back to Eden," Louch said. "Before the Fall."

"Shut up, Louch," Lee snapped.

"You have the same dream?" he asked.

"It's not the dream," she told him. "It's . . . it's seeing them reconciled."

". . . and we'll all work for ourselves, Mother," the girl was saying in a drowsy voice. "There won't be any bosses or wages and it'll be . . . so . . . great."

"Watch it," Curtis cut in. "She's slowed to a stop."

They watched the yellow head of curls settle slowly against the bars, touching Netta's sleek black hair. "That's the girl," Curtis said. "She has such a skinful of caffeine, it took her longer to fall asleep." He glanced at Louch. "Old philosopher," he said mockingly. "Are you ready to go in?"

"Give her a moment to settle into deep slumber."

"Quite a dreamer, this girl."

"Lay off, Curtis," Lee told him.

"Wipe your eyes."

She glared at them. "Go to hell, both of you cynical, cynical bastards." She fell silent. There was no way she could tell them that she'd never known her own mother. Nor was there time, now. And, besides, they'd probably sneer at her.

"How can you say that?" Louch demanded in a hurt voice. "What do we value most here, but human lives? And next to life, what do we cherish most but the . . . the artifacts of human genius. And in this place we have both. Our job is to save both. If we can."

"Then why make fun of that poor dumb girl?"

Louch gestured helplessly. "We all have such dreams, Leora. And then we lose them."

"How . . ." She struggled for the word. "How sad."

Louch smiled at her. "There is only one thing sadder." He began to strap on the Aqua-lung apparatus. "Never to have had the dream at all." He glanced at Curtis. "Coming?"

Lee watched them buckle up. Breathing oxygen through mouthpieces, they unlocked the door and disappeared into the depths of the Trocadéro.

58

Bert opened the closet to check the time on the electric clock with the olive-drab transmitter. A minute before eight in the morning. He set his wristwatch. 7:59.

In four hours, or less, the ransom would have to be paid into the post office at Benghazi. A message would be flashed across the Mediterranean to Marseilles, where a telephone relay would convey the news to the Ugandan embassy. It would be a routine message with the word "clear" in it. The embassy itself was empty today, because of the Easter holiday, but the Ugandan on duty would bring the message upstairs to the garret.

Bert stared glumly at the handsome young man he called Dris. The cramped position was beginning to tell on his muscles. So be it. In one corner, squatting on the floor as if it were desert sand, Khefte had loaded a small pipe and was deep into his own mysterious kif.

Bert shook his head. He switched on the CB radio and dutifully went through its channels, listening to each for a moment, in case an emergency signal was being sent. Nothing there.

He snapped on the television set and stood for a moment with his hand on the on-off volume dial, ready to switch off when, as expected, the screen brightened but produced no image. Paris television wouldn't be broadcasting till noon today.

But there was an image.

Bert twisted the volume knob higher. ". . . is safe,"

the announcer was saying, "I repeat, the young terrorist woman has been seized and the explosive has been defused. The Trocadéro is safe. So ends one of the most disturbing epi—"

Bert snapped off the television. He moved past Khefte and stared at the electric clock again. 8:01.

Bert sighed deeply. *Scheissdreck.* Ten million down the drain. And there were still commitments to fulfill to his sponsors, if he wanted to collect the rest of the payment. It was all right to melt away after such an affair, disappear into the netherworld, but his sponsors still owed him half the fee, five thousand dollars. It would go a long way toward helping Bert start something new.

He felt terribly let down. But it was a feeling with which he had learned how to deal. History was on his side.

"Awake, my brother," he muttered, nudging Khefte with his foot. The dark-faced young man came awake. "Wha'?" His voice sounded choked with the power of his hashish dream.

"They have removed the American girl."

"Wha'?"

"There will be no ransom."

Khefte was on his knees now, trying to get to his feet. "But how can this be?"

"What can be, is." Bert bent over the electric clock. Carefully, he moved the timer setting from 12 noon to 8:30 A.M. "Come, my brother. We have less than thirty minutes before it explodes."

Khefte was standing now, weaving a little, but growing more alert. "Then we must escape."

"By the route which you discovered." Bert opened the back window. "Lead the way, Khefte."

"And Dris?"

They both turned to stare at the bound man on the floor. He was awake, but his handsome face was expressionless behind the strips of black tape over his mouth.

"Our noble comrade will remain behind," Bert said.

"For the *flics* to torture." Khefte giggled.

"The lover and his beloved will be reunited," Bert said, "on the guillotine." He stared at the electric clock. 8:03. Moving to the closet, he closed the door on the timer and transmitter, then turned the key in the door and pocketed the key.

Khefte, moving a bit slowly in the aftermath of his kif, edged out onto the slate roof on his knees. Bert followed him. After a while they got to their feet. The April sky was leaden. It would rain this Easter Monday.

They moved quickly from roof to roof until they reached a courtyard near the corner of Poincaré and D'Eylau. Khefte led the way down to the ground and through an archway that let out onto D'Eylau.

"*Halte!*" a voice shouted.

Khefte had emerged into the street. Bert was several yards behind him, still in the archway.

Khefte began to run. Two uniformed police pounded past, guns drawn.

"After the Arab!" one of them shouted.

His pale white face as still as fallen snow, Bert waited in the archway. In the distance he heard a shout and then a shot.

Moving at a leisurely pace, he sauntered out onto the avenue and strolled into the Place du Mexico. There he walked along the Rue des Sablons as if he had plenty of time.

It was too bad about colored peoples, Bert thought. They carried danger on their faces. At the corner of Rue St. Didier, he hailed an early-bird taxicab and directed him far, far from the Trocadéro. He glanced at his watch. 8:10.

59

Things went quickly in Racine-12. With only a grunt of communication, Louch and Curtis unlocked the wall of bars at 7:40 and removed the wires that led from the detonator to the explosive charge inside the crate on which Leila Darcy sprawled, fast asleep.

Louch picked up a wall phone. Removing his Aqualung for a moment, he said, "Switch on the air exhaust system and send up the bomb squad as soon as the G/S clears."

Curtis eyed the sleeping women. "Naturally," he muttered to Louch, "you'll want to carry out the lighter one."

Louch gave him a broad grin before clapping the mouthpiece back on. "And naturally, you will want to carry *chère* Netta."

The elevator moved slowly down to street level. They carried the women into Hardy's office. At 7:52 Louch telephoned Vermeuil. "We've defused the bomb," he said. "The Trocadéro is safe."

"What?" Vermeuil's honking voice went up an octave. "Are you sure?"

"Absolutely. You can make your announcement to the press."

"Louch, this changes nothing between us, you—"

Louch hung up on him and turned to look at the sleeping women. Lee James had rolled up police jackets to form pillows for each of them. Then, borrowing Louch's handcuffs, she gently locked Leila's wrists together without awakening her.

At 7:55 two burly policewomen lifted Leila onto a stretcher and carried her, still sleeping, into a police wagon. "They're locking her away?" Lee asked Louch.

"After the usual medical examination, yes." He frowned. "For three days she's been behind bars. She's used to it by now."

Netta Irish murmured something and, when Lee bent over to listen, the older woman awoke. "Leila?"

"They've taken her away, Mrs. Irish."

"Will she be—?"

"They'll take good care of her," Louch assured her. He signaled to a policeman. "Take an unmarked car. Convey Madame Irish to the Ritz and make sure the maid puts her to bed."

"I'm not sleepy," Netta mumbled. And fell asleep again.

At 7:59, still breathing through Aqua-lungs, Louch and Curtis returned to Racine-12. The bomb squad had yet to arrive. Outside they could hear the singsong rise and fall of police sirens.

"The hero arrives, closely followed by the press," Louch said.

"I'd love to hear how Vermeuil explains it."

"You will, my friend, over and over again."

By 8:10, Louch had begun to experience that terrible depression that sets in once tension ends. Nothing about the case interested him anymore. He stood beside the open crate in which the K–7 had been planted. In the recesses of Racine-12 he could hear Curtis shuffling through paintings and moving around wrapped statuary. From time to time he would appear under an overhead light bulb and consult a piece of Hotel Ritz paper on which a list seemed to be written.

Louch had spent almost thirty years serving France and he felt as if he no longer had a client. With Curtis, it was different. His responsibilities still lay with UBCO and the Irish Collection. Bad idea, Louch thought, spending one's life in the service of an abstraction like one's country. Bad planning, since a country was no better than its politicians.

He watched Curtis moving swiftly from bin to bin of Racine-12. Most of it was leased to the Irish Collection, but one section seemed bare of art, a small triangular area walled off behind the usual vertical bars.

Louch began checking through the great ring of keys Hardy had made available to him. He fiddled through them until he found the one that fitted the lock of this separate triangular space. He unlocked the gate, stepped inside and stood for a moment before a wall of shelves, mostly empty. Here and there, on the lower shelves, at the level of Louch's chest, sat flat metal containers of the sort normally found in safe-deposit vaults, each box with its own padlock.

The boxes were of many shapes and sizes, but they had one thing in common, the initials "C.G." and a heraldic crest. Louch stooped to examine the design of the crest.

It consisted of a shield divided diagonally into two areas. In the upper section three stags leaped forward. The lower area showed a mailed arm and fist. A legend was lettered below the crest on a flowing, ribbonlike design: *"Nascoso sempre."*

He was beginning to get a pain in his back from bending over. Whoever used this strong room was quite a bit smaller than he was. Louch straightened up. For the first time since the bomb had been defused, he smiled. What small person would have a family motto, not in Latin, but in Italian?

Louch gathered up the dozen metal boxes. Their padlocks clanked as he carried them out of Racine-12 and set them down on the floor of the open elevator. He spat out his mouthpiece and called, "Curtis, haven't you finished?"

Curtis grunted something from deep inside Racine-12. A moment later he appeared, brushing dust from the sleeves of his sports jacket. He stared at Louch.

"Breathe oxygen," he said, his words distorted by his own mouthpiece.

"To hell with the sleepytime gas. Are you ready to go?"

Curtis nodded. Louch relocked the various doors and they went down in the slow-moving elevator. "Everything in order?" Louch asked finally.

Curtis eyed him. "Is that an official inquiry?"

"You ask this of a man about to be cashiered?"

"Because this," Curtis said, waving his piece of Hotel Ritz paper, "is a phony."

"What?"

"Oscar Ferguson's inventory. Fake."

"But the vault is filled with art."

"Greuze, some routine Renoirs, a few Bonnards, a de Chirico, some Signacs and about three dozen names I've never heard of. They may be valuable, but I doubt it."

The elevator had reached the street floor. Its doors opened, but the two men stood there, unmoving. "Curtis," Louch said then, "I don't understand."

"What did he hope to—?" Curtis stopped. "I've been out of the New York scene too long. I've lost track of the newer scams."

"Scams?"

"What's in the tin boxes?"

Louch picked them up from the floor and started out of the elevator. "I hope I live long enough to find out."

When they entered Hardy's office, the place blazed with light. Vermeuil was standing in the center of the room. TV cameramen with Arriflexes braced on their shoulders zoomed lenses in and out as assistants held bright lights overhead. Newspaper photographers circled the knot of people.

Louch watched for a moment. Nobody had noticed him. He set the metal boxes on the floor under a table, picked up a telephone and made contact with the Sixteenth Arrondissement police station.

"I want a pickup," he said quietly. "She calls herself a princess, one Claudia Carloni, short, spicy, probably staying at the Plaza Athénée or the George V. What charge? Since when do we need a charge? Have her brought here to me and no one else."

Curtis was tucking away the inventory list in his jacket pocket. "You didn't see this list," he muttered to Louch over the noise of the press people.

"And you," Louch said, "didn't see those boxes." He left the room.

A group of men carrying tools and a large peculiar basket of woven steel cable rushed past and entered the elevator. "The bomb squad," Louch called to Curtis and dashed after them.

"Can you tell us, M. le Ministre, how you solved the case?" a reporter was asking Vermeuil.

His scarecrow chest puffed out. "We have highly scientific meth—"

Curtis glanced at his watch. 8:16. He sidled around the edge of the mob scene until he found Lee James. Unnoticed, the two of them left the room.

". . . by following a correct strategy," Vermeuil was telling the reporters, "and by remaining firm in the face of terror. This has always been my policy and it always will be, despite the fact that there may be those within my department who . . ."

Outside in the hall, Curtis stopped Lee James out of earshot of anyone. "Tell me," he began in an undertone, "are you up on art fraud?"

"Forgeries? No."

"Not that. Suppose you owned valuable paintings. They're collateral, right? I mean, you could get a bank loan on the basis of them."

"Ye-es," she said slowly. "You mean, sort of hock them?"

"Don't let me put words in your mouth."

Lee James thought for a moment. "The big international galleries will actually buy your paintings for future delivery."

"How does it work?"

"Straight sale, nothing illegal. You get the money now and they own the paintings, but you specify that the things remain on your walls for, say, five or ten years."

"Why would a gallery do that?"

"Good business. They pay current prices. By the time you turn over the paintings, the market value has gone up. You've sacrificed that for cash up front."

Curtis stood motionless for a long moment. "And if the paintings weren't yours?"

"Curtis! You don't mean he—?"

"I'm still figuring it out. I think he sold each painting twice. Once the way you described, for a future delivery he never intended to make. Then a second time to someone else, let's say a dealer in the Middle East with clients who weren't too fussy about such things."

"Which is why he skipped when it looked like we'd be breaking into Racine-12," Lee said. "Or was he hoping the explosion would wreck everything beyond identification?"

"There's always some evidence, even after a real blast. No. I don't think he was in cahoots with the terrorists."

"Even though he had a way in to them through the Darcy girl?"

"You have an admirably warped mind," Curtis said. "He knew he'd have to split some day when the galleries called their notes due. But I don't think he'd be so amateurish as to try to bomb evidence out of existence. That might work with documents—" He stopped, remembering the boxes Louch had found.

"What's the matter?"

"Later." Curtis glanced at his watch. "Eight-nineteen. I don't want those bomb squad goons roaming all over Racine-12. We have to sit on this thing."

"Does Louch know?"

"Some of it. I don't want this leaking out. The whole Collection isn't here."

By 8:20 Curtis had returned to Racine-12. One of the bomb squad men, shining a flashlight into the interior of the open crate, called Louch over.

"What are these?" The man pointed gingerly at two gunmetal-gray objects the size of matchboxes that seemed to be fastened against the side of the steel drum in which the explosive had been packed.

Louch bent down. "How would I know?"

"Did the detonator wires go to them?"

Louch shook his head. "To these bolts here."

The bomb squad man stood up. "These are radio relays."

Louch's face went white. "Remove them."

"Not possible. Suppose this is wired negatively? It may explode *only* if removed. There are two systems, Louch. We don't know which the bastards are using."

The man waved in three helpers. They carefully lifted the steel drum out of the crate and lowered it gently into the basket of woven cable. They folded a flap of cable weave over the top.

All four of them stood there for a moment, then by some silent signal, they each lifted a corner of the basket and began moving slowly out of Racine-12.

The silence was appalling. So was the deliberate slowness with which they moved, a step at a time, toward the open elevator door. Curtis stepped behind Louch. "Do you think?" he muttered.

"I don't even breathe," Louch said.

"Leila, *mon amour!*" the radio squawked. "Moon of my sun, get out of there! They will destroy you!"

The four men carrying the basket of death didn't waver. They continued easing it toward the open elevator.

"I heartily repent of my folly." Dris's voice sounded cracked with passion. "We are babes in the wood, *mon amour.* They use and discard us, my own. The bomb! It will explode!"

Louch ran for the spiral staircase and started down it two steps at a time, with Curtis directly behind him. On Racine, the four bomb squad men had reached the elevator and were gently carrying their burden inside it. Although they had certainly heard Dris's words, nothing showed in their faces.

As he clattered down the stairs after Louch, Curtis checked his wristwatch. 8:23. At the base of the stairs, on the street floor, a police sergeant was running in from the Poincaré entrance of the building. He stopped short when he saw Louch.

"Well?"

The sergeant jerked his thumb over his shoulder. "They're in the Ugandan embassy. Number 13. Top floor. He's still broadcasting."

"Embassy?" Louch's face darkened. "How do we get in?"

"Vermeuil can get an authorization," the sergeant suggested.

"In a week's time." Louch's head jerked around. The elevator was in motion, descending slowly through the Trocadéro with forty kilos of explosive and two radio-controlled detonators. No basket woven of cable would contain such a blast. It was meant to contain low-level explosives like blasting gelatin or dynamite.

He glanced at his watch. 8:24. "Curtis, can you get inside the embassy?" Louch was reaching for his shoulder holster. "I can't send a *flic* inside."

"I'll give it a whirl." Curtis started for the Poincaré exit.

"Take this." Louch started to chuck his short-barreled Walther PPK to him.

"Never use 'em." Curtis ran out into the street.

He dashed across Poincaré under a dark sky rolling with clouds. He ran up the stairs to Number 13 and tried to open the door. Locked.

He hammered on the door, rang the bell. He could hear someone moving inside. *"Ouvrez!"* he shouted. *"Au feu!"*

A black man swung the door open, eyes wide. *"Au feu?"* he asked, glancing out at the street as if trying to locate the flames Curtis was shouting about.

Curtis shoved the door back into the man's face with a quick, stiff-arm motion. At the same time, Curtis snaked his foot inside and locked it behind the man's heels. The Ugandan fell backward and hit the floor with a solid thunk. Curtis dashed past him and ran up a flight of stairs. The man shouted something at him.

Inside the Trocadéro the elevator reached the street floor at 8:26. Slowly the doors opened. Four grim-faced bomb squad men moved at the same deliberate pace, trying to get the bomb out of the Trocadéro.

Down the hall, reporters shouted questions at Vermeuil. "Our unending vigilance," he responded, "our unflinching fortitude and our unparalleled intellectual superiori—"

Louch watched the men inching out toward the Kléber exit. Sweat rolled down their faces.

At 8:27, Curtis reached the garret. Dris had propped himself up on the floor. Somehow he had torn the strips of tape from his mouth, but they still clung to his cheek as he babbled into the microphone.

Curtis snatched it from him. "Where's the radio that triggers the bomb?"

Dris's dark eyes rolled in the direction of the locked closet. Curtis jumped across the room and rattled the door. He took a step back and landed a terrifying kick against the door directly to one side of the keyhole. The door shook but didn't budge.

The Ugandan who had followed him up the stairs paused at the entrance to the garret and stared first at Dris, then at Curtis. He seemed frozen to the spot.

Curtis stepped back again. Blond hair hanging

damply over his forehead, he measured distances and launched a second massive kick.

The door sprang open. The electric clock came into view. 8:28.

The four bomb squad men held the steel basket very steady as they moved past the corridor that led to Hardy's security office.

". . . and furthermore," Vermeuil was saying in his high, honking voice, "we French have no intention of yielding to any pressures whatsoever from outside the borders of our own land. Nor will we tolerate for a moment dupes and double agents who work from within the framework of our own security est—"

Two uniformed officers were hustling la Principessa Claudia Carloni in through the Kléber entrance. They managed to squeeze past the four men carrying the woven steel basket.

Louch held his watch up. 8:29.

In the garret at Number 13, Curtis was pleading with Dris. "You must remember," he begged. "It is one of two systems. One way, it sends out a continuous signal. If the signal is interrupted, the bomb explodes. The other system is that, at a given moment, it sends a signal and explodes the bomb. But which did he use?"

"I don't know." The handsome young man's voice wavered with self-pity. "I don't pay attention to such things."

"Yes, you do," Curtis insisted. "Describe how he hooked it up."

"He-he . . . arranged all this while I was unconscious."

"Yes, but you saw him set the times."

"He set a dial on the clock."

"Christ!" Curtis exploded, "that's all you can tell me?"

His mind raced back and forth through the meager

details. He was on his knees in the dust of the closet.
8:29:21.

On the ground floor of the Trocadéro, Vermeuil
was coming out of the conference. It was as if a malign
fate had summoned everyone to the same spot. Lee
James was watching the police escorting the Queen of
Blackmailers. And the four men with the bomb had
paused for an instant in order to maneuver their way
through the various surveillance anterooms that kept
the Trocadéro safe from intruders.

Louch began to wave people away. "Back," he called
to Lee James. "Go back."

Kneeling in the closet at the top of Number 13,
Curtis extended his finger like a pointer and traced
the circuitry. When this kind of timer reached its
setting, did it close a circuit?
8:29:41.

Or open it? But if it was used to time other things—
coffee makers, night-lights, wake-up radios—
8:29:51.

Curtis's right hand went to the alligator clips that
connected the olive-drab transmitter to the auto
battery. His left hand went to the electric clock cord,
plugged into a wall outlet. He took a deep breath.
8:30.

He pulled both sets of wires. The electric clock
stopped.

Kneeling, Curtis waited. He glanced at Dris. They
held their breath.

Louch watched the four bomb squad men maneuver the basket out the front door. He turned back
into the building and checked his watch.
8:31.
8:32.
8:33.

*   *   *

By the time Curtis got back to the Trocadéro, the press had cleared out. Louch was nowhere to be seen, nor was Lee James. It was just as well, since Curtis had Dris, his wrists still tied, in tow. Vermeuil would have been hard pressed to explain the scene. Curtis turned his captive over to a policeman. Then he went back to Hardy's office.

Someone had thrown open the shutters to the street without improving the dismal lighting by very much. Heavy clouds overhead seemed about to burst with rain.

Vermeuil was sitting behind Hardy's desk. Louch was standing at the window. In a corner, huddled in a sable coat, a tiny, attractive woman with heavily mascaraed eyes was working with a mirror and a lipstick brush, outlining her mouth in a pale mauve-brown color. She looked perfectly at ease. Curtis wondered if she were Vermeuil's wife.

". . . clear out your desk by noon," Vermeuil was telling Louch. "You'll face a board of inquiry tomorrow morning at ten A.M. And there is absolutely no reason why they won't recommend a term in jail for—" He stopped, his skull's mouth open, teeth glistening, as he registered Curtis's presence. "Yes?"

"I'm Curtis."

"I am aware of that. Get out."

Curtis glanced over at Louch. "Is this creep giving you trouble?" he asked in a street-argot French.

Vermeuil's mouth stayed open. Louch had an attack of badly stifled laughter. He calmed himself. "Curtis," he said very gravely, "you have helped us more than I can say."

"Out!" Vermeuil screamed.

Curtis walked over to him. Vermeuil got hastily to his feet. He towered over Curtis by a full head, but his skinny frame carried considerably less weight. Curtis made a sudden, violent gesture in the direction of the man's midriff. Vermeuil twisted sideways and covered up his groin, but Curtis had cut the movement short without touching him.

"Jumpy little devil, isn't he?"

"Your visa is hereby revoked," Vermeuil said. His eyes crawled sideways, measuring the distance to the door. "We have no need of American gangst—"

Curtis cut his words short by reaching suddenly inside his sports jacket, as if for a gun. Vermeuil jumped sideways and dashed for the door.

Curtis watched him disappear down the corridor. "Well," he said, "I was getting fed up with Paris anyway." He turned to Louch. "Who is this sexy lady?"

"A loose end." Louch turned and bowed courteously to the Princess. "Sexy lady, I have all your metal boxes. A dozen of them, I believe?"

She put away her hand mirror, placed a paper tissue between her lips and planted a mauve-brown kiss on it. "This Trocadéro," she said, "is not giving very good value for the money it charges me."

"I have not yet forced the locks on the boxes," Louch went on. "As you heard M. le Ministre say, I no longer have the authority to do so. But I will be turning over your little hoard to a colleague."

"Most unwise." Her huge eyes glittered at him. "May I see the boxes?"

Louch pointed across the room at the containers lying untouched beneath a table. The Princess got up and bustled over to them. She stared for a moment, then pulled out a smallish box. She carried it back and put it into Louch's hands. "Hold it, please?"

Digging into her bag, she brought out a ring of keys, selected one and opened the padlock on the box. Louch swung the lid open and began leafing through the documents inside. After a few minutes he glanced up at the Princess.

"Madame," he said softly, "I am in the presence of a true professional." He started to hand the container back to her but she stopped him.

"It's yours," she said. "Do I have your word that

the other ones will be returned unopened to Racine-12?"

Curtis watched the two of them for a long moment, the bulky Louch towering over the tiny woman with her glittering eyes. Neither of them spoke. Then, abruptly, as if released from an enchantment, Louch moved. He clicked the padlock shut and handed the box to Curtis.

"Hold this a moment. We're going back up to Racine-12."

Curtis watched him scoop up the remaining boxes. "If Vermeuil catches you . . ." Curtis let the thought die away.

"Vermeuil?" Louch's glance went to the box Curtis was holding. "He's no longer a problem, for either of us."

"Oh?"

"We won't be long. This way, Princess." With a faintly gallant air Louch led the way out of Hardy's office, his arms filled with metal boxes.

Ah, Europeans, Curtis thought.

He stood there, cradling the metal container in his arms. He'd been around this continent too long now. Time to find a different line of work. There had to be another way of making a living than by sweeping rich people's debris under carpets.

His glance was still fixed on the doorway through which Louch and the Queen of Blackmailers had disappeared. Slowly, grudgingly, Curtis grinned.

Ah, Europe.

PART NINE

AFTERWARD

60

By a quarter to nine Tuesday morning, Groark arrived at George Brown's apartment in the modern building on the Rue Jean Goujon. He helped Brown pack two bags, then called for his limousine.

As they waited for the driver, they talked briefly of several matters, mostly business. Neither of them mentioned the Trocadéro affair. It wasn't that Brown took defeats lightly. It was only that he had other, equally pressing problems on his mind.

"Round up local help," he told Groark. "I want that half-pint guinea broad found. I want Nicky sent home."

Groark indicated the packed bags. "To you? In New York? Or where?"

"I got an eleven o'clock on Air France to New York." Brown began pacing the floor. "Where's the fuckin' driver?"

"Any second, boss."

Groark stared out the big, sliding, plate-glass door to the rear terrace. The rain was still coming down steadily, light, sketchy lines of it, as if drawn almost vertically by a Japanese with a fine brush. Groark slid open the door to see how cold the day was.

Overhead, the sky was the color of old snow on a city street, a kind of smudged brownish gray. The air was damp. The chill began to get to Groark. It seemed to sink into his bones. He turned away as the doorbell rang.

"Finally," Brown grunted. "Let's get going."

Groark unlatched the door and swung it open.

Bert held the tiny Browning .25 in front of him. He held it in both hands, as he had been taught to do. This had the effect of concealing everything but the weapon's small muzzle.

Groark stepped backward. "What the hell?"

Bert looked past him. "Mr. Brown?"

Bert came inside and kicked the door shut behind him. He backed Groark into the room, then came all the way in himself, keeping to one wall so that he had both men in front of him. They stood for a moment like the points of a *Y*, with Bert and the Browning pistol at the base of it.

"You gotta nerve coming here," Brown began on a strong note of outrage. "The way you fucked up." Bert said nothing. "Whadya want, anyway?"

"Five thousand dollars."

Brown produced a barking laugh. "You already got five of my finest, for which I got nothing. Beat it while you still got your health."

Bert shook his head once. In the dull, flat light from the plate-glass sliding door he looked almost two-dimensional, as if the same artist who had sketched the down-slanting rain had quickly scribbled a blond, nondescript face on a chunky body.

Brown moved sideways a step. "Halt," Bert snapped. "Stand still. Put your wallet on the table."

Brown glanced at Groark. "This *djibrone* has big eyes."

Groark took a step in the opposite direction from Brown.

"I said stand still!" Bert's voice was high with tension. His s's had gotten thicker as bits of a German accent began to show through. "The wallet." He aimed the automatic at George Brown's belly.

On Bert's right, Brown deliberately took a second step away from Groark as he reached into his hip pocket. Between them they had now spread the *Y* into a broad *V*. It was becoming increasingly harder for Bert to keep both of them in sight at the same time.

"Neil," Brown said as he hefted the pale tan pigskin wallet in his hand, "I thought you took care of this little Kraut chiseler. Didn't you piece him off with ten?"

"Five when he did the radio job on the Trocadéro," Groark said. "That's how we located the dame's stuff on the fourth floor. And five more when he worked the scam."

Brown's heavy neck seemed to thicken dangerously. "Only it didn't work. I don't like getting hustled," he told Bert. "I piece off a soldier, he stays bought."

"But I am not your soldier," Bert said. "Put the wallet on the table."

Brown took the opportunity to widen still farther his distance from Groark. "Shtent shtill!" Bert cried out.

"Have it your way."

Carefully taking aim at the glass-topped table a yard away from him, Brown pitched the heavy wallet forward. As it landed, a gold-plated corner made a sharp ping. Bert blinked.

Groark had a five-shot Colt Cobra in his hand. His finger tightened on the trigger.

Bert wheeled left and fired twice. Two holes burst open in Groark's midriff. His narrow face seemed to grow more pinched as the Colt dropped soundlessly to the shag carpet.

Blood spurted from both holes. Groark grabbed at his belly and the blood oozed out between his fingers. He crumpled sideways onto the floor.

Brown stood perfectly still. The two shots had sounded more like the snappish barking of a small dog. He stared at Bert. "Take the money," he whispered. "I don't carry no piece. I'm clean."

Bert inched forward to the table and opened the

wallet. He took it back with him to his original position, against the wall. Awkwardly, with one hand, he leafed through the money. "Five thousand."

"Seven," Brown said softly. His hands had gone up in the air on either side of his head. His lips were as pale as his cheeks.

"Look, kid," Brown went on in a fast monotone, "take the money. No hard feelings. You had a good idea for hijacking that joint. You needed front money. You got it. I want you to know if you ever need more front money, you can come to me. Capeesh? You got another scam, I'm your man." His smile looked ghastly.

Bert frowned and started rechecking the wallet again. There was a certain German thoroughness in his actions. He had counted five. How could there be seven?

"Kid," Brown moaned softly, "I'm talking to you. I like your style. I'm glad you came to me. It's nobody's fault your idea went haywire. These things happen. It's business, that's all. Now, take the money and go, huh?"

"This time," Bert said in a severe, schoolteacherish voice, "our objectives happened to coincide. But next time, who knows?"

"I love the way you think, kid. I really do." Brown was trying to keep his glance locked on Bert. But his eyes wanted to crawl sideways.

Groark's right hand had reached the Colt. It slipped as he grabbed it with bloody fingers. He lifted it and fired once.

Bert spun sideways as the bullet cracked through his left arm between the elbow and shoulder. The tiny Browning went off in his hand, a reflex action.

Its bullet entered George Brown's thick throat an inch below his chin. It followed an upward course but didn't have the velocity to pierce through the skull.

Brown tried to catch the edge of the table as he sank to his knees. His eyes rolled up in his head. He fell forward on his face, the chromium leg of the table pressing cruelly into his thick cheek.

Bert twisted and started to shoot Groark again, but the two close-set eyes were shut and the Colt had slipped from his bright red fingers.

Shoving the wallet in his back pocket, Bert moved through the living room into a bedroom with a bath. He laid the Browning .25 on the edge of a porcelain sink. Then, carefully, he rolled back his left sleeve. The bullet had passed through. Blood was oozing, not pumping, from both entry and exit wounds.

He opened the cabinet over the sink and stared at the bottles, trying to focus carefully. Hydrogen peroxide.

He splashed it over his arm. Then he ripped open the packed bags and found one of George Brown's white-on-white Sulka ties. He twisted it as a tourniquet above the wound. He splashed more peroxide on one of Brown's white, Irish linen handkerchiefs with hand-rolled edges. This he tied over the two bullet holes. Using his teeth as a second hand, he tore strips of adhesive tape from a roll and secured the handkerchief-bandage in place.

He relaxed pressure on the tourniquet twice during this process, as he had been trained to do. Then he discarded his shirt and put on one of Brown's pale ivory shirts, monogrammed "G.B." on both cuffs and over the white-lace embroidery across the breast pocket.

Holding the automatic, he moved back into the living room. None of his shots had been loud, but the Colt's noise might have been heard. He moved carefully out onto the terrace. A fine mist of rain cooled his face. His arm had not yet begun to hurt.

He stared at the antennas clustered all over the German embassy building. After a minute, he let himself out of the apartment and ran down six flights by the service stairs.

Slipping out through the building's rear garden, he was soon lost in the endless, down-dropping slanted lines of chill April rain.

61

On Tuesday morning, Curtis finally located the Czech minister, who seemed only slightly the worse for having made an unannounced detour of several days somewhere between Vienna and Paris. Curtis returned to his flat off the Rue Washington in midafternoon and, when he checked his answering service, found four telephone calls from Netta Irish.

Curtis sat down in the brick-walled living room and stared at the rows of shelves on which his life was neatly set out. Not displayed. There was no way one could read much about the man who lived here from the collection of books and other things arrayed on the shelves.

He resisted the desire to make himself a drink. And, for some time, he resisted making a call to the Ritz. He didn't pretend to know anyone well enough to outguess them, but in Netta's case, he also had the feeling that he didn't want to know what was on her mind.

Eventually, telling himself that whatever else she was, she was still an UBCO client, he dialed the Ritz and asked for her suite. She picked the telephone up on the first ring.

"It's me," he told her. "Sorry I was out this morning."

"Can you come over?" Her voice sounded hoarse.

"I have a lot of catching up on paperwork here." This was true, but paperwork normally existed to be delayed. "I have to make a full report to New York."

"Can we come to see you?"

"Either way, I need the time to myself now." He paused for a beat. "We?"

"Tom Sandweg is here. You don't know him."

"Of him." Curtis thought for a moment. "Maybe you can put him on the phone now."

"But I still want to see you."

"Mm." He waited. "Let me talk to him."

A moment later a strong, positive man's voice made Curtis pull the telephone an inch away from his ear. "Curtis, can we get together for a drink? I want to do a proper job of thanking you for everything you did."

Curtis sorted through the elements of Sandweg's tone. Macho, sure, easy, the kind of man who never put off things. For whom paperwork existed to be done promptly. For whom there were no dreaded tasks, only jobs waiting to be successfully finished.

"I didn't do anything. Louch is the lad to thank."

"Louch isn't the one who kept the Irish name out of the press."

"Yes, he is. With a little prompting."

"We haven't been able to reach him," Sandweg went on smoothly. "He's out of his office today. We wanted to arrange a visit with Leila but nobody will tell us where she is or how we can see her."

"Louch can do it, once he's back in operation. Nobody's been getting much sleep these past few days. I suppose he's catching up." Curtis smiled wryly at the lie. Louch was spending the day fighting for his life against verminous politicals.

"Do you suppose she's all right?" Sandweg persisted. "One hears all sorts of stories about French police brutality."

"I'm sure she's all right."

"But we can't be certain."

"No," Curtis admitted. "The American embassy is your best bet."

"The hell you say. The cowardly bastards don't

answer my calls, now that they know what I want of them."

"Mm." Curtis thought for a moment. "If I find Louch, I'll speak to him about it." He gave the suggestion of an unspoken aftermath of: Then will you leave me alone?

"Do that, will you? Meanwhile, I have a call in to Washington, a friend at State. I'll get him to light a fire under the ambassador here."

"Do that," Curtis echoed. He listened for a moment to the silent sound of great wheels turning within the words Sandweg uttered. "And if that doesn't work, try NATO," he added, keeping the sarcasm out of his voice.

"Good idea." Sandweg muffled the phone at his end. Curtis tried to guess what Netta was telling him. When it cleared, Netta was speaking.

"Curtis, I feel so guilty bothering you with all this. It's strictly a private family matter and nothing to do with UBCO, but I think of you as a friend now."

Curtis's cynical smile gave a crooked downturn to the corner of his mouth. Did he want to see her again or didn't he? Was she something important to him, or just too rich for his blood? She lived in a welter of loose ends. Did he want to keep on picking them up for her?

"What about Oscar Ferguson?" he asked suddenly.

"Tom will attend to him later. Leila is our first priority."

"Did it occur t—" Curtis stopped. "What are you planning for Oscar?"

"When the publicity dies down, Tom will have him pulled in. Between the insurance company and our lawyers, Oscar will just have to make good on everything."

Quietly, Curtis added to himself. Funny how it was possible at this late date to feel sorry for an honest-to-God bastard like Ferguson. He'd almost wrecked the mighty Minton Irish Foundation. But even now, looted of its prize jewels, the foundation would some-how muddle through if everything could be kept under wraps. And Oscar would be squeezed as flat and dry as the sands of the desert.

No room for the little guy anymore. Curtis's smile grew more crooked. "Let me talk to Sandweg again."

"Yes?" Loud, masculine, in charge.

"Has it crossed your mind that you have to find Ferguson right away and keep him under wraps?" Curtis asked.

"Plenty of time for that."

"No time," Curtis contradicted him. "He can be turned into a material witness against the girl. Some-one may try to link him to the bomb scheme through Leila. She carried his proposal to the Arabs or some-thing. If the French can cook up that one, you haven't a prayer."

"My God." Silence. Then a fast recovery. "Good thinking, Curtis. What in hell's name would we do without you?"

"Let me say good-bye to Mrs. Irish."

"Of course."

When she got back on the line, Netta sounded con-fused. "What have you been telling Tom?"

"Details. He'll work it out just fine for you, Netta."

She took a while to answer. "He's a close family friend, of course. Leila's father's best friend. He's Leila's godfather. If anybody can keep her out of jail and get her back home—"

"What makes you think the French will let her go?"

"Tom says she's not of age. She was set up as a dupe, not as part of the conspiracy."

"Uh-huh." Her words rattled hoarsely in Curtis's ear. They had the ring, not so much of truth, but of gold.

"Curtis," she went on hastily, as if afraid he would hang up, "when will you be free?" Her voice lowered, perhaps to keep Sandweg from hearing her. "Can we have a drink tomorrow?"

"I'll call."

"Please do."

He hung up and sat staring at the telephone. If they kept Leila from talking, if they kept Ferguson under wraps, they had a chance. Otherwise, no go.

What the hell was he worrying about? How long did heiresses languish in jail, any jail, anywhere?

He made himself a strong soda and Johnnie Walker Red. As he sat sipping it, he wondered why this kind of work brought out his most cynical views of life. Was Louch this cynical?

It had seemed like good, clean work when he first took the job with UBCO. But it hadn't been clean, only new. And now it didn't even seem good.

He had a second drink and wondered if a vacation would help. Maybe pack a bag and rent a car. Elston would let the James girl cover for him while he took off.

62

Le Henri IV is a small wine bistro on the Place du Pont-Neuf, about two blocks from Louch's office on the Ile de la Cité. It is a modest place, frequented mostly at lunch. Some food is served at equally modest prices but the emphasis is on wine.

Lee James had gotten there shortly after five in the evening, when darkness was falling over the Seine. The rain had drained most of the ugly brown-gray from the sky, but a few drops still fell, widely spaced, making individual ripples in the water.

She sat at the bar and stared at the blackboard behind the counter, where the wines available that day had been chalked in quick, vigorous, hard-to-read handwriting.

Louch arrived a quarter of an hour later and escorted her to what was apparently "his" table near the window. "His" waiter came over and there ensued an excited interchange of French. For a moment Lee thought the two men were arguing, but she realized finally that the waiter simply had very strong opinions about today's best wine. As they discussed this most important matter, she watched two younger men come in, nod to Louch and proceed to play a pinball machine near the front door.

The neighborhood offices were beginning to empty now. She had no way of knowing how many of the men coming in worked at the Palais de Justice just behind Le Henri IV, and how many came from the nearby Préfecture de Police or, just across the river, the Hôtel des Monnaies.

Gazing out the window at the small triangular park that formed the prow of this shiplike island, she wondered whether Frenchmen always spent this much time choosing wine. But as she looked around at the other tables—there seemed to be no more than a dozen or so—she realized that waiters were staging similar arguments all over the room.

Louch finally settled for a '74 Cabernet Franc. "The owners," he murmured quietly to Lee, "are from the Loire Valley. So, of course, one pays a certain lip service to the wine of their region."

"Lip service?"

He glanced distractedly at her. "Did I say that?" He tried to laugh but his face, frozen in stiff lines, didn't respond at once.

"How did it go today?"

"Better than I expected." He was silent as the waiter brought two brimming glasses of wine. Louch lifted his. "To the—ah, what do you call them?—to the good guys."

Lee touched his glass with hers. "That's us."

He nodded and sipped, frowned, sipped again, then relaxed. *"Pas mal.* One can drink it." He watched her sample the wine. "I have been standing before the committee of inquiry all day. One's feet—" He broke off and sipped more wine. "Not bad at all. We may have a second glass."

"And did you have lunch?"

He shook his head. "Very delicate maneuvering. One needs on empty stomach when dealing with politicians, my dear. Otherwise one runs the risk of throwing up."

He rubbed the bulbous tip of his nose and finally managed a normal smile. "How they hated it all," he reminisced. "And, mind you, I didn't give them even one-tenth of what was in that little metal box."

"But what's the decision?"

"You must understand: the decision was really mine to make." He stared into the wine and his eyes lidded over. "Did I want Vermeuil dead or alive? *Enfin,* he agreed to tender his resignation for reasons of health."

"And there's no question you'll remain in the bureau?"

"But I will have been raised one rank."

"Louch! They gave you Vermeuil's job!"

He laughed quietly. "The American dream. No, dear girl. There would never be such a wild breach of protocol. Even now, two scoundrels of Vermeuil's political faction are fighting to take over the post."

They touched glasses again and silently sipped their wine. "Louch," Lee James said then, "you must be starving. Let's order something."

"Plenty of time."

"Well, then, I'm starving."

"Not for long, I assure you." He finished his wine and signaled the waiter. "To look at me one would think food played a major role in my life, but actually, I owe my weight to alcohol."

"One would never have guessed."

He glanced at her sharply. "Sarcasm, like sagacity, is unseemly in the very young."

"Louch, your liver . . ."

"Is perhaps as riddled as one of those black truffles the pigs dig up with their snouts. It doesn't look well for a young, shapely woman to worry about her companion's liver."

"You're being deliberately provoking," she told him. "Victory has gone to your head."

"The Tunisians have a saying, in French," he said as the waiter brought two more full glasses. "Or is it the Algerians? It's in the dialect. Most amusing. *'Ti bouffe, ti bouffe pas, ti crève quand même.'* You understand?"

"Not a word."

" 'You eat, you don't eat, you croak all the same.' "

"Croak?"

He gave her a pained look. "I am proud of my American slang. To croak is to die. Perhaps you are too young for croak."

She watched his face for a moment, and saw in it what she had seen the first night with him, at Mother's, when she had asked questions about the heroin traffic in the Golden Triangle. He knew something. Speaking of death brought it forward to his mind, but not quite on his face. Too good a cop for that. Something about her brother.

She decided not to ask. He would tell her one day. Knowing didn't seem as important to her now. "To croak," she said at last. "Not for us."

"Not tonight." He stared at her and produced a deep, satisfying, tension-releasing sigh. "We have a long way to go, you and I, before then."

63

Curtis was fast asleep when he heard the bell. He reached for the telephone, only to get a dial tone. He sat up and realized he was in his own living room on an easy chair. The lowered level in the Johnnie Walker Red bottle told him the rest.

Wincing at a hangover headache, he stumbled to his feet and went to the front door. Someone had rung the downstairs bell several times. Now he could hear footsteps on the stairs.

Curtis cracked open the door and watched Netta Irish come up the steps two at a time, long legs in tight leather jeans, big dark eyes fixed on the crack in the door through which she could see she was being watched.

"Tomorrow," he grunted, his head throbbing.

"You weren't going to call tomorrow." She went into the living room and stood there, surveying the place. "That last conversation of yours was the old Curtis soft-shoe. The brush-off part."

She picked up the bottle of Scotch. "Why am I fatally attracted to alcoholics?"

He frowned at her. "A man who has a drink is not an alc—"

"Who passes out in his own living room?" She went into his kitchen and he heard the sound of ice cubes in a glass. She returned with a drink for herself and none for him.

"Is this going to be some sort of inquisition?" Curtis asked. "It's after midnight."

She handed him her drink, let him sip it, then took back the glass and sat down in the easy chair he had just been using as a cot. "Are we all washed up?"

He brooded for a moment. "Did we ever get started?"

"You insulting bastard," she said in a tone of near-wonder. She stared into her drink and then sipped some. "Sit down, Curtis. You make me nervous, hulking over me that way."

"Back at the Ritz, in your own suite," he pointed out in as gentlemanly a fashion as possible, "you could be enjoying an evening of non-Curtis."

"Tom seems determined to fill the gap."

Curtis took the drink from her and sat down in another chair. "You ought to be used to that type by now."

"Dominant male. Always ready to shield the little woman from the world."

"Wants you for his very own?"

"Me and my voting stock."

"Smart Tom."

"Maybe he loves me for myself alone," she mused, "but having a lock on all those IBI shares would be even more irresistible."

"The foundation owns them now?"

"He's willing to give up his cherished bachelorhood for them . . . me." She laughed. "Tom Sandweg would remain faithful for five whole minutes. Not that I care. I mean, fidelity isn't everything. It isn't even anything." She stopped. "What happened to my drink?"

He handed her the empty glass. "Here."

"Well, the truth of it is, I don't want to get married. Especially not to someone who is going to turn me back into the little woman again."

"Wasn't Oscar doing that, too?"

"Oh, yes." She got up and went into the kitchen. When she returned, it was with two glasses of Scotch

and ice. "You don't have to be married to be domi-
nated. Although it helps."

He accepted a drink. "So what's your plan? Break
in here and start dominating me?"

"Curtis, you're a booby. I just want to get away
from Sandweg. Permanently. If you don't want to be
my friend, I'll move on."

She got to her feet again and went to the window,
glanced out at the damp little park under the tiny
electric lights. Then she walked back past Curtis to
the entrance foyer. "I mean it. Say the word and I'm
gone."

"Mm."

"That's not the word."

For the first time she caught sight of the two small
tan canvas suitcases sitting near the front door. "You
going somewhere?"

"Tomorrow morning," he admitted. "Got a car
rented."

"I was right," she pounced. "You never intended
to call me. You were running out."

"Taking a powder. Making with the heel and toe,"
Curtis went on more expansively. "Putting distance
between thee and me." He waved his glass in the air
and managed to spill Scotch on the floor. "Hightailing
it. Alone." He spilled some more and began singing
in a soft near-monotone: "I'll go my way by myself . . ."

The glass hit the floor without breaking. Ice cubes
shot out in several directions. Curtis looked despon-
dent. "Here," Netta said. She put down her drink and
helped him to his feet. "This way, Curtis."

Leaning on her, he allowed himself to be led into
his bedroom. She undressed him and put him in bed.
Then she undressed and got in beside him.

"Mm?" he asked drowsily.

"What time is the car reserved for?"

"Nigh. Nigh nay yem."

She set his alarm clock and switched off the light.

64

Certain that the entire underworld of Paris was looking for her, la Principessa Claudia Carloni had arranged for three tickets out of Le Bourget airport
aboard an Air Alsace twin-jet Fokker 614, nonstop
to Colmar.

Nico rented a car there and drove them the forty
miles south to Basel airport at Mulhouse. They took
a Swissair DC-9 to Milan, where Nico left. An Alitalia
DC-9 took them to Reggio Calabria. Nico had telephoned ahead so that a car and driver were waiting
to take them south and east along the Ionic coast of
the Mediterranean seventy miles to the beach town
where the Princess had her villa.

By Wednesday they were settled in. The villa staff
already thought it knew the routine. Late breakfast,
well after eleven in the morning. The tall young
American liked orange juice, and of all things, fresh
milk. Crisp bacon as well. What was one to do with
someone who ate the chunks of bacon that way, by
themselves? Barbarous.

By Friday, conscience had settled in and Nick
Brown was finding it difficult to sleep past dawn.
Waking at eight, the Princess saw him standing by
the huge arched window that looked down over olive
groves to the deep blue-green swell of the Ionic, where
the biremes of ancient Greece had swept the sea in
the old days, traversing their colonial ports on the
long route to Syracuse, last outpost of Magna Grecia.

"What is it, *caro*?"

She tried not to sound worried. God knew what she looked like after such a night. She had already felt for her false lashes, which remained in place through almost any exertion. "Keep the blind down, *carino mio.*"

He let it fall. The room darkened again, but he continued to peer out through the space between the blind and the marble frame of the window.

"I shouldn't be here," he muttered.

"On the contrary. You badly needed this rest."

He turned to her and she could see that he was about to tell her she had been giving him very little rest. But he was a gentleman, this strange boy, and she watched him stifle the thought.

He had been strong, but inexperienced. Now, after only a few days, she thought, he had made wonderful forward strides in technique. By the time he left her or she sent him away—whichever happened first— he would be one of the great lovers. Thanks to her. But she wouldn't be ready for farewells for many months yet.

He seemed to be trying to read her thoughts in the darkened room. Just as well he couldn't, she thought. The cruel sunlight comes soon enough into this young-old mating. She sank back in bed and pulled the sheets up around her neck and cheeks.

If ever I marry again, she promised herself, it will be to a blind man.

She smiled to herself. She and the blind man could grow old together. She would be forever young in his sightless eyes. "Princess," Nick Brown began.

"Claudia."

"Claudia, my family is worried as hell. I'm overdue at Williams. What I mean is . . ."

"You mean," she said in a flat voice, "you want to leave me."

"No!"

"Then stay, *amore.*"

"Prin— Claudia, I have responsibilities." His voice

sounded heavy with them. "Life isn't just screwing yourself blind."

She sat up in bed, suddenly interested. "You mean one can become blind by— Oh, I see. One of your jokes."

"I have to make something of myself," he went on doggedly. "I have a hell of a lot of things to do."

"Besides screwing yourself blind." She felt for her cigarettes on the night table, but failed to find them. "Are my cigarettes in the window, *carino*?"

He started to pick them up, then stopped. "That's another thing. You've got to stop smoking."

"Perfect. Meanwhile . . ."

He brought them to her, then sat on the bed beside her. "A lot of stuff is hanging over my head. I never did find Leila. My father's going to kill me. I owe Williams my thesis and it's a year late. They're going to drop me. Then what?"

"No *baccalauréat*?" She watched him nod miserably. Was this the time to tell him about the Trocadéro adventure? Or what Nico had told her over the telephone last night, that the Paris police had found the body of his father? Was there ever a time to tell a son such news?

His head was bowed. He sat staring at his hands in his lap. She took the cigarettes from him, then decided not to smoke. "What is a thesis?"

He looked shamefaced. "It's not really a thesis. A term paper."

"A piece of writing, is it?"

"I have all the other credits for a B.A. But I have to do a paper, a report, a long sort of . . ." He gestured helplessly. "Christ, Princess, I don't even have a subject."

"On anything you wish?"

"No. My major is poli sci." He turned to her. "Political science."

"In America there is a science for this?" She lay

back in bed and pulled his head down on her breasts. They lay quietly for a while.

"Life is hard for you," she said at last. "But occasionally you have great good luck."

His arms, lying at her sides, tightened slightly in a polite squeeze which took the place of the usual "you are my good luck" speech. The Princess, noting this nonverbal message, smiled up at the lofty ceiling, with its long, dark brown wooden beams. Such a gentlemanly young boy, and still mad about her. For now.

"*Caro*," she said then, "how much do you remember of Jack Kennedy?"

"Everything."

"But you were a baby when he was killed."

"I remember seeing it on TV, over and over again, for weeks."

"I could bring down here from Paris," she told him, "a great many documents, affidavits, notes, interviews, correspondence. From such material a student could write a very interesting thesis."

"On what?"

She felt his head lift up from her breasts. She looked down and their glances locked. She was giving away a million dollars in information. But what had it brought her so far, except grief? In any case, it was worth it. Love always is.

"You could work," she told him softly, "right here."

At the second level of the Eiffel Tower one waits in line for either of the two elevators that go higher. The mechanism is arranged so that as one car moves up with a load of arrivals, the other car carries back to earth those who have already visited the third level at the top of the tower.

Bert shuffled forward slowly as the elevator doors opened. He squeezed in beside one of the plate-glass windows. As the car moved up through the network of girders, he watched triangular flashes of Paris, jagged chunks of landscape, as if chopped up by a butcher.

At the top, the chill April breeze was more of a wind. He buttoned shut the collar of his raincoat. At one of the coin-operated telescopes he pushed two one-franc pieces into the slot.

He moved carefully, using only his right arm. There was no infection, but he didn't trust the butterfly sutures the Arab doctor had put in for him. If they tore loose too soon . . .

He focused on the top of the Trocadéro and a faint smile twitched across his flat face. The inner tower was so easy to see from this angle. So clear. Almost too easy.

Bert moved the telescope up and away. Moist air lay over Paris like a grayish blanket. Off in the distance, on the horizon beyond the Palais de Chaillot, he could see the upthrusting, blocky buildings of the

Défense business district. From this angle, the Bois de Boulogne seemed to lie right at their feet.

Slowly, he swung the telescope to the left and stared at the rounded, modern ORTF building where government radio and television originated. He moved the telescope to the right and examined the Arc de Triomphe for a moment, then, in the distance, the Sacré-Coeur and the Madeleine, the Tuileries, the Louvre, Notre Dame.

How efficiently the bourgeoisie grouped its treasure. Everything valuable within easy reach of modern technology. They made everything almost too easy.

Paris.

Rome.

London.

New York. All the same. All the valuable things collected, amassed, accumulated. Ready for him.

His arm had begun to hurt. Nevertheless, the smile on his face grew wider until it was—almost—a grin, as of a hungry man sitting down to a feast. There was a grating click inside the telescope and the view went blank.

Bert put more coins in the slot.